Centurion's Daughter

CENTURION'S DAUGHTER

by
Justin Swanton

Arx Publishing
Merchantville, New Jersey

Arx Publishing
Merchantville, New Jersey

First Edition

ISBN: 978-1-935228-05-9

Library of Congress Cataloging-in-Publication Data

Swanton, Justin.
  Centurion's daughter / by Justin Swanton. -- 1st ed.
    p. cm.
  ISBN 978-1-935228-05-9
  I. Title.
  PS3619.W364C46 2011
  813'.6--dc22

                                    2011013727

To my wife

Thank you for your invaluable help.

Acknowledgements

The following people made a real difference to the book in its final form:

My mother, for some very thorough proofreading

David Hulme, for his input on late Gallo-Roman civil and military society

A good friend, who does not want to be named but who I am mentioning here, as it was his input that, among other things, made it possible for me to give my reconstruction of the Battle of Soissons a ring of authentic detail.

PRELUDE

AD 464

After the assassination of his father, Senator Afranius Syagrius becomes Military Commander of Roman Gaul. He successfully resists all attempts at conquest by the barbarian tribes, who have occupied other parts of the dying Western Roman Empire.

AD 476

The last emperor of the Western Roman Empire, Romulus Augustulus, is deposed by his general, a barbarian mercenary named Odoacer. Scattered territories—still indisputably Roman—continue to hold out. Over the next few years all of them with the exception of Roman Gaul are overrun by the barbarians.

AD 481

At the age of 15, Chlodovech becomes king of the Salian Franks. He is committed to the conquest of Roman Gaul and the fusion of Franks and Romans into a new society. He spends the next few years consolidating his authority over the Franks and then begins preparations for the coming war. On its outcome hangs the future of western civilization....

Part I:
ARRIVAL

CHAPTER ONE

AD 486

The cart was traveling alone, at night, which was strange, and it carried a female passenger, which was more so.

It was the cold hour before dawn. The sky glimmered gray in the east whilst in the west the blackness of the night was touched by a hint of cobalt blue as the stars faded out one by one in preparation for the looming day. There were no clouds and with the moon already gone, the simple majesty of the paling dome above found its harmony in the earth below, where the mantle of black slowly resolved itself into the gentle curve of low hills unbroken by any crevices or rock faces, and undisturbed in their slow undulations by the thin mottling of trees scattered over them.

In such a setting the only suitable accompaniment was silence, for only silence could capture the eternal freshness of a land whose creation might have been yesterday or a billion years ago. In the predawn gloom the silence hung in the air like fingers poised over the strings of a lyre.

The silence was scarcely disturbed by the subdued noise of the cart: a regular clop, clop of hooves on flagstones, accompanied by an irregular grinding of iron-hooped wheels on the same surface. The stillness of the unroused countryside was not dispelled by the sound but, like a sleeper barely troubled in his dreams by some slight irregularity of the ground on which he lay, shifted slightly and made a small space through which it could move without disarranging the motionless order, closing behind it once it had gone.

The cart, the kind used by a merchant to deliver wheat or wine to an urban market, was drawn by a single horse and driven by a slave, since few merchants would take the risk of traveling themselves, unguarded, through open terrain. On the board at the front, the driver hunched forward, reins in his hands, intent on the blur of road in front of him. To his right, a mantle covering her head, sat the woman, who swayed slightly as the cart progressed over the irregular stonework.

3

The driver uttered a low curse and pulled on the reins, bringing the horse to a stop. In the dim gray of the road he could make out a large, black patch covering two-thirds of its width, probably a crater-like gap capable of holding them fast if he tried to drive over it. Carefully he edged the horse off the road onto the tufted meadow next to it and worked around by the flattest course back to the road again. At one point he asked the figure next to him to get down and make sure of the ground before them. She obeyed with a grace that gave away her youth, and the confidence with which she grasped the horse's bridle and led it herself showed her to be country bred, if not born. The driver did not thank her after she remounted the cart: they both knew their danger once the sun was up and thanks were superfluous in the elemental race for survival in which they were engaged.

The driver looked worriedly behind him at the eastern sky; the poor condition of the road had slowed him down and he was still six miles east of Soissons, the only walled town in the area. It would take more than an hour to reach it at the speed they were traveling. He hesitated a moment then, taking a short whip from a wooden socket next to him, urged the horse to a trot.

"What if we hit a pothole?" his companion asked.

"We'll have to chance it," he replied.

The horse was reluctant to pick up speed since it had been pulling the loaded cart all night, but the whip was a decisive argument. Neither driver nor passenger spoke during this final leg in the race against the dawn, but fixed their gaze ahead, occasionally glancing to the right and left as the hills around them imperceptibly took shape against the sky before gradually filling with color. The minutes passed; the light molded the land's features; the horse whinnied in protest as it clattered over the worn flagstones.

"There it is," the driver murmured in triumph, pointing ahead. They had crested a low rise and could see before them, just below the line where the land met the sky, the rambling outline of the town. It was not large: an uneven scattering of buildings of all sizes and shapes gathered toward the walls, built tall and thick to impress an invader before repulsing him.

He brought the cart to a halt, feeling already safe at the sight of that ring of security. It was only when the cart's wheels were stilled and the horse's footfalls had ceased that they were able to hear the approaching thud of galloping horses. The driver jerked his head around to look behind him. Scarcely visible against the darkened slopes of the eastern hills a group of horsemen could be made out bearing down upon them.

"The gods!" breathed the driver and laid the whip with all his strength on the back of his horse. With a shrieking neigh the animal jerked forward, straining at the weight of the cart until it reached a gallop as the leather cut into its rump. The driver could barely keep it on the road; there was no question of trying to steer around any obstacles. After his initial glance, he did not look back. As a man hunted by a charging bear knows he cannot escape and yet runs as fast as he can, so the driver strained every nerve of his will and body towards the town that, still three miles distant, he had no hope of reaching before being overtaken by his pursuers.

The girl said nothing, but after crossing herself hung onto the wooden board of the seat for dear life as the cart threatened to overturn from one moment to the next. Once she glanced back, and could make out the glint of a helmet on the head of the leading horseman and the shaft of a spear in his hand. She looked ahead and murmured inaudibly the words of a prayer. In her spine she could feel them drawing near a few seconds before being able to make out above the rattling of the cart the thudding beat of their galloping horses. She stopped breathing and waited for the sharp pain of a spear point between her shoulder blades.

"Stop, you fool! Stop!"

The driver hauled on the reins with both hands. In an eternity of five seconds the cart rattled, shook and came to a halt. The horsemen drew up round them. There was a moment's silence.

"You were bloody near the death of me," the driver managed to say, wiping the sweat off his brow to cover the trembling of his hands.

"If you're so blind you can't tell soldiers from barbarians then you shouldn't be steering a cart," replied a rider with the iron-crested helmet of an officer.

"How'm I supposed to recognize anything in this light?" the driver returned.

"Anyone behind you?" the officer asked.

"No. I left Reims alone. The only one who would chance it. No, I take that back. The only one whose master would chance it. Weren't you supposed to be our escort?"

The officer smiled slightly, twitched his reins and approached the driver's side of the cart. He leaned over to bring his face close to the driver's. The girl could see that his chin was unshaven and the wrinkles around his features were those of a man well past forty, but what caught her attention most were his eyes; there was something wrong with them: a hardness and opaqueness that repelled her.

"Now I want you to pay attention to me, slave," he said slowly. "Ten miles further away from town and I'd have cut your throat for what you just said. We left Soissons three days ago. We lost two men killing a bunch of Alaman raiders and we don't need lip from a piece of slave trash, you get me?" His voice was level and expressionless, full of menace.

The driver nodded, eyes downcast. The officer raised himself erect again in the saddle.

"What are you carrying?"

"Grain for the bakery by the town forum. Master Rictiovarus's, sir."

"How many carts should have come through?"

"There were thirty to go to Soissons, sir. Mostly grain but also some wine."

"Mm." The officer pulled on his reins and rode his horse alongside one of his men, evidently his second-in-command, and began to confabulate with him in a low voice. The girl, with attention off them for the moment, took the opportunity to examine the band of soldiery gathered round the cart. Their clothing was only partly military: all had army cloaks but no more than a third of them wore regulation tunics and trousers; the others had civilian clothing in various hues, caused as much by dirt as by dye. None, except the officer who had a mailshirt, wore any body armor. They all seemed to have helmets of which only about half were of standard Roman military issue. The rest were of uncertain origin—for the most part looking like modified barbarian helms. Every rider carried a bow and what looked like javelins or spears, but none except the officer had a sword. Their ages ran though the spectrum of active manhood: she noticed a few faces that were older than the officer, but even in the youngest she could see lines that belonged to an older man. All together there seemed to be about two dozen of them.

"Answer the Biarchus, girl," the driver muttered to her.

She darted her eyes back to the officer and met his gaze. He said nothing and continued looking at her, adding to her confusion.

"I'm...sorry, sir. I didn't hear what you said."

"Don't spend too much time admiring my men. They might end up appreciating it."

This brought a collective laugh and some fixed stares under which she dropped her eyes and gripped her seat. Her relief at being released from the terror of death was gone, replaced by a different kind of fear. The sun had just risen, and through a gap in the mounted men it caught her with the first rays of the morning. She was no more than sixteen or seventeen. She was not in any classical sense beautiful. Her nose was somewhat snubbed, her jaw a little heavy and her mouth lacked fullness, but one's attention was drawn to her eyes. Beyond the pale gray of the irises, which betrayed her barbarian blood, there was a depth of clarity which gave beauty to what was otherwise an ordinary face.

"My question was what are you doing on the open road?"

"I'm going to my father in Soissons, sir."

"Why couldn't you wait for a group with an escort?"

"I had nowhere to stay in Reims, sir. I'd just got there."

"That so? Where do you come from?"

"Near Tours."

"That far, eh? And why couldn't daddy go and collect you himself?"

"I've..." She hesitated, dropping her eyes to her moving hands.

"Speak up."

"I've never seen him before."

The officer's mouth opened in a lecher's grin. His teeth were yellow and brown, with here and there the gap of a missing molar.

"Got your mother pregnant in Tours, did he?"

At this the girl's face flushed dark red. She looked straight into the officer's eyes. He was surprised to see the flash of anger in her own.

"I was born a year after they got married. When my father left she worked hard to keep us and never married again. She's never been anything except a good woman." A gleam of tears appeared in her eyes, but she did not avert her gaze.

The officer looked a trifle disconcerted. The conversation was taking a turn that did not suit his position of crude superiority. It was time to end it without losing face.

"Why didn't you stay with her in Tours?"

The girl dropped her head to hide her face. When she spoke her voice was hardly a murmur. "She is dead."

The officer's features took on the appearance of a shrug. "It happens." He switched his attention to the driver. "Right. Carry on."

The girl raised her face to him. It showed a struggle between an earnestness born of urgency and a repugnance at speaking another word in the present company.

"Please," she said, "can you tell me where I can find my father? He's a centurion. This is my first time in Soissons and I don't know where he lives."

"What's his name?" the officer asked.

"Tarunculus."

Immediate recognition, and something else, flashed in the officer's face. Fixed on him, the girl did not notice the mutual glances and grins of the other men.

"Tarunculus," the officer mused, "yes, I've heard of him. Go to the forum

7

and ask anybody to point him out to you. You'll find him in no time."

"Is he famous?"

The unknown something became more pronounced, puzzling the girl.

"You could say that." A sound like a snort came from one of the soldiers. "What he says is known from one end of the town to the other." He turned to his second-in-command. "You'd say he's famous?"

"Yuh," the soldier replied, nodding and keeping his face straight. The officer turned back to the girl. "He's a big noise round here," he said, pursing his lips in a caricature of gravity.

It was evident that he was not going to clear up the mystery, so the girl dropped her eyes again. With a glance of command at his men, the officer followed by the troop of cavalry started up the road in the direction the cart had come from. The girl could hear their fading laughter as the driver set off again for the town. Neither said anything until they were out of earshot.

"Bastards," he finally blurted. "I'd almost prefer meeting barbarians."

CHAPTER TWO

The carthorse was an old animal and his insane gallop had brought him to a condition bordering on collapse. The driver let him complete the final distance between them and the town at a slow walk, secure in the knowledge that the region around them was safe, at least for the moment. Freed from the tension of fear, he became garrulous, taking his slave's revenge on the free classes in the only way he could, by rating the military and the men who ruled them.

"...and the rest of the army is no better, I tell you. Call it an army? I've seen better-armed bandits. Half of 'em *are* bandits too. Picked up by patrols and recruited, just like that. Paid a fat wage, out of the taxes of us poor beggars. Not that I pay taxes, 'f course, but master does and we feel it when it comes to mealtime..."

From their elevated position she could make out the rectangular shape of a walled barracks on the west side of the town, one wall of which formed part of the city walls. The forum lay more or less in the center of the town. Its east side was straddled by a civil basilica and its west side by the atrium and porch of a church.

"See the basilica over there? It's full of clerks and scribes and quaestors and whatnot. What does Syagrius need all *them* for? Why not put 'em in the army and let 'em have fun with real troublemakers instead of coming down on the rest of us. Half the taxes fatten their purses in any case...."

On the south side of the town there was another large building. The girl could not make out what it was, guessing it to be the dwelling of Syagrius himself. The one other prominent building appeared to be the baths. In between the main structures, like restless waves amongst rocky islets, were the narrow streets and crowded tenements of the town.

They descended to the valley floor and drew near the spread of buildings outside the limits of the walls. As they reached them the driver fell silent, as if he had just entered a cemetery. Before them rose houses, shopping booths, tenement buildings—all dilapidated or in a state of patched repair, and many partly or wholly roofless. The more intact buildings were inhabited, shown by the clutter of wares laid out for sale in front of them, mixed with barefoot urchins, tattered beggars and listless women. The girl noticed the lack of bustle amongst the dwellers. There was a heavy quiet about them, like that of a chronic invalid who senses he must die and closes in on himself in an instinctive effort to stave off death for as long as possible. As the cart's squeaks and rattles rippled in the muted air, she could see on their faces and in their eyes the unmistakeable stamp of endurance without hope. She understood the driver's silence. It would take only a slight shift of fortune to toss them both into those moribund huddles. She turned away from their incurious gaze and looked up at the approaching walls with a lead pellet of fear in her bowels.

They reached the town gates, massive iron-latticed portals recessed between two stone towers. A guard detached himself from a knot of soldiery and sauntered over to them. His dress was similar to that of the cavalry: a helmet, a green tunic with trousers tucked into leather boots, an oval shield, a spear and no body armor.

"From?"

"Reims," replied the driver.

"Just you?" the guard asked. "Where're the others?"

"They didn't leave. They're waiting for the escort."

"What's she doing with you?

"Took her chances."

The guard lost interest and waved them on before returning to his group. The driver grunted his contempt for the military and urged the horse through the gates. As they slowly made their way towards the forum ahead, the girl's senses, heightened by her feeling of dull dread, fixed on the details of her surroundings. The buildings—apartments for the most part—looked tired and old, but at least were structurally intact. She saw gaps in the quarried stonework of several edifices, filled in with irregular rows of bricks, and wondered why fresh stone could not have been cut and inserted instead. Avitus, her patron, would have done so at his country villa. He could not bear shoddy masonry and would have whipped his builders for this kind of negligence. When it came to architecture he was a perfectionist, having the money and means to make of his dwelling on a small scale as fine a piece of Roman craftsmanship as any in Rome itself.

Her flickering attention turned to the people and she noticed that although the streets were lined with a display of human poverty similar to that outside the walls, there were pedestrians whose purposeful activity showed that the town's economy still had some vigor in it. The aimless shamble of a beggar went side-by-side with the steady gait of a tradesman. The town still possessed the working sinews of urban life, but it came to her with a dim sense of surprise that the general indigence was as prevalent here as everywhere else she had been. Soissons had nothing to show for being chosen by Syagrius as his capital. It was as poverty-stricken as the other towns she had passed through on her journey. Her feeling of dull dread grew.

Inching past the columns of the basilica, the cart made its way gradually around the sides of the forum, along one of the narrow thoroughfares to which horse and donkey-drawn vehicles were confined, the central space being given over to pedestrians and open-air stalls. The crowded lane was full of street sellers, hucksters, peddlers, criers offering solid and liquid refreshment, carts, wagons, serious shoppers, idle onlookers, beggars, pickpockets and anyone else commercially connected in some way with his fellow townsmen. They had reached the beating heart of the town, the clamorous hubbub of human intercourse where men bought, sold, worked, trafficked, cheated, stole, loaned and gave, all with a diligence and haste having the appearance of enthusiasm, all masking a desperation to keep poverty at bay. The girl, unused to towns, gripped her seat as her fear coalesced into the conviction that she did not belong here, like a whelp that had been thrown into the wrong litter, pressed against the side of some strange and pitiless creature that would soon sniff her out as alien and tear her to pieces.

"You can hop off here."

A clot in the wheeled traffic had forced the driver to stop, giving him the opportunity to offload his passenger.

"Where...where are you going?"

"Baker's. Just ahead," he said, pointing.

"I must find my father...I don't know where to look for him."

The driver gave her a quick glance of pity. "Let me give the cart in and then we'll go and look for him, eh?"

The girl's face lightened with relief and she settled back on the board. The driver craned his neck, trying to make out the obstruction. "Shall I go and see what the trouble is?" she asked. He grunted his assent and the girl, gathering up her courage, climbed down from the security of her seat.

Edging past the wagons and carts she reached a small crowd gathered round the cause of the delay: a horse in harness had collapsed and lay sprawled on its side whilst its owner beat it in an attempt to get it on its feet again, laying on his whip more furiously as the creature's convulsions lessened and its breathing became increasingly spasmodic. At last, after a final twitch or two, it was still. The driver looked at it, bewildered, and the crowd momentarily fell silent before the untidy monument of death.

"And that's what will happen to all of us if the barbarians get here."

A block of flats rose opposite the spot where the horse had collapsed. From a first-storey window the speaker leaned out, hands on the windowsill, using his elevated position as a public rostrum. The girl had a good view of him: middle-aged, with a powerful, paunched torso and a mass of thick, white hair rising above the scored authoritarian features of his face. He had the *prima facie* look of an orator and his voice was stentorian.

"I say it again, that's what will happen to us if the barbarians get here. Kill the men, rape the women and dash the infants against the ground. They'll put the town to fire and the sword if they get past the walls, and they *will* get past if there aren't enough men with guts to defend 'em. D'you think all your moneymaking and merrymaking will help you then? D'you think your wine and wenching will save you then? Do you?" The heavy cadence of his voice died away in a rhetorical pause.

"They'll do in the meantime," came the voice of a man, who held up the amphora he had been carrying. His jibe was accompanied by scattered laughter.

"And how much time will that be?" continued the extemporary orator. "Why d'you think the legions've been doubled in size in the last year? But the army's not big enough yet. The Franks are nearly ready to move, and what are you doing about it, eh? What are you doing? Nothing! It's time to remember who you are. You are Romans, the inheritors of a glorious past..."

"Speak for yourself. I'm a Gaul," the same voice interrupted.

"You are Roman citizens and so Romans, and you have the same duty your forefathers did who held out in the Capitol against the barbarians. They didn't give in but stood fast until fortune favored them, just like fortune will favor us if we do the same. Each one of you has the sacred *duty* to join the army and fight for kith and kin and show what stuff you're made of. And when you do remember that you're fighting for Rome, just like Rutilius said:

Yea the sun himself, in his vast course,
Seems only to turn in your behalf.
He rises upon your domains;
And on your domains, it is again that he sets.
As far as from one pole to the other spreads the vital power of nature,
So far your virtue has penetrated over the earth.

For all the scattered nations you created one common country.

The crowd was getting bored and began to disperse. "Crazy old goat," the driver growled, and then found a couple of bystanders to help him unbuckle the dead horse from the shafts and drag it off the thoroughfare.

"Give it over," the heckler called out one more time, shouldering his amphora and continuing on his way.

"Fight for Rome. There's only one Rome and that's something we must never forget. She is our mother and our swords are at her service and our lives too, if necessary."

The crowd was nearly gone and the wheeled traffic resumed progress. Heckling increased from the few idlers left of the vanished audience. It dawned finally on the speaker that he had become a voice in the wilderness and he withdrew back into his apartment. The girl made her way to the driver and climbed up alongside him, giving him a brief account of what she had seen.

"Yes, I heard him," the driver interrupted. "Nutty as a fruitcake."

A narrow street running from the forum let to the back entrance of a courtyard around which were clustered an assorted collection of buildings that made up the bakery. The driver drew up the cart next to what looked like a small barn, which the girl recognized as a grain storeroom. With the help of a couple of slaves he unloaded the sacks of wheat. The girl stood quietly under the arcade shading the back wall of the mill room until they were finished.

"That's all done," he said. "Wait there." And he disappeared in the mill room.

After two or three minutes he reappeared and tilted his head for her to follow. "Let's go and get some breakfast."

She went after him through a ramshackle wooden door into a space that she instantly recognized as the communal kitchen-cum-dining room for the establishment's slaves. A hearth, holding the glowing embers of a fire, sat squat by the wall opposite the door. Above it hung an assortment of spoons, knives, pots, saucepans and other utensils. A few sacks of grain and flour were lined up against the wall to the right, and an amphora leaned against the corner to the left of the hearth. Two scored and pitted tables, flanked by equally decrepit benches, occupied the middle of the room. At one table an old woman with a faded apron—evidently the cook—and a very old man were seated opposite each other over bowls of wheat porridge. The woman glanced up.

"Yes?"

"Just in from Reims with grain. Master Rictiovarus said we could take breakfast," the driver replied, looking at a pot suspended from a tripod over the hearth. The old woman nodded and resumed her meal. The driver spied several stacks of bowls on a shelf and took down two, along with two wooden spoons from an adjacent pile. Giving a bowl and spoon to the girl he helped himself from the pot and sat at the table with the old man. The girl followed his example, placing herself next to the old woman.

"Travel all night then?" asked the old man. His words were a little indistinct, as if he had just filled up with wine. Then the girl realized that he had no teeth.

"That I did, and we had a time of it," said the driver expansively, ripe with his fresh traveller's tale. In between mouthfuls he held the two old slaves' attention, making the high point of his story the moment when the Biarchus was about to cut off his head. "Then I looked him straight in the eye, I did, and he saw I wasn't a coward. He wasn't going to make *me* beg for mercy. I looked at him, like *that*"—and he stared fixedly at the old man—"and he backed off then and there. You could see he hadn't come across anybody like me before, hah!" And he finished off the last of his porridge.

At this point the old woman seemed to notice the girl's existence for the first time. "She come with you?" she asked, pointing.

"Uh. From Tours," replied the driver, holding a pitcher of water and getting up to look for a cup.

"That's far. What's your name, girl?" the old woman asked.

"Aemilia," the girl replied.

"First time in Soissons?"

"Yes."

"It's been six months since I was last here," interjected the driver, who had returned to the table. "Master Galbus owned the bakery then."

"He packed up and went down south to Toulouse," said the old woman. "We came with Master Rictiovarus."

"Why did he leave?"

"He wanted out before the Franks marched in and stuck a spear in him."

"Get off! They wouldn't do that," the old man scoffed.

"He wasn't taking any chances."

"Well, he jumped from the frying pan into the fire, didn't he?" said the driver.

"Never. Living's good under the Visigoths, anyone'll tell you that," she said with emphasis. "They took over Toulouse when I was a girl and the town's still doing all right. They don't tax a body into the ground; they just take their slice and leave the rest of the cake on the plate. Master Galbus was a smart rat, jumping off the boat while there's still plenty of time. He's sitting fat in Toulouse, that he is."

"Think the Franks'll attack Soissons this year?" queried the driver.

"They well might," the old woman surmised.

"I spoke to a soldier at the Pheasant Tavern," interjected the old man. "He was tanked up and talking. He said their king ... Klovicus..."

"Chlodovis," the old woman corrected.

"That's him. Said he was spoiling for a fight. Reached his manhood now and can't wait to get stuck into Syagrius. They'll only follow a king if he takes 'em where they can knock off heads. Syagrius is the big apple and they know it. Chlodovis wants him before the Visigoths get him, and he don't like it that his dad, Chilperic..."

"Childeric," the old woman corrected again.

"Aye, him. That Childeric helped Syagrius out against the Visigoths all those years ago when they tried to take the province. Reckons it's his turn now to help himself."

"Savages, all of them," said the old woman, curling her lip.

"Maybe, but at least they're better than the Alamans," said the old man. "I met someone from Trier after the Franks took it over who said life's not so bad there. They don't like towns much and live outside of 'em. Of course nobody's fixed the place up since it was sacked."

"We'll see how much they don't like towns when they get here," said the old woman. "They'll stay long enough to get their hands on everything they can carry away, you wait."

"Why doesn't your master join Master Galbus in Toulouse if it's that bad?" the driver asked.

"Hasn't got the money. He bought this place for a song and it still cost him everything he had. How many bakers can make a living in Toulouse anyway?"

"He could move down to Bordeaux."

"Think it'll be any easier there?"

"I don't see why not."

The conversation degenerated into a mild bickering and the girl, left in peace with a stomach filled with warm porridge, found herself becoming overpoweringly drowsy. Her eyes closed unconsciously and she lost the thread of the discussion as the slaves' voices retreated into a background murmur. She was unaware of her head beginning to loll.

"Wake up!" A jab in the ribs shook the girl back to the gray room. She opened her eyes to see the two men grinning at her. The old woman was not smiling. She seemed to lack the facial muscles for it.

"Time to be going," said the driver.

"I must find my father," she replied, confused.

"I told 'em that. What's his name again?"

"Tarunculus."

The two old slaves looked at each other. "Him!" croaked the old woman. "That cracked old pot's got a daughter!"

"It's her first time here. She hasn't seem him before," said the driver.

"Maybe it's another Tarunculus," suggested the old man.

The old woman turned to the girl. "Was your father a soldier?" she demanded.

"Yes."

"There you are," she said to the old man.

"Please, where does he live?" the girl asked.

"In the Aurelian Flats," the old woman replied, "next to the forum on this side. Wait a while and you'll see him in the plaza. Fancies himself another Horatio, going to save the Empire. He gets up on the steps and goes on like a bullfrog about glorious Rome and kicking out the barbarians and whatnot. He's as mad as they come."

"That's the one we passed on the way here," said the driver with glee. "He was carrying on from his window. You could hear him for half a mile."

"They've told him to shut up any number of times," the old woman continued, "but he just starts up again a day or two later. They won't lock him up. Ex-officer. But just any of *you* try playing at Cato and see what happens to you. They think they're little gods." The sour lines on her face deepened.

The driver raised himself up and stretched, giving a yawn. "Well, now you know where to find him," he said to the girl. "I'm going to bed." He turned to the old woman. "Is it the granary loft again?"

She gave a nod. "I'll get you the bedding."

The girl hesitated as the other two rose from the table. The old woman began collecting the bowls and spoons. "You can't sleep here," she said, taking them to a larger washing basin. "The master won't allow it." The message was clear; it was time for the girl to go. Grasping her bundle, she thanked the old woman for the breakfast, earning a glance of surprise, and then bade the driver and the old man goodbye. "Good luck," said the driver and then, as if moved by a momentary flash of pity, he added, "If you want a lift back to Reims, hop on tomorrow when I'm out the gates."

"Thank you," she said, and left them.

CHAPTER THREE

The Aurelian Flats were careworn without yet having reached dilapidation. Standing in front of them, the girl had no difficulty identifying the window from which the improvist orator had spoken earlier, but it was a long time before she could summon up the courage to pass the open entrance to the inner courtyard, ask directions from a flat dweller she met leaving his apartment, and then mount the stairway to the upper story.

He is my father, she thought, and took a moment's comfort in that; and then, he is mad and he left my mother, and her fear returned; and then, what if he isn't my father like the old slave thought? and then, he *must* be my father, he was a soldier; and then, he spoke about loving Rome, he will love me; and then, he did not love my mother, he left her; and finally she was in front of the door.

It reminded her of the door at the baker's kitchen. Her eyes took in the irregularities of its scored, wooden surface as if she were studying a map in some remote wilderness. Gaps between the planking, rounded and frayed edges, lines and cracks making patterns that resolved themselves into a horse's head—that poor horse!—and the corner of building—Master Avitus was careful about repairs, very careful—and the edge of a dove's wing—it would be interesting to be able to fly, far away—and then her hand was raised, fingers bunched into a fist. It paused in the air and moved a fraction away from the pockmarked surface, and then it came down, twice. She waited.

"Yes? Who's there?"

She was committed. "I'm looking for Centurion Tarunculus." Her voice was clear, with just the slightest waver in it.

The door opened and he stood before her. He was older than she had surmised when seeing him from the street. She guessed him to be about sixty. His tunic and trousers were stained and she noticed a barely perceptible tremor in the hand that held the door half-open. The arm

17

behind the hand was powerful though, as were his shoulders. The lines of authority that an assertive will had carved on his face were stronger than they had first appeared, and now almost overpowered her. The harshness of his features, however, was belied by his eyes: there was a touch of sadness in them that was out of character with the rest of his face.

"What d'you want?" The voice was suspicious.

"I wanted to find you..." It was becoming increasingly difficult for her to control the shake in her voice.

"Well you've found me, so what's your business?"

"I'm Aemilia."

There was the briefest expression of surprise in his eyes and then shutters came down, presenting to her the opaqueness of a stranger.

"So? Common enough name."

"My mother was Gisela."

"That's a common name for a barbarian. Get to the point."

"Sir....are you my father?" The words took every ounce of effort she had left to pronounce them.

The man laughed, a short guttural sound. "Nice try, wench."

"But sir...."

"Try your luck elsewhere," he interrupted. "You're healthy and you've got two hands. Go and earn your keep."

"I'm not...."

"Stop wasting my time." And the door slammed in her face.

She stood before it for a full minute before turning and slowly moving towards the staircase, feeling her way unsteadily down it to the arched entrance. She sat down on the lowest step to rest. She could not think. The leering horror of nightmare was upon her and all she could do was hope she was inconspicuous to passers by. Seconds, hours long, turned into minutes. Minutes, ages long, became hours, and still she did not move. No one paid her any attention except for one or two flat-dwellers who gave her a curious glance as they went past her up the stairs. The sun rose high in the sky, drenching the street and buildings and their confused tangle of detail with a bright, horrible clarity that she could not escape. Finally, after an eternity, the numbness of her mind gave way to scattered thoughts that coalesced into the ghost of a resolution: she would go to the church and beg for help to return to Avitus' villa and hope somehow to avoid the groping hands of the senator. It was a hopeless plan but better than no plan at all.

"You still here?"

The voice was a shock. She spun her head around. He was coming down the stairs with a slight limp. She rose up, unthinkingly, and he

19

stopped halfway down, looking at her.

"I've nowhere to go, sir."

"What d'you mean? Where do you stay?"

"I came from Master Avitus' villa, near Tours. This is my first time in Soissons, sir."

The man said nothing, and the girl became aware of the pause.

"Master Avitus, eh?" he said finally. "D'you still think you're my daughter?"

She looked down in confusion. "I don't know....if you've never had a daughter then I suppose I can't be."

There was a second pause, longer than the first.

"I'll have to check your story. I'll write to Avitus. In the meantime you can stay in the kitchen. If you are my daughter I'll fulfill my obligations as a father. If you aren't, I'll thrash you from here to the town gates, is that clear?"

Relief, like an overpowering wave, flooded through the girl's being. "Yes, sir. Thank you. Master Avitus will tell you I told the truth."

"Come." Without another word he turned and remounted the stairway. She picked up her bundle and followed him. From the corridor she had time to glance briefly down at the courtyard, where a slave was hanging up the tenants' washing to dry, before hurrying to catch up with Tarunculus. Passing through the door behind him, she found herself in a large room in the middle of which was a table and two wicker chairs, of simple design but in good condition. Against the wall to the right of the door were two large chests, presumably for clothing and other personal effects. Beside them a lampstand with a clay oil lamp stood against the wall. Two windows on the opposite wall gave out on to the street running along the forum. But the most striking feature was the row of book cases lining the wall on the left side of the room. Two had shelves holding books and three had diamond-shaped pigeonholes filled with scrolls. The collection was scarcely smaller that the private library of Avitus and she realized it was worth a fortune. Tarunculus turned and noticed her eyes fixed on his literary treasure.

"Mind you don't touch any of it," he said. "It's taken me a lifetime to gather and I don't want it damaged by someone too ignorant to appreciate its value."

"I can read," she said quietly.

He turned his gaze full on her. "Who taught you to do that?"

"My mother, sir."

On the table a scroll was laid out. Tarunculus beckoned to her. "Come here. Now read this." He pointed to a line of text.

"'Give ear to me, Queen of the world which you rule, O Rome, whose place is among the stars,'" she read. "'Give ear to me, mother of men, and mother of gods!'....It's the poem of Rutilius! Rutilius Namantianus. The one you were reading this morning from the window."

There was a silence. "Where did you read Namantianus?" he asked.

"There was a scroll of his poetry in Master Avitus' library," she replied. "Lady Avita let me use the library when I was not waiting on her."

"'Waiting on her?'"

"Yes sir. I was one of her attendant girls. We helped the Lady dress and set her hair and arranged her jewellery."

His eyes narrowed slightly. "Are you a slave?"

"No, I am not!" she said with emphasis, pulling back her shawl to show her ear lobes unmarked by any slits.

"Right. No need to get fresh. There's many a slave who's better off than you are right now. Why did your master dismiss you? Were you giving cheek?"

"He didn't dismiss me, sir. I left of my own choice to come and find you."

"Leave a position like that and with a mother to look after in the bargain? D'you expect me to believe that, girl?"

It was more than she could take. A great heave of anguish broke through her self-control: her throat tightened with pain and tears came unbidden. "My mother is dead," she said, voice breaking at last. She covered her face and wept freely and uncontrollably, beyond caring what anyone thought. In her grief she did not notice that he had moved to the window and had his back to her, concealing his face. After a time she was able to get a grip on herself and stop weeping.

"When did she die?" he asked when she was quiet again.

"A month ago, sir. The physician didn't know what was wrong with her. It was like a fever." Looking up she noticed that his head was bowed. "I would have come to you earlier, but the Lady Avita would not let me go until a replacement was found." She flushed saying this, but he did not see it.

He remained standing at the window. She stood by the table, waiting for him to speak. He turned around. "Right. Let's show you the kitchen. Through here," and he passed through a doorway opposite the bookcases into a room smaller than the one he had left. A brazier squatted in the corner to the right of the doorway. Next to it and on shelves above an untidy array of cooking utensils, cutlery and crockery were scattered. On a shelf a loaf of bread shared the space with leeks, carrots and some small earthenware jars evidently meant for spices. Beside them, another lampstand with its clay lamp stood by the wall. A window pierced the wall opposite the brazier. Across from the doorway another entrance led into the bedroom that she could see was as small as the kitchen.

"I'll get a straw mattress until I can find a bed for you," he said. "Your things can go in the corner by the window. You can wash in the basin over there when you need to. Have you eaten today?"

"I had breakfast at the miller's."

"Buy some fruit at the forum and we'll have it with bread for lunch. Later you can prepare supper. Can you cook?"

She nodded.

"Good. Make some soup. I eat at sundown." He fell silent and gazed away abstractedly, as if forgetting her existence. She waited a few moments before speaking.

"Shall I go now?"

"Go where?" He glanced at her.

"To the forum."

"Oh, yes. D'you have any money?"

"I spent all of it getting here."

"When did you arrive?"

"This morning. I travelled through the night on a grain cart from Reims."

"How many carts came in?"

"Just one, with the driver and me."

"Did you have an escort?"

"Just for part of yesterday. Some guards from the Reims garrison came with us until afternoon then went back."

A hint of a grin crept up the corners of his mouth. "Plucky girl."

They returned to the dining room where Tarunculus opened one of the chests from which he took a small leather bag. Untying it he extracted a silver siliqua. "Here. Mind you bring the right change—an apple costs one follis and a pear costs two. And don't dawdle. The forum is full of pickpockets."

"I'll be as quick as I can," she said, and left him.

The rectangular plaza of the forum was flanked on its two longer sides by shaded walkways running along dozens of tiny shopping booths. In the central space a scattering of covered open air stalls clustered together in outward-facing rectangles. Winding through the crowd she eventually found a fruit shop and bought three apples and a pear. Fatigue began to reassert itself and her eyes closed involuntarily whilst she waited for the shopkeeper to give her the change. On her return something caught her sleep-dulled attention: a covered litter carried by four strong-bodied slaves. As it passed she could make out the features of a woman, middle-aged, finely-dressed and loaded down with a rich collection of jewellery on her wrists and about her throat. She wondered vaguely who she was.

"That's it," said Tarunculus, sifting through the money she gave him. "Any trouble?"

She shook her head. "Nothing happened, except a litter went by with a rich lady."

"That'll be the empress."

"Empress?" Despite her tiredness her curiosity was aroused.

"Her Majesty, I should say. Married to the nephew of Emperor Avitus—same family as your master—who was on the throne back in '55. The emperor's own family gave up their claim to the throne, which makes her son the rightful heir to the purple. Aegidius and Syagrius didn't recognize any emperors after Avitus, except Majorian, and he had no children."

"Is her son here in Soissons?"

"That he is. Stays with his mother at the governor's Residence." He scowled. "An idler layabout you never saw. He thinks that being emperor-elect is enough without having to live up to it. The way he carries on, lounging around, scented and all, you'd think we were living in Caligula's time, when the empire could get on even with a mad fool at the helm. Damn it, we need men now, not wet motherboys. Thank the gods we've got Syagrius. He's the man to lead us if only that mob out there"—he jerked his head contemptuously at the window—"wake up and realize they'll lose everything if Clodovis comes. Their only chance is to join the army *now*. Not later but now." His voice had risen and the last syllables boomed through the room. The girl sensed she had become an audience and waited for an oration.

"And if they don't wake up soon—mark my words—he'll crack down on 'em, hard, like Her Majesty cracks down on her serving girls..."

Suddenly he paused. "Now there's an idea," he said, raising a finger. "Waited on the Lady Avita, you said?"

Surprised by the sudden change of topic, the girl took a moment to gather her wits.

"Yes, for two years. I worked in the kitchens and stables before that."

"I'll ask Her Majesty if there's a place for you. I know her. She's always had a high regard for me. If I recommend you from Avitus and with an education to boot, she's sure to take you on the spot."

The girl was too tired to speculate on this potential change in her fortunes, other than feeling a vague sense of alarm at the thought of working for someone of the same family she had left. She wondered briefly if she should tell Tarunculus the full story of her leaving Avitus, and decided it would have to wait until later. Odd, she thought, that Avitus had never spoken of his empress relation.

"I'll mention you when next she passes me by in the forum. She stops to greet me from time to time. She's a fine lady, a true highborn....steady!" He caught her arm as she began to sway. "What's with you?"

"I'm sorry sir. I'm just very tired."

"Right. It's a day and night run from Reims. We can't expect you to have a soldier's stamina, can we? You can use my bed. I'm off to my armory shop. I don't like leaving the slaves alone for too long—they've got a big order to finish. I'll bring a mattress on my way back."

"Thank you."

He had already left as she made herself ready for sleep, taking off her sandals and removing her shawl. Hearing the door creak, she opened her eyes and saw him re-enter the apartment, lift the lid of one chest, take out the moneybag and depart with it. As sleep rushed in on her the thought drifted through her mind that he still did not believe she was his daughter. She comforted herself that Avitus would at least convince him of that, before sinking into a sweet, dreamless oblivion.

CHAPTER FOUR

When she awoke the light was dim in the bedroom. She was confused and for a few seconds did not know where she was. Realization seeped through in stages: Soissons—Tarunculus—the apartment—and finally, preparing the evening soup. She lifted herself up and, sitting on the edge of the bed, tied on her sandals. Entering the kitchen she saw a straw mattress placed near the window, and on it, Tarunculus fast asleep. For a moment the thought crossed her mind that it was late for an afternoon siesta and then she applied her attention to the brazier. Raking through the ashes with a twig taken from an adjacent pile of bracken she found a glow that she gently blew to life, adding small twigs and chips of wood until a modest flame flickered. Fetching down a small ironware pot she filled it with water from an amphora in the corner. She piled together a selection of vegetables on a wooden slicing board and was about to peel them when she was interrupted.

"What d'you think you're doing?"

She turned and saw him looking at her, leaning on an elbow.

"Just getting the soup ready, sir," she answered, showing him the vegetables.

"Soup? Now?"

"Yes. It's nearly dark."

He chuckled. "You've got the day back to front, girl. It's dawn."

"Dawn?"

"Yes, dawn. You've been out like a candle since yesterday afternoon. I had half a mind to wake you but left it. A body works better when it's fresh—less chance of bungling things." He heaved himself up, rubbing sleep from his eyes. "Leave the fire. Here's a siliqua. Go and buy some more fruit and we'll have breakfast." He passed her the coin. She took it and made for the door and then turned back, hesitant.

"Lavatory's on the ground floor. Ask a slave," he said, reaching for his sandals.

25

The fruit shop she had visited the previous day was open, and its owner, recognizing her, was inclined to make conversation.

"From outside Soissons then aren't you?"

"Yes. How did you know?"

"I can always tell a body from the accent. You're from the south, Arles maybe?"

"Tours."

"There you are. I wasn't far wrong. Never am."

"Have you lived here long?" she asked.

"All my life. The family's been in Soissons since my grandfather's time. He moved here in '23 when times were better."

"Where did he come from?"

"Tirocinium. The village council told the imperial agent they couldn't pay the land tax—they'd had two bad harvests—and the agent told them pay or else. It was my grandfather who said to him, 'Come here with your men to collect it and you won't find a soul to collect it from.' They come, and the whole village was gone, every man, woman and child of 'em. Some moved to town, some became serfs at a villa. One or two became brigands as they shouldn't have. They were done in in no time, the fools."

"Is it hard for you now? The town seems very poor."

"That's Syagrius's doing. Pushing up the taxes to pay for that ragtag army of his without forking out a nummus from his own pocket. He's richer than any of those lord high senators down south and he's as grasping as the worst of 'em. I'm telling you, he treats the whole province like his private estate. You pay your rent, you do as you're told, or out you go. When the Franks come do you think anyone's going to cry about it? I'm one that won't, I tell you."

"Do you know the empress?" she asked.

He gave her a quizzical look. "Who?"

"She's the rich lady in a litter with a lot of jewellery. I saw her yesterday."

"Oh, *her*. Lady Julia. Who told you she's an empress?"

"Someone did."

The shopkeeper scratched his stubbled chin. "Come to think of it, there's one or two who call her that for a joke. An uncle or something of hers was emperor years ago and she likes people to remember it. Got her nose higher in the air than anyone, even Syagrius."

A customer entered the shop at this point, cutting short the conversation. Aemilia took the basket of fruit and made her way back to the apartment with an abstracted expression on her face. *There's one or two who call her that for a joke.* But she was certain Tarunculus had made no joke. It did not make sense. Then again, it was her second day here and she had everything to learn.

Once inside she put aside her thoughts and set about preparing breakfast with a will. When the table was covered with bread, wine, fruit and two plates with knives she called Tarunculus. The two ate in silence for a few minutes and then he pointed his knife at her, elbow on table. "Until that job with Her Majesty comes through, have you thought about what you're going to do in the meantime?"

"What would you like me to do?"

"I've been thinking about it. I have a slave from the landlord doing the cleaning and cooking but I don't trust him. You can't trust any of 'em. They're thieves, the lot of 'em. You can take on his chores. They're easy—a soft shift, we'd call it in the army. You can read. Can you write too?"

"Yes."

"Good. I've got some copying you can do when the chores are done. I'm making up some pamphlets that I want to pass around to right kind of the people. The more copies you can make the better. I've started handing them out in the forum but I want to do it all over the town. We've got to *wake up* these people before it's too late. It's an important work you'll be doing."

She nodded her understanding.

"You can start after breakfast. Clean the rooms and then begin the copying. I'll show you how to do it before I go. Any questions?"

"No, sir...just one thing. Will I have some free time this afternoon?"

"Of course. You're not a salt mine slave. D'you need more rest?"

"No, I've had plenty. I'd like to visit the church next to the forum."

"The church?" He looked at her curiously. "What for?"

She felt uncomfortable. "I'd like to pray there."

"The pious Christian, eh? Just like your m..." He caught himself. "Right. Do as you like. If you're not taking any rest, then go during my siesta. I prefer it quiet here then." He arose and, leaving her to clear the table, began rummaging through one of the chests, carefully bringing out sheets of clean parchment and a wooden box. Once the table was cleared he placed these on it and took a small scroll from his library. When Aemilia came in from the kitchen the scroll was laid open with the sheets of parchment next to it. A quill pen and a clay inkwell had been taken from the uncovered box and were neatly arranged beside the sheets.

"Here," he called to her. "Read this passage."

She bent over the roll and began to read the paragraph next to Tarunculus's finger.

27

Fellow citizens and Romans,

Many times in her history, Rome has been threatened, attacked and besieged by enemies whom she has always overcome. In the Punic wars she was attacked by the barbarous city of Carthage, and even though her armies were several times defeated by Hannibal, in the end she triumphed.

How did she do this? Not by bribery, for Carthage had greater riches than Rome, nor by the endless talking of ambassadors and diplomats, for it was the unyielding resolution of the Senate never to parley with an enemy on Roman soil, nor by a quick and easy victory, for it took ten years to beat Hannibal. It was by the determination and sacrifice of her citizens that Rome finally overcame her enemy.

What they did then we can do now. Thirty years ago the Roman army under the great general Aetius defeated the hordes of Attila, as we all know. None of the barbarians could stand up to the Huns and yet Aetius beat them and sent them running back east.

The only enemies we have now are those same cowardly barbarians. Let us show the resolution our forefathers did and we will do for the barbarians what Aetius did for the Huns.

Fellow citizens and Romans, now is the time to fight for your city and for your country. Join the colors, take up arms, and do your duty.

"Think you can make good copies of it?" he asked, once she was finished.

"I think so," she replied.

"Good. You can start after the cleaning. Mind you don't throw up too much dust. I'll be back at noon." And he was gone.

Once the rooms were swept and dusted Aemilia settled down to the task of copying out the extract. Turning through the scroll, she found the rest of it to be composed of similar exhortatory pieces written in the same consciously rhetorical style, and guessed that they were all Tarunculus's own compositions. Her handwriting was clear but slow, and she became absorbed in the work, taking care above all that the passage would fit neatly on the sheets of paper without either being cramped or leaving too much space. As she became confident her mind gradually freed itself from the mechanics of producing a neat script, and focussed on the sense of the words. Playing with the paradox of a barbarous city, her imagination responded with an image of a vast, wooden settlement, a sea of thatched roofs and palisade fences, full of fierce warriors, the fiercest of which was Hannibal, a huge, hairy brute dressed in skins and astride a great warhorse.

The hordes of Attila produced in her a more objective picture, for she had listened to descriptions of the Huns from those who had heard from others who had fought them. Short, with strange, slanted eyes, and teeth sharpened to points to tear the raw meat they cured under the saddles of their horses, they were half animal, half demon. Her imagination made them shriek like wolves as their hosts thundered across the green pasturages of Gaul. She felt certain they could not speak any language; there was no question of even attempting to parley with them. And then Aetius, standing calm and dignified, like an emperor, with his massed rows of legionaries before him, against which the ravening Huns broke themselves like waves on rocks.

She was halfway through her ninth copy when Tarunculus returned.

"Not bad," he said, leafing through the completed sheets. "Finish that last copy and then you can make lunch."

Later at table she asked him, "Did you go to the forum?"

"Not today. I went to my shop in Fullers Street."

"I didn't know soldiers had shops."

He bit off a piece of bread and chewed for a moment or two. "Some do. In the old days the retirement payout was good and you could buy a piece of land, but not now. I was discharged in '78—they were reducing the army then—and I opened an armory shop. I was able to get my hands on the tools from the old fabrica. Did some metalwork in the army before I was made centurion."

"What do you make?"

"Spears, helmets, war darts, shields, and all suchlike. A lot of private armory shops supplying the army in Soissons now. Syagrius can't get enough. I know how important we are so I give as much on credit as I can."

"I heard people say that the Franks might attack Soissons this year."

"Aye. Syagrius knows it. He's played a clever game of politics with 'em, playing their chiefs off against each other, but sooner or later it'll come to a fight, and when it does we'll be ready. Won't be long before we have the equipment. Then we just need men with guts. And training," he added as an afterthought.

"Will you have to fight if the Franks come?"

He sat up erect and gave her a hard look. "D'you think I'll hide under the bed? I haven't been a young man for thirty years but I can still hold a sword. Here, I'll show you." With that he rose up and went over to the chests. Opening one, he pulled out an object wrapped in linen cloth. Pulling off the covering he held up a military longsword, three feet in length. It gleamed in the midday light.

"See this? I had it at the Catalaunian Fields where we stopped Attila. Ran it through the guts of a Hun standard bearer on his horse. Like *that*." He lunged forward with the blade, startling the girl, and gave it a half twist in the air. "He was dead before he hit the ground. We showed the bastards." Wrapping the sword carefully in its cloth, he replaced it in the chest. "Always thought I would need it some day so I kept it after discharge. You don't get swords like this anymore."

"Mother never told me you'd fought the Huns."

The pupils in his eyes contracted and, seeing it, Aemilia felt a flash of pain, regretting her words.

"It was a long time ago. She must have forgotten it." His easy manner was gone and he averted his eyes from her. "You'll be going to the church, then?"

"Yes, after I've finished the dishes."

"Leave them for later." He got up, and Aemilia read in the gesture a dismissal. She arose awkwardly and made for the door. Closing it she caught his eye on her with an expression on his face she could not identify.

The atrium of the church consisted of a large courtyard flanked by colonnades. In the middle of the central space a statue—Aemilia guessed it to be an apostle—was set on a tall base. She paused at the entrance to take in the details of the mosaic set in the wall above the main doors. She was sensitive to beauty and the mosaic was beautiful. Christ in majesty stood on a cloud in the middle, flanked by two apostles that she recognized as St. Peter and St. Paul. To the sides of them were other figures including one who held a miniature of the church in his hands, evidently the patron who had paid for the building. At the ends of the composition were two women which Aemilia again had no trouble identifying: the church of the Jewish and the Gentile converts.

The coolness and silence of the church's interior was in marked contrast to the bustle of the forum. The central nave was flanked by two rows of columns supporting round arches, above which rose on each side a wall pierced by large windows. Two wide walkways ran between the rows of columns and the outer walls of the church. Having crossed herself at the font she walked down the nave toward the altar, behind which she could see

a raised stone seat, occupying the middle of a semicircular apse. Glancing around, she saw what she was looking for: to the left of the altar on the side wall, a picture resolved itself as she drew close into an image of the Madonna and Child, considerably darkened by the smoke of oil lamps that hung from the ceiling. She knelt down amongst half-a-dozen other devotees and began to pray. Her Faith was a simple one, absorbed from the cradle as part of the order that had structured her life, but it was not merely ritualistic. Beneath the formulae of the prayers that she murmured lay the perception of a God who knew and cared for her.

When she was done she whispered to a woman next to her, "Where can I find the priest?"

"What do you want him for?"

"I want to go to confession."

"The bishop's hearing them. Through the door over there."

The door led to a vestry. Walking up and down in it was a round ball of a man, his fatness accentuated by his shortness, reading a scroll held open in his hands. He wore a priest's toga with a stole hanging from the one shoulder. On his round and boyish head floated an incongruous wad of black, curly hair. She stood by the door and waited. He noticed her and paused in his stride.

"Yes?" The tone was of pleasant interest.

"My Lord, can you hear my confession?"

"Certainly. Close that door."

He pulled up a stool and sat down. She knelt beside him.

"*Dominus sit in corde tuo et in labiis tuis ut rite confitearis omnia peccata tua. In nomine Patris et Filii et Spiritus sancti.* Amen. Now then, let's have it."

"Forgive me for I have sinned. I last went before Easter, on Palm Sunday. I want to confess that I told a lie." She hesitated.

"Go on," he said encouragingly.

"I lied to my father. My mother died and I've come to Soissons to stay with him. I told him I left the service of Master Avitus after the Lady Avita had found a replacement for me. It isn't true. I ran away."

"Are you a slave?" he asked.

"No," she said, showing him her earlobe.

"Ah, you are a serf."

"That's what Master Avitus says. When my mother came to him she was a free woman and she never became a serf. But after she died, Master Avitus said I had stayed on his villa all my life and that made me one. He told me serfs can never leave the lands of their Master without their permission and he wouldn't give it."

"Can you tell me why?" the bishop asked gently.

"He...he tried to...touch me, when I was alone in Lady Avita's bedroom. I ran out then. I was afraid he would try again. I had a little money saved up. I left at night and came here as quickly as I could before he found me. But now I don't know what to do, My Lord. My father is looking for a position for me with the Lady Julia and she is related to Avitus. If she finds out, she will dismiss me and I'm afraid that will make him angry. Should I tell him now?"

There was a pause. The bishop looked ahead, meditatively.

"Mmm...you're going to have to tell him sooner or later. Who is your father?"

"Tarunculus."

He darted her a sharp look, and after another moment's hesitation seemed to come to a decision. "Don't tell him just yet. I take it he's written to Avitus?"

"Not yet, but he's going to."

"The post is slow. It'll be weeks before a reply comes back. Tell him then. Anything else?"

The rest of her confession consisted of peccadilloes. The bishop gave her a small penance — "just an Our Father, my girl" — and dismissed her. As she was going out he called after her: "You can always come here if ever you need help, remember that."

"Thank you, My Lord," she said simply, and left.

CHAPTER FIVE

When she returned to the apartment, the door was locked and Tarunculus gone. He must be in the forum or in his shop, she thought. She would try the forum first.

Wandering around the crowded plaza she eventually glimpsed, at the far side, the litter she had seen the previous day. Acting on a hunch she made her way over.

A bejewelled hand holding a closed fan emerged, accompanied by a word of command. The slaves turned with the litter and made their way slowly toward the civil basilica on the east side of the forum. Aemilia followed it at a discreet distance until she spotted Tarunculus standing at the base of a broad flight of steps leading up to the basilica's entrance. She hung back in the crowd, waiting to see what would develop.

"Good day to Your Majesty." Tarunculus stood by the litter. Its gauze curtains were drawn back and Aemilia had her second glimpse of the Lady Julia. She was in late middle age and her skin hung in loose, heavy folds under her eyes and around her neck, its flabbiness somehow accentuated by her make-up and jewellery. There was a firmness in her eyes, however, that contradicted the initial impression of dowdiness.

"Ah, Tarunculus. You wouldn't happen to have a copy of the last volume of Strabo's *Histories*, by any chance? My boy is asking about them." Her accent seemed a little stilted to Aemilia, unlike the unconscious ease and dignity of the patricians she had known.

"Afraid not, Your Majesty. There's that copy of Terence I loaned him. If he's finished with it..."

"In good time, in good time. Well I won't keep you any longer."

"Just one thing if you please, Your Majesty."

"Yes?"

"I have a daughter just arrived from Tours. She worked as lady-in-waiting for the Lady Avita. She is currently occupied as a scribe for me, but she would be available if a position ever came up."

Lady Julia gave him a look of renewed interest. "A daughter? How fascinating! And a scribe too. I never knew you were married."

"It was a long time ago, ma'am. Military duties kept me from seeing them much."

"Indeed. Is her mother here?"

Tarunculus's expression took on a flat quality. "She passed on, ma'am."

"How sad. Well, I shall certainly consider your daughter if a vacancy should arise."

"Much obliged, Your Majesty."

Again the hand and the fan. "Up."

Going up the stairs the two foremost slaves held the poles of the litter at their sides whilst those behind them raised them to their shoulders, thus keeping the box level up the incline of the staircase. At the top, the litter disappeared into the basilica and Aemilia went forward to meet Tarunculus. He grinned.

"Job's in the bag, sure as sure. She goes through her girls like old clothing. She'll be asking for you in no time."

"Is she difficult to work for?"

"No more than any other highborn lady. She's particular, that's all. Do your job well and she'll keep you. She can't abide idlers."

Her fatigue and fears were past, leaving room for a little nerve of pride to be piqued. "I'm not idle."

"I can see that. Sunning yourself in the forum, eh?"

"I came looking for you, sir. The door was locked."

"I thought you'd still be in the church. Those old women take more time over their prayers than a priest at his sermon."

Aemilia did not reply, and followed him back to the apartment. "Carry on with the copying," he ordered her once they were inside, "I'm off to the shop."

Alone again, Aemilia sat down to her task, fingers and eyes settling into the by now familiar routine, and for the first time since her mother's death, peace pervaded her mind. The anxiety that had never been far from her evaporated, leaving her with a sense of safety—more than that, a barely conscious feeling that her life was taking a direction, where to she could not guess and did not need to. The future could be left to Providence, leaving her free, at long last, to be content with the present.

The sun was lowering in the west when she heard a knock at the door, two sharp raps. Leaving her pen and parchment she went over and opened it. A small man with a short beard and nondescript features stood waiting, holding a sealed scroll.

"Can I help?" she asked.

"This is the residence of L. Cornelius Tarunculus?"

"Yes."

"Message from the Lady Julia Avita." He held up the scroll. "Is he in?"

"No. He'll be back soon. Shall I take it?"

The messenger hesitated. "I'm supposed to deliver it to him in person."

"He's my father."

He glanced at her with interest. "That's all right then, ma'am." There was a new touch of deference in the voice. He was no longer a slave speaking with peremptory familiarity to another slave. Aemilia felt a twinge of regret.

"Thank you," she said, accepting the scroll.

"G'day ma'am" and he turned to leave. She had a momentary desire to say something that would establish the old comfortable rapport she had always had with slaves, having been so like one herself. The moment passed. There was nothing to say. She sighed and closed the door. Leaving the scroll on the table she resumed her copying and was busy at it when Tarunculus arrived.

"You can leave that. Time to prepare supper."

"There's a scroll for you, sir," she said, pointing. "Arrived from the Lady Julia."

"So it's come," he said with satisfaction. Breaking the seal he unrolled it and began to read.

From Her Imperial Majesty Lady Julia Avita to Centurion L. Cornelius Tarunculus. Greetings.

It is my hope that this epistle finds you in good fortune and health. Following our conversation, I have given consideration to the offer of your daughter as lady-in-waiting. I am pleased to inform you that such a position is currently vacant at my Residence, following the dismissal of one of my girls for insubordination and other misdemeanors. Please inform your daughter to present herself for an interview at midday tomorrow, at the Governor's Residence. She is to bring with her any epistle of reference she has from her former employer.

Signed by my hand
Lady Julia Avita

"In the pot," Tarunculus said. "All we need to clinch it is a letter from Master Avitus. He must have given you something when you left his employ."

Aemilia's heart skipped a beat.

"He did not, sir. It didn't seem necessary as I wasn't going to take up a position of lady-in-waiting again."

A moment of doubt crossed Tarunculus's face.

"He was busy and I didn't trouble him for it." Strictly-speaking that was the truth, she thought.

Tarunculus gave a shrug and turned his eyes back to the scroll. "Can't be helped now. I'll write to Master Avitus asking for a reference and tell Lady Julia it's on its way."

"That will be fine, sir."

He leaned over the table to inspect her work. "You've got a neat hand. You say your mother taught you?"

"Yes, from when I was five."

"Did she tell you how she learned it?"

Aemilia hesitated. "She said you taught her, sir."

"Aye, so I did. She knew nothing when I found her. Merchant's daughter. Did you know him?"

"He died when I was three."

Tarunculus scrutinized her face. "D'you know where his money went?"

"Mother said the Romans took it."

"Did she say anything else?"

"No. Just that."

"Aye, well, that's the way of things. Anyway as I was saying, I was the one who taught her. All the education she ever got she got from me. My pay wasn't coming through then and I had to sell a book or two to make ends meet. Her father bought 'em all up for her. I'd visit and talk about the books with him. Your mother and I got on speaking terms and we eventually married. She asked me to teach her then—her tutor was useless. She worked hard at her lessons, couldn't get enough. We went through Virgil from start to finish. Wasn't interested in Ovid though." He chuckled. "Too raunchy for her. Here," he went over to the shelves and pulled out a book. "She got me to buy Augustine. She told me his prose was good."

"I don't think there's been anything better since."

He gave her a look. "I see you spent a lot of time in the library."

"Quite a bit, sir." Aemilia flushed. "Lady Avita encouraged me. She said she wanted some educated female company."

Tarunculus gave a grunt of disapproval. "Wasn't her husband good enough for her? In principle, I don't hold with women getting too educated. They start getting above their station—telling their men what to do, and that leads to no end of trouble. Women are made for the home, I've always said. Those who need to write can hire a scribe. Those who are too poor to hire one don't need him anyway. I tell you, that's been the curse of the Empire: women with too much education twisting the men round their little fingers. In the old days they did as they were told, and if they didn't the men divorced them, without any silly Christian scruples. That's the way it was and it worked. But once the Empire became Christian, aye, *that's* when the trouble started."

Perhaps it was the newness of her situation, too embryonic for the habitual restraint to have developed that prevents people of a very different mental cast from speaking their minds to each other in the way they might to a stranger. Whatever it was, Aemilia did not keep silence as she would have done had any man spoken thus in the past. "What trouble was that?"

"It's obvious. The emperors became weak, the men lost their backbone and the barbarians got past them. When the women became men the men became women, eh? Remember that."

Aemilia had the curious impression that Tarunculus was quoting. She thought for a moment.

"Didn't all that start before the Empire became Christian? As I remember the emperors persecuted the Christians because they were afraid they would be disloyal to them, and they were afraid because the barbarians were already invading the Empire."

"That's crud, girl. Did your mother tell you that?"

"No, it was something I thought of myself."

"Well don't do too much thinking. You're not made for it. The Empire went soft because the Christians stopped the men from keeping the women in line. It's as plain as the nose on your face. Nature made men to lead and women to follow, and if a woman tries taking the upper hand, then by the gods I know how to put her in her place!"

He stopped suddenly and there it hung in the air between them—the question that had been present from the moment she arrived, the question that she did not dare ask and he would not answer, and she sensed now with a slight surprise that it was a question that troubled him as much as it did her: the question of *why*. Why had he abandoned his wife and daughter and gone all the way to the other end of Syagrius's realm? Why in seventeen years had he never seen or contacted them? She was nerving herself to pronounce the question when he abruptly ended the moment.

"Come on, girl. We're wasting time. Take a fresh sheet and write the answer as I dictate. '*Centurion L. Cornelius Tarunculus to Her Imperial Majesty Lady Julia Avita. Greetings...*'"

She bent to the task with a troubled look in her eye.

The evening meal was a silent affair. Tarunculus drank his bowl of vegetable soup with an abstracted and sour expression. At the end he seemed to mellow a little, remarking on the finer points of Aemilia's penmanship. "Take more time over the O's, girl. Make them full and round"—he traced a circle in the air—"and take care they connect neatly."

"Who are you giving the sheets to once I've finished them, sir?"

"Told you. The right kind of people. Anybody who can read and looks like he matters or can hold a spear. The people here have forgotten who they are. Soissons used to be an important place. Its fabrica supplied the spears for the standing army in Gaul, then the rest of the equipment after the other fabricae closed."

"Is that why Syagrius made it his capital?"

"No, it's because of the walls."

"The walls?"

"They're short," Tarunculus explained. "There's not too much of 'em to defend. A small garrison could hold the town forever. Not like the big cities. The walls were too long and there weren't enough troops to man them. That's what happened at Trier. Count Paulus learnt the lesson and left most of Soissons outside his walls. Syagrius only needs two or three cohorts to hold it, and he's got two whole damned legions. I tell you, nothing can beat him. We have to make the people understand that. Barbarians don't know a thing about siege warfare. They haven't got the equipment or the patience for it. They'll never take Soissons, never!" And he thumped a fist on the table.

Aemilia started, and Tarunculus grinned. "I'm frightening you am I, girl?"

"You just surprised me, sir."

"Well then, that's enough surprises for tonight, eh? Don't want you a bag of nerves tomorrow when Lady Julia interviews you. Make sure you address her correctly. Curtsy and call her 'Your Majesty' whenever she speaks to you. She's imperial family and she must be given the proper respect."

"I understand."

"I know fools laugh at her and say she's too big for her boots, but they'll laugh on the other side of their faces before long." He pointed a finger at her. "I know why Syagrius keeps her here in Soissons. Not just because she's blue blood. There's another reason."

He paused, as an oracle about to unburden himself of a great truth.

"He's got his eye on her son. When the time's right, mark my words, he'll make him emperor!"

CHAPTER SIX

The Governor's Residence was small compared to analogous buildings elsewhere in the defunct Empire. A white-walled complex with ochre tiled roofs, it abutted against the walls on the southern side of the town. Approaching it from the forum, Aemilia reached the gateway of the Residence's stables, where a groom directed her to the main entrance round the corner.

At the entrance doorway a guard, similar in dress to the cavalry officer she had met outside Soissons, asked her business.

"I've come to an interview with Lady Julia," she replied, holding out Tarunculus's sealed epistle.

"Stay here," he said, taking the epistle and entering the building. A few minutes later a young slave girl appeared and beckoned to her. "This way."

The short entrance passage led to the room-sized space of an atrium, in the middle of which a small, square pool lay open to the sky. Around the central space ran a covered walkway, with pillars on one side supporting the roof whilst the wall on the other was spaced with doors leading to adjacent rooms. At the far end of the atrium a wide passage led to another, larger open space—a peristyle with an enclosed garden from what Aemilia could see from her vantage point.

"Wait here," the slave-girl told her. "When the mistress is ready she'll call for you."

"Will I have to wait long?"

"As long as it takes." The girl glanced at Aemilia with a dismissive look. Aemilia was puzzled for a moment and then looked down at her clothing, realizing that its rural simplicity had placed her a notch below the fine white linen of the attendant girl. She showed the hint of a smile as the slave disappeared down the narrow passageway.

She stood where she was for some time, seeing only the odd figure passing across the entrance to the enclosed garden. She went over to the pool and looked in. A dozen fat, sluggish goldfish meandered between water lilies and ornamental rocks that rose from a bed of light gray pebbles. A boring life, she thought, but at least they are well-fed and have no fears. She crouched down and lightly touched the water with her finger. Three of the fish came up, quite tame, hovering near for a morsel of food. She let out a slow sigh. *I shouldn't be afraid; there is a bigger hand looking after me if I could just see it.*

"They're not partial to fingers."

She glanced around and quickly rose up, flushing with embarrassment.

"I'm sorry, sir. I was just looking at them."

"Don't worry. I won't report you."

A youngish man stood in the wide passage. He was overweight without being fat. His lips were disconcertingly red and his eyes had a heavy expression of inertia. He wore an elaborately embroidered tunic and trousers—not of linen, but of some finer material. Aemilia guessed him to be about thirty.

"I'm here to see the Lady Julia, sir."

"'The Lady Julia.' Tch, tch."

" I mean...Her Imperial Majesty."

"The old girl's very particular about that. A girl has to forget it once and she's out on her ear. Are you the replacement?"

"I suppose so, sir. Her Majesty asked me to come to an interview for the position of lady-in-waiting."

He leaned against a pillar and appeared to reflect for a moment. "I don't know why she sent Lavilla packing. I thought she was quite good. Where're you from?"

"The Avitus villa near Tours, sir."

"Oho. The plot thickens. Did you work in the villa?

"Yes, sir."

"Doing what?"

"I was lady-in-waiting to Lady Avita."

He snapped his fingers. "That's it then. She wants some up-to-date gossip on the family. Got any choice scandal to give her?"

Aemilia hesitated. The young man grinned.

"That would be telling, eh? Well I won't pry. I couldn't give a damn about what they get up to anyhow. What brought you here? Did you come for the job?"

"No, sir. I came to stay with my father."

"A good enough reason I suppose." He seemed to be getting bored. "Maybe I'll get round to pumping you after all. Just make it more interesting than a poacher stealing the pheasants." He turned and went down the passage without looking back, leaving Aemilia alone again in the atrium.

Half-an-hour later the attendant girl caught Aemilia's eye from the far end of the passage and beckoned her with her finger. Joining the girl, Aemilia followed her along a walkway running round the carefully groomed shrubs and trees of the peristyle's formal garden, open, like the atrium, to the sky. The walkway was separated from the garden by a low wall. On the side facing the garden, frescoes had been painted of pastoral scenes—a shepherd holding a lamb, dogs chasing a buck through undulating grass, storks and swans drinking at a pool. She followed the girl up a flight of marble-covered stairs and along another passage, at the end of which was an ornately carved wooden door. The girl knocked softly and waited.

"Enter."

She opened the door and passed in. Aemilia stood at the doorway.

The girl curtseyed. "The new girl, Your Majesty."

"Good. Bring her here."

Aemilia entered. Lady Julia sat in a delicately carved wooden chair in the middle of the room whilst a slave girl stood behind her styling her hair. The room itself was sizeable without being overlarge, and was furnished with a bed, a heavy wooden cupboard, a chest of drawers, a table and two or three brass stools, all as elaborately molded as the chair. What caught Aemilia's attention most, however, were the walls. Every square inch of them was covered with fresco paintings depicting pillars supporting architraves, and beyond them doorways leading to balconies themselves giving out to sumptuous woodland scenes. They were very realistic, and succeeded in giving the room a grandeur its dimensions would otherwise have denied it.

"Come forward, girl."

Aemilia did as was told and curtseyed. "Your Majesty."

"It's all very well your father telling me you were a lady-in-waiting, but without a letter of recommendation I have no idea of what you can do. Can you style hair?"

"Yes, Your Majesty."

"Massage?"

"I have done a little, Your Majesty."

"Manicure?"

"Yes, Your Majesty."

"Mm. Well I suppose that will do for the moment. I will need you as a manicurist and you can help Sylvia"—she indicated the girl behind her with a lift of the head—"with styling. Vipsania will show you your quarters. That is all."

"I will need to get my things from my father's flat, Your Majesty."

"Very well."

Aemilia curtseyed and turned to go. Lady Julia held up a finger.

"Oh, one other thing. For how long were you at the Avitus villa?"

"I've been there all my life, Your Majesty."

"Indeed." The word was drawn out and gratified.

Aemilia hesitated, wondering if any more questions were forthcoming. Lady Julia flicked a hand loosely at her. "You may go."

Once outside the door she turned to her guide. "My name is Aemilia."

The girl didn't answer. At the bottom of the stairs Aemilia stopped and paused a moment. She was inclined to let it go, to let distance answer coolness, but she was aware of a familiar deeper urge within her to bridge the gap between herself and her acquaintances by any means possible. She faced the girl.

"What's going to happen to Lavilla?"

There was surprise and a flicker of pain in the girl's face. "She'll have to find some work outside the town."

"She can't be a lady-in-waiting again?"

The girl's eyes showed a glint of anger. "Nobody will take her after what the Mistress said about her."

"Whatever it was, I'm sure it wasn't true. Was she your friend?"

"Yes."

"I'm sorry, I really am."

The girl turned to face her. "Why did you come here anyway?"

"I came looking for my father."

"But why'd you leave your last position?"

Aemilia looked quickly around and then went up close to her and whispered in her ear. She nodded with a look of understanding.

"Can't be helped then. Come. You'll be sharing our bedroom. I'll show you where it is now."

"I haven't got very many things to get. They won't take up much space."

At the bottom of the stairs the girl paused to look her over.

"You'll have to have a better dress than that."

"I haven't got anything else."

"I'll lend you one of mine until Urganilla can make one up. She's the seamstress. You'll have to pay for it though, since you're not a slave."

"I don't have any money. Perhaps it can come out of my wages."

The slave girl gave her an amused look. "You won't be getting any *wages*. You'll get board and lodging and from time to time *Her Majesty* will

44

give you a gift if she...thinks you deserve it."

They had reached the slaves' quarters: a narrow passage with small bedrooms on either side. The one they entered had three low wooden beds with just enough space between them to move about.

"What do people think of her?" Aemilia asked.

The girl glanced out into the passage and then closed the door. "She's a stuck-up cow, that's what she is. That's your bed over here. 'Wife of the Emperor's nephew.' We get it all day long. Yes, Your Majesty. No, Your Majesty. Three bags full, Your Majesty. It's enough to make you want to bring up. I tell you, she's only here because her own family wouldn't put up with her."

"Why does Syagrius keep her? Is she related to him?"

"No she's not. There's them that say he wants to make her son emperor, but I don't hold with that. I think he can't see that she's just an old bag of hot air. He doesn't have to put up with her like we do. Do you know that just the other day I was holding the mirror for her and she said I wasn't holding it right and she grabbed it from me and hit me over the head with it, just like that. Nearly broke it too. I've still got the bump to prove it. Here, look."

Aemilia found herself looking at a rounded portion of scalp under hair parted by the girl's fingers. Suddenly a wave of mirth rose up within her and she stifled a laugh. The slave girl looked up sharply.

"Sorry. I can't help myself. It just looks so funny..." The girl hesitated and then the two dissolved into laughter. Taking a large wooden comb from a shelf, the girl stuck her nose up high and pulled a sour face. "Youuu aah totah-ly inn-competent, dyouuu youu heah me?" And she swished the comb down through the air. Aemilia sat on a bed and held her sides, tears starting from her eyes. Eventually the two pulled themselves together.

"What was your mistress like?" The girl asked. "Did she ever clop you with a mirror?"

That provoked another peal of laughter. It was a few moments before Aemilia could reply. "No, she wasn't like that at all. She was good to me. We used to talk a lot about all sorts of things."

"Did she know about..."

"No. I didn't tell her. She couldn't have done anything about it anyway." Aemilia became grave. "Vipsania, Don't tell anyone what I told you. Lady Julia mustn't find out."

"All right. I won't tell, but she'll find out eventually."

"I know, but it should be all right then. Promise you won't tell. It's very important."

"I promise."

45

A slave stuck his head in the door. Aemilia recognized him as the messenger who had come to Tarunculus's flat the previous day. "Lady Julia's looking for you. Better get a move on." He glanced at Aemilia before disappearing.

"I've stayed too long," Vipsania said. "Now I'm in trouble."

"Go on," Aemilia said. "I'll find my way out."

As Vipsania was leaving Aemilia called to her. "Who is the young man in the embroidered tunic? The one with the shiny material."

"That's Ennodius, Lady Julia's son. Be careful of him. He's got his eye on the girls."

"I'll be careful. Goodbye."

Once outside Aemilia made her way back to the forum. The distance was not far. The circumference of the town walls was so small one could walk from one end to the other in less than half-an-hour. As she passed through the forum entrance she heard a distinct voice rising above the hubbub of sellers and the clatter of wheels over flagstones. Entering the plaza she made out a stocky figure standing on the steps leading up to the basilica, in front of a small group of onlookers.

"...and I speak as a Roman to Romans, a countryman to countrymen. This is the time to show you're proud of what you are. Rome is the greatest city in the world, never forget it. It was Rome that gave you everything you have. Who built the cities? Who built the roads? Who made the forum and the houses you live in, eh? Rome did! You've got to stand up for it and fight for it. Your ancestors are all looking at you to see if you will show yourselves worthy of the names you have. They're looking to see if you've got the guts they had."

One elderly idler put an arm around another. "Rufus here's got 'em all rolled in one," he said, pointing at his companion's wide and wobbling belly.

Tarunculus came down the steps and pulled out a wad of papers from a bag strapped round his waist. Aemilia recognized the sheets she had copied. "Doesn't matter how fat he is if he can use a spear," he said. "He can do time on the walls."

"Did my time," said the fat man. "Frontier guard I was."

"About forty years ago," his companion snorted.

"That's still honorable service." Tarunculus said.

"Lot of good it did me," the fat man replied. "We didn't get our pay for a year and we all went home. I came out as thin as Octavian here."

"Get off. You were always fat."

"I was not."

46

"Were too."

"Can you read?" Tarunculus interjected.

"No, never learned," the fat man replied. "You talk to Octavian. Educated like a highborn, he was. He did his letters and learned to write 'em too. He wrote my name all nice and neat, as good as any of those scribes at the basilica. Show him, Octavian."

"How'm I supposed to show him when I haven't got a quill and parchment, eh? Don't be a fool." He turned to Tarunculus. "That doesn't mean I can't do it. I can read all right, as well as the next fellow. What's it about anyway?"

"It's important," said Tarunculus, "but you'd better be telling the truth. I'm not giving these out for wrapping sheets."

"I say I can read means I can read. Did a bit of scribe work when I was a young 'un, till my eyesight went off. I screwed up my eyes to make out the words until I got such a headache I couldn't sleep at night. Not a wink. The Master says to me, 'You'll be in the grave in a year if you keep that up. Go in the kitchen,' he says to me. I told him, 'I can manage.' I didn't want to work in the kitchen, not with the cook. He was a terror, that one. Come the full moon you couldn't do anything with him. He says, 'You're scouring the pots the wrong way,' and he'd throw one at you. Nearly broke my head with one, he did. I didn't want to work with him but there was nothing I could do. The Master said so and that was the end of it."

"Can you read now?" Tarunculus interrupted.

"That's what I've been saying..."

"Then take one of these and stop wasting my time." And he thrust a sheet in the old man's hands. "Who else can read?" he called out.

There was a moment's silence.

"Well come on," he said. "Don't tell me you're all a pack of uneducated slaves."

"I'm not a slave," said the ex-soldier.

"I'm not either," said his companion. "Got my manumission twenty years ago, I did."

"What I want to know is who else can read, by the gods," Tarunculus's voice was near a shout.

No one else was willing to own up to literacy, and the small knot of spectators loosened and drifted off. Aemilia went up to Tarunculus.

"There's not a grain of grit in their bodies," he said with contempt. "I don't know why I waste my time with 'em. It's like talking to blocks of wood. They'll hop though, when the Franks come next month. That'll wake 'em up."

"The Franks are coming here?"

"That's what I said."

"Are they going to attack the town?"

"Not just yet, girl. Chlodovis is coming to see Syagrius. Aulus tipped me off. Ten to one he's throwing down the gauntlet. He might even challenge him to single combat. They like that kind of thing."

"Maybe he's just coming to make a peace treaty."

Tarunculus threw back his head and roared with laughter. "A peace treaty! Barbarians making a peace treaty! Spent your life in a convent, girl? Barbarians don't make peace treaties. All they understand is war. They've been straining at the leash ever since Chlodovis became king, and now he's ready to let 'em loose, but it looks good for him if he tells Syagrius first. Shows that he's not afraid of him."

"What will Syagrius do?"

A kind of grim, exultant joy crept into Tarunculus's voice. "He's been getting ready for this for years. He won't lie down and surrender like they did at Nice. He'll take him on and show him what we're made of. We're going to thrash that arrogant cub right back to the Rhine. I tell you, this is when everything will start changing. We need just one victory and the people will realize that Syagrius is the man to follow. Once he's beaten the Franks it'll be the turn of the Visigoths, and when he's got Gaul under his control, Odoacer'll be next and then...Rome. It's starting, girl—I tell you, it's starting now."

Aemilia glanced back at the old ex-scribe who was squinting at the sheet, holding it as far as he could from his face. His friend grinned at him, screwing up his eyes in imitation. The old man scowled and threw it away, stomping sourly along with his companion laughing at his side. The discarded sheet landed on a flagstone and rested there a moment until a light breeze caught it and tumbled it over and over, away to the center of the forum, where a stronger wind seized it and blew it up into the air, spinning it over the roofs of the buildings and out of sight.

Aemilia looked down and Tarunculus was already gone, striding with a limp back to his apartment. She hesitated for a moment, feeling an odd twinge of sadness and then, shrugging it off, followed him.

PART II:
HANDMAID

Chapter Seven

Settling down in her new post at the governor's Residence was not as difficult as Aemilia feared. She had won over Vipsania as a friend, and she soon mastered the idiosyncrasies of service with Lady Julia, a task made easier by her being of chief interest to her as a source of information. This Aemilia handled as best she could, feeding her details about the Avitus family that were titillating without being damning. On the whole she did it well. She discovered that the Lady had, if not a sense of humor, at least a sense of the ridiculous. Her account of how Avitus had stepped back in the atrium to admire a new bust of himself and fallen backwards into the pool provoked from her the nearest she could come to a laugh, a kind of staccato cackle.

That anecdote earned her first 'present' from Lady Julia, with which she was able to buy a white linen tunic dress from the house seamstress. She showed it to Tarunculus who grinned. "There's my girl. Now you look like you belong to the highborns. Not like those rags you came here in." Aemilia noted that it was the first time he had used 'my' when speaking of her. The sense of happiness it gave lasted well after she had returned to the Residence.

It was not long before she was on easy terms with the slaves of the household. The initial novelty of her status as freeborn and daughter of the town eccentric soon wore off—she had grown up amongst people like these and she understood them. They saw no trace of social snobbery or eccentricity in her and smoothly fitted her into her natural slot in the hierarchy of the place: a little above the cooks, below the Chamberlain, and roughly on a par with the guards.

As she became more proficient in the minutiae of her employment so she became busier. When Lady Julia saw that Aemilia could manicure her nails quickly and with precision, she ordered her to help the slave girl Sylvia style her hair. Styling was an intricate job; her mistress wanted an elaborate coiffure and rounded on Sylvia for being an imbecilic dolt who knew nothing about hair except how to wash it, and not even that properly. Aemilia instinctively grasped what Lady Julia wanted and was able to suggest improvements—curls in this direction, braids higher up—that were to the Lady's liking. Her greatest achievement was to hold up the mirror and watch the Lady admiring herself without her disapproving either of the hairstyle or of the way the mirror was held.

Thus filled, the hours multiplied rapidly, turning into days, which gradually lengthened into weeks. During that period she saw little of Lady Julia's son and nothing of Syagrius. The governor was away in the west, bargaining with the Britons and Saxons. The slave who had delivered Lady Julia's missive to Tarunculus's apartment told Aemilia the background story. Nearly sixty years earlier the dying Empire pulled its last troops from the provinces of Britain. One of the British Magistrates, Vortigern, made himself king and brought Saxon mercenaries across the Channel to help him contain an invasion of Picts, who were raiding Roman Britain from the bleak lands north of Hadrian's Wall. The Saxons came, settled in the land he gave them in return for their services, and then rebelled against their paymaster. Vortigern could not stop them. Neither could his son Vortimer after him, nor anyone else. From the green fields of Kent they spread west and north, pillaging towns, burning villas, and driving the Romanized and unwarlike Britons before them.

When a revolt of serfs cut the Gallic province of Armorica from Roman rule, a British chieftain brought his men over the Channel to subdue it, initially in the name of Rome. The Britons could not match Saxons in combat, but unorganized serfs were easy meat, and the peninsula was soon theirs. The new kingdom of Brittany, independent of Rome, expanded eastwards as more Britons arrived from their devastated island, gradually encroaching on the shrinking territory of Imperial Gaul. After consolidating the remains of the Roman provinces into a single domain, Syagrius had made a treaty with them, fixing the common frontier. But the bargain was old, and the times had changed.

Of more concern to him, though, were the Saxons. Encouraged by the success of their kinsmen in Britain, Saxon raiders had landed further up the coast from Brittany, pillaging far into Roman Gaul and beginning the same process of conquest their compatriots were achieving across the Channel. Count Paulus had gathered every soldier he could find, enlisted the help of the Frankish king Childeric who was still an ally of the Empire, and beaten the Saxons decisively. Reduced to the status of vassals, they had remained in uneasy allegiance ever since. It would not be long before they realized Syagrius could no longer keep them in subjection.

Indeed Syagrius, resting against the teeth of the Frankish wolf, could not afford to fight either Britons or Saxons now. He was trying to strike a deal with them, to convince them that a triumphant Chlodovech posed more of a threat to them than he ever would, thus securing his flank before taking on his real enemy in the north. He would be back soon enough, the slave continued, to deal with the Frankish embassy.

Aemilia had been at the Residence for nearly a month when he came. It was midmorning. She was filing Lady Julia's fingernails in her bedroom when Vipsania came through the door without knocking. "Your Majesty, My Lord Syagrius has arrived," she blurted out.

"And your manners?" the Lady queried sharply. "Are we being invaded by barbarians that you cannot remember to knock?"

"I'm sorry, Your Majesty."

"Now go out and try again."

Flushing, she went out and knocked. "Come in," said Lady Julia. She re-entered and stood waiting by the doorway. "Your Majesty."

"That's better. Now go and tell the Lord that I am in my bedroom if he wishes to see me."

Half-an-hour later the door opened and Aemilia had her first sight of Syagrius. From her childhood, she had imagined him rather like another Aetius—tall, noble, Roman—the imperial ideal of the ruler and soldier. Seeing him at last in the flesh was a surprise.

He was balding, of medium height and had a slight paunch. His mouth and chin had the lines and firmness of a man used to ruling, but the effect of strength was offset by his eyes: they were darting and wary, harried almost. Aemilia noticed that he wore a military tunic and trousers and had a sword buckled at his side, but no cuirass or helmet. Then it occurred to her that he would have taken them off on entering the building.

Lady Julia signed to Vipsania who brought up a chair. Syagrius eased himself into it and glanced at the girl. "Get me some wine," he said, waving her away.

"Was the journey tiring, my Lord?" asked Lady Julia.

"Very. Four hundred miles in five days without stopping. I'll die before I make a journey like that again."

"You could not have left sooner?"

"I had to wait for an embassy from Britain. They found out I was with Budic and sent over a man. That held me up a fortnight before I could get back to the business here."

"Is it certain the Franks are coming?"

"Of course. That's why I got back so damn fast. Staterius tells me they'll

be here the day after tomorrow."

Lady Julia crinkled her lips in disdain.

"Can we expect them to come when they say they will? They have no notion of punctuality."

"In this case I expect them to arrive right on time. They're not coming for a picnic." Syagrius's expression shifted, taking on a touch of irritation that showed in his voice. "I want to see Ennodius. The servants tell me he's nowhere to be found."

"Indeed. I believe he went to the baths."

"I sent for him there. They couldn't find him."

"Doubtless he went home with one of his friends. Perhaps you could try Ricovicus's house."

"I have neither the time nor the inclination to nanny him, my Lady. When he comes, inform him that I need to know where he is at any hour of the day or night. We are living in uncertain times, you understand, and a young man's...habits can no longer be left to his own whims."

A brief glance of mutual comprehension passed between the two.

"I shall speak to him the moment he returns," the Lady spoke. "Indeed it seems to me that it is important that I do so?" There was just a hint of a question at the end of her words.

"It may be."

Vipsania re-entered bearing a goblet of wine. Syagrius took it from her and drained it in one practiced movement, handing the empty goblet back. He gazed moodily before him. Lady Julia dismissed the girl with a movement of her hand.

"We don't have much time," he said after a long pause. If his delegation's coming now that means his army is ready to march, perhaps already on the move. It could be here in a week."

"Good Lord." Lady Julia seemed genuinely shocked.

"I have to stall him."

"You could offer him money."

Syagrius gave a short grunt of a laugh.

"He thinks he can have all the money he wants by marching in here and taking it. He won't be bought off. I must find another way."

Lady Julia examined her carefully polished nails. "How much time would be required?" she asked.

Syagrius considered. "The legions have taken on as many recruits as they can handle. That puts them at three thousand men in all—at the most. I need to bring in every jack man I can from the town garrisons and coastal forts, get the landed senators to give me their guards and conscript a militia.

At least two months." He shook his head. "He'll never wait that long."

The Lady laid her hands on the armrests of her chair. "Well, my Lord, we must see what fortune brings."

Syagrius appeared to become aware of Aemilia's presence. "You've got a new girl, I see."

"Yes." She took hold of Aemilia by the wrist and brought her round in front of her. "You'll never guess who she is."

Syagrius shrugged.

"She's Tarunculus's daughter, can you believe it?"

He glanced at Aemilia with a spark of interest. "The mad centurion? I never knew he had a daughter."

"Neither did I. It appears she has just arrived in Soissons. Her mother died recently, it seems."

"Where are you from?" Syagrius asked.

"The Avitus villa, my Lord, just outside Tours."

"What were you doing there?"

Aemilia felt confused. "...We always lived there, my Lord. My father was busy in the army and didn't have much time to see us."

"The devil he was," said Syagrius. "He hasn't been in the army for years." His look showed comprehension. "His kind is too much taken up with saving the universe to have time for anything else." He paused a moment, as if considering. "Still, he might come in useful. He is a centurion and he's had battle experience. I'm going to need every man like that I can find."

"He's too old," objected Lady Julia.

"I'm not thinking of sending him into battle. He can train conscripts and put a bit of enthusiasm into them. Does he still go on in the forum?"

"Yes, he hasn't stopped. I wanted to speak to you about it. It is all rather embarrassing, you know. It's time something was done about it."

"Let him carry on with it. The common crowd swallows that kind of thing hook, line and sinker. If he can stir up some 'patriotism'"—here Syagrius chuckled—"then so much the better. I don't want recruits running away the moment they catch sight of a Frank."

"Nonsense. Your soldiers will follow you anywhere."

Syagrius rubbed his chin. "I'd like to think so. I had an interesting chat with the British messenger about the state of affairs in Britain. It seems they've at long last found a leader who can fight. A cavalry commander who knows what he's doing. They say he lives in the saddle and that his men follow him to the ends of the earth."

"Is he their king?"

"No. Ambrosius rules still."

"Ambrosius? I would have thought he had died by now."

"No doubt he's old. He's been king for, what...twenty years? Too old for any personal campaigning. The man he's got he employs rather like a commander-in-chief. Brought him south from the Wall apparently. The fellow's clever. He uses cavalry since the Saxons don't have any, and he hits them at fords, when they're trying to cross rivers. Infantry are at their most vulnerable then."

"Do I know him?"

"He is called Arthur."

Lady Julia shook her head. "I've never heard of the name. Not that one hears much from Britain these days. The island was only half-civilized in any case, and it's almost completely barbarian now."

Syagrius arose. "There are times when I would rather be there, my Lady. The sea at my back, some good, heavy cavalry with me on either side, and only Saxons on my front. Well, good day to you."

"Good day, my Lord."

For a while Lady Julia gazed abstractedly ahead, saying nothing, and Aemilia stood behind her, not daring to speak. Eventually the Lady stirred. "There is nothing for it. I must do it," she murmured to herself. Then she looked up sharply at Aemilia. "Did you hear what I said?"

"Yes, Your Majesty."

"You will keep it to yourself, is that clear?"

"Yes, Your Majesty."

"And now finish my nails, girl."

Half-an-hour later Lady Julia dismissed her. Closing the door carefully behind her, she turned and drew breath sharply in startled surprise. Ennodius stood just one foot away. He cautioned her, finger to his lips.

"Caught you by surprise, didn't I?" he whispered with a grin.

"I didn't expect to see you here, my Lord," she replied in a low voice. She was not going to whisper like a fellow-conspirator.

"I know. We need to talk. Not here. Follow me." He set off down the passage. Aemilia did not move. He glanced back, and beckoned her. Seeing her reluctance he came back. "Just to the garden. I need to know what's been said about me." Slowly she followed.

The main garden at the back of the Residence covered an area larger than the building itself. For Aemilia it was the most beautiful part of the dwelling. A high wall, elaborately frescoed with woodland and pastoral scenes surrounded a huge rectangular space, far larger than the garden in the Residence, in which a profusion of every tree, herb and flower flourished, criss-crossed by neat paths and spaced by ornamental pools framed with white pillars. A peace lay suspended in this perfect blend of nature and architecture, and Aemilia had come here more than once, remembering with a pang a more tranquil time on a distant villa. It was then, in the early evenings when the garden was deserted, that she wept for her mother.

"Just here."

They stopped at the central pool. There was no one in sight. Aemilia felt uneasy. Ennodius gave her a disarming smile.

"All right, spill the beans, girl. Am I in trouble?"

She hesitated. "Lord Syagrius was looking for you, My Lord."

"Yes I know that," he chuckled. "That's why I'm here. Staterius interrupted a very pleasant rendezvous. How the devil he found out where I was I don't know, but what I want to know is, how is the mighty Lord? In a bad mood?"

She felt her way. "A little perhaps, My Lord. He was impatient to see you."

"Why did he want to see me?"

"I don't know, My Lord. He didn't say."

"Well then, what did he say? He was with the old girl long enough."

She took a breath. "It's not my place to discuss such things, My Lord. I think it much better if you ask Her Majesty or Lord Syagrius rather than me."

The dull eyes lit up, whether with anger or amusement Aemilia could not tell. "Oho. A close one." She shifted as if to return to the Residence. He continued, "I admire that, believe me I do. It's good to come across a servant with some spunk."

"May I go, My Lord?" she asked.

He ignored her. "Look, everyone here knows everyone else's business. It's perfectly natural—the way things are. I know the old girl likes you and I've got no doubt she'll end up trusting you. Now, if I make it worth your while," he reached inside his tunic and produced a small cloth bag which he shook, producing a clinking sound, "perhaps you could keep me up to date. What do you say?"

"I cannot change what I said, My Lord."

He put the bag away and gave her a look of appraisal. "More fool than you look, girl."

"It would be wrong."

As the words came out she regretted them. She had gone beyond the protective formality of the servant-master relationship and put herself on a level of moral equality with Ennodius. She chided herself that she had allowed her pride to be piqued again. *You are a lady-in-waiting in a highborn's house,* she thought, *why can't you remember that?*

Ennodius smiled, and sat down on a stone bench. She remained standing before him.

"Yes it would," he agreed, "but try to understand, I have to do everything I can to look after myself. I may look like I'm sitting pretty in the lap of luxury, but don't be taken in by appearances. I'm only here because my noble lord Syagrius thinks he can use me. The moment he decides I've outlived my usefulness, out I go."

Aemilia was silent. Ennodius went on.

"You may think that because I'm important I'm popular, but the truth is I have very few real friends. That's why I tried bribing you. I didn't think I could appeal to your better nature. My mistake. Look, Aemilia..."

She stiffened. He noticed it and paused.

"Well I'm not going to call you 'girl' indefinitely. Aemilia, help me and you won't regret it, I promise you."

"I can't help you in that way, My Lord," she said.

"Will you help me in any way you can?"

"I don't see how I *can* help you."

"There are ways," he replied, his eyes fixed on hers. She was silent. He gave a sigh. "You don't trust me, do you?"

She averted her head, confused as to what to say.

"Aemilia," he went on in a softer voice, "you're a good girl, I can see that. I've spent my life looking for someone like you, someone I can depend upon. You must know what it's like with the big families: all the immoral cloak and dagger that goes on under the appearance of"—the tone was mocking—"good breeding."

Her eyes flicked back at him. He had struck a nerve. Aemilia remembered Avitus in the bedroom, and the moment when the mental deference of a lifetime had disintegrated, replaced by she knew not what.

"You have to get used to living that way just to survive," he went on. "Everyone I know is like that: dishonest, untrustworthy...generally immoral. But you're different. You say what you mean. I know I can trust you. Won't you trust me? I would never ask you to do anything wrong, of course."

A sense of affinity with Ennodius rose up in her. She looked at him directly. "Anything I can do for you I will, My Lord." There was feeling in the words, with just a slight emphasis on the 'can'.

"That's all I ask," he replied. "And now run along. I've got an interview with Syagrius that had better not wait." He stood up. "Friends?"

She could not say why, but for some reason his last word troubled her. She murmured something indistinct and turned, walking away. She did not look back and so did not see the grin on his face, like a gambler in a tight game who had just thrown two Venuses. As she disappeared into the Residence he pulled out the coin bag and tossed it up, catching it.

"A little patience and free of charge," he said to himself.

CHAPTER 8

By the next day the news that the Franks were coming was common knowledge and an air of tense expectancy settled upon the Residence. Lady Julia was absent for the first half of the morning and Aemilia took the opportunity to go and see Tarunculus, finding him at the apartment. Omitting Syagrius's tag of 'mad centurion,' she related his plans for a militia and the need for men like Tarunculus to train them.

"You say he mentioned me?" Tarunculus asked, leaning forward, arms crossed on the table.

"Yes, sir, he did."

"Ha! He knows I'm the one to whip those scum into shape. You can make a soldier out of anything. You just need time and discipline, discipline, discipline." He emphasised each of the last three words by jabbing his finger down on the table. "When does he want me there? I'll have to make arrangements for the shop and re-enlist at the barracks. Does he want me there today?"

Aemilia felt a trifle embarrassed. "He didn't say exactly when, sir." She wondered if she should have mentioned Syagrius so soon.

"No matter. He'll send a messenger. Today. I'll have to go to the shop now. Anything else you can tell me before you go?"

Aemilia hesitated before answering. "He did say the army of the Franks could be here in a week."

Tarunculus stared at her. "A week? By Hades." He thought for a moment, chin on palm. "I can't train recruits in a week. They'll be a mob when they go out."

"He said he's going to try and delay them."

"How?"

"He didn't say."

Tarunculus's features settled into a confident mold. "If he wants me to train recruits then he knows I need time to do it. He'll think of something. I've seen him in tighter holes than this and he always gets out. It's not ours

63

to worry about."

Aemilia remembered the darting eyes, the weariness, the weighed-down determination. She became aware of a tiny stab of sadness within her.

"I must be getting back, sir," she said.

Tarunculus got up and came round to her. She stood up in surprise. He put his hands on her shoulders.

"From now on you call me 'father.' Is that clear?"

She looked at him wide-eyed. "Yes, sir," she said, and then, "yes, Father."

He patted her cheek. "That's my girl." He stepped back. "You don't get much time out. How safe are your things at the Residence?"

"Quite safe," Aemilia replied. "I know all the slaves there and nobody would take anything of mine."

"Even something valuable?"

"Even if it was valuable. They're not like that."

Tarunculus went over to the bookshelves, took out a brown-covered volume and brought it back to her. "You said you liked Augustine. Here. Only on loan, mind."

She was dumbfounded for a moment, and then suddenly hugged him. "Thank you, Father," she said. Surprised, he patted her awkwardly on the back.

"Now, then," he said, "no getting carried away. I've never read it myself. Come on, now."

She stood back and took the book from him. In the joy of the moment she did not notice his sudden discomfort. He looked away from her. "You'll be late back if you don't get a move on, girl."

"Yes, Father. Thank you. I'll take good care of it, I promise."

"That you will, or you'll buy me another."

"I'll try and see you tomorrow."

"Aye, if you can. Be off, now."

"Goodbye," and she was gone.

Holding the book tightly she made her way back to the Residence. The guard at the entrance greeted her familiarly. "Hello, Aemilia."

"Hello, Galbus. Is the Lady back?"

"Not yet. What you got there?"

"A book from my father." She showed it to him. "Isn't it beautiful?"

The guard pulled a face. "Just old parchment to me. Mind that Ennodius doesn't see it. He likes books and he don't give 'em back either, from what I've heard."

"Nonsense. Why would he want a book that much?"

"Vipsania says he wants to be more educated than the rest of 'em. That way they'll respect him, she says."

"But why is he worried about respect? He's a highborn."

The guard looked at her conspiratorially.

"Highborn don't help if your purse is flat. The Lady's got no money except what Syagrius gives her..."

"Hasn't she?"

"Nope. Not a nummus. She had a big fight with the family and they cut her off."

"What did they fight about?"

"There's them that say it was the will. Her husband's. He changed it before he died and gave everything to his nephews. They had in mind to give her an allowance, but she wasn't having any of that. She says, you give me it all, it's mine, she says. They tell her where she can jump and—oop!—she jumps here."

"Oh," said Aemilia.

"If you ask me, *that's* the reason she acts so high and mighty. An empty pot makes the most noise. But she's careful around Syagrius, that she is. Doesn't boss *him* around, not her bread and butter."

"She would be extra-careful if he's going to make her son emperor."

The guard gave a snort. "Can't see him doing that. What do we need an emperor for? We haven't had one since Augustiekins and we've done well enough without. Anybody who's crying for one can go off to Constantinople, that's what *I* say. Emperors did us no good when we had 'em, and anyhow what's there left to be emperor of?"

"But Gaul is so big, Galbus. I travelled right across it and it went on forever. It's easily big enough for an emperor."

The guard smiled paternally. "You're still young, girl. You haven't been around much. What the Visigoths and the Burgunds and Odoacer's got's bigger, and *they* don't go round making emperors. Mark my words, if Syagrius puts up an emperor, they'll jump on him like jackals, that they will. They won't stand for it. They'll say he's getting too big for his boots. I'm telling you, Syagrius's kept what he's got because he talks their lingo and keeps his head down. If he starts getting high and mighty..." he pulled a finger across his throat.

There was a pause. Aemilia looked downwards. "Is something wrong with your leg?" she asked, noticing him shifting uncomfortably.

"Aye. Just a corn. Too much standing."

"I know a good salve for that. I'll find it and give it to you."

"I wouldn't say no, but you can't come into the guards' quarters."

"I know, but Pollux won't mind if we meet in the kitchen when you're off duty. When Lady Julia dismisses me I'll send you a message."

The guard grunted his assent. Then looking over her head he straightened up.

"Here she comes. In you go."

Aemilia glanced around to see an approaching litter. She went through the entrance, hurrying to her quarters as fast as decorum would allow. She arrived to find Vipsania sweeping the cramped room.

"The Lady's here," she said, putting the book on the shelf above her bed. "I'll finish sweeping if she calls you."

"Nearly done," Vipsania replied. "Is that a book?"

"Yes. From my father."

She looked at her curiously. "What's he giving you a book for?"

"I can read," said Aemilia, flushing.

"Get off! You never told me."

"It doesn't matter."

"Yes it does. It means you're educated and all, just like the highborns. I bet they wouldn't like it if they found out."

"Lady Avita didn't mind. She let me read her books."

"She's different. Look at Her Majesty. She's so proud of little Ennodiekins' education. 'He's read all the old books,' she says, 'and he knows big pieces of 'em off by heart too. Say something for the man, Ennodiekins,' and off he goes, spouting some nonsense from Caesar or Cicero or whoever."

Aemilia giggled. "Oh, go away," she said, lifting up a bed so the girl could sweep underneath.

"If she finds out you can do it too she'll see red. You'll never hear the end of it."

"Oh, she knows already. My father told her I was doing scribe work for him."

Vipsania paused in her sweeping and glanced up. "Scribe work? You mean writing and all?"

"Yes."

"You shouldn't be a lady-in-waiting," she said, resuming her sweeping, "you can do better than this."

Aemilia put the bed down. "I'm happy here, Vipsania. I've only ever been a lady-in-waiting and before that I was in the stables. I'm not looking for any more."

"Well, I still think it's a waste."

The door opened and Sylvia came in. "Lady's back," she said, looking at Aemilia, "she wants you." A mouse-like, moody creature, she had cooled toward Aemilia when the Lady's preference for her had become manifest. Aemilia had tried all she could think of to break through the crust of jealousy, but without success.

Aemilia left the room and made her way to Lady Julia's apartment.

"Wash my feet," Lady Julia ordered when she arrived. Aemilia noticed mud splattered on the Lady's sandals. She fetched a basin, towel and sponge and set them down in front of the Lady's chair. Untying the left sandal she lifted the Lady's foot into the basin and then began to rinse it down with the wet sponge.

"The streets are in dreadful condition," Lady Julia complained, "I simply cannot understand why more effort isn't taken to..."

"*Vervlaks!*" Aemilia uttered the exclamation involuntarily as she knocked the basin, slopping out some water.

Lady Julia glanced down at her. "Careful, you clumsy girl."

"I'm sorry, Your Majesty. I'll clean it up."

"What did you say?"

"I'll clean up the water, Your Majesty."

"No, I mean that barbaric word you used."

"It's just an expression, Your Majesty," Aemilia replied, mopping up the spilt water with the towel. "It means 'oh, dear.'"

"Indeed. Where did you learn it?"

"From my mother, Your Majesty." Aemilia began to feel uneasy.

"Wasn't your mother a Roman?"

"No, Your Majesty...she was a Frank, the daughter of a merchant in Tours."

Lady Julia leaned back in surprise. "A Frank! Whatever next!" She paused a moment. "So you can speak their language?"

"Yes, Your Majesty."

The Lady leaned chin on finger and her expression became abstracted. Aemilia hesitated.

"Carry on, girl," the Lady ordered, and resumed her musing.

After both feet were washed and dried and a new pair of sandals fetched and tied on, Lady Julia broke her silence. "Put away that bowl and come here. I have something important for you to do."

Aemilia did as bid and stood in front of the Lady.

"Now listen carefully. The Franks arrive today. Tomorrow you are to tell anyone who asks that I have given you the day off. You must then go to their campsite outside the city and tell Chlodovis their leader that I wish to see him, but you must make it clear to him that he must ask to see me.

Tell him I have important information for him but it must not look like I sought him out myself. Do you understand? He must ask to see me."

Aemilia was wide-eyed. "I understand."

"You must speak to him alone, in private."

"Yes, Your Majesty."

"Now repeat what I said."

Aemilia did so.

"Good. The most important thing is that *no one* must follow you. *No one* must know where you have gone. Can you manage it?"

"I...I think so."

"Just put a shawl on and keep your head down. You've been here only a month so no one will recognize you."

"Yes, Your Majesty."

"And one last thing, girl," Lady Julia leaned forward with a hard look in her eyes. "Should you repeat any of this to anyone you will lose your position immediately. Nor will you obtain another. Do I make myself clear?"

A memory of the squalor outside the walls on her arrival at the town took hold of Aemilia's mind with the soft touch of fear. She looked down. "I understand, Your Majesty."

Lady Julia's expression was satisfied. "Good girl. I needn't mention that if you do exactly as I have said there will be a little reward for you."

"Thank you, Your Majesty." *I do not want your reward,* Aemilia thought. *What are you getting me into?*

"Tomorrow you are free until sunset. A recompense for your hard work. Start telling the slaves. You may go now."

"Yes, Your Majesty." Aemilia curtseyed and turned to leave.

"Oh, and I want you here this afternoon for a styling. After my siesta."

Aemilia curtseyed again and left.

She sought out the main garden and sat down to collect her thoughts. It was evident that there was something wrong in Lady Julia's reasons for wanting to see Chlodovis, something she wanted to hide from Syagrius. Aemilia could not imagine what it might be. Her fear spoke to her: If Syagrius finds out that Lady Julia is talking to the Franks without his knowledge, and that you helped her do it...Then common sense interposed: What can Lady Julia do that would really make Syagrius angry? She's just a pompous old lady. Fear spoke again: Syagrius is like a cornered boar, you saw it in his eyes. If anybody does anything behind his back how do you think he will react? He'll be furious, he'll order his soldiers to...Then common sense: It's true, he may, but you cannot refuse to obey the Lady. You must just make sure nobody finds out. Trust Providence. Then fear: If what you're doing is wrong, Providence won't protect you.

That gave her pause. Finally she sighed and arose, uncertain what to do, and walked slowly back to her quarters.

After lunch Aemilia went to the kitchen to see the chief cook, Pollux. A heavy, solid man, entirely bald, with a head that jutted forward like a wrestler's, and permanently covered with a film of sweat, he had a bark and a selective bite. Aemilia was on easy terms with him.

"Do you have any bread left over?" she asked him.

"What for? You hungry?"

"It's not for me. It's for a friend."

"You giving to the beggars? That's the Church's job. Why d'you think they got deacons?"

"It's just for one person, Pollux."

"And if they find out? What happens to me, then, eh?"

"Nobody will mind. You throw the old food away anyhow. Besides, I won't tell them. I'll keep it in my shawl."

The cook hesitated. "Who's this friend?" he demanded.

"It's Lavilla."

"Oh. She still in Soissons?"

"Yes. She hasn't got any family that she knows about. She's looking for work."

The cook turned back to a pot bubbling over the hearth. "It's a shame the Lady send her away like that. All right. You take but not too much." He stirred the contents, ignoring Aemilia as she helped herself to a stale half-loaf from the big table in the middle of the kitchen. Wrapping it up in a cloth she took it back to her room. She was stashing it on the shelf above her bed when Sylvia came in.

"What you got there?"

"Food," Aemilia replied, showing her.

"That's not allowed."

"It's not for me, it's for Lavilla."

The girl considered this.

"You still shouldn't. It'll make trouble."

Aemilia sighed, smoothing out a stab of irritation within her, and got down from her bed. "She doesn't have any work, Sylvia, and she's got no one to go to. I have to help her until she can earn money somehow."

"I don't want trouble."

"There won't be any. This is food Pollux would've thrown away. He doesn't mind." She added as an afterthought, remembering Lady Julia's instructions, "I'm taking it to her tomorrow morning. Her Majesty gave me the day off." Then she bit her lip, remembering to whom she was talking.

"The day off? You are in her good books."

"I didn't ask for it."

The girl shrugged her shoulders and lay down on her bed. Later Aemilia thought about her whilst going up the stairs to the Lady's room for the afternoon coiffure. She realized she did not know where she stood with her, nor what the girl, prompted by jealousy, might do. *Strive to be on good terms with everyone,* St. Paul had written. *I am striving,* she thought, *but with someone like Sylvia I just don't know what to do.*

The afternoon styling was a strange affair. Lady Julia did not mention the Franks, and treated Aemilia with her usual mixture of indifference and petulance, with a small word of praise at the end on viewing the completed structure. As Aemilia was taking her leave the Lady gave her a folded piece of paper. "Let no one see this," she said. Opening it later in the main garden Aemilia found it to be directions to the Franks' campsite.

Lying on her bed that night, her thoughts went back to Sylvia. If you had been like her, saying little, never smiling, not being especially good in your work, Lady Julia would never have made you her favorite and put you in this danger. You'll be alone outside the town, going to barbarians. What will they do to you? Romans are their enemies and you're just a serving maid. Will you be able to make them understand the importance of your mission before they decide to...

She shivered slightly and turned in her bed, clutching her blanket tightly to her although it was not cold. If you're doing wrong and Providence doesn't protect you.... At this point she refused to think any further but turned to God, beating off fear with trust until her thoughts settled into relative calm. Finally, when she was tranquil, the thought crept into her mind: You cannot know whether the Lady is doing wrong, but you can do no wrong in obeying her. Her reasons for seeing the Franks are her business, not yours.

With that she was content, and could, at last, fall asleep.

CHAPTER 9

Aemilia awoke early, when the light was still dim. She knew Lady Julia wanted her message delivered to the Franks before they saw Syagrius, and had willed herself, adding a prayer, to waken before the dawn. She dressed quickly and quietly, tying up the half-loaf she had taken from the kitchen in a cloth. The guard at the entrance was mildly surprised that she was leaving so early.

"Her Majesty's given me the day off. There're a lot of things I need to do," she said by way of explanation.

Except for a few beggars and open-air stall keepers setting up their wares, the streets and the forum were deserted. Stopping in the plaza, she took a moment to read Lady Julia's directions, then made her way to the east gate. The gates were shut from sunset to sunrise and finding them not yet opened, she sat in a nearby doorway until a sentry with a trumpet blew the morning watch call. She was first through the opened gates, but no one paid any attention to a serving girl in a brown mantle holding a nondescript cloth bundle.

She walked a mile along the Reims road and then stopped to take out the sheet with the directions. The sun rose above a wall of low clouds on the horizon, and the morning dew sparkled in the grass. Aemilia looked up: the clouds were pink and the sky cream with the soft light of the young sun. She became aware of the silence around her, of the great motionless sweep of the natural world, keeping its delicate and immovable balance in the eternity of the present moment. She put down the bundle and stretched her arms above her, feeling the gentle touch of sunlight on her skin, and then, suddenly and inexplicably lighthearted, she did a few steps of a country dance. Coming to herself she chuckled at her own frivolity. *The mission, the mission,* she thought, opening the paper, *time for the mission.*

Finding the mile marker a little further on, she left the road and struck north along a mule track, following it until it began to wind between two low hills. "The hill on the right," she murmured, scrutinizing the paper. Its

71

contours were broken by an irregular belt of trees round its base. Through these she would have to go, finding the campsite somewhere near the summit.

She sensed all at once her solitude. The town was out of sight and she was utterly alone, beyond the reach of help. Her carefree mood evaporated and a finger of fear began to press inside her chest. She scanned the trees differently. Who was in them? Had she been seen yet? If she turned and hurried away quickly and quietly there was a chance she would not be noticed. What to do, what to do?

She stood, irresolute. Why continue with this? What was right about it? But to turn back, be dismissed by Lady Julia, face her father in disgrace, with nowhere to go if he cast her out...What was the right choice? She did not know. Time passed and then, irrationally, or rather, beyond reason, the conviction seeped to the surface: *nothing for it but to go on.*

Her mind made up, she slowly made the sign of the Cross and started up the grassy slope toward the trees. The dew-beaded grass soon soaked the hem of her dress but she was hardly aware of it, gazing ahead and thinking of the desperate race in the grain cart just a month before.

Coming to the wood now, a gap just there. No sign of anyone. Where are they? Now under the trees. The gap is deceptive: there is a lot of brush and undergrowth to work around, fallen branches, rotting logs. The mantle and bundle catching on twigs, slowing her down. And all the time total silence. No breeze in the leaves, no birds, nothing. Ahead the trees thinning, giving way to open pasture. Still not a soul in sight. Where on earth can they be? Out in the open again, approaching the summit. Nothing to be seen except a few irregular boulders. One straight ahead, a black silhouette against the dawnlight...

Her heart lurched. The boulder moved, took the shape of a man and began to come down toward her. It was far too late to run now. She stood still, gripping her bundle, and let him approach. At fifty yards he stopped, scanning the trees behind her.

"Who are you? Why did you come here?" he called out in Frankish.

"I must speak to your king," she replied in the same language.

"You are alone?"

"*Ja.*"

He was suspicious. "Why do you want to see him?" he demanded.

"I have a message for him, sir. I come from the house of Syagrius."

"You are from Syagrius? Does he send girls as messengers?"

"He did not send me. I am from someone else in his house."

The Frank considered this for a while. Aemilia began to register his

appearance. Long blond moustaches, no beard, a striped blue-and-white tunic, brown trousers cross-gartered below the knee, leather shoes. A pointed Frankish *spangenhelm* protected his head. He held a round shield on his left arm with a pattern of red and black spirals painted on it. His right hand grasped a short, wickedly barbed spear. From his belt hung a strange, curved axe. He appeared to be young.

"There is nobody with you?" he asked again.

"Nobody," she replied. "I came alone."

That seemed to decide him. "You come up here," he called out.

She made her way up the slope and stood before him. He scrutinized her curiously.

"You are a Frank," he said, lifting his spear and pointing it at her face. Her heart gave another lurch. "You have the eyes of a Frank." In her confusion she did not understand him.

"Gray," he said in explanation.

"My mother was a Frank."

"Why are you living in Roman land?"

"My father is a Roman."

"You do not look like a Roman. They are darker."

"Those are Gauls. My father is from Rome."

"*Ag so?*" He turned, his curiosity satisfied. "Come with me," he said

73

over his shoulder, "I will take you to Chlodovech."

Aemilia nearly had to run to keep up with the loping strides of the warrior. They crested the hill, and there, slightly below them on a small plateau, lay the Frankish camp. Several dozen horses were corralled in a crude enclosure made of felled young trunks and lopped off branches. Near them thin tufts of smoke wafted from four or five smouldering campfires. There were no tents. A number of Franks sat round the fires eating breakfast, bread it seemed though Aemilia could not be sure from her distance. She saw more figures scattered round the plateau and realized there must be sentries on the other slopes.

As they approached the campsite Aemilia tried to divine which of the figures was Chlodovech. No one individual stood out. Their attire was similar, that is to say diverse in the Frankish fashion. The detail of each Frank's clothing was different from the others. Certainly they were fond of color. Blue, ochre, brown, yellow, green in various patterns made them seem like bright flowers transplanted to the gently rolling contours of northern Gaul. Their weapons seemed equally diverse: axes, spears, and swords were strapped to their sides or lay not far from them. As Aemilia drew near one or two lifted their heads to look at her with mild curiosity before returning to their occupations. Absorbed by the strangeness of the scene, she forgot her apprehension.

Around one campfire sat a group of half-a-dozen Franks. Aemilia's escort went up to them and spoke to a very young man with a chainmail corset seated in the middle of them. He turned his eyes to Aemilia and beckoned her. She went forward.

"You want to see me," said the youth in Frankish.

For a moment Aemilia had no words. The king of the Franks seemed barely out of his teens. She groped for the right expression in Frankish. "My Lord, I must speak to you alone."

He glanced to his right and left. "Why can you not speak here?"

"My message is for your ears only, My Lord."

Irritation showed in the young features. "I will not play this Roman game. Syagrius will not give me something to hide from my warriors. You give your message here," he said, finger pointing downwards in front of him.

Aemilia did not hesitate. "Yes, My Lord. I come from Lady Julia."

"Who is she?"

"She is staying at the house of Syagrius. She is from a great family."

"Which family?" Aemilia saw the shrewdness in his eyes.

"The Avitus family. There was an emperor Avitus many years ago."

He shrugged. "There is no emperor now."

Aemilia briefly weighed telling him of Syagrius's plans for Julia's son and decided against it.

"Good. So what message does she have for me?"

"She said you must ask to see her. Then she will have something important to tell you."

"So?" He tilted his head quizzically. "Why cannot she just come here herself?"

"I don't know. She said it must not look like she wanted to see you, but that you wanted to see her."

"*Ja*, this is a Roman game," he chuckled. His men joined in his amusement. He rubbed his chin, considering. "We will play it."

"Shall I tell her you will see her?"

He nodded. "*Ja*. But you are a Frank, are you not? What are you doing with Romans?"

"Her father is a Roman from Rome," interjected her escort.

"He speaks Frankish?" Chlodovech asked.

"No," she replied. "My mother and I spoke it in our home."

"So you speak Latin with your father?"

She began to redden. "...he was not there."

"What did he do, your father?" asked the young king, with a glint in his eye. "Did he put his hands on a Frankish girl?"

"They were married," she said.

There was a pause. "Oh, *ja*? That is good then. Some of my Franks are married to Roman girls. The Visigoths do not allow it, but it is no matter to me. When I have Syagrius's lands the people may marry as they choose." He mentioned this casually, as if the Frankish conquest of Roman Gaul was something so evident it did not need any emphasis. Then he noticed her bundle. "You bring me a present?" he asked.

She brought the bundle in front of her. "No, this is just food I am taking to a friend."

"Your friend is a beggar?"

"She is a serving-girl, like me. She used to work where I work, but now she has no living."

"Show me." She opened the cloth, revealing the half-loaf. He grunted. "Not much."

"It is all I could get."

He turned to her escort. "Merovec, give her a loaf and take her to the bottom of the hill." Then turning back to her he said, "Tell this Lady Julia I will send a messenger today, but she must not waste my time with nothing."

"Yes, My Lord," she replied, "and thank you."

Later at the mule track the Frank bade her goodbye. "Off you go, little Frank."

"He is kind, your king."

He grinned. "*Ja*, he is good, until you make him your enemy. Then, chop." It was clear he admired Chlodovech tremendously. She held up a hand in farewell. He reciprocated and turned back up the hill. She walked slowly back to the milestone, collecting her thoughts. She had not been at the Frankish camp for long, yet that brief time had sufficed to pitch overboard lifelong notions of barbarians. She had no doubt the Franks were dangerous, but they were not brutes, and they had a king who was utterly unlike the powerful Romans she knew. He ruled, that was clear, but he did not make his authority a pillar to bear him loftily above his subjects. It was all very new to her. She opened the bundle and looked at the bread Chlodovech had given her. It was oval rather than round like a Roman loaf, heavier and made of darker flour. She wondered how she was going to explain it to Lavilla. *I'll just have to tell her a traveller passing by Soissons gave it to me*, she thought. *That is the truth after all.*

The visit to Lavilla depressed her. The girl lived in a dilapidated apartment building outside the walls. She had been given breakfast and board in a small cupboard of a room near the top of the building by the landlord in exchange for ten hours of work each day scrubbing the floors of the apartment block. The landlord had made this arrangement with her because she had come to him well-dressed and he did not think she would be tempted by the miserable possessions of the other tenants. The girl was pathetically grateful for Aemilia's visit and fell upon the bread the moment it was put on the bed. She did not know what she was going to do. Both her parents were dead and she had no other relations that she knew of. Working for any of the wealthy families in Soissons was out of the question without a reference from Lady Julia.

Together they went through every occupation they could think of. Lavilla did not have the necessary skills for an employable trade nor, Aemilia suspected, looking at her gaunt face and thin frame, the stamina to stay where she was. Working for a noblewoman like Lady Julia was a trial, but it was a sheltered existence nonetheless. As they examined the possibilities, exhausting them one by one, Aemilia felt a presence, slight but insistent, filtering into the room through the cracks in the door, the floorboards and the angled ceiling. In her mind's eye it thickened imperceptibly, settling on the girl sitting next to her, binding itself with an air of mockery to her fragile resolve, like a chronic illness still young and tender. She was in a spiral that would drag her down as surely as cancer unless help came to her. She could not save herself. Aemilia stood up.

"I'll find an answer," she said.

"How will you do that?" the girl asked.

"I don't know, but I will."

She left with the promise to return with more food and made her way back to the forum. She had no idea how she was going to fulfill her pledge to Lavilla. The bishop at the church had told her to come to him if she needed help, but she doubted he would be able to do much beyond the odd handout. Soissons was poor and the Church did not have much to give. If she pressed the case on him, he would agree to ensure that Lavilla did not starve, she felt certain, but it was not primarily the question of food that troubled her. Penury was not just an affair of the stomach. She was afraid of what it would do to Lavilla's mind: eating away her hope, breaking down her small stock of self respect, making her vulnerable...

The Franks must take the town. The thought came suddenly, unbidden. She stopped, startled. Never, she thought. Impossible. How could Lavilla be safe with them? What were they?

For a few moments she contemplated the absurdity of the notion that such a thing should be desirable and then, inexplicably, there arose in her, like a great wave, the love for all the things she had known and cherished since consciousness first opened in her. The cool and graceful architecture of the villa; the sweep of its fields interspersed with trees, oak and ash and pine; the row of stables she had cleaned and the horses she had known; the old cook, Melanie, who had been almost a second mother to her; the kindness of her first mistress; the excitement of learning how to read, and the books she had devoured—they tumbled through her, a collection of images of everything that was dear to her, all familiar, all roots in the tree of her life, all Roman. It was not something that she needed for a moment to debate within herself. It was a sentiment, simple, irrational, certain. As she stood in the great open space of forum, seeing the colonnades around her for the first time as familiar and not strange, she became aware that, against all reason and circumstance, she was a patriot.

She chuckled to herself. *I couldn't even lift my father's sword,* she thought. She hesitated between going to the church immediately to tackle the bishop on Lavilla's behalf, or returning first to Lady Julia to relay Chlodovech's message.

The Church won't go away, she thought, and started back for the Residence.

Chapter 10

Lady Julia was alone in her room when Aemilia returned. After glancing to see there was no one outside in the passage, the Lady resumed her seat and ordered Aemilia to stand before her. Her habitual sharp aloofness had given way to a restrained eagerness, amounting almost to anxiety.

"You have seen Chlodovis?"

"Yes, Your Majesty."

"And?"

"He will send a messenger to you today."

A sigh escaped from the Lady. "Good. Now what is he like? Describe him to me."

"He...is very young, Your Majesty."

Lady Julia gave a snort of irritation. "I know *that*, you foolish girl. He is twenty years old. What I want to know is, what kind of a man is he? Is he intelligent, a fool, what?"

Aemilia proceeded uncertainly. "He seems very direct, Your Majesty. I had to give your message to him in front of his soldiers so that he wouldn't have anything to hide from them."

"A sense of honor, then," interjected the Lady.

"Yes, I think so, Your Majesty. I wasn't with him very long, only a few minutes. He also seems...very confident."

"About what?" the Lady queried sharply.

Aemilia deliberated. "I...he gave me the impression that he did not think he would have any difficulty taking over the province..." Her voice trailed away. Why did speaking feel so treasonous?

"Headstrong," commented the Lady. "That can serve our turn." She spent several moments ruminating on the news she had been given and then turned her regard to Aemilia again. "What else can you tell me?"

Aemilia described the appearance of the Franks and the disposition of the camp, emphasising their vigilance. At the end of her account, Lady Julia leaned back in her chair with a satisfied look.

"Good, you have done well. Open that casket on the table and bring me the bag you see in it."

Aemilia complied. Lady Julia opened the bag and extracted several silver siliquas. "Take these," she said, holding them out, "and remember, you are to speak of this to no one, do you understand?"

"Yes, Your Majesty," Aemilia replied, her thoughts on Lavilla.

"Now go. I want you away from the Residence when their messenger comes. Do not return until this evening."

"Yes, Your Majesty." Aemilia curtseyed and left.

Aemilia quitted the Residence as quickly and discreetly as she could, not wanting to explain her return to the building after purportedly having left it for the day. To the door guard's query she said by way of explanation: "I remembered something I had to do for Lady Julia," and hurried away to avoid further conversation.

She decided to seek out Tarunculus and see if she could be of use to him. Finding the apartment door locked with no reply to her knocking, she made an effort to remember where he had said his shop was. It seemed an age since he had mentioned it: Field Street...Fitters Street...Fullers Street. That was it, Fullers Street. Once outside the flats, she asked the first bystander she met, a fat, middle-aged woman with a basket, for directions.

"You're new here, love," the woman replied.

"I came just a month ago."

"You shouldn't be alone in times like these."

"I'm not alone. I have family in Soissons."

The woman looked her up and down. "Well-to-do it seems. Have they been here long?"

"Yes." Aemilia was disinclined to tell this inquisitive woman anything more about herself. "Is Fullers Street far from here?"

The woman's eyes narrowed slightly and her tone became a fraction more formal, less friendly. "Nothing is far in Soissons. It's by the barracks, that way," she said, pointing up the street. "Ten minutes if you've got good legs."

"Thank you," said Aemilia, giving her a nod and starting off in the direction she had indicated. A month before she would not have been curt with such nosiness. Since she could remember it had been the norm for people to know what they wished about her private affairs. It was something that they and she had taken for granted. But now, there had been a shift. The crust of her world had slipped into a new configuration that was like and unlike the old. The rock under that crust was jostling and grinding as great forces strove with one another, seeking a new equilibrium, and the ground felt different under her feet. Like all the truly fundamental mutations underlying the theater of human existence, the change was almost imperceptible. She was barely aware of it and when it did reach her consciousness she considered it, let it go as an enigma and gave it no further thought.

The armory shop was built into the corner of the outer wall of the barracks building. On the wall over the wide arched entrance, the sign 'Tarunculus Armorer' was painted in neat, red letters, doubtless by Tarunculus himself.

The entrance gave into a deep room in which three smiths sweated in front of two large, glowing brick kilns. Wooden poles, six feet long, were stacked against the wall. In a wooden crate were what looked like spear or arrow points. Spear points, Aemilia decided. They were leaf-shaped and rather too big for arrows. A number of large, flat, shields were stacked against the other wall, all oval in the standard Roman style. On each were painted four red bars, intersecting in the middle, and set against a yellow background. The smiths were working on helmets, several of which lay on a table near the kilns. They were round, with large, hinged jaw guards on the sides and a hinged neck guard on the back. A ridge of iron ran over the top of each helmet, from front to back. Fascinated by the detail of the weaponry, it was a second or two before Aemilia noticed Tarunculus, seated behind the shop counter entering figures on a scroll. She went over to him and her shadow fell on the parchment. He glanced up with an irritated expression that softened when he recognized her.

"Didn't expect you at this hour."

"The Lady gave me the day off as a reward."

"A reward, eh? So she's taken to you. I knew she would." He laid down his quill. "Come to have a look at the shop?"

"Yes, Father," the word still sounded strange, "and also to see if there's anything I can do for you during the day."

"Aye. No good you being idle." He stood up and came round the counter. "We're in the middle of an order now, standard arms for a centuria—a hundred men. That's Arbogast. He's been with me from the beginning." The smith paused in his hammering to acknowledge Aemilia. "Nestor next to him, and Primus." The first gave Aemilia a momentary smile, the second nodded briefly without pausing in his work. "I've had Nestor for three years. Primus I got three months ago."

"Did they come from the army too?"

"What d'you think, girl? D'you think Syagrius'd let 'em out before they're twice the ages they are now? Not bloody likely. They're slaves."

"Oh," said Aemilia.

"I bought 'em and trained 'em from scratch. Useless idlers when they came here, but that didn't last long, eh, Primus?" The slave glanced up, the line of his mouth stretching to what Aemilia guessed was supposed to be a smile, though there was no mirth in it and the expression in his eyes was wary. "Nothing like this for enforcing discipline." Tarunculus had picked up a centurion's cane and held it with one hand, slapping it on the palm of the other. He gave Aemilia a grin. "Another souvenir from the army."

Aemilia said nothing. An image flickered through her mind, a memory from years ago, when she was still a small child. A slave had been caught stealing an ornate silver knife from Senator Avitus's study, one the senator used to open sealed scrolls. The slave's hands had been bound together and then tied to a rope which was thrown over the branch of a tree and used to haul him up until his toes barely touched the ground. He had then been flogged until he was unconscious, and left hanging for the rest of the day. He died the following morning. The entire household had been obliged to witness the flogging. From that time on there had been no thefts in the Avitus villa. It had been days before Aemilia's nightmares had faded and weeks before her fear of undergoing the same fate had subsided to the level of intermittent background unease. But it was from that time that the resolve in Aemilia never to become a slave or a serf became permanent, for serfs could be punished in the same way.

The sound of snapping fingers brought her back from the memory.

"Seen a ghost, girl?" Tarunculus queried.

"No...I was just distracted, that's all."

"Mmh. Any more news from Syagrius about my training recruits? I've had no message yet."

"I've heard nothing. He didn't say when he would speak to you, just," she paused to recall the conversation between Syagrius and Lady Julia, "that he would need every man like you he could find." The nearest slave, Primus, looked up quickly, and then brought down his hammer with more than usual force.

Tarunculus gave a shrug. "Well then, we wait. Chances are he won't be calling on me until he's seen Chlodovis and got the lie of the land. No sense being impatient."

"Is there anything I can do here?"

"Nothing yet. You'd best be going back to the apartment and getting on with the copying. You know where to find everything. Here," he pulled a key from a pouch in his tunic, "let yourself in. Bring it back before you return to the Residence, mind."

"Yes, sir."

82

"'Sir' is it now?"

She flushed. "Yes, Father."

He gave her a pat on the back. "There's my girl. If you're hungry, help yourself to whatever's there. Off you go, now."

"Goodbye, Father." Somehow the words were an effort.

Her walk back to the forum was slow as her mind was full of Tarunculus. She did not want to put him in the same category as Avitus, but her nascent affection for him could not get past the cane he had held in his hand. It doesn't mean anything, she thought. He would never use it on me. But her unease would not dissipate: He is my father. But what did he mean when he said he knows how to put a woman in her place? Did he beat my mother? Did he ever love her? He wasn't moved at all when I told him she had died.

She reassured herself again: He loves me, she thought, he is proud of me because I am doing well with Lady Julia. This did not quiet her troubled mind: The Lady will find out that I ran away and then what will she do? She might dismiss me and that will make him angry at me for lying to him. He might beat me then. Her mind leapt to Lady Julia: She will not dismiss me, she thought. She hates her family and I'm useful to her. She may want to use me to contact the Franks again. But of this she was not sure. The shame of being a runaway servant might be too great and tip the scales against her. Nothing was certain. The sense of security she had felt over the last few weeks had vanished, and with it the feeling that she was on some sort of definite path.

She stopped walking. She was nearly resolved to go back to the workshop and tell Tarunculus everything. He accepted her as his daughter now and would surely understand her reasons for acting as she did, but for some inexplicable reason she could not make up her mind to turn back. Standing stock still in the middle of the street she became aware of queer looks from one or two passers by, and resumed her progress towards the forum.

Having entered the flat she collected the necessary writing materials, opened the scroll she had copied from previously and settled down to the task of making more copies. It was late morning when she decided to break for an early lunch. Glancing into the kitchen she found only an old cabbage and some leeks on the shelf. With no inclination either to prepare these as a soup or to eat the soup once prepared, she quit the flat and went off to buy a small loaf from a bakery, with perhaps an apple or a pear to go with it. After making her purchases, she spent some time passing from shopping booth to shopping booth. The day was warm and she was not inclined to return immediately to the apartment building.

Finally making her way back, she mounted the stairway and reached the first floor corridor. She was surprised to see Ennodius leaning against the door of the flat.

"The old girl's been looking for you," he said.

"I was in earlier, sir," she replied. "I went out to buy some lunch. Does she want me now?"

"Wants you two hours ago," he answered, grinning. "Looks like you're in trouble."

"She did give me the day off," Aemilia murmured, hesitating in front of him.

"Not any more," he said, standing aside to let her unlock the door. "There's been a real to-do at the Residence. The Franks came and wanted to see *her* of all people. 'Ze Lady Jul-ya of ze A-*vit* family. Ve vant her.' That pulled her nose up three inches. Well, she talks to them, all hush hush, and it turns out that Chlodovis wants to see her himself." He paused and looked at her quizzically. "Any idea why?"

She shook her head truthfully. "None at all, sir."

"Chlodovis won't come into the town," he continued. "She has to go out to him. But she wants you with her. Can't imagine what for, can you?"

Again she shook her head. His questions were beginning to make her uncomfortable. "Couldn't she have just gone with one of the other attendant girls?"

He grinned again. "Right in the middle of her morning toilet? She'll be seeing a king, even if he's only a barbarian king, and she won't go until she's preened and dressed herself to the nines. And those Franks were too stiff-necked to wait for her. They went back to their camp right away. But I'm guessing she's probably ready by now. She had the slaves looking all over for you—I found Adeodatus here and sent him off. I had a hunch you'd be back for lunch. Pretty clever of me, don't you think?"

"You needn't have waited for me, sir," she said, unlocking the door and passing in.

"Just doing my bit for the old girl," he replied standing by the doorway.

Aemilia stowed her provisions in the kitchen and then, taking a shawl, returned to the front door. Ennodius made her uncomfortable. Without actually obstructing her, he seemed to be in her way, standing a fraction closer to her than she felt he should. She locked the door and then stood perplexed, holding the key.

"Got a problem?"

"The key," she replied, "I'm supposed to give it back to my father before returning to the Residence."

"Give it to me. He works by the barracks, doesn't he? I've got nothing to do today—I'll amble over and give it to him," he said, extending a hand to take it from her.

Aemilia did not move, troubled. Tarunculus had entrusted the key to her and her alone, and she pictured his ire when someone else, especially someone he despised, appeared with it in his possession. Still, there was nothing else to be done. Lady Julia could not be kept waiting. She thrust the key into his hand and made her way down the passage as quickly as walking would allow.

"Trust me, Aemilia, he'll get it safe and sound," Ennodius called after her with a chuckle as she disappeared down the stairs.

On reaching the Residence, she found Vipsania standing at the front entrance. "Hurry up! Lady Julia's waiting for you in Syagrius's office. There's been a real rumpus—Franks coming to see her and all, and now she wants you to go with her to see them. I can't imagine what it's all about, can you? Wouldn't surprise me if she already been doing a little talking with them hush-hush, though why they should be interested in *her*'s anybody's guess."

Aemilia did not reply to Vipsania's stream of talk, but hurried with her through the main atrium to the reception room that bordered it. A guard stood before the closed door, the taciturn Odo.

"She's in with Syagrius," he grunted in reply to Vipsania's query. "Don't rightly know'f I should be interrupting 'em."

"Lady Julia wants Aemilia now," Vipsania urged.

"Right. I'll see what they say," the guard replied, knocking on the door.

At the command to enter the guard opened the door and, after a brief explanation, waved Aemilia in, closing the door after her.

Syagrius stood in the center of the floor, whilst Lady Julia sat on a chair in front of the governor's vast, green, ornate marble desk. Besides two or three white marble statues in wall niches, and some elaborate drapery, there was little else in the room.

"Your Majesty, My Lord," said Aemilia, curtseying.

"Stand here, girl," Lady Julia ordered.

Syagrius's eye followed Aemilia as she made her way to the Lady's side.

"Why are you taking her with you?" he queried. There was a flicker of suspicion in his glance.

"I do not intend to go out in the wilds on my own, My Lord." The Lady's manner had a touch of patient condescension.

"Mmh." Syagrius paced back and forth for a minute or two, saying nothing. "This is a very strange business," he resumed finally, "I cannot imagine what Chlodovis would want with you."

"I must confess that no one was more surprised than myself. I can only guess that he wants to speak about some matter or other, but not directly to you."

"That might be true," the governor mused. "He has come to issue me a direct challenge, either to battle or personal combat, and he cannot speak to me personally of anything else in front of his men."

"Then it remains for me to find out what he wants," Lady Julia continued. "Indeed, this may well be the occasion for me to aid your cause in some way."

Syagrius spun around. "That is possible, but do not make any promises or agreements with him without first consulting me, is that clear?"

"Indeed not, My Lord," said the Lady, wide-eyed. "I intended no such thing. Come girl," she continued, rising. "It is time for us to go."

"I'll detail an escort to accompany you," Syagrius said.

"Thank you, My Lord."

Syagrius's eye followed them out the room.

The Lady stopped by her chamber and let Aemilia fasten on her most practical walking sandals. At her order, Aemilia summoned her litter to the entrance of the Residence. Lady Julia climbed into the box, signing to Aemilia to walk behind her. Preceded by four guards, the cortège made its way outside the town walls. The Lady dismounted when they reached the mule track and, having commanding the guards to remain beside it and keep an eye on the knot of curious stragglers who had followed them, went on accompanied only by Aemilia. Once they were out of earshot she turned to her.

"I need you as an interpreter. It is vital that what I have to say be not misunderstood in any way. The Latin of those barbarians is deplorable! And their chief is worse from what I hear. Savages, all of them. Their own tongue is little more than the grunting of pigs and I shall certainly never stoop to learning a word of it."

Aemilia was silent.

"I shall impress upon you this once, girl, that what transpires between me and the Franks you shall relate to no one. No one at all. Is that clear?"

"Yes, Your Majesty."

Chlodovech was waiting for them at the base of the hill with a band of warriors. They were all on horseback and looked beyond the two women at the country around.

"Tell him we are alone," Lady Julia hissed.

"There are just the two of us, My Lord," Aemilia said in Frankish to the young king. "The escort is by the road."

He searched her eyes for a moment. "I see you tell no lie. This is the Lady Avit?"

"*Ja*. This is she."

The Franks dismounted and approached them. Lady Julia, without averting her eye or moving an inch from her stiff and regal pose, murmured, "Which one is their king?"

"The young man wearing the chainmail," Aemilia replied.

"Speak when I tell you," the Lady replied in an undertone.

Chlodovech stood before Lady Julia and briefly inclined his head. "My Lady, greetings," he said in heavily accented Latin.

Lady Julia inclined her head in her turn, just a fraction. "Tell him I give him my greetings and hope he is in good health." Aemilia did so.

"Why you see me?" Chlodovech replied, cutting short the formalities.

The Lady turned to Aemilia. "Speak as I speak." She turned back to Chlodovech. "I wish to make you an offer—Your Majesty—that I think you will find very much to your advantage." She paused, and Aemilia translated.

"What—offer?"

"We know you are about to attack the lands of Syagrius and you have come to challenge him to single combat, is this not so?"

Chlodovech gave a brief nod of assent.

"He will not accept your challenge of single combat, that is certain. You will have to fight him in the field."

Chlodovech shrugged. It was clear he expected as much.

"He is not ready to meet you in battle now. If you come, he will not fight you. He will keep his soldiers in the towns and you will have to besiege them, one after the other. It could take months, even years. You will have no glory of a single victory."

Chlodovech eyed her narrowly. "Why you say this to me?"

"Syagrius has spoken to me. He will fight you on the field when he is ready. He needs more time to prepare, that is all."

Chlodovech put his hands on his hips. "Good, you say he fight later, not now. But if he fights and I win, afterwards he is behind his walls and I have nothing."

"He will not shelter behind the walls. If he fights and loses, I will open the gates to your men."

Aemilia gasped and glanced at the Lady. "Translate, girl," she said evenly. Aemilia did so, stumbling over the words.

Chlodovech's eyes became narrower. "How you do this?"

"I have spoken to the garrison commander. He has agreed to do

whatever I say in the event of a defeat."

Chlodovech tilted his head with an expression of wry surprise. "You Romans," he said after a pause, "how you make empire, I do not know." Then he looked shrewdly at the Lady. "Why you do this for me?"

"There is something I want from you. When you rule in Soissons you must agree to give into my possession a portion of land I will indicate to you."

The words, translated by Aemilia, caused an expression of genuine astonishment in the face of Chlodovech.

"Land? But you are great family. All you great families have plenty land. Why you want more?"

"It is what I wish—I have reasons for desiring this land."

Chlodovech crossed his arms and gazed downwards, considering.

"Think," the Lady continued. "In this way you may have glory and all Gaul from a single battle."

Chlodovech glanced up at her. "How much land you have now?"

The question was unexpected, and for the first time the impenetrable self-possession of the Lady began to unravel. Her eyes glanced away.

"I do not think....it is not important. Do you accept my offer or not?"

A grin crept up the corner of Chlodovech's mouth. "How much time Syagrius want?"

"He told me two months."

"I give him three. You tell him that, *hein*?"

"You agree to my conditions then?" the Lady said, with an undertone of urgency filtering through the erect dignity of her demeanor.

Chlodovech remounted his horse, followed by his men. "I do as you wish, but I tell you one thing. You are a woman, and we Franks, we learn always to respect women. But if I come and find the doors of Soissons shut, I cut your head from your body, *verstaan*?"

Lady Julia's face went white and her mouth stayed open, silent. The Franks urged their horses toward the hill without a backward glance. Eventually the Lady stirred.

"Savage! Brute! Barbarian!" she said in a shrill, tight voice. "Speaking to me in that manner! He should have his skin whipped from his flesh. It is unendurable! I shall tell Syagrius not to spare his life, not if he should beg for it." Aemilia noticed a slight trembling in the Lady's hands as she spoke. It was a while before Lady Julia finished her outpouring of invective against Chlodovech and seemed at last to come to herself. She glanced at Aemilia, as if recalling her existence, and then set off back toward the litter without another word.

CHAPTER 11

On reaching the Residence, Lady Julia turned to Aemilia.

"If Syagrius should question you, you are to repeat the conversation between me and that barbarian, but leaving out everything I said about what would transpire should there be a defeat. You are to emphasize the fact that I attracted that brute to the idea of a quick victory and thereby made him agree to wait for three months. You are to say nothing else. Is that clear?"

Aemilia nodded.

"Now go. Remain in the building. I may have need of you later."

Left alone, Aemilia made for her bedroom. There she found Vipsania agog with curiosity, plying her with questions the moment she walked in. When Sylvia came a little later she asked if the meeting between the Lady and Chlodovech went well, the importance of the event overcoming her repugnance for Aemilia. A few slaves wandered in, wanting to know what had happened. For the first time in her life Aemilia was a minor celebrity and she wished with all her heart that it were over.

She could say nothing other than that the Lady had ordered her to be quiet. She saw that this rankled. The universal contempt for Lady Julia coupled with the habitual freedom slaves had in discussing the private affairs of their masters made her silence seem unreasonable, even insulting, to them. One by one they drifted off, dissatisfied. Eventually only Vipsania was left.

Aemilia, sitting on her bed, put her head in her hands. She felt her eyes filling with tears. "Oh Vipsania, what am I to do? I can't speak about what happened—I don't dare."

Vispania sat on her own bed and clasped her arms around her knees, looking at her. "Is it that important?"

"It is! I wish I'd never met Lady Julia."

"Nothing for it then. But they're all going to think you're getting stuck up now that you're in the Lady's best books."

"I know, but I can't help it. I didn't ask her to take me as an interpre…" Aemilia stopped, biting her lip.

Vipsania was sharp. "A what? An interpreter?"

Aemilia said nothing.

"You can speak Frankish, then."

Aemilia remained silent.

"*Are* you a Frank?"

Aemilia looked up at her. "I'm half Frank, but don't tell anybody, please."

Vipsania looked at her appraisingly, and then gave a smile. "I won't, but you're smart keeping it to yourself. How did Her Majesty find out?"

Aemilia told her.

"*Vervlaks,*" Vipsania mimicked, when the account was finished. "What an ugly word." And she repeated it, exaggerating the rolling 'r'.

"It's not ugly."

"It is."

"It isn't."

"Is."

"Isn't."

Aemilia stood up, red-faced. Vipsania laughed in glee. "I made you cross! I made you cross! *Verrrrvlaks!*"

Whump! The pillow hit Vipsania square in the face, cutting short her mimicry. She squealed and seized the pillow off her own bed. The two girls swung away at each other until, exhausted and giggling, they called a truce.

"All right," Vipsania said once she had caught her breath, "don't be so sore about it."

"Sorry," Aemilia said, sitting with her pillow clasped on her lap, "I didn't mean to get angry. It's not so important, really. It's just that I grew up speaking Frankish. We always spoke it to each other at home. It's just—normal to me."

"I suppose, if you say so. Did your mother come from Frankland?"

"No. Her grandparents did. Her father became a merchant. My mother told me that he started by trading between the Romans and the Franks and then later between the Romans and the Visigoths."

"Was he rich?"

"He was fairly rich—not very rich like a senator."

"Where's all his money then?"

Aemilia paused. "The Romans took it. They said he was a dangerous alien and requisitioned everything he had. Mother said it was just an excuse though—they wanted his money."

"That's sad," said Vipsania, musing.

The door opened and a slave's head appeared in the doorway. Aemilia recognized Procopius, Syagrius's messenger. "Heard the news? Chlodovis is coming now to challenge Syagrius. Everybody's going outside the walls to see it. Aemilia, Her Majesty wants you right away." With that his head disappeared.

"I must go," Aemilia said, flurried and anxious.

"All right. I won't ask you any more questions about what happened, but I'll say what I think. I think the Lady's sticking her nose into business that doesn't concern her and that she's going to cause a lot of trouble. That's what *I* think."

"I'll see you later," said Aemilia.

She found Syagrius in Lady Julia's bedroom. The governor gave her an appraising look. Lady Julia's expression had not changed from the angry grimness of her return journey. She ignored Aemilia and turned to Syagrius.

"I cannot understand why you just do not kill him now, My Lord. He has only a small escort and he is far from his lands. Surely one need not have moral scruples over such a deed? He is a savage and must be treated as such. They are more like wild animals than men and must be dealt with accordingly. If he should die the Franks will be no further bother to you."

"My Lady," said Syagrius slowly, without turning to her, "I am not in the habit of explaining my policies to others, but since Chlodovech has treated with you I will make an exception in your case." Aemilia noticed a sudden flush of red in the Lady's cheeks.

"When it comes to combat the Franks have a sense of honor that it is vital to respect. Chlodovech has not yet united all the Franks under his leadership. He has only the tribes on this side of the Rhine. For me to break the safe conduct implied in a face-to-face challenge would be taken by every Frank as a personal betrayal. They would all rally behind Chararic or some other king and come down on me with all the anger of a northern gale. I would be facing an enemy twice the size and with ten times the fury of the one I confront now. Do you understand?"

Lady Julia was silent.

"We shall speak of it no further. It is time for me to go and hear what Chlodovis has to say." With that he gave the Lady a brief nod and quitted the apartment.

Aemilia waited. The Lady gazed ahead, features set, for a minute or two. Then she turned to Aemilia. "Clean my feet, girl," she said.

"Are we not going, Your Majesty?"

Lady Julia turned on her. "Going? Going where, you numbskull? Do you imagine I would have any interest in what that unwashed heathen will be bawling out in the wilds? Don't be a fool. Now do my feet and mind your place."

Aemilia fetched the basin and towel in silence. The Lady eyed her irritably. "Call Sylvia and keep out of my sight for the rest of the day."

"Yes, Your Majesty."

Aemilia was grateful for Lady Julia's petulance. Pausing only to give the order to Sylvia, she hurried out of the Residence and made for the eastern gate as quickly as she could. Passing through it she continued along the road that led between the decaying buildings outside the walls and into the open land beyond.

There, in the first field bordering the town limits, she found a crowd, held in check by a line of soldiers. Beyond them stood a knot of horsemen, Syagrius in the middle, waiting. The Franks had not yet come.

To the left of the road ran a line of trees and bushes. If I can work my way around to them, I can see the Franks up close, she thought. Walking northwards as quickly and discreetly as she could between the crumbling buildings, she found a field of wheat just beyond them, the stalks tall enough to hide her. Using the sun as a guide she struck eastwards through the field until she judged she had gone far enough. Making a right turn south she continued until the field gave way to the shrubbery of the copse she sighted earlier. Her judgment had been good. She was about twenty yards from Syagrius and his escort, and only a dozen yards from the road itself. She had a grandstand seat in the drama about to be enacted.

She waited for what seemed a long time, seeing and hearing nothing, and began to wonder if the Franks out of mistrust had decided not to come. Then she heard the faint clop of horses out of sight on the road. After a few minutes they came into view. It seemed to her that all Chlodovech's escort was with him—several dozen warriors on horseback, axes and spears in hand, gathered around their chief.

Aemilia held her breath and kept still, gazing through the leaves of a bush at the approaching horses. She was not afraid but she did not want to be noticed by the Franks. About twenty yards to the left of her vantage point Chlodovech drew rein, his men on either side of him. She was roughly halfway between the two groups. There was silence for a moment. No one had seen her.

"I have come to challenge you, O king of the Romans," said Chlodovech in a loud, clear voice. He spoke in Frankish.

"What is your challenge?" replied Syagrius in the same language, with just a slight accent.

"I go to war with you," replied Chlodovech. "There shall not be two kingdoms, but only one. We will fight each other now, you and I, for the two thrones. If you win, you shall rule Franks and Romans. If I win, I shall rule them both. What do you say?"

"You are in your first youth," replied Syagrius evenly, "and you wish to fight an old man? Is this just? If I should challenge one of your boys, a youth half your height, would you say I had done honorably?"

"If a man is brave and knows how to hold a sword he may yet win," replied Chlodovech with a shrug.

"Nonetheless I shall not accept your challenge to fight body to body," Syagrius said. "Have you any other challenge to give me?"

"We will do battle," Chlodovech returned. "But I will prove that I seek no unjust advantage over you. You shall choose the day of battle, any day from now until the end of the third month, and you shall choose the place. Come, is that not fair to an old man?" His warriors laughed.

Syagrius waited for silence, and then a little longer. Aemilia realized he was thinking.

"Very well. I accept your challenge. We shall do battle at the end of the third month on a field ten miles from here," and he pointed northwards.

Chlodovech smiled. "I shall be there. Do not be late."

Syagrius switched to Latin, his voice rising: "I shall come with all my men, young king, and you shall learn what it is to fight Romans. From this day forth I pledge my life and honor that there shall be no end to this war until your people are my subjects, for your lands are Roman lands and I will have them back again!"

His voice rang out over the fields, clearly audible to the crowd behind him. Aemilia noticed several bystanders stirring. Chlodovech's face went white, his lips set in a taut line.

"It is as you say, Roman," he replied, also in Latin. "There shall be no truce and no mercy. The day I lay hold of you is the day of your death."

There was silence. The parley was over. Aemilia looked through Chlodovech's escort, trying to recognize their faces. She caught sight of the warrior who had escorted her to the Frank's encampment. At that same instant he saw her. She realized she was leaning forward out of the foliage.

"*Wie?*" he uttered, raising his axe. Aemilia realized she must act immediately.

"*Nee, Dis net ek,*" she called out, pushing her way through the shrubbery. Chlodovech glanced her way and, recognizing her, muttered a command to the Frank who had seen her. He reined his horse over.

"What are you doing here, little Frank?" he asked.

"I came to see Chlodovech", she replied.

"Do you love danger so much? I might have thrown my axe and split your head in half."

"But you knew who I was."

"*Ja,* lucky you came out the bush. If you had tried to hide..."

"Why should I hide? I'm not afraid of you."

He looked at her with a grin. "That is true. You are brave, little Frank."

"Merovec! We go." Chlodovech called out.

"Go well," he said. "When we come again, don't hide in bushes. We will be looking in them for Romans." And, nudging his horse's flanks with his heels, he set off after Chlodovech.

"Go well," Aemilia murmured, watching the group of horsemen make off down the road. *I'm not afraid of you. I wanted you to see me. Why did I do that?* When they were about a hundred yards away she heard the thud of horses' hooves behind her. She turned in alarm. Syagrius and his escort gathered around her.

"You're Lady Julia's handmaid. You were speaking to them," he said.

"Yes, my Lord," she replied, curtseying.

"How do you know Frankish?"

Aemilia felt her mouth go dry. "My mother was a Frank, my Lord."

Syagrius gazed after the retreating Franks and then swept his glance over the undulating fields before turning it back to her.

"Is that why the Lady chose you to accompany her?"

"...yes, my Lord. She wanted to make sure that there was no misunderstanding between her and Chlodovech."

"That is reasonable." He paused, and then his features relaxed. "You're plucky enough. Take after your father, I suppose."

"My Lord."

"Reminds me. Tell him he has a commission from me. He is to report to barracks first thing in the morning. Rank of Centurion. I'll detail an army smith to run his shop." Without waiting for any response from her he turned to his entourage. "Right, let's get back. We have a lot of work to do. I want all dispatch riders ready and mounted in half-an-hour." The party made off, leaving Aemilia alone again.

For a full minute she did not move. She realized it had been close. Syagrius had suspected Lady Julia of something underhand in her dealings with the Franks, of that she was sure, but for some unknown reason his suspicions had not settled on her. The Franks had been in the area for only a day. He could easily have ascertained that she had been absent from the Residence that morning. What kind of alibi could she have offered to explain it? Where could she have gone except to her father's apartment and what would he have told the governor except the truth—that he had not seen her until midmorning although she had quitted the Residence before sunrise. If questioned, what likelihood was there that the guards at the Reims gate would not have remembered her as the first through that morning? Inexplicable fact upon inexplicable fact, doubt solidifying into certainty....

You're being looked after, she thought to herself, and then, with a start of amused comprehension, realized it was the exact truth. It was comforting, and with it she felt the return of an almost intangible sense of direction.

Looking up, she saw several onlookers from the dispersing crowd gazing at her curiously. She sighed, and started back for the town. *I might as well have shouted to everyone in the forum that I can speak Frankish,* she thought. But at least she had some good news to tell her father.

CHAPTER 12

From the day of the challenge time seemed to speed up. The practical business of everyone, whatever his occupation, was henceforth directed towards one end: war with Chlodovech.

The people had begun to fear him. As the knowledge of Syagrius's proclaimed intention of taking the war into Frankland became widespread, so did the conviction that the governor, in a fit of bravado, had succeeded only in turning the Franks from opportunistic, would-be conquerors into an implacable foe.

On the same day, posters were affixed to the walls in the forum and criers announced that universal conscription was to be levied on every able-bodied man of military age in Roman Gaul who could not prove his profession to be necessary to the welfare of the province. From that day too all criminals were pardoned on the condition that they enlist for a minimum period of three years, and any and every street beggar who was sufficiently able-bodied was rounded up and taken to the barracks for rudimentary training.

Aemilia went directly from Syagrius to Tarunculus's shop. The afternoon was far advanced when she arrived, and she found him in a good mood: the weapons order and the payment for it had both been delivered on time. He waved aside the subject of the apartment key as something of no importance and it was not mentioned again.

After Aemilia had finished relating the details of the parley, Tarunculus punched fist in palm and grinned. "He's given 'em no choice," he said, "It stuck in Chlodovis's throat that his father was the last barbarian to be a Roman vassal and Syagrius's reminded him of it. It would've been a slap in the face for him."

He noticed Aemilia's puzzled expression. "The Franks were federates of Aegidius—that's Syagrius's father. Aegidius used Childeric—that's Chlodovis's father—to beat off the Visigoths when they attacked the province back in '64. Childeric stayed a federate right till his death in '81.

That's why Chlodovis is so damned set on beating Syagrius. Wants to show everyone he's not a lackey—and Syagrius just told him he damn well is one.

"Now the people will *have* to fight—or get their throats cut. There'll be nobody telling the garrison commander to open the gates because they're getting hungry, like they did at Avignon." And he spat on the floor.

The news that he was a commissioned centurion again did not make him leap for joy, as Aemilia half-expected. Instead, he leaned back against the wall on his stool, with an expression of settled satisfaction on his face, amounting almost to peace. He said nothing for a full minute, gazing ahead. Finally, he turned his regard on her.

"I'll whip those scum into shape in three months, see if I don't. I'll make a soldier out of every last ninny of 'em. They'll wish they'd never come near a barracks." And he chuckled at the thought. Then, looking past her shoulder he called out, "Primus! Come here!"

The slave in question left off whatever he was doing with the others at the back of the shop and approached his master, standing deferentially before him.

"I don't need three slaves in the shop. Arbogast and Nestor can work overtime from now on. You're joining the army."

An expression of dumb surprise came over the slave's face. "Army, Master? But I know nothing about fighting. I..."

"You'll learn. You know how to do what you're told, don't you? That's all you need. Report at the barracks tomorrow morning first thing. Ask for the commanding officer of the slave's centuria. He'll tell you what to do from there."

The slave was silent, unmoving. Tarunculus glanced at him. "Back to work." There was just the slightest edge in his voice. The slave moved off promptly.

"Army will sort him out," said Tarunculus, turning back to Aemilia, "Faster'n staying here with some idler to run the shop when I'm away. He needs a firm hand, that one, and he'll get it, by the gods."

Aemilia's eyes strayed after the slave. He was standing at the back of the shop, gazing into space with the expression of one who does not see what is in front of him. One of the other slaves spoke in an undertone to him, but he did not answer. She turned back to Tarunculus.

"...and I want you to do as many as you can in your spare time, girl. When Her Majesty gives you time off. They're important now, understand? We must get them to as many to the people as we can."

Pamphlets, Aemilia thought. "Yes, Father," she replied, and hesitated, debating whether to continue with what was on her mind, but thought better of it. "I must be going. Her Majesty will be expecting me."

"Aye, to be sure."

"I'll see you when I can."

"Evenings, girl. I'll be busy all day at the barracks, unless you come by at midday."

"Yes, Father. Goodbye."

She walked back wearily to the Residence. Much had happened that day and she was tired, but her step was heavier with the realization that she could do nothing for Tarunculus's slaves. Possibly later, when she was established as his daughter beyond any threat, but that would be too late for the one he had earmarked for the army, and even then she doubted she would ever be able to change his mind on that subject. It was true that some Christian and even pagan slave owners were kind toward their slaves to the point of sparing them any real misery, but she knew quite well that one didn't acquire slaves in order to take pity on them. They were there to be useful in any way their master saw fit, and no one would query Tarunculus's judgment in sending his most recent acquisition to the army. The realm of Gaul needed soldiers now more than it needed blacksmiths, from wherever it could find them, and his act could only be commended as one of self-sacrificing patriotism. But she remembered the slave's unseeing eyes and was troubled, more deeply than she ever recalled being.

On returning to the Residence she learned that the Lady Julia had no need of her services just yet, probably not for the rest of the evening as Vipsania and Sylvia were already with her.

That night, after the other two girls had gone to sleep, she took her bundle from off the shelf above her bed. Wrapped in an old garment she found what she was looking for: a book, small with surprisingly fine pages, comprising a complete New Testament. She had told no one of it. It had been given to her by Lady Avita just before she left the villa. The Lady had never said why she chose to give Aemilia such an obviously lavish gift, and Aemilia wondered whether she knew what had happened between her and Senator Avitus.

Sitting on her bed, she opened the book and turned the pages until she came upon the First Epistle of St. Peter:

Slaves, be subject to your masters with true deference, not only to the good and gentle but also to the difficult. For it is commendable if, for love of God, a man endures sorrows, suffering wrongfully. Where is the merit in putting up with the troubles your sins bring upon you? But for you to suffer with patience in doing good is something of great merit to God. For you are called to this, because Christ also suffered for us, leaving you an example that you should follow his steps.

Aemilia sighed and closed the book, replacing it in the bundle which she lodged back on the shelf. Lying down she recalled in her mind the image of the enlisted slave. Primus, she remembered, was his name. Gawky, undersized and with a noticeable hunch, she imagined him with a spear in his uncertain hand, facing the Franks...tall, powerfully built, with their barbed harpoon-like spears and axes, born for war. He will have to endure death, she thought. Is he Christian? Does he understand that it is commendable before God to suffer such a fate patiently? What if he is a pagan, and does not know why his life must end thus? Questions, questions, for which she did not have the answers.

She was about to extinguish the lamp when a thought came to her. Reaching up, she carefully took down the heavy tome Tarunculus had given her, and opened it on the bed. She spent some minutes turning the pages until she came to the passage she was looking for:

In this way was man made by God. 'Let them rule,' said He, 'over the fishes of the sea, and the birds of the air, and over everything that creeps upon the earth.' He gave him reason, and made him lord only over those without reason: not over man but over beasts.

Not over man but over beasts. She reread the phrase twice before going on.

Hence the first holy men were shepherds rather than kings...And therefore in all the scriptures we never read the word 'servant', until such time as the just man Noah laid it as a curse upon his offending son. So that it was guilt, not nature, that was the origin of that name...

Sin therefore is the mother of servitude, and first cause of man's subjection to man; which nevertheless comes not to pass but by the direction of the Highest, in whom is no injustice, and who alone knows best how to measure out His punishment to man's offenses. He Himself says: 'Whosoever commits sin is the slave of sin'; and so even if many religious Christians are slaves to wicked masters, those masters are not free, for that to which a man is addicted he is slave of. And it is a happier servitude to serve man rather than lust: for lust (putting aside all other passions) practices extreme tyranny upon the hearts of all who serve it, whether it be lust after power or carnal lust. But in the stable ordering of society, wherein one man is under another, as humility benefits the slave so does pride damage the one in authority. But take a man as God created him at first: he is neither slave to man nor to sin.

Neither a slave to man nor to sin. Her eyes paused over the words as if reading them for the first time. She read on:

Therefore the apostle warns servants to obey their masters and to serve them with cheerfulness and good will: to the end that if they cannot be made free by their masters, they can make their servitude a freedom to themselves, by serving their masters, not in deceitful fear, but in faithful love, until iniquity is brought to an end, and all man's power and rule made void, and God only is all in all.

All man's power and rule made void. Could that come to pass in this world? Slaves, and men's power over slaves, would be what it was for as long as men sinned: it was sin that made a world that allowed slavery.

Then a memory came to her, of Chlodovech sitting beside a fire amongst his warriors, as one of them, indistinguishable from them in everything except the fact that he was their king. Could that be what Augustine meant? But how could pagan Franks be nearer than Christian Romans to living as God originally intended men to live? The emperors had been Christian since Constantine, and the Empire itself had been thoroughly Christian in its laws since Emperor Theodosius, nearly a century before. Wasn't a hundred years enough time for an empire to become what it professed to be?

The lamp was burning low and it was fully dark. She replaced the book on the shelf and made herself ready for sleep. As she drifted off, a phrase passed through her mind several times, as if she was speaking to herself: *I am not the slave of Avitus.*

It was a comforting thought.

CHAPTER 13

In the following weeks little changed in the practical details of Aemilia's daily routine. Her brief moment of prominence as Lady Julia's assistant in her meeting with Chlodovech was swallowed up in the greater drama of Syagrius's confrontation with the Frankish king.

Aemilia soon realized, however, that although Lady Julia continued to make use of her skills, she was no longer her favorite. There was a distance, a frostiness, that overlaid the old woman's bouts of moody aversion and restoration of favor. At times, it almost seemed to Aemilia that the Lady was wary of her, an impression that persisted despite the incredulity of her reason. After all, what can *I* do to her? Aemilia thought. She knows that if I say anything it would be worse for me than for her. She knew that when she told me to go and see Chlodovech.

But her uneasiness in Lady's Julia's presence did not abate, nor did the hidden, flickering fear that eventually, the Lady would dispense with her services.

The erosion of her own standing went parallel with the rise in the standing of Tarunculus. Holding forth from the pedestal of a statue, in stained tunic and sandals, he had been the town eccentric. But now he wore military boots, thigh straps, an army tunic and trousers, chain mail vest, military cape and a helmet at a period when, for the first time in decades, the citizenry took the army seriously.

As a commissioned officer, Tarunculus saved his oratorical powers for his conscripts. Outside the barracks his speech was stiffly and strictly official. More than ever, he longed to harangue the populace. It was now, he told Aemilia, that somebody was needed to tell them where their obligation lay, but his sense of duty forbade him to do as a soldier what he had done as a private citizen. He did not realize that his reserve, more than anything he could have said, earned him a new and grudging respect from those who had formerly made him the butt of their jokes.

"I hear he's whipping them into shape good and proper," said the fruiterer Aemilia had met on her first day in the town. She had taken the opportunity of some free time during Lady Julia's absence from the Residence to nip down to the forum and buy some fruit and vegetables for Lavilla, whom she now visited regularly with provisions.

"That he is," interjected a bystander. Aemilia recognized the old ex-frontier guard, Rufus. "I went down to the barracks to have a look. Said I might be interested in signing up so they let me in. The quartermaster remembered my fort and we got talking about old times. He was an Circitor from Cologne. Surprised me to see him still in the army. He must be over sixty if he remembers my old camp. Doesn't look it, though."

"You see Tarunculus?" asked the fruiterer.

"That I did," answered the ex-guard. "No problem finding him. Just look for the voice," and he chuckled. "He had 'em standing to attention like posts and in squares straight as a floor-plan. 'About—turn!' he goes. 'By the left—quick march!' It was good to see it. I like a smart march past, that I do."

"Think they'll do for the Franks?"

"Aye, if they fight as good as they drill. But I reckon that's your problem."

"How's that?"

"You can drill a body until it marches in its sleep, but that doesn't mean it won't run like a chicken when the heat's on." The old soldier shook his head. "They can left turn, right turn, about turn till they fall over, but they're still green."

"Did you run away the first time?"

"I might've," admitted the old soldier, "but we had some tough veterans with us. Kept us together. I couldn't bolt so long as they were steady. There aren't many of their kind left now."

"Is Tarunculus going out with the recruits?"

The old soldier pulled a face. "I don't see it. He's too old. He can't walk properly, and you have to run on a battlefield."

"I reckon he'll manage," said the fruiterer.

The old ex-guard shrugged. "That may be, but I don't see it."

Tarunculus had agreed to let Aemilia take his writing materials to the Residence. She borrowed an old breadboard from Pollux and, at odd free moments during the day and for most of the evening, she sat on her bed, perched it on her knees as a writing surface, and copied out a steady stream of Tarunculus's pamphlets. Late at night, with a stiff back, she finally extinguished her lamp.

Sylvia ignored her, more with indifference than hostility since she had become aware of Aemilia's loss of status with Lady Julia. But Vipsania was puzzled. One night when she was in bed and Aemilia had just finished a parchment, she tackled her:

"Why do you do it?"

"Do what?"

"Spend so much time writing that nonsense."

"It isn't nonsense."

"It is. Strabo read it to me from a copy he got. It's all about Rome and bringing back the empire. It's rubbish."

"What's rubbish about it?" said Aemilia, with a sudden flash of irritation that surprised her.

Vipsania leaned forward. "Aemilia, there isn't any empire any more. It's gone. And Strabo says that Syagrius'd be mad to take on the Goths. He says they're not like the Franks. They're all on horses—they'd ride right over him. That's what happened when they beat Valens—or Valentine, or whoever it was—and broke into the Empire. That's what he told me and he should know. He's a soldier after all. We're never going to get Rome back."

Aemilia sat up from her work and leaned back against the wall. In her mind was a faint vision of a tree-shrouded villa with a hearth-warmed kitchen, and a library full of wonders, and a smiling Lady. She gazed ahead in silence.

"We have to try. I don't mean we have to go to Rome, but we must fight for what's good here. They say Rome's falling into ruins, and everywhere else. Only here there aren't ruins..." Then she stopped. Vipsania gave her an amused look. "No, I don't mean that. I mean that there are good things, things *worth* keeping, that are carrying on only here."

"Like what?"

Aemilia paused, unable to convey in words the impressions in her mind. "...like books. Barbarians aren't interested in reading and writing. If they come here, there'll be no books left."

Vipsania shrugged. "I'm not interested in books either."

"But you should be. There are wonderful things in books, things you never thought of and also things you've never seen or heard about. There's so much they can tell you. "

"Fat lot of good if you can't read."

Aemilia put the board aside and clasped her knees. "I remember," she said, "when I first became lady-in-waiting to Lady Avita. It was night and she asked me to wait on her during a small house party she was having—just half-a-dozen friends for the evening meal. There was a visiting poet there, a young man who could sing as well as declaim poetry. He gave a recital from

Virgil—the Georgics—which he sang to the lyre and flute. The Lady had musicians accompany him. Vipsania, it was the most beautiful thing I ever heard. I wasn't just hearing Virgil's poetry—I was right inside it, like in a world of beauty and grace and goodness. I never forgot it, and afterwards I saw everything around me differently. It's as if...I don't know...Virgil showed me how to look at ordinary things in a way that made them not ordinary any more. The Lady noticed it. That's when she told me I could read her books." Aemilia looked down, embarrassed. "I'm sounding silly."

"No, it's not silly," said Vispania, "though I can't say I understand it much. But I've already told you that you shouldn't be here. Getting the work done, keeping the mistress happy—doesn't leave much time for listening to poets and all." Then she grinned. "Was he good-looking?"

"You wretch!"

"What's wrong with that?"

"He was fat, bald, had a big wart on his nose and his teeth were crooked."

"Liar!"

"Then don't ask."

Vipsania did not bother Aemilia again about her copying, except now and then to strike a rhetorical pose in their bedroom, to which Aemilia responded by pointing to an imaginary wart on her nose.

It was about a week later that Lady Julia summoned Aemilia to her bedroom.

"Have you told anyone of what transpired at the meeting?" she asked peremptorily.

"No, Your Majesty, no one."

Lady Julia regarded Aemilia for a few moments, then appeared satisfied. "Good. Now I want you to find Ennodius. He was supposed to let me know of his whereabouts at all times, but he has not done so. I must see him before midday—he has an important meeting then. Get him here before midday without fail. Tell no one what you are doing. Understood?"

"Yes, Your Majesty," said Aemilia, curtseying before quitting the apartment. She realized that Lady Julia had made herself responsible to Syagrius for Ennodius, and that the Governor clearly wanted to see her son. Delegating the task of finding him to anyone else risked the disappearance of Ennodius reaching Syagrius's ears. The Lady did not want to cross him. He was increasingly on edge, with a temper that flared at anything that looked like neglect of his orders.

Aemilia had no idea where to start looking. She could not simply ask around, as that would make Ennodius's unauthorized absence common knowledge. She had seen little of him since their meeting at Tarunculus's apartment, and was unfamiliar with his habits. She sat down on a stone bench in the main garden and put her head in her hands to think. Where on earth would she begin her search? Then a fragment of conversation came back to her—Ennodius talking to her, here in the garden: "...Staterius interrupted a very pleasant rendezvous. How the devil he found out where I was I don't know..."

That's it, she thought. *I must find Staterius.*

Syagrius's chamberlain was a man close on seventy—dignified, deferential, reserved, the perfect servant. Responsible for the smooth running of the household, he made it his business to be aware of everything that took place within its precincts, and above all, of everything that the prominent ones residing in it did. There was little that escaped his observant eye, and what did was soon known to him after some discreet enquries. Aemilia felt instinctively that she could trust him not to divulge her mission to Syagrius or anyone else.

She found him in his personal office, a small room next to the larger atrium, where he attended to the financial affairs of the Residence. The door was always open, and she knocked to get his attention. The old man raised his head from a parchment he had been perusing.

"Yes?"

"May I trouble you sir? Just for a moment?" Aemilia was somewhat overawed by him.

"Certainly. What is the matter?"

"The Lady Julia sent me to give a message to Ennodius and—well—I don't know where he is. Can you help? I think it's important..."

Staterius regarded Aemilia for a few moments. There seemed to be just the faintest hint of amusement in his expression, but Aemilia wasn't sure. He put down the quill pen he had been holding and sat back, as if considering.

"The Master, I believe, is currently at the Majorian flats in Paulus Street. The area is rather insalubrious. I could send a messenger..."

"No, thank you, sir. The Lady asked me to find him myself."

"Very well. He is in a ground floor flat. To the right through the main entrance."

"Thank you, sir." Aemilia curtseyed and turned to leave.

"I would be careful about entering the apartment too precipitately," the chamberlain continued, picking up the quill pen and turning his attention to the parchment. "It might be a little—impolitic."

A bystander outside the Residence directed her to the flats and on the way there she debated what to do. She did not want to enter the apartment Ennodius was visiting at all, never mind precipitately, but it was uncertain how long his rendezvous would last. Lady Julia wanted him by midday and it was already late morning. She was still uncertain what to do when she reached the apartment block. It was an old building, and had a seedy, run-down look caused as much by the negligence of its tenants as by its age. Aemilia stood a long time under the worn stonework of the arched entrance before finally entering into the central courtyard. Washing lines were strung overhead. Idle tenants leaned over the balconies of the upper two floors, and barefoot children played on the dirty stones of the central yard. She felt uncomfortable and had nearly made up her mind to leave when, inexplicably, a strange anger came over her. She approached one of the children.

"Can you tell the man in the flat over there that someone wants to see him."

"What will you give me?" said the urchin.

She extracted a follis from a bag within the folds of her mantle. "Here. Hurry now."

The boy ran across to the door and knocked. It opened a crack and he spoke to an unseen occupant. After a few moments he ran back to Aemilia.

"Says he's coming." he said, and waited hopefully.

"I gave you a coin," Aemilia said. "Go play." Her anger had not abated. The boy shrugged and trotted off. Time passed. Finally the door opened and Ennodius came out. He caught sight of her and turned to speak to someone behind him. Aemilia had a glimpse of a woman's face framed by a mop of dishevelled, black hair, and then the door closed. He sauntered over to her.

"How did you find me?" he asked.

"Staterius told me," she replied.

"The man is supernatural. If I died, he'd know in which part of Hades I was."

Aemilia was silent. Ennodius glanced at her. "Well? What's the story?"

"Your mother sent me to find you. My Lord Syagrius wants to see you."

"Does he just? Well then, it's come." Ennodius paused and then, glancing around, continued in a stage-whisper, "The old boy's going to make me emperor."

"You, emperor?"

"Yes. About time too. I've waited long enough for it."

Somehow Aemilia could not contain herself. "Why is he going to make you emperor?"

"Because he needs a figurehead. Someone to stir the enthusiasm of his loyal subjects."

"But why you?"

Ennodius glanced at Aemilia curiously. It had begun to occur to him that she had abandoned her habitual reserve.

"Because he's clever, that's why. If he makes himself emperor he'll just look like another upstart. But taking someone with an emperor in the family tree looks much more authentic, something that people can take seriously. I'm the only available candidate, so—I get the job."

"And what will you do as emperor?"

Ennodius paused before replying. There was something odd about Aemilia's mood.

"Improve my wardrobe—lots of purple—make speeches, wear some armor now and then, put on a bit of a show. That sort of thing." There was a silence. Then suddenly Aemilia turned and hurried towards the entrance.

"What's the matter?" Ennodius called out.

Aemilia stopped and turned. "You're not fit for it!" she said. She continued on as quickly as she could without glancing back, and so did not see the astonishment in Ennodius's face.

As she threaded her way through the crowded streets her anger abated, and a sense of disbelief at what she had done came over her. *I must be insane,* she thought, *I'll lose my position for certain now, if I ever had a chance of keeping it. What did I get angry for? What's wrong with me?*

She could not return to the Residence, not yet. She needed to be alone, somewhere she could think. In the forum it came to her where she could go. Making her way to the church she entered into the cool silence of the nave and sat on one of the benches placed against the wall for the ill and infirm. She looked around. There was no one except herself in the building. Shafts of sunlight filtered through the windows above the arched colonnades, breaking up the floor into a pattern of light and shade. She studied it. Light and shade. Cream and gray. Neither one nor the other, but both, and possessing a finesse that came from being both. Neither a floor plunged in shadow, nor a surface drenched in sunlight like the plaza outside. Something in between: two colors, each bringing out the beauty in the other.

Then a cloud passed overhead and the light dimmed, becoming softer, more diffuse, molding itself around the perfectly proportioned pillars, the ornate capitals, the carefully balanced arches that lined the central space of the nave. Aemilia was suddenly aware of the sense of depth, of perspective, that the reduced light gave to the church. It seemed to grow in stature as the perfection of its design became manifest. There should not be too much illumination here. She remembered an old pagan temple she had seen when a child, half-ruined but still substantially intact. The interior had had no light at all, except what a torch could provide. The pagans had worshipped outside, her mother had told her, under the sky and the sun, never once entering the building. It had not occurred to her to ask why they had done so, and why the Christians had not imitated them. Now she began to perceive the question and the answer together. We are children of the light, but our light is not the light of the noonday devil. A fragment came to her, from the gospel of Matthew:

> ...at the hour when dawn broke on the first day of the week Mary Magdalen and the other Mary came near to see the tomb. And suddenly there was a trembling of the earth, because an angel of the Lord came to the place, descending from heaven, and rolled away the stone and sat over it...

Early in the dawn, when the light was dim. That was when the Son of Man showed what he truly was, rising from the dead.

Aemilia got up from the bench and went up the front of the nave where she put alms in the slot of a small chest in front of the Madonna, kneeling to say a prayer before quitting the church. In the atrium she stopped a few minutes to look at the mosaic of Christ above the church's main entrance.

I still don't know why I got so angry, she thought, *but look after me whatever happens.*

CHAPTER 14

During the next few days, Aemilia waited to be summoned into Lady Julia's presence and dismissed. She had already mentally rehearsed what she would say to her father, not knowing what his reaction to the news would be. But for the rest of that day, and the next, and the day after that, the Lady's attitude to Aemilia did not change, unless it were to be a shade less cool. It gradually dawned on Aemilia that Ennodius had kept her outburst to himself. Why, she could not imagine. Perhaps, she thought, he had found it amusing rather than insulting. If so it was the last time he would have that kind of entertainment from her. She would be doubly on her guard now, a model of correctness and deference.

The news spread through the household that Ennodius had spent two hours closeted with Syagrius, and the more perspicacious of the slaves divined why.

"He's going to do it," Galbus told Aemilia. The guard was in the kitchen during off-duty, sitting on a bench whilst Aemilia wrapped a bandage round his foot. "Wouldn't have believed it, but Staterius dropped a hint to Procopius who passed it on to me."

"Who's going to do what?" Aemilia asked.

Galbus leaned forward and dropped his voice confidentially. "Syagrius. He's going to make that dandy son of Lady Julia emperor—begging your pardon, 'Her Majesty'", and he bowed his head in mock deference.

"She really will be Her Majesty then."

"Aye. She can't wait for it. She'll have us genuflecting each time we see her, I wouldn't be surprised."

Aemilia pulled a wry face and gave a shrug, turning her attention to the guard's other foot.

"It's going to be a bad lookout for us," Galbus continued. "The Visigoths won't like it."

A remark by Vipsania teased Aemilia's memory. Something about the Goths... *They're all on horses, they'll ride right over him...*

113

"Do you think they'll attack us?" she asked.

Galbus considered a moment. "Not right yet, I reckon. If Euric'd been alive, he'd have done something. But his son Alaric's still just a boy, not a proper king yet. He won't be throwing his weight around for a while. I'll bet a solidus Syagrius's counting on that."

"You think?" interrupted Pollux, pausing from slicing meat. "Wait till it happens, then bring your solidus, eh? In Spain a gladiator makes an auroch angry before he kills him. Waves a cloth in front of his eyes, then he charges. Sometimes he gets the auroch, sometimes the auroch gets him, but always the auroch charges." He picked up a dishcloth to illustrate. "Syagrius, he waves a big cloth, with 'emperor' on it. You think the Visigoths stay at home? No, no. They come."

"Then just feed them what you feed us. That'll do them in."

The cook snorted and resumed cutting the meat. Galbus stood up and gingerly tested his feet.

"A lot better, I reckon," he admitted.

"We must do it again tomorrow," Aemilia said. "The oftener the better."

"Aye. If Pollux can put up with the smell," he said, pulling on his boots and tying the shin straps.

"You make my food taste bad."

"I can't make it worse than it is."

"Off with you."

Aemilia had not been able to see much of Tarunculus during this period. Travelling alone at night to and from his apartment would have been dangerous, and during the day he was fully occupied with his century of recruits at the barracks. Just once, at midday, she was able to take off enough time to pay him a short visit. Being a centurion's daughter was enough to admit her through the main gates. The parade ground was immediately beyond it, where several groups of men were being drilled by their officers. Tarunculus, as the old ex-frontier guard had said, was easy to find: his voice carried over all the others. He was training his men to form a shield wall: shields in front, overlapping, with spears bristling over them.

"Faster than that, you snails! Think the Franks are going sit and wait for you? Now...on my orders...turn *right*. Slowly, slowly, hold the line, *hold the line*....Halt! A bit better, but they'll still be kicking your backsides before you're halfway there. As you were. We'll do it again."

Aemilia stood under the shaded arcade that surrounded the parade ground and waited. The recruits seemed to be a mixed bag: some very young,

others almost old. They were hesitantly trying to take their cue from each other, shuffling uncertainly from one position to the next. How long *does* it take to train a soldier, she wondered. Would three months be enough?

Finally Tarunculus stood them at ease.

"You're getting there. You've a way to go yet—I want that line straight, and after lunch I want you to turn side-on before I count ten."

A murmur of groans came from the body of men.

"'ten-*shun!*" The company stamped heels together. There was a moment's silence.

"Half midday lunch forfeited. Any further complaints and you lose the other half. Stand to attention until dismissed."

Tarunculus turned his back to the men and strode over to the arcade towards Aemilia. He grinned at her.

"Come to see your father put the fear of Hades into 'em, eh?"

Aemilia looked past him at the recruits. It was a hot day, the sun blazed earthwards from a cloudless sky and she could see, even at this distance, the gleam of sweat on their faces. They had obviously been drilling all morning and had their eyes on Tarunculus, waiting for him to dismiss them.

"They seem tired, Father."

"They should be. Been at it since sunrise."

"Isn't that too much?"

"If they're still standing, nothing's too much." He pulled off his neckerchief and wiped his sweaty brow. "This lot should have been broken in gently. Six months training, a nice, easy post in a fort, a few skirmishes and no big battles before a year is up. That's what it should be like. But what's going to happen is that they're going to leave here and be thrown into the worst day of their lives. They're up against Franks." He looked at her for a moment. "I've fought 'em. Tough bastards." He turned to survey his men. "I haven't got time to mother this crowd. They'll get all they can take, and then a bit more...Dis-*missed!*"

The men broke ranks and headed precipitately for the canteen building at the far end of the parade ground.

"Heard you met the Franks," said Tarunculus, turning back to her.

"I did. Lady Julia took me with her."

"How'd you find 'em?"

"...I think you're right. They seem very tough. Also they have spears with barbs, like fishing hooks."

"Aye. A Frankish trick. That way you can't pull the spear out and throw it back." Aemilia winced. "But they're still barbarians. No real discipline. All they know how to do is charge, and if that doesn't work then they break and run. We've just got to hold against them long enough and they'll turn tail, sure as I'm here."

"You think our men will hold?" asked Aemilia softly.

Tarunculus didn't immediately answer, but leaned against the arcade wall and rubbed his leg, glancing across at the disappearing recruits.

"They need spirit. Guts," he said finally. "Something that'll make 'em fight no matter how hot it gets. It comes with time, but they need it now."

"Something to inspire them?"

"Something like that."

Aemilia hesitated, then make up her mind. "I heard that Syagrius is going to make Ennodius emperor." Tarunculus gave her a sharp glance. "Syagrius spent two hours with him, and everyone says it's because he's going to make him emperor, soon."

"Is that so?" said Tarunculus, with slow emphasis.

"We'll be an empire again."

"So we will. They won't be asking any more why they're risking their necks for a damn province. You don't know when Syagrius's announcing it?"

"No." She glanced at his leg. "Is it painful?"

He paused in his rubbing. "This? Just an old arrow wound in the knee. Got it years ago and it's stiffened up the joint a bit, but that won't stop me moving with the best of 'em when the time comes." Aemilia realized that Tarunculus expected to be with the army in the coming battle.

"I know a salve that would help it," she offered.

"Much obliged, but I don't need help," Tarunculus replied. "When I'm in bed and breathing my last then you can bring all the potions you can think of. But I'm not in my dotage yet, girl." With that he stood away from the wall and started off across the parade ground. He stopped after a few paces and turned back.

"You're a good girl," he said, then continued on.

It was on the following day that Aemilia found a note from Ennodius inside her copy of the New Testament: *The old girl is out tomorrow morning. Come and see me then in the Theater. Third Hour. Be on time. Ennodius.*

It was something she had been half-expecting, half-dreading. She wanted no further dealings with him, but had been able to do nothing other than allow a frail hope to bud that he had lost interest in her after her outburst, preferring the pliant company that, in his position, it was so easy for him to procure.

She debated the option of refusing the rendezvous. Theaters were virtually abandoned buildings. Nobody bothered with plays any more. Mass entertainment in the larger cities of former Roman territory focussed on the circuses, where chariot racing was a passion, the more so since gladiatorial contests had long since been outlawed. The theater of Soissons was used for rare social events—such as a speech by the governor intended for the more affluent section of the populace—on which occasions it was swept out, patched up and decorated with banners and pennants. The rest of the time it was left as an arena for the contest between Roman architectural solidity and the ceaseless beat of time, with no doubt as to the outcome. No waifs or strays lived there, as the building's design did not suit habitation, making it the perfect place for a private tête-à-tête. And that was the last thing Aemilia wanted.

On the other hand agreeing to see Ennodius was not necessarily dangerous. Aemilia lacked experience, but she had the dim notion that he was not likely to mistreat her. Even though he was the son of a highborn, there was still a limit to what he could get away with—the more so that he was now emperor-elect. Her memory cast back to that age long ago when she had been subject to Avitus. Even he had not dared to take advantage of her whilst her mother was alive. *He must have thought I would agree to it once I was alone*, she thought. *Even he couldn't* force *me to do what he wanted.*

She made up her mind. The following day she took a basket after breakfast and told Vipsania she would be buying provisions for Lavilla. "Something a bit nicer than the food Pollux throws out."

"Maybe I should come with you."

"Don't bother. Her Majesty might come back unexpected. I'll tell Lavilla you give her your love."

Pausing at the forum to procure the ingredients for a vegetable dish, Aemilia continued on to the theater. It lay outside the walls, to the west of the town center, in an area whose buildings had once been well-to-do, but had long since decayed into a state of near-ruin that had a touch of melancholy in the evening light, but was merely seedy in the frank glare of the morning. The theater nestled among the old buildings, its floor plan forming a half circle, with the entrances at either end of the flat side.

Aemilia remembered a fragment of conversation with Lady Avita, when the subject had been Rome and its great buildings. The Romans, Lady Avita told her, had copied the theater design—like so much else—from the Greeks, who had originally taken a concave piece of hillside and molded it into semicircular tiers of seats, with a raised platform before them, for their religious rites. The rites had gradually incorporated music, monologues, and finally, actors, until the original religious purpose was submerged under the dramatic presentations that replaced it. The plays started by glorifying the gods, then humanizing them, and finally reducing them to mockery. Augustus, who wanted the Roman gods respected, forbade the construction of any stone theater in Rome. In time the Romans ceased to take their deities seriously, and theaters were built everywhere until interest in theater died along with the old gods.

Aemilia passed under the tall, pillared entrance and approached the central stage. All around her, rows of worn stone seats rose up. There was no one else in sight. Behind the stage rose an architectural facade, pillared and arched, with several blind doors and a balcony on the first floor, designed as a backdrop to the dramas and comedies that would never be put on again. It was quiet. Aemilia sat down in the first row of seating and waited. Time passed.

"Up here."

She glanced up in surprise. Ennodius leaned over the balcony, holding a manuscript.

"Came early, did you?"

"You asked me to be on time, my Lord."

"Good. No, don't stand. I need you as an audience, and audiences sit. Go on, don't be shy."

Aemilia reluctantly took her seat again.

"I suppose you're wondering what this is all about." He paused. Aemilia looked downwards, saying nothing. "Don't worry. I'm not going to hand you over to the tender mercies of the old girl for that little remark of yours, though I admit it was a bolt out the blue. No one's ever told me I'm not fit for anything before."

"My Lord, I apologize."

"No need. You made me curious, that's all." Aemilia glanced up. "I wondered what you meant by it. How is one supposed to be fit to be a puppet emperor? I pumped the old girl and it came out you could read and write. That got me thinking. I waited until the coast was clear and then had a look in your room. And guess what I found? Your copy of *City of God*. Someone who reads the heavyweights, and a girl too! Then it all fell into place. So here I am to prove I can do it."

"My Lord?"

"Give a first-class speech, and my own composition too. Modelled on Cicero a bit, I admit. You've read Cicero?"

Aemilia nodded.

"Good. Here goes."

Ennodius began to declaim. Aemilia quickly realized he had been trained in rhetoric. He enunciated his phrases in a clear voice, carefully mixing emphases with pauses. The sentences were balanced and nicely rounded. The meaning—what she could grasp of it, since her attention was held more by technique than content—was high and imperial, and reminded her of Tarunculus's oratory. The overall effect was polished, artistic, contrived and lifeless. After half-an-hour it came to a climax, and Ennodius finished it with both arms raised up. Then he leaned them on the balcony balustrade and grinned.

"What did you think of that?"

Aemilia was silent.

"Well? Never heard oratory before?"

"I've heard my father, My Lord," she replied, glancing up and then down again. She stood and picked up her basket. "May I go now?"

Ennodius's grin faded. "I suppose you could do better yourself? All right, come up here and try it. And what your father does is called haranguing, not oratory. Come up then."

"My Lord, I would rather not."

"Of course you would, if you're the expert."

"My Lord, you've been trained in rhetoric. I have not. Please."

There was a pause. "Well, you spotted the training at least...all right. Tell you what. You go and *write* the sort of speech you think I should deliver. I'll be giving it in the forum, Syagrius's told me, once the army's ready to go. I'd prefer here but there's not enough space. It's during my coronation. Something to stir the troops. See what you can come up with."

"You don't need me to write a speech!"

The grin was back. "*You* said I wasn't fit for it. It's up to you to show me what fit is. Here, this might give you some ideas." And folding up the manuscript, he dropped it over the edge of the balcony onto the stage below. Aemilia hesitated, then mounted the steps at the base of the stage and picked up the folded wad of parchment.

"I think three days should be enough time. Come and find me then"— the grin broadened—"at the Residence." And he was gone.

Aemilia stood for a minute or two, waiting until she was sure Ennodius had really left. Then she turned to face the vast curving tiers of seats. Her thoughts moved at lightning speed: ...*fellow citizens and Romans...crazy old goat...you are Romans, Roman citizens and so Romans...speak for yourself, I'm a Gaul...now is the time to fight....*An image of the fruiterer:....*when the Franks come do you think anyone's going to cry about it? I'm one that won't, I tell you....*Then a memory of Syagrius, chuckling:....*the common crowd swallow that kind of thing hook, line and sinker....*Tarunculus, contemptuous:....*that* *mob out there....*And then Ennodius:...*how is one supposed to be fit to be a puppet emperor?...put on a bit of a show....*

A great mental weariness overcame her. She dropped her head and glanced at the manuscript in her hand. *I can't,* she thought. What had he said? "Something to stir the troops." Just tell them all to go home. That should do it.

Then it welled up in her again: not a loyalty—more than that—a great, unarguable adhesion to a world that she had grown up in and learned to love, a world whose evils disturbed her to the very core of her being, yet one she would not give up, simply because she perceived that for her there was no other. The Franks were not savages, but if they came what would there be? The ruin of the treasury of her mind and—it flashed through her thoughts like a bolt—her inevitable fall into destitution. No, no. No.

I should have more faith, she thought. She unfolded the manuscript and smoothed out the sheets. Lady Avita had been mercilessly satirical about the turgid rhetorical style that was endemic to the educated class, and this was a first-class example of it.

Aemilia sighed. Never mind getting him to say something the people will listen to, she thought, how will I make him stop waving his arms about like that?

PART III:
THE UTMOST

Chapter 15

For the next two days Aemilia put out of her mind any thought of writing a speech. Her periods of spare time during the day were limited to Lady Julia's sorties from the Residence, which were not frequent. That left the evenings, which she devoted to copying out Tarunculus's pamphlets. These she passed to one of his slaves, Nestor, from time to time. Once, she asked after Primus.

"Reckon he's doing all right, ma'am," he said.

"Did you see him?"

"That I did. Managed to look in at the slaves' quarters whenever I need to see the Centurion."

"Is he happy?"

"Reckon he's doing all right."

Aemilia did not press him. Only, as he turned to go, she added, "Tell him I send my greetings." The slave's profile paused momentarily before he answered, "Will do that, ma'am," and then took his leave.

It was only when the evening of the second day was far advanced that Aemilia forced herself to consider the speech Ennodius had demanded. She felt only aversion at the thought of supplying him with another source of amusement, but knew she had no choice. He held her fate in the palm of his hand. Lady Julia might have a mother's lucidity about her son's shortcomings, but that did not stop her doting on him. She had seen them together, Ennodius treating his mother with a casual flippancy which she would not have believed possible had she not witnessed it with her own eyes. The Lady had him on a leash, but the leash was long. A single critical word from him would be mortal.

She had found half-a-dozen blank sheets of parchment—evidently supplied by Ennodius—under her *City of God*. She took one and laid it on the breadboard. Dipping her feather quill into the clay inkwell perched on the edge of the board she wrote:

I appeal to you all, dear countrymen

125

And then:

We are all Romans together

And again:

We are gathered together to fight for that which we love

She stopped writing and carefully put the quill pen back in the inkwell and then stood, placing the board on her bed. She paced, back and forth, between the beds. Sylvia was asleep. Vispania opened a drowsy eye.

"Can't you sleep?" she asked.

"Just thinking."

"What about?"

"Oh, just what I have to write."

"Save the world tomorrow," and she turned to face the wall.

Aemilia paced for a while longer and then sat on her bed again. Putting the board on her lap she took up the quill pen and resumed writing, this time not stopping until she extinguished the lamp nearly an hour later.

The next day Aemilia kept an eye open for Ennodius. Having to attend the Lady and be ready to answer a call from her at a moment's notice, would leave her only enough time between chores to find him and give him the speech, which suited her. He could laugh at it in her absence.

At midday a messenger arrived with a supper invitation for Lady Julia, from the wife of one of the foremost merchants of Soissons—unexpected, as the Lady received few such invitations. Ennodius came in shortly after, and Lady Julia discussed it with him whilst Aemilia curled her hair with hot irons.

"The word is getting around, my boy."

"What word's that?"

"Your little secret is out. An invitation to supper from Aedia Ricovica. Here, read it."

Ennodius perused the missive, then shrugged.

"I suppose so."

"Count on it. The first of many."

"Well, it's nothing to grin about. Ricovicus is a provincial bore. Whenever his wife wants to wake him up from his afternoon siesta, she jingles a couple of coins. That gets him going: 'What! What! Someone's pinching the grocery money!' I watched him once while I was waiting for his daughter. He was asleep in a chair with his head leaning back and his mouth open. His tongue had slid to the back of his throat and he couldn't breathe. He gave a big snort, nggh! and half woke up, lolling his head forwards so he could breathe again. Then he fell asleep and leaned his head back—and couldn't breathe. Nggh! It went on like that until she came in and spoiled my fun."

"Well the invitation expressly includes you."

"They want to pair me off with their ugly daughter. I'm not interested and in any case I can do better than that. You'll have to give my excuses."

"I think, my boy, that it is better that you come." Aemilia heard the note of authority in her voice.

"Did I tell you that I received a missive from Symmachus?" Ennodius spoke diffidently, but Aemilia could detect the tension between the two.

"Indeed?"

"Oh yes. He mentioned that his daughter is of marriageable age."

"Did he?" There was a gratified emphasis in the words. Symmachus was one of the foremost of the Curia senators, the inner circle of the senatorial body that lived in Rome and managed the city's municipal affairs. They had immense prestige, backed by equally immense wealth.

The Lady deliberated a moment. "Very well. I shall give your excuses to the Ricovici."

"Suits me. I don't want to have to turn their girl down in front of them. When do you go?"

"Before sunset. They take supper early, it seems."

As he left, Ennodius caught Aemilia's eye out of Lady Julia's field of vision and winked at her, mouthing the word 'garden'. It was to be a rendezvous after all. Aemilia felt troubled.

"Pay attention, girl!" the Lady said sharply.

Aemilia's mind returned to her task.

The sun was low in the sky when Lady Julia summoned her litter and left the Residence. The moment she was gone, Aemilia took her speech to the garden, hiding it along with Ennodius's own composition in the cloth she used to carry food to Lavilla. She found Ennodius seated on the same bench he had used before.

"Very prompt. I was afraid I might have a bit of a wait."

"Here it is, My Lord," said Aemilia, extracting the two speeches from the cloth and pushing them into Ennodius's hands. "May I go now?"

"Not so fast. I want to read it first." Leisurely, he opened Aemilia's composition and began to read. His expression of good humor turned to an amused astonishment before he had finished with the first sheet. He continued half-way through the second and then looked up with an incredulous smile.

"I can't say this!"

Aemilia said nothing, eyes downcast.

"I mean, I won't even be there! I'm just supposed to give them a rousing oration: long live the Empire, long live Syagrius, and that's it." He shook his head, like a patient schoolmaster. "This is ridiculous. Sorry, girl, you'll have to try again."

"What is ridiculous?"

They both looked up. Syagrius approached them, a expression of query on his face. Ennodius stood up. "My Lord..."

"I was looking for you. They told me you were in the garden."

"Yes, My Lord. We were discussing my forthcoming speech for the coronation. Aemilia here is well read, so it turns out, and not too impressed with my own efforts. This is hers. We were discussing its merits—or the lack of them."

"Give it to me."

Ennodius handed him the manuscript. Aemilia fixed her eyes on the mosaic paving, hands crossed in front of her. There was silence for what seemed an eternity as Syagrius read the speech through, and then reread it. When done, he said nothing for a few moments.

"Clever. No rhetoric. Just the one thing you can say to them that'll make any real impression. What do you have there?"

"My own speech, my Lord."

"Let's have a look at it."

He read the speech, this time without comment, and then handed both back to Ennodius. He looked away for a moment before speaking.

"You'll give her speech at your coronation." He glanced at Aemilia with a hint of amusement. "All of it." Ennodius's face seemed to set. "You realize, of course, that for it to have its effect, you'll have to do as it says."

"But...my Lord..."

"But what? Did you think you were to be emperor at the price of a few fine words and nothing else? It's time for you to earn your keep."

"But I know nothing about soldiering!"

"You don't need to. You just need to be there. That's what I'm making you emperor for, after all." Syagrius gave a wry smile. "I should have thought of it myself." He gave Aemilia an appraising look. "You keep on surprising me. Always more than you appear. Well done."

"Thank you, My Lord," Aemilia replied, and then took courage in both hands: "But My Lord Ennodius's speech is quite suitable. He is very proficient in rhetoric, I heard him..."

"You heard him? He read his speech to you?"

She glanced at Ennodius. "...yes, My Lord."

"Before you wrote your own?"

"Yes, My Lord."

Syagrius looked at her keenly.

"And? How did his strike you? Tell me the truth."

Aemilia hung her head, not knowing what to reply.

"As turgid and overblown perhaps? High sounding phrases that pass completely over the head of the listener? Correct, contrived language with the odd archaic term thrown in here and there? In short, as you said, a very proficient show of rhetoric?

"And what did you do? Write a speech that went completely against it in content and style, producing something that no rhetorician would dream of writing, and that might just have an effect on the crowd….if it's properly delivered."

Syagrius glanced away again, considering.

"Ennodius, I want you to rehearse this speech with this girl. I regret having to oblige you to do so but I'm afraid I do not have the time to pander to anyone's sensibilities. You are to rehearse it with her and you are to follow her advice. The day before the coronation you will give the speech before me. Is that clear?"

"Clear, my Lord."

"And keep in mind that it's not pleasing me that matters. What matters is that it is effective with the troops. You understand that your life could depend on it."

"I...understand."

Syagrius turned to leave, and then turned back as if struck by an afterthought. "Do it in strictest secrecy. And tell your mother the girl is to have all the time she needs to help you with it." He was gone before Ennodius could reply.

Ennodius remained unmoving. Aemilia felt she had to speak. "My Lord, I'm sorry..."

"Look what you've got me into! How could you write this? How could you possibly think I could give it, knowing what that meant! Were you out of your mind?"

"I..."

"Well? Were you trying to make a fool of me?"

"I wrote what I felt! It's what I would say and do in your place. I expected you to laugh at it and throw it away. I never expected Syagrius to read it!"

Ennodius was brought up short by Aemilia's outburst. His anger subsided and anxiety crept into his eyes. "What am I going to do now?"

A flaming sense of purpose overrode Aemilia's guilt and pity. She looked directly at Ennodius. "My Lord, we're going to win! With men like my father training them, they can't lose. They just need...inspiration. They need to have their heart in what they're doing. You can make them feel like that. You can. You can. You'll be the emperor. You're the one to do it."

For a moment Aemilia could see a spark flicker in his eyes. Then his look travelled downwards. Aemilia realized she was gripping his arm. She let go with a slight sense of confusion.

"I'm sorry, My Lord. I spoke out of turn."

There was the hint of a grin. "You did, but you're getting used to doing that."

There was a silence. "I think I should be going," Aemilia said.

"Yes. Well, perhaps we can start tomorrow."

"...as you wish, my Lord."

"I'll let you know."

"My Lord."

Ennodius said nothing further and Aemilia took it as permission to leave. She walked quickly from the garden to her room, which she found empty, and threw herself on her bed, staring up at the sloping ceiling above her. She did not move for a long time. She could not think. Her mind was awash with the vast certitude that Ennodius and Syagrius together had shaken loose her last fragile grip on her niche in the order of things, a grip already weakened by Lady Julia. She now floated in a dangerous, undefined space between them, like a skin boat tossed by waves between sharp rocks, liable to be splintered at any moment. Her emotions veered between elation and leaden fear, and in the midst of her wildly fluctuating moods, she hardly noticed the realization that Syagrius was forcing the utmost out of Ennodius, as he was out of the populace of Soissons, by giving him no choice. Triumph or die.

Gradually, her mind began to adjust to her new situation. There was no doubt whatsoever that it was all over with Lady Julia. Any criticism of Ennodius would have been enough to get her discharged. And now she was instrumental in putting his life in danger. Her services—henceforth no more than a pretence—would be dispensed with the moment the need to keep up appearances had passed. The Lady would dismiss her three weeks from now, howsoever things went. It was time to start looking for other employment.

Then an image came to her: the brief moment when she saw the spark in Ennodius's eyes. The wages of sin is death, but just for a fleeting instant there had been the stirrings of life, a faint touch from without that had lifted him, however briefly, from his moribund absorption with himself. That spark must be struck again, fostered into a steady flame and not allowed to go out. Later, much later, it might be made to rise beyond a speech and a battle.

The room was now quite dark. Aemilia rose up and felt for the lamp on the shelf above her bed. Finding it she worked her way carefully to the door and opened it, admitting the dim light from the passage lamps. She lit hers from one of them and returned to the bedroom, replacing the lamp on the shelf. Then she gave her thoughts to the speech. It would need more work: she had written quickly and had not revised it. Suddenly she smiled. Syagrius is a wonder, she thought. He is forcing the utmost out of me as well.

CHAPTER 16

Three days before the coronation, Aemilia finally had the opportunity to slip away from the Residence and go to the town's civil basilica. Lady Julia had received another invitation, this time for lunch, from a town worthy. Since the midday meal was a far less protracted affair than the evening *cena*, Aemilia knew she would have to hurry. She had never been nearer the basilica than the base of the flight of marble steps leading up to its front entrance. Mounting them she passed through the vast doorway.

The interior—the largest she had ever seen—looked very much like a church. She knew, as well as anyone else, that church design was modelled on that of a basilica. Lady Avita had told her more: many older churches were simply basilicas converted for the purpose. The Lady, who had a smattering of Greek, had added that the word basilica meant 'king's house' in that language. The building was, like so much else in the Roman world, an import from Greece.

Looking around, Aemilia saw the familiar central space flanked by colonnades. There was even an apse at the far end—in churches the place of the bishop's seat, here the place for the chair of the presiding magistrate, for the basilica, among other purposes, functioned as a courthouse.

The interior was full of people, and noisy. Above the two colonnades running down each long side of the building she saw people looking over a balustrade, and realized that there was a higher level. As she drew nearer the apse, Aemilia noticed a trial in progress. A magistrate, suitably attired in a toga, reclined against the armrests of the backless *sella* and listened to a lawyer, whilst a scribe sat at a side table taking notes, with a small crowd standing deferentially before them. It was difficult to tell who the accused and the accuser were, and in any case she did not have the time to indulge her curiosity. She caught sight of a man hurrying by holding a scroll—he looked as if he worked there—and touched his sleeve. "Please sir, can you tell me who I should speak to about employing a scribe?"

The man, rather small and overweight, didn't understand the question.

"Eh? You want to employ a scribe?"

"No. I want to offer one for employment."

The man thought a moment. "Don't rightly know if they're employing anyone now, but you can ask for Vegetius: he's Master of Scribes. Upstairs—that side." He pointed up at the balustrade.

"Thank you. Where do I find the stairs?"

"Outside. Through that door over there."

Aemilia's gaze followed his finger. The interior side walls were lined with wooden booths, rather like the rows of small shops on the sides of the forum, in which officials in their various capacities sat behind tables and conducted their official business. Aemilia was heartened by the observation that a lot of it seemed to involve writing. Record-keeping clearly played a large role in Syagrius's bureaucracy.

She spotted the small, wooden door between the booths. Passing through it, she climbed a narrow stairway running up the outside wall to the level of the first floor. Reentering the building she found a perambulatory running along the side and rear walls, flanked on its outward side by booths set against the walls, and on its inward side by a balustrade that overlooked the din and bustle below.

She felt out of place here. This was a part of the building that did not deal directly with the general public and she was the only woman present. She steeled her nerve and asked for Vegetius. A passerby pointed to a wide booth at the end of the perambulatory. She approached and found a middle-aged man, balding, portly and—this surprised her—with a good-natured face, seated behind a desk, talking to a slave standing before him (she noticed the slit earlobe). She stood by and waited. After a few moments the Master of Scribes dismissed the slave and noticed her.

"Yes? Can I help you, ma'am?"

"Yes please. I was told you were the one to talk to about employing a scribe."

He seemed momentarily taken aback.

"Do you ever employ scribes?" she persisted.

"Well...yes...we do, on occasion, for temporary work. It depends on the need. But mostly we just buy them. From larger households, you understand. You don't find an educated slave in the marketplace. Do you want to sell me a scribe?

"No. I want to offer one for employment."

He seemed to think for a moment. "You might just have come at the right time. With all these preparations we've had a good deal of extra work. But we can't offer much in the way of pay. You're certain you don't want to sell your scribe? You'll be paid well for him."

"No. I don't have a scribe to sell."

"Then if I may ask, ma'am, who is your scribe?"

"Me."

His eyes widened in astonishment.

"I can read and write," Aemilia continued, "and I've done scribe work already for my father. He can vouch for me."

"And who's your father?"

"Centurion Tarunculus."

This time his mouth fell open. "You're his *daughter?*...But if you don't mind my asking, why come here? Surely he's in a position to keep you without you having to earn a living."

Aemilia looked downwards. "He may not always be." She glanced up and caught his eye, which showed an immediate flash of understanding. Then the Master of Scribes looked away, uncertain.

"Problem is, we've never employed a woman before. It's just not done." He paused and then slowly shook his head. "Don't see how I could get it past them, I'm sorry."

"There's one other thing." Aemilia dropped her voice. "I can speak Frankish."

He looked at her sharply, then gestured with his hand. "Say something."

"*Ek is 'n Frank. Ek kan die taal flot praat,*" she replied, after a moment's thought.

There was long silence. Finally he spoke. "I can't promise anything now, but come to me later,"—he put a slight emphasis on the 'later'—"and we'll see what can be done. In the meantime, here." He pushed a sheet of parchment and an inkwell towards her. "Write your name and what you just said in Frankish." Aemilia leaned over the table and did as asked, using Latin letters phonetically as best she could—Frankish was not a written language. As she was finishing he whispered to her: "Tell no one about our conversation, understood?"

"Yes sir," she replied.

He smiled. "Goodbye. Let's hope that I don't have to see you again."

"I do hope it," she replied and took her leave.

Going down the outer stairs she thought over the Master of the Scribe's parting words. What was the likelihood she would return? If Syagrius triumphed then she need never work again. When Lady Julia dismissed her she would tell Tarunculus why. She would even tell him of the Lady's treason. She was certain he would not turn her out.

But if Syagrius lost...

Her mind cast back over the previous two weeks. The rehearsals. Ennodius had not wanted to return to the theater as it did not sufficiently guarantee secrecy. He had tried to persuade her to come to a small one-roomed apartment he rented in a remote part of the town outside the walls. Aemilia had turned the suggestion down out of hand.

She had debated the problem in her mind of where to go throughout that day and the next. She had then approached Lady Julia. It had been the hardest thing she had ever had to do. The Lady had not been hostile, as Aemilia had expected. Her reaction had seemed indifferent, and Aemilia did not know what lay behind that inscrutable mask. She had acquiesced immediately to Aemilia's request. From then on all rehearsals took place in the Lady's bedroom with the Lady present.

They had been a purgatory. Lady Julia had not ridiculed her as she half-feared. Throughout every session she had sat in her chair, looking away and saying nothing. This, more than anything else, worked to unnerve Aemilia, nonetheless she kept at her task. She had no hope of winning the Lady's approval, and her disapproval did not matter anymore.

She succeeded in getting Ennodius to learn the speech by heart, but that was the extent of her progress with him. The initial spark raised in him on the day of their meeting with Syagrius had not returned, and nothing she could do would re-ignite it. By turns frivolous and irritable, he read and reread the speech like a grammar tutor reciting his pupil's first effort at composition. Aemilia could make nothing of him. The rehearsals had meant to be a daily affair. The last one had taken place five days ago. Aemilia felt sick at the thought of them.

Once, Syagrius had met her, as if by chance, and asked about Ennodius's progress. She had tried to say something good without being positively untruthful. He had listened to her without comment and then continued on his way. She had no doubt that her tone of voice had conveyed far more than her mere words did.

Absorbed in her reflections as she walked through the hall of the basilica, Aemilia did not notice a figure standing in her way until she had nearly bumped into him. She looked up with a start. "I'm sorry."

"Fancy meeting *you* here."

Aemilia recognized him instantly: the cavalry officer who had stopped her cart outside Soissons. He grinned.

"Your dad's doing alright? I hear he's shaking 'em up at the barracks."

"Yes sir," she said, and made to pass on.

"You're on the up too, I hear. Right in Lady Julia's secrets, eh?"

Aemilia started. He noticed it, and his grin grew broader.

"Don't worry love, I won't be telling anybody."

"I don't know what you're talking about," she said, glancing at him and then away.

"That's right," he said. "We don't know anything. But a little bird told me that Her Mightiness isn't the only one who can make a deal with the Franks. Ha! ha!" He guffawed on seeing Aemilia's fear.

She glanced around. "I must go, please," she said.

"You do that, love." He put his finger to his lips. "Not a word to the Centurion, eh?" He winked as she passed him.

Aemilia walked quickly away, dread in her bowels and confusion in her mind. How had he found out? If he knew, how many knew? Would anyone tell Syagrius? *Had* anyone told Syagrius? What should she do? She had never seriously thought of the implications of Lady Julia's deal with the Franks. At the time she had taken for granted that there was nothing she could do about it and that, in all events, its execution was unlikely to materialize. Now the notion dawned on her that she had the obligation to reveal the Lady's treason to Syagrius if she did not want to share in it. For a moment the thought gripped her. The speech was a tired joke: she could do more for the cause of Roman Gaul by making Syagrius aware of the treachery that, she realized, had spread beyond Lady Julia's dealings with the Franks.

But the thought lasted only an instant. It would mean Lady Julia's death, for certain, and Ennodius's too, perhaps. No, she could not be the cause of that. There was nothing to be done. She dared not tell her father, and there was no one else she could trust. She had no other choice but to hope that the traitors, whoever they were, would be cautious enough to prevent their and Lady Julia's treason from reaching Syagrius's ears. It was an uncertain hope. Syagrius had praised her, and in his pre-emptory way trusted her. If he found out that she had a part in those dealing with his enemies...good Lord, what would he do to her?

She walked quickly down the basilica's stairway, almost knocking against a pedestrian as she did so. The entrance to the church's atrium was on the other side of the plaza, and Aemilia was inclined to go across. But it was late—she would have to be back at the Residence soon. Another time, she thought. I should speak to the bishop. He will tell me what to do.

"Well, well. Pupil meets the master again." It was Ennodius. "Haven't seen you for a while. Bored of the rehearsals?"

"My Lord."

"I'm rather bored of them myself. The whole thing's ridiculous, you know. What got His Lordship to suggest the idea I can't guess. I wouldn't have bothered at all if the old girl hadn't insisted on it. She told me to play along. But I'd say it's time to call it quits, wouldn't you?"

Aemilia said nothing.

"Time's up anyhow. He wants to see me today. Hush, hush. In his reception room."

"But I thought there were still two days...My Lord." Aemilia's voice showed her agitation.

"Not any more. Two hours, more like. As soon as he gets back from the camp." The influx of detachments from all over Roman Gaul had by now far exceeded the billeting space in the barracks and a temporary camp had been set up outside the town. Syagrius was often there, organizing and overseeing the formation of his army.

Ennodius looked at her curiously. "You're pale as a sheet. Seen a ghost from Hades?"

"I'm fine."

"Don't worry. I'll be a credit to you."

"I must be going. Her Majesty..."

"...is due back any minute, I know. We can't have her finding out you go for a jaunt every time she's out."

Aemilia reddened.

"Don't worry. Everyone's entitled to their fun. I'm just off to have mine." He gave her an ironical bow and made off.

Aemilia remained motionless. *Syagrius knows,* she thought. *He's going to tell Ennodius and then arrest Lady Julia and me. What will happen to me?* A vision of Avitus's slave, hanging from a tree branch and covered in blood, came into her mind. No, no. Not that. But maybe he doesn't know. Maybe he's just impatient and wants to see how good Ennodius is now. How will I know? It's not too far to Frankland. If I leave right away I can hide in the bushes in daytime and walk at night until I get there. Chlodovech is kind and that warrior, Merovec, is kind too. They will take me in. But if Syagrius doesn't know then it will be for nothing. What will Tarunculus think of me? He is so proud of me. He gave me Augustine's book. I can't do it to him. I must find out if Syagrius knows. *Think.*

A few moments passed, then an idea came to her. She considered the details. Audacious, yes, but possible. Syagrius had a guard at the entrance of his reception room only when he himself was in it. At other times the room was unguarded and the door unlocked, since the interior contained nothing of importance or value small enough to be taken out unnoticed. She remembered the drapery in the room. It hung from ceiling to floor, between the niches and the windows, in broad, deeply-folded strips. It might just be possible to hide behind one and hear whatever was said. The difficult part would be getting in and out of the room unnoticed.

The plan was far more foolhardy than Aemilia realized, but in her turbulent state of mind she judged it the most sensible thing to do. If Lady Julia queried her absence she would just have to think of some excuse. But now there was no time to waste, and with her mind made up, she set off for the Residence as quickly as she could.

CHAPTER 17

The reception room bordered the large atrium which Aemilia found momentarily deserted. Glancing briefly around, she carefully pushed open the heavy, ornate wooden door and slid swiftly inside, pulling it shut behind her as quietly as she could. The room was empty. She moved over to the drapery and examined it. No good. There was not enough space behind it—it would bulge out, revealing the hider. She looked around the room, spare and Spartan in its magnificence. There. At the far end was a marble statue of an emperor, Avitus she guessed, placed on a pedestal large enough to hide her. The pedestal was set in a niche in the back wall. She went up to it and looked behind. Yes. Enough room. Glancing behind her one more time, she hitched up her dress, clambered over the pedestal, squeezing past the statue and letting herself down into the narrow space behind, just wide enough to conceal her if she crouched down. Bracing her heels against the niche wall and her knees against the pedestal, she waited.

Time passed. She grew anxious. Every second that went by made her absence more noticeable. Lady Julia might have sent slaves to look for her. She had been seen re-entering the Residence. They would be wondering where she had disappeared to. As her agitation at Ennodius's news subsided, the sense of her folly grew on her. What on earth did she think she was doing?

Her mind went back to the cavalry officer: "Her Mightiness isn't the only one who can make a deal with the Franks." What deal? What were they plotting? Lady Julia's arrangement with Chlodovech had not threatened Syagrius's cause, quite the opposite, but these others—would their treason cost him the battle?

Her tumbling thoughts slowed, came to a standstill, and there was a stillness in her mind. Then, from the depths of her will the conviction arose: *I must tell Syagrius.* It would cost Lady Julia her life, and perhaps her own too, but it would have to be done. She was prepared to let the Lady's treason pass since it harmed no one, but the treason of a man like that officer—who knew what harm it would bring? She could no longer be silent. She must get out of the room now and find the governor before he saw Ennodius.

She had straightened herself and was gathering the nerve to climb out of her hiding place when, without warning, the door opened. She ducked down and held her breath, not knowing if she had been seen.

"We're not to be disturbed." It was the voice of Syagrius, giving the guard outside the door his orders. There was a sound of sandaled feet that approached and moved to the left, towards the table. Then came a rustling of parchment. "Come, Ennodius, I want to show you this."

"What is it, my Lord?"

"A map of the battlefield. Here. Our main infantry line will be along the base of this hill, just below the treeline. The right taken up by the levies and Auxilia troops. The archers to their left, and then the Plumbarii. The legions will form up behind the Plumbarii, with a dozen ballistae to their left. The ballistae will be ordered to target Frankish chieftains, and Chlodovis if he comes near enough. The horse archers will form up to the left of the infantry line. Chlodovis will expect all this. He'll line up his infantry opposite our infantry—probably two lines of heavy infantry with a screen of skirmishers—and his cavalry opposite our cavalry. His cousin Chararic will form up on his left, outflanking our line."

"What will we do about him?"

"Nothing. Chararic has sworn me undying friendship. At the critical moment he promises he will turn against Chlodovech."

"Why will he do that?"

"I promised to support his bid to become High King of the Franks in Chlodovis's place once Chlodovis is deposed, which will happen if he loses the battle. Chararic will become an ally, or at least neutral, for the foreseeable future."

"Are you sure you can count on him, My Lord?"

There was a moment's silence.

"No, I'm not sure, but I am sure he will do nothing until he is certain which way the battle is going. Which brings me to the real point. The horse archers will needle Chlodovis's cavalry until they charge. Behind the horse archers six hundred heavy cavalry will be waiting. Chlodovis doesn't know I have them."

There was a short laugh from Ennodius. "Neither did I My Lord. Where did you find them?"

"That is the big secret. The equipment was made in Brittany by army smiths from Britain. My men trained in Brittany under British cavalrymen. No one knows about it. I spoke to their commander himself, Arthur.

The smiths and training were a free loan. His only condition was that I guarantee the territorial integrity of the Britons in Brittany."

"Is he the British king?"

"Practically. Ambrosius lets him do whatever he wants. The apple of his eye, it seems. There'd just been a truce between him and the Saxons, so he was free to give us his help."

"Why *is* he helping us?"

"Because he and I are fighting for the same thing—our Roman civilization. We understood each other perfectly. Once I have beaten the Franks and secured our position in Gaul then I will be free to help him, if he needs it. The Britons appealed to my father nearly thirty years ago, but he was not in a position to help them then. I would like to be able to do what Aegidius could not. I said as much to Arthur. We shook hands on it."

"Now—this is the important part, Ennodius—when Chlodovis sees the heavy cavalry he'll think I've sprung my trap. I'll reinforce the conviction by hiding a force of light Illyrican cavalry in the woods nearby—just here—but making sure he sees them. Chlodovis will let his cavalry go in regardless. In any case he won't be able to stop them once they charge. He'll see that I have fewer heavy cavalry than he does and he'll calculate that he can win or at least lose slowly whilst his infantry win the fight against our main line. He knows as well as I do that everything depends on the battle between the infantry.

"I'll wait until his cavalry are locked in combat and then I'll spring the real trap. Another six hundred heavy cavalry hidden further away in these woods to the west, behind the Frankish line. They will emerge and charge the Frankish cavalry in the rear, scattering them. The cavalry will then regroup and charge the Frankish infantry in their flank and rear, rolling up their line.

"But here's the point. The Frankish infantry will break only if they are engaged in front. The cavalry will not be able to face the Franks on their own. Our infantry must defeat the first Frankish line and engage the second. That means that they *must* fight hard and long—long enough to give our cavalry time to break the Frankish cavalry, form up behind the Frankish line, and charge. The plan will work *if* the infantry are prepared to stand up to the Franks, and for that I depend on you."

"What do you want from me?"

Syagrius did not answer. There was a sound of measured steps, from the table across to the other side of the room, then a pause.

"I shall speak honestly with you. I have ruled for twenty years, and in that time I have played the part of the artful politician. That is how the people see me...no, it's the truth as you know well enough. Financially I've come down hard on them. God in heaven, you think I can't see the penury of the province? I've taken every follis I could squeeze out of them to raise this army and I am perfectly aware how much they resent it. I'm cast in a mold and it is too late to do anything about it now. They will obey and respect me only as far as is necessary, and not a jot further. That is the principal reason why I can never become emperor.

"But you are different. The people respect legitimacy and you have the best claim to the title, but more important than that, you are an unknown quantity. Your private escapades are unimportant: there is nothing particularly outrageous about them and they will be quickly forgiven and forgotten. The people are prepared to believe the best of you if you are able just to convince them. And that, my friend, is up to you. I cannot do it for you and I cannot make you do it. You must do it yourself. All I can say is that I will make you emperor, and once you are emperor I cannot unmake you, nor do without you. You will be as necessary to me as I am to you. Do you understand me?"

"I do, my Lord."

"You needn't call me 'my Lord' any longer. On the day of the coronation I will resign from the position of Governor and assume that of Commander-in-Chief. You will be the Lord here. I will simply be a general. I will retain power, I don't deny it, but it will be a power effective only in conjunction with your power. We will be two sides of the same coin. So come, take my hand. You are not my subject any more—you are my friend."

There was a moment's silence, then Ennodius's voice: "You can count on me."

"We are one in this?"

"Yes."

He has lit the spark. Aemilia, forgetting her danger, raised her eyes above the pedestal. Syagrius had Ennodius's hand in a firm grip. The younger man looked steadily at the governor. Aemilia, seeing him, finally understood where she had gone wrong. Ennodius was able to catch another's purpose of will if he was given just one thing, something that lack of means and maternal domineering had denied him all his life: self-respect. Syagrius must have realized it. Aemilia began to perceive the true greatness of the man, who could find and touch the hidden chords that moved men when they needed to be moved beyond custom and brute obligation, and so held together the dissolving bands of loyalty in a province that should long since have gone to its grave.

Syagrius turned towards the table. Aemilia dropped down again.

"We set out the day after the coronation. Messengers tell me the Franks have gathered at Tournai. That's four days march from here."

"We'll be ready for them."

"We will. They're not going to be as many as I feared. We have around ten thousand men. Chlodovis will have between fifteen and twenty thousand, nearer fifteen thousand if his other cousin Ragnacar doesn't join him. Once his cavalry are out the way his infantry won't stand up to twelve hundred heavy horse. We'll knock the wind out of them."

"Do you think Chlodovis will fall for the trick?"

"He will, and when he sees what is happening it will be too late. That's what I'm counting on."

"I'm almost looking forward to it."

"Well, I'll admit I've been looking forward to it for a long time. Rather like throwing dice with a bit of lead under the Venus, don't you think?" There was a sound of laughter.

"It's a clever plan."

"Not original, I have to admit. Hannibal did the same thing at Trebia. Wiped out an entire Roman army. If it worked for him there's no reason why it shouldn't work for us, eh? Come, let's go and get some wine. You'll keep all this to yourself, Ennodius?"

"Not a word to a soul, I promise—not even my mother."

There was a chuckle from Syagrius. "Oh, she can keep her counsel, I'm sure. It was my impression that she was less than enamoured with Chlodovech at that little meeting they had, even though she managed to get him round her little finger. A remarkable woman, your mother. Come." There was a sound of footsteps followed by a pause. "Oh yes, I nearly forgot. Your speech. Your description of me was very flattering..."

"But redundant, I understand. Well, I have the other one."

"It'll do."

Aemilia heard footsteps again and then the door opening and shutting. She counted slowly to a hundred and then emerged from behind the pedestal. Stepping quickly over to the door she put her ear to it and listened. Silence. Squinting through the keyhole she could see nothing. She took a deep breath and opened the door. No one outside. She closed it quietly and made for her bedroom which she found empty. She sat on her bed and, after recovering her calm, gave herself to thought. Treason or not Syagrius would win the battle, that was clear. If Ennodius had not known about that special heavy cavalry then it was certain the conspirators did not either. The cause was safe. She would not have to see Syagrius after all.

About half-an-hour later Sylvia came in.

"Oh, there you are."

"Is Her Majesty looking for me?"

"No. Vipsania's with her." Was there a hint of satisfaction in Sylvia's voice? Glad at my fall from favorite, Aemilia thought. Well she's welcome to enjoy it. Sylvia went across to the shelf above her bed, adjusting her comb and other bric-à-brac on it. She did not speak. Aemilia was used to her habitual taciturnity and thought nothing of her silence. Her mind flew back to the reception room. Ennodius, Syagrius, Arthur...

"Did you go to see Lavilla?"

"Not today."

Sylvia reached within her dress and pulled out a pouch. She took a small coin from it and gave it to Aemilia.

"Give this to Lavilla from me."

Aemilia took it, surprised.

"Sort of a present. It's her birthday soon."

"I'll see she gets it."

Sylvia turned and left the room without another word. Aemilia looked at the coin. It was a follis, not much, able to purchase half a loaf of bread. Aemilia knew that Sylvia received little from Lady Julia, who had never once in her hearing given the morose girl a word of praise. The follis would be one of the few she possessed, a widow's mite indeed. She thought about Sylvia. In all her time at the Residence the girl had hardly spoken to her except out of necessity. Her resentment at Lady Julia's preferment of Aemilia had given way to indifference once that preferment was gone. There had never been any hint of friendliness. And now this.

Aemilia slipped the coin into her own pouch. It was a little thing: a few words from a jealous rival and a gift a beggar would scorn, but enough to put the drama of the reception room out of her mind, or rather to reduce it to something transient, trivial almost. Ennodius and Syagrius were off to do great things, Lady Julia would have to be endured a few more days, and she would need to find out Lavilla's birth date and give the present to her. Best to do it on the day itself, she thought. That would be nice.

CHAPTER 18

On the morning of the coronation Aemilia was up early. Lady Julia required a toilette that was to be the last word in imperial magnificence, and of her three girls Aemilia was the best at creating the intricate hairstyle necessary for such an occasion. The ceremony was set for midday. After three hours work by Aemilia the lady pronounced herself satisfied and the girls passed on to the dress, using irons warmed on coals to press carefully stylised folds into the garment against hand-held wooden pallets. It had to be done and redone until Lady Julia, surveying herself in a huge brass mirror specially brought into her room for the purpose, finally approved. The attendant girls were then sent to dress in their best in order to accompany the Lady to the forum.

"Not you," she told Aemilia.

It was not long after Lady Julia left that a messenger arrived from the barracks, a slave in uniform, bearing a missive for Aemilia. Called to the main atrium, she took it from him, opened it and read: *Come to the barracks urgent. Tarunculus.*

"Does he want me now?" she asked.

"Yes, ma'am," he replied. "You're to come with me."

She detoured quickly to her room to fetch her mantle and then the two made their way to the barracks through streets thick with people.

"Did he say what the matter was?" she asked, heart thumping and mind dancing with fearful surmises.

"Nothing to me, ma'am," he replied.

At the barracks entrance they found a crowd of curious onlookers. "She's to come in," her escort said to the gate guards, indicating Aemilia with a jerk of his head. One of them, a biarchus, nodded and waved them through.

Inside there were soldiers everywhere. Soldiers packing their baggage and laying them in rows; soldiers tying saddles to horses; soldiers loading supplies onto requisitioned grain carts, or sitting on benches, stools or anything convenient, polishing their armor; soldiers, some in chain mail, some in leather jerkins, others in simple tunics and trousers; soldiers carrying heavy spears, light javelins, bows, large, weighted darts, and equipment she could not recognize. Their number seemed infinite: they filled the parade ground, and Aemilia could see more clustered around the barracks buildings beyond.

"This way," the messenger said.

She followed him across the parade ground, flushing at the curious stares the men all around gave her, until they reached a long dormitory building at the other end. The soldier knocked on a plain wooden door and waited. A voice she recognized answered. "Enter."

She followed the soldier into a small, simple room. Tarunculus stood, facing the window, arms crossed. The soldier saluted him, hand straight and fingers touching brow with palm facing inward. "Sir."

Tarunculus returned the salute. "You may go." He waited until the soldier was out the door before turning to Aemilia. "I have a question to ask and I want a truthful answer out of you, girl." His face was black.

Aemilia felt her chest constrict. "Yes, father."

"Did you tell *anyone* of my leg injury?"

Aemilia was confused. "What injury?"

"You remember. I told you I'd taken an arrow in the knee years ago and that it'd stiffened the leg. I want to know if you repeated that to anyone. Did you?"

"No, of course not!" Aemilia replied, surprise and relief flooding her in equal measure.

Tarunculus studied her face. "You sure of that?"

"Yes! I wouldn't dream of repeating anything you'd told me in confidence, father, truly I wouldn't."

He looked at her for a few more moments and then turned away. "Aye. Well, then there must be some other explanation."

"Explanation for what?"

"My orders. Got 'em today. I'm to stay behind—command of the main gates." He fell silent.

"Is that bad?"

He turned on her angrily. "Don't be a fool, girl. I trained 'em. I know them. They know me. And now they're under some jumping jackass who got his promotion a month ago. They'll be like a chicken with its head cut off. Can't they see that? " He crashed his fist down on the table next to the window. "I told the tribune I need to be with 'em. He didn't listen to a bloody word. I can march on a battlefield as well as the next man. That's where I should be, not sunning my backside at the gates! If he thinks I'm a grandfather then why in Hades was I told to train 'em, eh? Do they think *that's* easy, standing twelve hours a day, seven days a week. Let *him* try it!"

Tarunculus went on, pacing back and forth, until his anger gradually subsided. Aemilia could see men glancing at them through the window. She kept still and waited, saying nothing. Finally he stopped and looked at her.

"I've waited years for this. Years. There's nobody who can know what it is to me." He turned and gazed through the window at the preparations beyond.

"You've done your duty, father. No one expects more of a soldier than that." The words came spontaneously. Tarunculus glanced at her.

"Staying behind will be your duty too. The Franks might decide to attack the town while the army's away. They'll need you then."

There was a minute's silence. Finally Tarunculus stirred.

"Aye, true. I would have had it differently, though." He took in a breath, his expression lightening a fraction, and turned to her. "Off to the coronation, then? You'll have a front seat with Her Majesty on the stage."

"No. She needs only two girls. She's taking Vispania and Sylvia."

"You've not gone and put a foot wrong with her?"

"I've done nothing wrong."

"Then it's a shame you should miss it. Come. There's still time to find you a good place with the civilians." Without further ado he made for the door. Aemilia followed him.

"Won't it be crowded already?" she asked as they crossed the parade ground.

"No doubt. But we'll see what we can do about that."

The two walked rapidly toward the forum, Tarunculus striding in front, surprisingly quick despite his limp, and Aemilia stepping rapidly behind. As the crowds grew denser, Tarunculus raised his voice: "Make way! Make way!" Confronted with a centurion, the people did not hesitate, moving to the right and left and glancing at Aemilia as she passed. *They must think me a senator's daughter at least,* she thought.

A line of soldiers cordoned off the central space of the plaza, reserved for the centuriae soon to march in, but to the sides there was space left for the citizenry. A wooden dais had been constructed in front of the steps leading up to the civil basilica. Tarunculus, followed by Aemilia, pressed through the crowd to a point on the side of the forum nearest the dais.

"There," Tarunculus said. "You'll get a good view from here. Be able to hear the speeches too with luck if this mob leaves off yapping."

"Are you staying?"

"No, worse luck. My command's effective from midday. I must be at the gates then. Keep your ears open and let me know what's said, eh? There's a good girl."

He turned to one of the soldiers lined up round the central space. "You're with which cohort?"

"Twelfth Flavian, sir."

"Apollinarius's command?"

"Yes sir."

"I know him. Keep an eye on the girl. Anyone touches her it's civil disturbance. Understood?"

The soldier's mouth twitched slightly. "Understood, sir."

Tarunculus put his hand on her shoulder. "Come and see me afterwards."

"I will. Goodbye father."

Without another word he made off.

Left alone, Aemilia looked around. Along the rank of guards the crowd was packed. She would never have been able to get to where she now was unaided. A thin cover of cloud left the forum bright but not unbearably hot. It was early autumn and a cool breeze sifted amongst the dense throng gathered to see their new emperor. She studied the dais. It was entirely covered in brightly colored linen cloths. At its center wooden steps led up to a wood and cloth baldachino, under which a throne had been placed, an ornate, gilded affair, backless and with armrests, rather like the magistrate's chair in the basilica. There were a few other chairs behind the baldachino, but these were as yet unoccupied. Guards stood around the base of the dais.

Aemilia's eyes wandered back to the forum. All round the edge of the open space, poles had been erected from which hung pennants. She studied one nearer to her. The fluttering canvas bore an eagle and lettering that took her time to decipher as the pennant moved and twisted in the breeze: S.P.Q.R. *Senatus Populusque Romani.* The Senate and People of Rome. The initials of the ancient Republic, transplanted into the Empire that had succeeded it. Painted onto the standards of its legions, written into its records, carved onto its monuments, surviving cataclysms that had brought the society that bore it within a hair of oblivion. But here it was, still high, still proud, despite everything. It moved her. *We have a past again,* she thought, and felt a touch of reassurance.

Time passed. The half-concealed sun reached its autumnal meridian. The crowd grew restless, sensing delay. Then without warning, through the cleared main entrance to the forum, the army came marching in.

The heavy Comitatenses of the Second Britannica and First Flavia legions arrived first, infantry with chain mail corsets, oval shields and long spears, the elite of Syagrius's foot soldiers. With them came the Plumbarii, dart throwers, similarly attired. Aemilia, seeing them, felt a strange jolt of excitement pass through her limbs. These were the two legions that had survived the collapse of the Empire in the West. It was the Second Britannica, originally the old Second Augusta, that had taken part in the conquest of Britain by the emperor Claudius, afterwards garrisoning the island for three centuries until it was withdrawn to protect the threatened provinces in Gaul. It had been the best of the old Empire's legions, never defeated in battle. The First Flavia, a border legion transferred to the mobile army, had also remained intact through the decades of turmoil that had broken up the Western Empire's military machine. Now here they were, two formations that could outfight any barbarian force their size. In perfect order they formed up, centuria after centuria, before the cloth-covered stage.

Then came the *Auxilii*, lighter troops, carrying arms similar to the Comitatenses but without chain mail armor. Then came the archers, bows in hand and quivers at their side, wearing helmets and leather jerkins. Then the cavalry, rather like the detachment that had stopped her on her arrival at Soissons, but all in regular uniform and carrying bows and javelins. They did not seem to be the special heavy cavalry Syagrius had spoken of in the reception room. Aemilia guessed he was keeping them hidden from Frankish spies until the battle itself.

Other troops arrived, of types she could not identify. Some bore no arms: she guessed some of them to be the ballista crews. Rank by rank the plaza was occupied, companies forming up in straight lines, with regular gaps between one group of men and the next. The crowd was silent, awed by the spectacle. One bystander near Aemilia, an old man, said to his neighbor: "If I was a Frank I wouldn't be smiling, that I wouldn't."

"Sure not," came the reply.

Lastly came the militia, less uniformly dressed and equipped than the regular troops, but marching with the same professional discipline. They filed in behind the other troops, taking up the last of the open space. The plaza was filled with thousands of men come to see their emperor crowned and hear what he had to say to them.

Aemilia felt suddenly sick. *Dear Lord, he's going to give my speech.* The folly of it almost made her stagger. What she had written in a moment of emotion, for no other eyes than Ennodius's, expecting no other reaction than his incredulous amusement, would now be spoken to these men, to hearten them the day before they went out to fight and die for their world. Insane. Insane. Insane. He must have written another. Syagrius could have

written one for him. Anything but hers. The men would laugh at it, know it had been written by a fool, or rather be saddened, seeing they were being made fools of the day before they went out to die. She dropped her head, face red with shame, overwhelmed by the enormity of what she had done. *Let it not be mine,* she prayed silently.

The tramp of marching feet was stilled and the crowd fell silent, expectant. Minutes passed, then with a shrill blare of clarions, the doors of the basilica were opened and Syagrius, in full uniform and preceded by the legionaries of his personal guard, came forth. He was accompanied by Ennodius, dressed in ornate armor, and the high-ranking officers of the army. Aemilia recognized a tall, thin man, with a face much like a bust of Julius Caesar, as Albinus, commander of the town garrison. She looked at him closely but could make out no discernable expression in his features. The others were unknown to her. They came out in a group, confident, dignified, resolute in the assured manner of experienced military men, down the basilica steps and onto the dais. A cheer went up from the crowd. Behind them came the dignitaries and more important officials of Syagrius's realm, preceded by Lady Julia, with Vipsania holding a parasol and Sylvia a fan. They took their places behind Syagrius and his officers lined up along the front of the dais. Syagrius raised his arms for silence. A minute passed and the hubbub was finally stilled.

Syagrius spoke. He had a powerful voice that carried over the vast space of the plaza. "Soldiers of the army and citizens of the province, today is an important day, a day that we will remember as the most important of our lives. It marks an end and a beginning. First, an end. For twenty years I have labored to preserve this province from the destructive power of the barbarians. My father, who received his office from the Emperor Avitus, did the same before me. All know that my family have spared nothing in the defense of this land, such that today we remain free, proud and Roman. But now the time has come to lay this burden on the shoulders of another. I declare that on this day I resign the office of governor, holding only that of Commander-in-Chief. From this day forward my service to you will be on the field of battle."

There was a murmur of surprise from the crowd. Syagrius paused, letting them take it in. Then he continued. "I do this because from today the province of Gaul will exist no longer. On this day there is a new beginning. Ennodius Flavius Julius Avitus, grand-nephew of the great Emperor Avitus from whom my authority came, is here before you today to be crowned Emperor. From this time henceforth, there is no longer a province of Gaul. It has become the Roman Empire of the West restored!"

He paused again. There was some scattered clapping, and a few individual cheers. The soldiers remained, as they had been from their arrival, motionless and silent. Aemilia studied Syagrius's face. Was there a slight smile at the corner of his mouth? She could not be sure.

The crowning was a simple ceremony. The bishop of Soissons came up onto the dais holding a vial. His short, fat form was unmistakeable—it was the same bishop she had confessed to on her second day in the town. Aemilia felt a fleeting moment of surprise. Why was Remigius, Bishop of Reims and the most important churchman in the province, not here? The bishop gave the vial to Syagrius who poured a little oil from it onto Ennodius's head. It was the anointing: customary with Christian emperors in imitation of the anointing of the Jewish kings of the Old Testament. Ennodius sat on the throne under the baldachino. Then a slave brought a purple cushion bearing a golden circlet. Syagrius took it and, with a grand gesture, placed it on the head of Ennodius. Then, standing to one side, he spoke out, "Behold your Emperor!" The crowd cheered, briefly. The soldiers remained silent and unmoving.

Ennodius stood up and stepped forward, raising his arms for quiet, though it was hardly necessary as the noise of cheering had nearly subsided. Aemilia stared at the plaza paving, face white. There were a few moments of silence. Then Ennodius spoke, his trained voice reaching easily to the far end of the plaza.

"Men. You're all probably wondering what on earth someone like me can have to tell you. Well I can tell you that I've been in uniform before. I did a year as a fort tribune so I know what the inside of a camp looks like—and what the food tastes like."

Aemilia's eyes snapped up to Ennodius. She hadn't written that. She caught the face of the guard in front of her: his mouth had a slight grin. Ennodius continued:

"I know some of the jokes too. Have you heard this one? There was a soldier who was about to go into battle. His friends asked him, 'Aren't you afraid?' He said, 'No. If things get really bad I've got something I can pull out that will stop the enemy dead in their tracks. They won't think of attacking me once they see it.' The other soldiers asked, 'What is it?' He told them, 'A white flag.'

That joke was hers. It was clear that her speech had been touched up. She felt relief. The guard's grin was broader this time, and she caught the snort of a laugh from one or two of the soldiers standing nearer her.

"I suppose you're all thinking that once I've finished this speech I'll be sitting here in comfort while you all go off to fight the Franks. Well I've got some news: I'm coming along. The bad news is I don't have a white flag, but it doesn't matter because I won't be needing one.

"You are all a fine lot of soldiers and you're going to teach the Franks that if they think they can just walk over us, they're going to think again. How many of you have been in a fight before? Give me a show of hands. Some of you are holding a spear, so that's all right. Just raise the spear."

The soldiers hesitated, glancing at each other. Ennodius grinned, hands on hips. "Go on. Don't tell me you were all hiding behind a bush! Raise hands." Now he was being spontaneous, not following the speech at all.

The laughter was louder now. A forest of hands and spears went up.

"Good. I can see you're all tough lads. You remember what it was like in your first fight. You were scared out of your boots and almost ready to run away, but the commander didn't run and the other men didn't run, so you stayed where you were and fought until the fight was won. Well, that's how it'll be with the Franks. I'm going to make you a promise, and the promise is this: that however hot it gets, however bad things seem, I will not run away. And I expect you to stick by me. Will you do it?"

This time the soldiers cheered. Ennodius waited a minute or two and then raised his arms. The men fell silent.

"The only thing you have to do is remember your training. It hasn't been easy. It's been tiring, even exhausting, and I know that at times you've wanted to give it all up and go home. But keep this in mind: you've been drilled by the best soldiers of our Empire and you can be sure that if you follow their orders, you can't lose. There's one thing you must know about Franks. They're good fighters, nobody denies that, but they have no training. They only know how to charge, and if that doesn't work then they break and run. All you have to do is stand firm against them. You remember Aetius at the Catalaunian Fields? The Huns were much worse than the Franks but our soldiers didn't move. It was the Huns who did the moving: back east at full gallop."

More laughter, men turning to each other and giving a thumbs up. Ennodius paused again, continuing only when they were attentive. The silence was utter now, every man still to catch each word. As Ennodius spoke it seemed as if the words came spontaneously, from his heart, so much conviction there was in his voice. No one, Aemilia thought, would guess that I wrote every one of them.

"Long speeches are for rhetors, and I'm not here to give you a load of rhetoric, so I'll finish now. We didn't start this war, and we're not fighting for glory or power or riches. We're fighting to protect that which we love: our homes and our families."

There was a murmur of assent. Aemilia realized how much the people had feared the Franks, ever since Syagrius had mortally offended their king. Feared what they would do when they came, angry and relentless, to wipe that injury away. And now they had an emperor who they perceived understood their fear.

"We didn't start this war, but we're going to finish it. We're going to fight and keep on fighting until the Franks are back behind the Rhine, and our lands are safe again!"

The soldiers and the crowd cheered, longer this time. Ennodius stretched his arms out to them.

"We are Christians and Romans together. The victory I win will be yours. The spoils I gain will be yours. I am your Emperor and your happiness is mine, your peace is mine, and your burdens and hardships are mine. And I swear before God that I have been made Emperor for one purpose only: to do what I must to ensure that the burdens and hardships you have endured end with this war. That is my duty, and before God, I will do it!"

A roar arose from the plaza. Ennodius's arms remained stretched wide to receive it. The tumult went on, seemingly endless, with shields, spears, swords, hands raised, caps flying, accompanied by a sound of cheering that gradually resolved itself into a mighty chant: *Vivat Imperator*. Long live the Emperor. The old man, standing near Aemilia, slapped his neighbor

on the shoulder and shook hands with him, before resuming his cheering. The spark that Aemilia had first lit and Syagrius rekindled was now a mighty forest fire. *There is no doubt any more,* she thought, *we will win the battle.* Her conviction turned into an exultant joy, and waving towards the platform she chanted with the rest: Long live the Emperor. It carried her, strong like a heady wine: Long live the Emperor. An identity, a hope, not to be denied: Long live the Emperor. On and on she chanted with the others, only dimly aware that the sentiment she felt now was not the one she had when she wrote the speech. *Vivat Imperator.* Thus to be Roman.

Finally, Ennodius and Syagrius left the dais, re-entering the basilica. The troops reformed ranks and marched out the forum, cheered on by the crowd. It was almost a triumph, as if the battle had already been fought and won. The last soldier left and the crowd began to disperse, its mood festive, each talking with animation to his neighbor. Aemilia found herself alone again. She did not know anyone around her, and she had not quite lost her reserve to the point of speaking like a familiar friend to total strangers. She looked around at the clustered groups scattered over the plaza and stirred herself. Nothing for it but to return to the Residence on the unlikely chance that Lady Julia would call for her services. Two days, three at the most, and she could quit her post, once the battle was over. She had made up her mind to tell Tarunculus of the lady's treachery, dissuading him from reporting it since there was no way she could prove it. He would remain in service. She had no doubt he would be needed to train more men for the ongoing war against the Franks that Syagrius intended to wage.

She knew what she herself would do. She stood between two worlds. The minds of the ordinary folk around her she understood, having lived as one of them herself. The aristocracy were aloof from them and had no grasp of what was really in their hearts. She could make it known to them. She could make an Ennodius or a Syagrius touch them. She knew the words for it. She had done it today and she could do it again. She could—as far as it lay in any one human being—pull them together. Syagrius had seen it and brought Ennodius to see it too, and the people—dear Lord, how they had responded!

Would she tell Tarunculus that she had written the greater part of Ennodius's speech? One day, perhaps, when he knew beyond any possibility of doubt that she was telling the truth. He would be proud, so very proud of her then. She had done her best for his cause.

Lost in reverie, she entered the Residence, and was making for her bedroom when Odo the guard caught sight of her and signed her to come over.

"He's looking for you."

"Who?"

"Syagrius. Wants you now, chop-chop. Reception room."

Nonplussed, Aemilia made her way to the room. Another guard stood by the door. Aemilia recognized him.

"Hello, Theodore. Is the Lord inside?"

"Aye. You're to go in as soon as you come."

She knocked on the heavy, carved wooden panelling.

"Enter."

She turned the handle and went in. Syagrius, still in uniform, sat behind the marble desk. A lamp burned on it, presumably to give light though the room seemed to her bright enough from the thinly overcast sky outside.

"My Lord?"

"Close the door."

She did as bid and approached the desk, curtseying. He surveyed her for a few moments before speaking.

"Your speech. Do you have any copies besides the one Ennodius had?"

"Just one draft, My Lord. The one I gave him first."

"Go and fetch it."

She curtseyed again and left the room. Hurrying to her bedroom she brought down her bag from the shelf onto the bed, and fished out her copy of Augustine. The parchment was sandwiched between the pages of the book. Pulling it out she returned to the reception room, the speech hidden in the folds of her mantle. She knocked and re-entered. Syagrius sat, waiting.

"You have it?"

"Yes, My Lord."

"Bring it here."

He took and opened it, perusing through it. "A very successful speech."

"It was my Lord. He gave it so well." She laughed. "*I* started cheering."

His eyes continued their perusal of the manuscript.

"Did anyone help you compose it?"

"No, My Lord. I wrote it on my own."

His eyes glanced away, towards the windows, the statues, the drapery, and then came back to her.

"You are to tell no one you wrote it, is that clear? Under pain of imprisonment."

Aemilia's heart lurched. She could not speak. Syagrius moved the pages of the manuscript near the lamp. A corner touched the flame and the dry parchment took. He held the sheets carefully until they were ablaze before dropping them on the floor.

"I want it equally clear that this is the first and last time such a service will ever be required of you. You are a handmaid. A servant. That is your station and in that you will remain. Do you understand?"

"...My Lord." Her voice was barely a murmur, shock giving way to the sudden sting of tears.

"No need to upset yourself. You have done well and you will be rewarded." He took a small bag lying on the side of the table and pushed it toward her. She looked at it and at him.

"Take it. Fifty siliquas."

She stretched out a hand and then withdrew it.

"Thank you My Lord, but I do not need it."

"No? Very well. But bear in mind what I said. You are to speak to no one."

"My Lord." She curtseyed, and hesitated.

"You may go."

She left the room, eyes wet, earning a glance of surprise from the guard outside the door. Once in her bedroom she sat on her bed, hands on her lap, and let the tears run down her face. So quiet and demure she was that none would have guessed at the anguish within her: a mind and a will and a heart given without reserve—given and taken and then tossed back, with a bag of money. A pain worse than any jilting. It was thus that Vipsania found her. She sat next to her and put an arm round her shoulders. "Aemilia, what's wrong?"

A sob escaped. "...nothing..."

"What's happened? Someone gone and dumped you?"

Aemilia did not reply. Gradually her weeping subsided and she was able to pull herself together. "I'm sorry...making a scene...so silly..."

"There. No need to say sorry. Just dry your eyes. Your face is all wet. I've got a clean cloth somewhere...here, use that."

After a minute or two Aemilia was more or less composed again. Vipsania took the damp cloth from her and put it away before sitting next to her again.

"Now, tell me about it. I won't repeat it to a soul, that's a promise."

Aemilia took a slow breath, hands together under chin. "I'm sorry Vipsania. I wish you hadn't come in. I just can't tell you. I daren't."

Vipsania looked at her sharply. "Is it more of that Lady Julia business?"

"...something like that."

"Are you in trouble?"

"No."

"And you can't tell me about it?"

"No. I'll go to prison if I do."

There was a silence. "That bad then? Well I won't ask any more questions. But perhaps you should think of moving on."

"It's not like that. I'm not in any danger."

Vipsania let her breath out through her teeth in a low whistle. "I wouldn't be so sure of that. If someone's mentioned prison to you and you're mixed up in something big, then who's to say you're safe, eh?"

Aemilia remembered Syagrius's proffered money and her refusal, and felt the sudden, soft touch of fear. Would Syagrius think his threat had been enough? She stood up abruptly and walked to the other end of the narrow room, then turned around.

"It's true. It is something big. I know too much, but I've done nothing wrong."

"*Wrong's* neither here nor there. Anyone who can use prison to shut you up isn't going to find you a judge before he tosses you in."

"Oh, go away. That isn't going to happen."

"Who's to say? I think it's time you moved on."

"I've nowhere to go."

"What about the Franks?"

Aemilia paused, surprised. It was the same idea she had had, just three days earlier. Vipsania, seeing she had made an impression, went on: "Your mother was a Frank and you can speak the lingo. You've got their eyes too. Franks are supposed to have gray eyes. When you went to see them with the old dragon, how were they?"

"They were kind to me."

"There you are. Natural place to go."

Aemilia was silent, arms crossed, for several moments.

"...no. I don't think it's come to that. Not yet. Besides, I don't want to go there."

Vipsania stood up, brisk. "My old man used to say, 'if you got two choices, take the best choice. But if you got no choice...'" She made for the door. "That's all *I've* got to say."

Aemilia grasped her arm. "You're a real friend...thank you."

The slave girl looked at her, then smiling, hugged her. Drawing back, she spoke, *sotto voce*. "One of the wall guards is a sweetheart. If you need to get out at night, I can charm him up."

"I'll keep it in mind," Aemilia said.

CHAPTER 19

By the time Aemilia awoke the next day, the army had already left.

"Marched out before dawn," Galbus said. They were in the kitchen, after breakfast. Aemilia was applying ointment to Galbus's feet, whilst Pollux plucked chickens in preparation for the midday meal. He did not pause in his work, hands pulling out the feathers. "They go quick," he said.

"Had to. They've got ten miles to march, with baggage and all. They'll want to reach the battlefield well before sunset and set up before the Franks arrive. I hear the Franks've been on the march for three days already. They'll get there tomorrow."

"Ennodius—he go with them as he said?"

"Aye, he's gone. Spent the night at the camp with Syagrius."

There was a lull in the conversation. Pollux finished the chicken and started on another. "He make a good speech," he said. "Is it true what he say?"

"What's that?"

"That he was a tribune before."

Galbus shrugged. "First I heard of it, but it must be true. Why make it up?"

"I was here when they first come. They got no money. His mother comes from a small merchant family who go broke. His father's family tells them to get out. So how does he become a tribune, eh?"

"They must've had friends in the army."

Pollux gave a snort. "Friends? Them? Where are their friends? *I* say he make it up."

"Well if he did, he did. It's no matter now."

Later, Aemilia went out to the main gates. Lady Julia was out for the morning, and in any case she knew she would not be called for. On the way she fell to musing. *A small merchant family.* She would never have believed it if it had not been Pollux who said it—Pollux, who in twenty years at the

Residence had seen and heard everything. He would be certain of a fact like that.

She reached the main gates, whose road led north. They were manned, not by the casual knot of three or four soldiers she had met on her arrival at Soissons, but by a squad of guards on both sides of the massive gates and on the towers above.

"Excuse me. Where can I find the centurion?" she asked one of the men standing by the great stone gateway.

"In the guardhouse, gate tower," he replied. "But no civilians allowed in."

"I'm his daughter. Could a message be sent to him?"

"I'll see, ma'am."

A short while later the soldier returned. "You're to come up."

She followed him through a small doorway set in the tower on the left of the gates. A narrow spiral of stone steps led upwards, eventually reaching a room above, which she entered through a hole in its wooden floor. Along one wall there were wooden brackets, holding dozens of javelins. Further along she could see leather quivers filled with arrows. Logs were piled up against another wall. She briefly wondered what they were for. An arched entrance led out onto the walkway of the section of wall that spanned the gates between the two towers.

"This way."

The soldier went out onto the walkway. Aemilia followed. There, gazing over the battlement to the north, arms behind his back, was Tarunculus.

"Sir."

He glanced at the soldier and at Aemilia. "Very good." The soldier saluted and returned the guardhouse, descending the stairway once again. Aemilia moved next to her father.

"Any news?" she asked him.

"None. There won't be, not until the battle's done."

The sky was heavily overcast and the air chill. Aemilia pulled her mantle more closely around her shoulders. Low hills on the horizon marked the limit of the wide valley in which Soissons lay. She could see no movement. All was quiet. She became aware of the absence of sound and glanced around behind her. Even the usual bustle of the town was stilled: everything seemed to have paused, waiting. She turned back and remained standing next to her father. Neither spoke for some time. In the silence Aemilia looked at Tarunculus out of the corner of her eye. His gaze was abstracted, faraway, serene almost. He seemed unaware of her standing beside him, or rather, aware and not troubled to speak just yet, content for her to share in his tranquillity. *If only I could*, she thought, *if only I could*.

"It was a fine speech he gave the men, I heard."

"Yes, father."

"I wouldn't have thought he had it in him. Blood will out, that's all one can say. Senator's son. Good Roman family."

Aemilia was silent.

"I remember when Avitus went to Rome to become emperor. Back in '55, after the Vandals had gone. We'd beaten the Huns just before. Only troops around who had any clout, so we got him chosen."

"Did you go to Rome then?"

"No. Not part of his guard. Wish I had. He'd have lived longer."

"What happened to him?"

Tarunculus grimaced. "That swine Ricimer had him assassinated. Avitus made him Commander-in-Chief in Italy and then the bastard turned against him. That's what you get for trusting a barbarian. If Avitus'd lived long enough he'd have been a great emperor." He sighed. "Ah well. Some things aren't meant to be. I would like to have seen the city again."

"When were you last there?"

"That'll be.....what, forty years ago? I'd just finished training and they sent us to Gaul. Reinforcements for the Gallic Field Army."

"Where did you live in Rome, father?"

"Trastevere. Wrong side of the Tiber. Didn't bother us though. Give me a straight fight with any one of those loudmouths from Velabrum and I'd knock 'im flat every time." He glanced at her with a grin. "That's when I was a lad. They'd come over the Aemilian bridge to our side and wish they hadn't." Aemilia's eyes widened. Tarunculus noticed it. "Aye, to tell the truth, that's what gave me the idea for your name."

"A bridge..."

"The Aemilii were a good old patrician family. I had that in mind too. Your mother wanted to call you Caecilia, after some Christian saint or other. She came round in the end. That's when I bought her that copy of Augustine."

"Did you ever take her to Rome?"

"No. I wish I had. We didn't recognize any emperors after Majorian so I had no chance of going back. But one day you'll see it, my girl. There's nothing like it in the world."

He leaned forward on the battlement, chin on fist. "I remember the day my father took me into the imperial palace on the Palatine. I was twelve then. It's the biggest damn building you ever saw. He left me in an atrium and I got wandering. In no time I was lost. I tried to look like I knew where

I was going but one of the Candidatus Guards stopped me and wanted to know what my business was. He was big enough for a man—must've been six foot tall—but to me he looked a giant. I told him I was lost and he took a shine to me. Made me come with him to the guardroom and showed me how to hold a sword. When I got it right they all had a good laugh and said I was a born soldier. I told 'em that was all I ever wanted to be. I remember it like yesterday. The big fellow put his arm on my shoulder and told me to come back when I was old enough and he'd recommend me. I tell you, I walked out of the palace feeling like I was already a man. I had to wait four more years before I could enlist. It seemed like forever. I trained in the meantime. My father taught me everything he knew."

"Your father?"

"Aye. Didn't I tell you? He was an ex-soldier himself. Served under Stilicho. His father was a soldier before him. And his. There's always been soldiers in the family."

"What did he do after the army?"

"Ran a tavern for soldiers. They'd come and have a flagon and talk. I'd serve 'em and keep my ears open. I heard some tales, I did. Believed 'em all too." He chuckled. "I remember one fellow, old Rusticus. He was an ex. A wall guard from Britain. He filled me with stories about the monsters north of the wall. 'There was one', he said, 'that had heads like a hydra. *That* was a problem. If you chopped off one head the others would rip you apart.' So I ask him, 'What did you do?' And he tells me, 'I got the smith to make me a sword a hundred feet long. I take this long sword up to the wall and I yell out: come on you coward!' He says hydras hate being called cowards. The hydra comes and he gives the sword one big swing—like that—and lops off all the heads at once. But there's one head left that he misses, and it goes for him. So I ask him, 'What did you do then?' He says, 'You're forgetting, boy, I got two hands: my special long sword in one and my regular service sword in the other. I got his last head with the service sword.' He could spin a yarn, he could."

A breeze started up, blowing the cold autumn air over their faces. Aemilia drew the corner of her mantle across her front and over her opposite shoulder. Tarunculus noticed.

"Feeling cold, girl?"

"Not really, father. This is a warm mantle."

He smiled. "Aye, well, take care. We don't want you catching a chill."

He resumed his gaze at the distant horizon. "Your mother'd come up often in Tours. I was on the wall there too, for a while. She'd bring up something each time. A little cheese, dates maybe, if there were any in town. Not her round cakes though. I told her she'd have to save those for off-duty. That would be pushing officer's privilege too far."

"She taught me to make them. I could make some for you, if you like."

"Did she then? That would be grand. I got to be very partial to them."

"She said mine were as good as hers."

"I doubt that. There's no one who could bake like your mother. She was a treasure."

His words trailed off. Surprised, Aemilia glanced at his face and saw the sadness in it. He did love her, she thought. I must ask him.

"She never said anything bad about you," she said.

He glanced at her and then looked away.

"Why did you leave?"

"She never told you?"

"No. She just said you were in the army and couldn't come."

"Aye. That's true enough, as far as it went. But there's more to it than that." He seemed to deliberate for a moment. "You must understand, girl, that the first duty of a soldier is obedience. If you don't have obedience you have no discipline, and if you have no discipline...well, then, you have no army. I did what I did because I was ordered to. A soldier never, never questions his orders. Never. Do you understand?"

Aemilia nodded.

"Doesn't mean I liked what I had to do, but I had no choice. I was ordered out of Tours by the magistrate and I had to go."

Aemilia waited, then asked, "Couldn't you have come back?"

"Aye...perhaps...but things were difficult between her and me. It wasn't possible then. Time passed...what with one thing and another I never got round to it." He paused, and went on. "She did not agree with my going."

"Why didn't she go with you?"

"It was to do with her father. He was wealthy. Had as much as any merchant in Tours. Lepidius—he was town magistrate then—wanted his money. He gave out the story that he needed to bribe off the Visigoths and didn't have enough. It wasn't true. They weren't moving against us then. Your grandfather wouldn't give him what he wanted so he got up some charges against him and had him arrested and his property confiscated. Him being a Frank made it easy. The judge upheld the charges and he was convicted."

"What happened to him?"

"Imprisoned. Six months. It might've been worse but I put a word in for him to the magistrate. He agreed to reduce the sentence but on condition that I go before the trial. I told your mother that was the best I could do, but she wouldn't budge. Someone must look after him when he comes out, she said. And her own mother too. They didn't have a nummus left to their name. I told her bring her mother along, but she wouldn't hear of it."

"Did she think you hadn't done enough?"

"She kept on that I should speak up at the trial. I told her don't be a fool. Lepidius wanted his money and nothing would stop him. It would've been the end of my commission if I'd tried. But she wouldn't listen. Said I had to stand by her family. And so we parted. I learned later that they'd found a place at Avitus's villa. I knew she was all right then."

A guard came up to them and saluted. "Sir, a rider coming."

The distant speck of an approaching horseman brought their conversation to an end. Tarunculus sent Aemilia down with the guard. She stood next to the gate and watched the mounted messenger pass through and go on in the direction of the barracks.

He did what he could, she thought, on her way back to the Residence. Why was mother so hard on him? I wouldn't have been. I would have gone with him and then come back later for grandfather when he was released. Then everything would have been well. Why didn't she do that? He loved her. Why did they have to part? A nameless doubt crept into her mind.

I will stand by him, whatever happens, she resolved, and with a tiny start of surprise realized that she felt no comfort in her resolution.

She reached the Residence and was greeted at the main door by Galbus. "Her Majesty just came in," he said. "Seems she wants you after she's changed."

I do cut it fine, she thought as she entered the building.

166

CHAPTER 20

The time in Soissons before the battle, Aemilia moved around with a peculiar feeling of detachment, observing the details around her with the eyes of a newcomer from a distant country. She spoke little, and noticed that everyone else did the same. Conversation was broken by silences. The inhabitants of the Residence watched, waiting. There was a heavy quiet everywhere.

Lady Julia was brief with Aemilia.

"You have told no one of what I said to the Franks?"

"No one, Your Majesty."

"Syagrius has spoken to you?"

Aemilia dropped her eyes. "Yes, Your Majesty."

"Good. I was of a mind to dismiss you after you put my son in such an absurd position, but I have since reconsidered. You shall remain as lady-in-waiting."

"Thank you, Your Majesty."

"It is understood, of course, that you will have nothing further to do with Ennodius."

"Yes, Your Majesty."

"You may go."

Aemilia was at a loss for what to do. She could not leave the Residence for as long as Lady Julia might call on her services. She went back to her bedroom and brought down the board and writing materials. Placing them on her bed she picked up a pamphlet she had been copying. *Romans, remember your forefathers. Remember their courage and guts.* She sighed and put it down, then replaced everything on the shelf. She felt in her bundle for her New Testament and pulled it out. Opening it, she tried reading at random.

Then I heard the count of those who were sealed, a hundred and forty-four thousand of them, taken from every tribe of the sons of

167

Israel. Twelve thousand were sealed from the tribe of Judah, twelve thousand from the tribe of Ruben, twelve thousand from the tribe of Gad, twelve thousand from the tribe of Nephthali, twelve thousand from the tribe of Aser, twelve thousand...

She closed the book. Standing up, she began to pace slowly up and down in the narrow space. Up and down, up and down, hands gripping elbows. Not thinking, not praying, just pacing, with a great, inexplicable leaden emptiness within her. Up and down, up and down. Having no sense of passing time, caught in a vast, frozen present. Just pacing, since keeping still was unendurable.

She wanted to be alone, not to have to speak to anyone. She made her way out to the garden. The leaves had begun to drop from the trees and made a pattern of orange and brown and yellow on the ornate mosaic paving. The colors held her eyes, as did the spider's web of veins on each leaf. She studied them minutely: a universe of lines, thinning and dividing and branching out, in patterns almost but not quite symmetrical.

"Coming for lunch?"

It was Vipsania, calling to her from the end of the walkway.

"No. I'm not hungry. Go on without me."

"Are you all right?"

"I'm fine, really. Go on. I'll wait in the bedroom in case Her Majesty calls."

"She's gone out again. To the barracks."

"Do you know how long for?"

"Quite long. She's going on from there."

Aemilia waved. Vipsania reciprocated and disappeared back into the Residence. Aemilia resumed her scrutiny of the leaves for a few minutes and then began pacing again, up and down, along the walkway. Finally, after a quarter of an hour, she went to the bedroom, put on her mantle, and left the building.

It was a Sunday and the forum was almost deserted. The pennants with their imperial inscription fluttered idly from the poles lining the central plaza. Aemilia approached the dais below the basilica steps. Its drapery had been removed, exposing the wooden framework. She examined it. It had been rather crudely constructed, beams and planking sawn off unevenly. She peered underneath at the criss-cross lattice of rough wood. It had been erected *in situ*, and the ground below was covered with a scattering of chips and sawdust, the latter already beginning to be dispersed by the erratic breeze.

She straightened up and turned toward the church at the other end of the forum, but then stopped. She was rarely able to go to the Sunday Mass—a deacon would come to the Residence with Communion for those who wished—and she had been able to come to the church herself only infrequently. Now was a good time, yet she felt a curious reluctance. To be alone, to be in the company of no one, of nothing; to speak to no one, of nothing: so the void within her spoke. But the void itself was unbearable.

She turned away and went on toward the nearest forum entrance. An old beggar was sitting by the archway. She had seen him there often before. He was thin, bent and always had two or three poorly-made brooms for sale. An uneven, earthenware alms bowl lay on the ground before him. Aemilia walked past him and then hesitated. She turned back, drew a coin from the purse within her mantle and, approaching the old man, placed it in his bowl.

"Thank you miss. Buy a broom?"

"No," she answered, and continued: "Why did you come today? There's nobody here."

"Always come miss, rain or sun."

"Do you get much?"

"Enough to get by. Better when there's not too much bustle."

"Why's that?"

"Who's going to see me in a crowd? A crowd's busy. No time to stop and give anything. On quieter days they've got time to look around, and they see me then. You saw me."

"That's true. Did you make anything yesterday?"

"Not a nummus."

She bade him farewell then passed through the archway and went on down a street. Without really knowing where she was going, she continued in the direction of the north gates. On reaching them she glanced up a moment at the towers above, and then approached the arched gateway. The guard she had met earlier recognized her and gave a nod. "Ma'am."

"I'm just going out for a little," she said.

"I wouldn't go too far, ma'am. We're under orders to close the gates at any sign of the Franks."

"I'll keep it in mind. Thank you."

A few hundred yards brought her from the walls to the last ruined building of the municipal boundary. Beyond were open fields, scattered with bushes and copses of trees. She walked along the road until a bend round a clump of pines hid the town from view. Leaving the road, she picked a path through the shrubbery until she was under the gentle, speckled light of the trees. The ground was soft with pine needles and the odd twig snapped under her feet, but other than that there was no sound. The lightly moving air blew a slight touch of peace within her, easing the leaden paralysis in her heart.

She stopped and stretched her arms out, fingers splayed, then slowly took a deep breath, and another, and then another. The breeze grew stronger, swelling the trees with a gentle rustling that filled her ears like a stream running over rocks into a mountain pool. She drank the sound in, eyes taking in the speckled undulations of light that filtered through the swaying branches above her head. Bit by bit, the hard core of sickness within her was softened, diluted and leached out. *I am back. I am back. I am come back. I will not go so far from you again. I will not go so far from you again.* It was some time before she realized she was praying. She remained still, speaking within herself the words that came until her peace of mind was fully restored. She then knelt down and made the sign of the cross.

Standing, she debated a moment within herself what to do: I can carry on walking, now, to Frankland. When I'm there I can write and tell him I'm well. He'll be happy if he knows that. But she dismissed the thought. I must stay with him. He will need me if things go badly. Then she remembered the cavalry officer in the basilica and felt a touch of anxiety. She hesitated, pondering. I must talk to the bishop now, she thought. I've left it too long.

Thus resolved, she made her way back to the road.

There was a sharp coolness in the interior of the church that felt different from the freshness of the open air. She found, to her surprise, that the building was nearly full. A deacon knelt before the altar, chanting a litany, to which the people rhythmically responded *Libera nos, Domine.* Lord deliver us.

From famine and pestilence.
Libera nos, Domine.
From the scourge of war.
Libera nos, Domine.
From all evil.
Libera nos, Domine.
She knelt on the floor and joined in the responses until the litany was finished and the deacon began another. Then she whispered to the woman in front of her: "Is the bishop hearing confessions?"

"He is. Over there."

There was a long queue outside the sacristy door. Aemilia joined it and waited. Time passed. The deacon finished the litany and began a third. Aemilia looked around at the kneeling crowd. Some had their hands clasped in front of them, some hugged their arms to their sides. Some kept their eyes shut whilst others had them open, gazing at nothing in particular, or fixed on the mosaic in the apse, depicting Christ standing by the river of life and flanked by the saints of the two Testaments. Everyone was praying in earnest, each in his own way.

As the penitent in front of her went in, Aemilia gathered her thoughts. A few minutes passed and it was her turn. She walked in.

"Close the door."

The bishop was sitting on a stool. Aemilia approached him and knelt at his side.

"*Dominus sit in corde tuo et in labiis tuis ut rite confitearis omnia peccata tua. In nomine Patris et Filii et Spiritus sancti. Amen.* Now then, spill the beans."

"Bless me for I have sinned. The last time I went to confession was here, when I first came to Soissons."

"Very good. Go on."

Aemilia told him. She related her first visit to the Franks and her subsequent role as interpreter for her Mistress. She described her initial fears and how she had resolved them, letting them subside until her encounter with the cavalry officer in the civil basilica revived them. She told of her idea of leaving Soissons for Frankland, and her decision to stay for her father's sake. She wondered whether she should tell him of her part in Ennodius's speech, and decided against it. It doesn't concern confession, she thought.

Finally she was done. There was a moment's silence, then the bishop spoke. "You *are* a one for puzzles."

Aemilia glanced at him and saw concern and—was it amusement?—in his eyes.

"Yes, My Lord."

The little round man stood up and moved over to the single, high arched window.

"Have you heard from your last master yet?"

He remembers, she thought. "Not yet, My Lord. I don't think any post has been coming through lately."

"No, probably not. It will though, sooner or later."

Aemilia was silent. The bishop remained by the window, gazing through it. He said nothing for some time, then sighed. He turned around.

"Bishop Remigius is on good terms with Chlodovis."

"He is? I didn't know that."

"It's not well known. I know it because he is my brother and tells me everything. He sent him a letter of congratulation when he became king. Since then things have soured between Syagrius and the Franks and the good bishop has had to be careful, but I know he wishes Chlodovis well. I can't say, really, but I think he may have hopes for him."

Aemilia remained silent.

"Myself, I am Roman, born and bred. I haven't heard of any good the barbarians have done for our poor old Empire. Just look at Africa! I hear stories from there that you would not believe. Those—*Vandals*—are persecuting the Christians to the death. I know the martyrs are the seed of the Church, but if they keep it up much longer the Church over there will be seed and nothing else. It's tragic. It's the country of Augustine! And it's not much better anywhere else. The Visigoths, the Burgunds, the Heruli— if they're not pagans they're Arians, and look at what the Arians did to the Church. We are living in dark times, maybe even the end times."

He paused and gave a wry smile. "It's a subject I tend to ramble on about. Never mind. The point is that Remigius is well disposed towards Chlodovis who I believe is well disposed towards him. Chlodovis may be a pagan, but he has no axe to grind with the Church. That may be of help to you in time to come."

"How will it help?"

"Well...Syagrius has always struck me as being more a politician than a general. I really can't believe he intends an all-out war against the Franks. I think he'll be content with just a victory. That being the case, Frankland will be there whether he wins or loses this battle, which means you will have somewhere to go if you need to, and it should be possible to include you in a messenger party from Remigius to the Franks. I'm not promising anything, mind, I'm only saying don't do anything rash just yet. If you need to—shall we say—disappear in the interim, that can be arranged too."

Aemilia felt a deep relief settle within her. "Thank you, My Lord."

"Don't mention it. You've been very badly used by her Ladyship. It's about time you had some help."

"Should I tell anyone what she did?"

"No. I've always preferred mercy to strict justice. If her head is going to leave her shoulders, let it be someone else who arranges it. Perhaps the barbarians will be good for something...and don't repeat *that* to anyone either."

"I won't, My Lord." Then a thought occurred to her. "Should I leave anyway? I would if it wasn't for my father."

"Yes...your father. If all goes well you won't need to stay with him, but if things go badly he'll have great need of you, and I don't just mean materially. Who knows? You may be able to do what your mother could not."

"My mother?"

The bishop glanced her way and then averted his gaze. "Never mind. An old story."

"He told me about what happened to my grandfather. The magistrate was after his money and had him falsely accused. Mother wanted my father to try to get him freed but he said there wasn't anything he could do."

"Mm."

"He also told me the magistrate agreed to free grandfather if he left Tours. He went but mother wouldn't go with him. She found a place for them at the Avitus villa after that."

"That's true."

Aemilia's eyes widened in surprise. "You *know* about this, My Lord?"

"More or less. It was an acquaintance of mine who arranged the position at the villa. The Lady Avita is a good woman. Lord knows what would have happened to your mother if it hadn't been for her."

"She was very kind to me too."

"No doubt, but come, let's hear your other wickednesses. I've got a queue out there as long as the church. Nothing like an invasion to get people thinking about eternity. Maybe the barbarians have their uses after all."

He heard the remainder of her confession and absolved her. She had risen from her knees and was turning toward the door when he said: "Keep your ears to the ground. If there's any hint of danger come straight here."

"I will," she said, then added, "but what will you do if they come looking for me?"

"Be very surprised to see them," he said. "Go in peace."

CHAPTER 21

The following day seemed as dry and aimless as the fallen leaves nudged here and there by the autumn breeze. For the first half of the day Aemilia was occupied with Lady Julia, who ordered her—and her alone—to pack three trunks of her most valuable possessions. This took up the greater part of the morning as she kept changing her mind about what should be put in them, requiring everything to be taken out and repacked, and then taken out and repacked again. Aemilia realized that it was a symptom of her interior agitation. Great boulders were rolling against each other and she was between them, not knowing where they would settle. She rounded sharply on Aemilia often, and once, just for a moment, her speech dropped to plebian colloquialisms: "A body can see you never packed a thing in your life, that you haven't!" She came to herself, returning to her frosty hauteur, and ordered Aemilia to fold and place her violet gown in the trunk for the fifth time.

In the afternoon Aemilia found the ingredients for her mother's honey cakes and with Pollux's help, prepared and baked them in the kitchen oven. The latter was a tricky operation, requiring that hot coals be placed in the small, rectangular space in the center of the oven bricks until they was sufficiently heated, after which the coals were removed and the cakes quickly inserted. It had to be done just so, otherwise they would burn, or bake unevenly. Pollux knew his oven and the cakes came out perfect, moist and golden-brown. At her insistence he tried one.

"Not too bad," he said. "Your mother teach you, you say?"

"Yes."

"Nearly as good as what my mother do, long time ago."

"Where...?"

"She dead. Many years. She teach me how to cook. I work on a villa in Spain then I come here. You stay with your mother in a villa you say?"

"All my life."

"A shame she die."

"It was very sudden. A kind of fever." Aemilia began to remove the other cakes and lay them on the table, describing the symptoms of her mother's last illness as she did so. Pollux looked at her sharply.

"You listen to me," he said. She turned around. "Whatever happens, you don't go back there. Not ever. Understand?"

"Why?"

"She blue round the mouth when she dead?"

Aemilia stopped what she was doing. "Yes. She was."

Coming closer he lowered his voice. "That was not fever. Done to her. Understand?"

"Good God." She sat heavily on a bench, staring in front of her. "But why..." Even as she uttered the question she knew the answer, realizing, too, that she had always half-suspected. The shock took time to lessen, and when it did her heart was wrenched with pity. Deprived of her home, abandoned by her husband, murdered by her master, with only her daughter to mourn her passing. Aemilia was overcome by a sense of tragedy and futility: a life that should not have been so. Pollux looked at her shrewdly.

"He not a good man. But he cannot touch you here. One day he stand before God and then his money is nothing."

"He was cruel."

"Your mother with God. Nothing can hurt her now."

"But she should not have died like that."

"God take her when the time is right. Maybe it make you come here for a reason."

Aemilia hung on to that thought.

Waiting until Lady Julia had left for an evening invitation she took the cakes to her father. It was early dusk and the light was dim when she found him in the barracks. He was having supper with the other garrison centurions so she sat outside on a bench next to the parade ground until he came out.

"I baked you some honey cakes, father," she said, showing him the bundle.

"That's kind of you, girl", he replied, sitting down beside her. He took one cake and chewed it meditatively. "As good as your mother's."

"The cook helped me."

"Aye." There was a silence for a few moments.

"...there's news?"

"Messenger came in not long ago. The Franks've arrived and pitched camp. They'll fight tomorrow. We'll know by midday—afternoon at the latest." His face was grim.

"We'll win, father," she murmured.

"I don't doubt that, but I wish by all the gods that I was there. They told me: train my century to do a shield wall. Nothing loose or flexible. That means Syagrius's using 'em in the front line as an anvil. They'll be where it's hottest. I should be there!"

The two remained in silence for a long time. Aemilia thought somberly of her mother. Finally she rose up. "I must be going. It's getting dark."

"To be sure. I'll see you back."

At the Residence she bid him farewell.

"I'll come to the gate tomorrow if I can," she added.

"Aye, you do that."

The next day dawned cold and overcast, a presage of the coming winter. Aemilia was finishing breakfast with the slaves in the kitchen when Vipsania, who had spent the early part of the morning with Lady Julia, came in and sat down next to her.

"Looks like we've got time off again," she told Aemilia as she took a small loaf and broke it in half.

"Is she going out?"

"That she is. To the barracks."

"Any idea how long she'll be gone?"

The girl shrugged her shoulders. "Ask Procopius."

Aemilia caught sight of the messenger slave as he was about to leave the Residence. "Some time, I imagine," he said, in reply to her query. "She's going to a meeting of the garrison officers." He looked at her. "You know anything about it?"

Aemilia flushed. "I didn't know about a meeting," she replied.

She returned to her bedroom and had just put on her mantle before leaving to see Tarunculus when there was a knock on the door. She opened it. One of the stable boys, Gerontius, stood outside.

"Soldier wants to see you," he said.

"Where?"

"At the stables. I have to give 'im a horse. Orders from the Centurion at the north gate."

"Who? Tarunculus?"

"Aye. I'm not s'posed to tell anyone, 'cept you. Looks like something's happening."

Aemilia said nothing further but followed the boy to the stabling rooms. These normally held a dozen horses, but on arrival she found only two. Beside the larger horse stood a garrison *Limitaneus*, whom she recognized from her earlier visit to the northern gate.

"Good day, miss."

"What's the matter?"

"Can't say I know. Just that the Centurion told me to find you and bring a horse at the same time. Said I should requisition it quiet-like and he would do the talking afterwards. He wants to see you now. Says you can ride."

"I can. He wants me to take the horse to him?"

"Aye. I'm to walk with you and answer anybody's questions. Are you ready to go, miss? Stable lad's saddled it up an all."

Bewildered, Aemilia led the mare out into the small stables courtyard and through the wide gate that opened onto the street, passing Galbus who looked at her curiously and slowly returned the salute the *Limitaneus* gave him. Mounting the horse she followed the soldier at a walk. The glances of passers by made her increasingly aware of the oddity of her situation: what on earth was Tarunculus up to? Did he have the authority to commandeer a horse in this manner? What did he want with her?

On arrival she dismounted, gave the reins to her escort and was led up the narrow stairway by another soldier. Tarunculus was waiting in the guard room at the top. "Good. That will do," he said to the soldier, dismissing him. "Come with me," he told Aemilia, jerking his head for her to follow.

Outside on the walkway Aemilia followed Tarunculus to a section of the wall as far from the guards as possible. The wind flapped through the folds of her clothing, muffling any words they would speak. Tarunculus leaned on the battlement, scanning the gray horizon to the north. "Now listen to me," he said, without glancing at her, "I've heard that Albinus is taking control of the town and giving Syagrius the boot. I wouldn't have believed it if it hadn't been Aulus himself who told me. The bastard said I had to go along with it or be clapped in irons."

So it's happening at last. Aemilia felt a sick apprehension. Had Tarunculus finally learnt of her part in it?

"He said Syagrius will lose the battle for sure, and this is the only way to stop Chlodovis from pillaging the town and killing everyone in it. I told him, aye, right, it's not my business to interfere, I'll just do my job here. He bought it and left.

"Now listen, girl. Syagrius has got to be warned, but I can't trust a man here to do it. You have to go yourself."

"Me?" said Aemilia, unbelievingly.

"Aye, you. You can ride, and Syagrius knows you. Give your name and he'll see you. Here." From his sleeve Tarunculus withdrew a piece of parchment. "These are directions to the camp. Just follow the northern road until it drops into a valley with a river. That's where they'll be. You can get there in less than an hour if your horse is good. Tell Syagrius what's happening. Tell him I'll open the gates for him when he gets back, and I'll kill anyone who tries to stop me. You've got all that?"

"...yes."

"Go like the wind. Someone might report you and put two and two together. Don't let anyone catch you."

"I won't." There was no time to think, weigh up consequences. She simply had to do what her father said.

Tarunculus turned to face her. His features showed the hint of a smile. "There's my girl. Don't be afraid. You'll manage. It's a great thing you'll be doing, remember that."

"I'll do my best." She tucked the parchment into her tunic. Tarunculus placed a hand on her shoulder.

"Go, quickly."

She turned and, without a backward glance, made for the guard room. Descending the stairway she took the reins from the soldier and remounted the horse.

"Trouble, miss?" he asked, seeing the fear in her face.

She didn't answer. Pulling on the reins and digging her heels into the horse's flanks, she turned towards the gates.

She had ridden a number of times before at the villa, helping the master groom exercise the horses, but she was hardly an experienced rider. After passing through the gate she urged the horse to a full gallop. Her mind was wholly focused on adjusting to the rhythm of the horses' strides, gripping the horse's mane and using her knees to steady her seat on the saddle, trying not to put her weight on her hands and risk pitching forward. *No point in this if I fall off,* she thought. *Keep your balance, keep her on the road, let her know you are the master.*

After a time she found a kind of familiarity with the insane recklessness of what she was doing and began to feel a little more confident. Her horse was strong and used to speed, but it was not temperamental.

The land north of Soissons was relatively flat, with a few low hills near the town, past which an undulating plain spread out toward an irregular line of distant hills. In the soft, overcast light, the dark autumnal green-and-brown of the ground became part of the gray sky above, the cold wind blending the two into a great expanse of fresh, rain-tinted coolness that swept over Aemilia as she galloped down the stony path. Confidence gave way to exhilaration. *Come,* the land and air and sky said to her. *I come,* she answered. *I come, I come.*

About three miles from Soissons she finally reined in the horse, giving it a chance to wind itself. Around her, the open land receded from the road to dark irregular lines of forest and, further off, a mist-hazed horizon. She glanced back. The road itself was empty save for her. She was alone.

She pulled out Tarunculus's parchment and unfolded it. *Follow the road for ten miles until it drops down into a small valley between two hills. A stream runs through it. The camp will be there. Or it will be on one of the hills. Don't leave the road until you see it.*

The horse had recovered its breath and was cropping grass on the roadside. Reluctantly it left its meal and at Aemilia's urging picked up speed to a trot, which she hoped would leave it reasonably fresh on arrival. She did not know if she would find the battle already fought and lost, and she might need to escape.

The trot is a more bouncing gait than the gallop, and Aemilia spent some time trying to remember the few, rudimentary lessons the villa groom had taught her, rising up and down in the saddle in rhythm to the horse's stride. After a time she got the idea and could focus her attention on the land ahead of her, looking for any sign of the army or its campsite.

Time passed. She began to feel uneasy. This was the day of the battle and she did not know how late in the morning it was. Battles could start at any time of day. The great Roman General Scipio Africanus had once deployed his army before the sun rose, though he waited hours before actually fighting. She resolved to turn back immediately if she saw soldiers coming in her direction unless she was certain they were not stragglers.

She approached an area more thickly wooded than she had hitherto passed through. Beyond it were hills, though she could not be sure if they were the ones Tarunculus had described. The road entered a belt of forest. She slowed her mount to a walk and passed cautiously under the trees, glancing from left to right for any signs of a possible ambush. But save for a light wind, it was as still as the day she had made her way through the wood to see Chlodovech for the first time.

The forest thinned out and she emerged into open ground again and there, before her, with the road dropping down towards it, was the camp.

Bringing the horse to a stop, she examined it. A rectangular wooden stockade fronted by a ditch and pierced by two gates surrounded an area filled with tents of different sizes and shapes, arranged around a group of larger, white tents in the center. From her vantage point she could make out figures moving around in the camp grounds, but there did not seem to be as many as she had seen at the barracks on the day of the coronation. The army had either already left the camp or was still asleep under canvas.

Nudging the horse's flanks she made her way down into the narrow side valley that led to the wider valley beyond, through which a thin sliver of river traced its path about two miles away. It was not long before she reached the south camp gate. She stopped a good twenty yards short. A group of what appeared to be militia, dressed in an assortment of clothing, with only their spears and helmets to show their military status, stood guard at the entrance.

"Where is My Lord Syagrius?" she called out to them.

"Who are you?" one of them called back.

"I have a message from the town. He knows me. Where can I find him?"

"Where's the regular rider?"

"There's trouble in the town. He couldn't come. I have to see him now. It's very important."

The guards confabulated for a moment. Then the speaker raised an arm and pointed up the hill to the right of the valley.

"Up there. There's a path at the top. Then through the trees to the other side. That's where they are."

"Thank you."

Pulling on the horse's reins Aemilia left the road and pressed her mount as quickly as it would go up the grassy slope. The incline was not steep and she soon crested the flat-topped hill. There, as the guard had said, was a broad path recently hacked through the grass and leading to the spread of forest that ran down the northern slopes. She sensed that time was running out. The troops had gone to deploy for battle and were perhaps already fighting. Driving her tired mount to full gallop she made for the gap between the pines and passed into the shadow of the trees, barely noticing the ground beginning to slope downwards. It was not far, perhaps three hundred yards or so, before she suddenly emerged into open ground again and saw the army.

Below her, drawn up in a slight curve that followed the contour of the hill, were two immense lines of men. The scale of the deployment momentarily stunned her—it was far greater than she could have imagined. Even seeing the troops in the forum at the coronation had not prepared her for the sheer size of an army arrayed for battle.

She cast her mind back to the dialog between Syagrius and Ennodius in the reception room. Yes, there were the Comitatenses of the Second Britannica and First Flavia legions making up the rear line. To their left was a line of ballistae, heavy bolt-throwers, whose missiles could pierce through several men at once, and then a mass of cavalry, partly screened by the trees of the forest from which she had emerged. The glint of sunlight on their

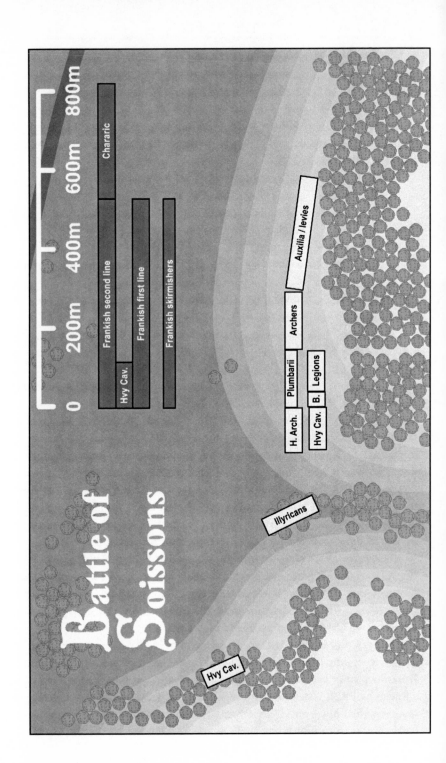

body armor showed them to be the heavy cavalry Syagrius had kept secret from the Franks until now. They stood in three rows, each two horses deep, with gaps between each row.

The forward infantry line was three or four times longer than the rear line. Its left flank was made up of the dart-armed Plumbarii, who formed a thin screen in front of the legions. To their right were the archers, and then the levies and Auxilia, who formed the right flank deployed just below the treeline.

On the left of the Plumbarii, in front of the heavy cavalry, was a loosely-spread line of horse archers. There would be two more groups of horsemen hidden in the woods on the long spur of hill further off to the west, but from her vantage point Aemilia could see no sign of them.

North of the Roman infantry lines, less than half a mile away on the valley floor, were the Franks. Two deep lines of warriors, one well behind the other, matched the width of the Roman deployment, with a third, separate line to their left that spread far beyond the Roman right. To the Frankish right, in the gap between the infantry lines, a mass of cavalry were waiting, evidently a counter to the Roman cavalry deployed opposite them.

Aemilia was able to make out a thinner line of Franks, more loosely spread out, in front of the two lines of warriors, and surmised them to be archers or something similar, though it was difficult to see much detail at this distance.

Coming to herself, she recalled her purpose: she had to find Syagrius quickly and deliver her father's message. Scanning the ground behind the army she spotted a small group of cavalry a few dozen yards up the slope from the legions. That must be him.

Urging her mount to a trot, Aemilia descended from the forest at a westerly angle down the slope, straight towards the troop of horsemen below her. When she was within a hundred yards of them, three riders detached themselves from the group and made for her. She reined in her horse and waited. They approached, spears leveled, and drew up in front and on either side of her.

"Who are you?" demanded the one in front.

"I was sent by my father, Centurion Tarunculus. He commands the north gate at Soissons."

"Never heard of him."

The horseman to her right spoke up. "I know him. He trained the recruits at the barracks."

The first horseman turned his attention back to Aemilia.

"Why did he send you? Why not a regular courier?"

"Sir, there's trouble in the town. He had to send a message without anyone knowing."

The horsemen glanced at each other. Then the second spoke up, "He's still with the cavalry."

"Can't take her there now," replied the first. "They'll be moving at any moment. Our orders are to stick with the Emperor. She can stay with him until the battle's done." He turned his horse. "Come on."

They made their way along the grassy slope to the knot of cavalry. Aemilia recognized Ennodius: his attention was fixed on the scene before him. The first rider drew up alongside him and spoke a few words. He glanced back at her, his eyes widening in surprise.

"Aemilia! What on earth are you doing here?"

"My father sent me, My Lord."

"What for?"

"I have a message for Syagrius."

"You've no time to give it to him now. Tell it to me."

Aemilia reined her horse in as close to Ennodius as she was able, and leaned across to him. "My father says that Albinus will take over the town and remove Syagrius. They asked him if he would go along with it. He said yes and sent me to warn Syagrius. He says he will open the gates for Syagrius when he returns."

Ennodius looked at her for several moments, saying nothing. Then he turned his gaze back to the scene before him. "It doesn't matter."

"What?"

"What matters is what happens here. If we win, Albinus won't dare move against Syagrius. Don't bother him with the news just yet—he needs to have all his attention on the battle. We'll tell him afterwards. He can execute Albinus at his leisure."

Execute Albinus. Without a doubt they would question him first and find out about Lady Julia's involvement, and then about her own. Fear wrapped a tendril around Aemilia's throat. She shook it off. There was nothing that could be done about it.

Over the wind the murmur of a clamor reached her ears: a faint cry that rose and fell. With it came a sound as of a vast drumming. One of the cavalry guards turned to Ennodius. "Doing their warcry, My Lord, and hitting their weapons against their shields. They'll be coming now."

For a full minute the cry lingered on the wind, then, drifting like a heavy mist over the land, the thin line of Frankish skirmishers approached the Romans.

Aemilia did not hear the command that let loose a rainstorm of arrows upon the Franks. She saw figures fall. It took a moment for the truth to impact on her mind—within her sight men were wounded, dying, dead. All she had read about the epic clash of arms, the renown of great soldiers and the glory of battle melted before the reality like wax in a fire. War was about men killing other men; it was not about anything else. Her stomach and throat tensed. She wanted to stop it, but she could not.

After a few moments the Frankish skirmishers reached their own bowshot range and stopped to shoot back. A number of them ran closer and hurled javelins at the front ranks. In their turn the Romans added darts and javelins to the blizzard of arrows enveloping the Franks. More and more fell and finally, as if on a signal, the survivors broke and ran.

The horse archers surged forwards after them, individual horsemen pausing now and then to shoot arrows at the retreating Franks. Their pursuit followed up all the way to the main Frankish lines which became their next target.

Some moments passed. Finally, through the front Frankish line, the Frankish cavalry charged. The horse archers ceased shooting and turned, making for their lines at full gallop with the Franks close behind.

With her attention on the horsemen, Aemilia did not immediately notice what was happening in the center. Once the remnants of the Frankish skirmishers had retreated through the main lines, the frontmost of these began to advance rapidly towards the Roman infantry. At the same time the Frankish cavalry halted in their pursuit of the retreating horse archers. There was a murmur from the riders surrounding Aemilia and Ennodius.

"What's happening?" Ennodius asked

"The Franks have stopped their charge," replied the one who had spoken to Ennodius earlier. "First time I've ever seen barbarians do such a thing…My Lord." Aemilia heard the note of concern in his voice.

The horse archers reached their starting positions and began milling around, slowly reforming their line. Aemilia sensed that Syagrius's plan had met a hitch: the Franks were not doing what was expected of them.

Thwunk, thwunk, thwunk. The noise startled Aemilia. She glanced to the left. The ballistae, enormous crossbow-like weapons mounted on wheeled bases, were firing their missiles at the Frankish line. The bolts flew with incredible speed over the heads of the Plumbarii and disappeared into the enemy ranks, with what effect she could only imagine.

A few moments later, the archers loosed on the Franks, followed shortly after by a volley of large war darts from the Plumbarii. Then, as the Frankish first line drew near, Aemilia heard the centurions crying out an order. "Second line!"

With trained discipline, the archers in the front rank wheeled about and retired through the files, moving up the hill to form a new line further back. The archers of the second rank loosed an arrow then repeated the manoeuvre of the first rank. The third rank did likewise, then the fourth. Slowly the sixteen-rank deep line of archers retreated up the slope, shooting continuously. The Franks facing them came on slowly, shields up against the withering rain of arrow fire.

The Auxilia line in the meantime turned about and scrambled up to the forest. From her vantage point Aemilia could see the Auxilia nearer her enter the trees and then reform just behind the outermost trunks. The Plumbarii did not move. The archers continued shooting.

The line of warriors paused, as if gathering its strength. The chant of a warcry rose to a crescendo, died away, then rose again and the Franks threw their franciscas.

Aemilia remembered the strange, curved axe hitched at the side of the Frankish warrior, Merovec, she had met on the hill. Tarunculus had later told her about it. "They throw it before they charge. Nasty piece of work. It'll go through a helmet or a shield if it's thrown right. You always let the light troops take it—never let the bastards throw 'em at the main line. Archers can stop it though: they pull back and keep shooting. Makes 'em keep their shields up so they can't throw."

Men fell by the score in the skirmish line in front of the legions. Their screams reached Aemilia, setting her heart pounding. "Can't we help them?" she cried out to Ennodius. He said nothing.

"Those who are down are dead," replied a rider. "The others will live if they run."

On the right flank the Auxilia had suffered less from the axes, partly shielded as they were by the tree trunks. A scattering of fallen bodies indicated that only a few axes had been thrown at the archers.

Before her the Plumbarii were fleeing back to the main line with the Franks surging up behind them. Aemilia heard the centurions call out another order. "Aim high!"

As the Franks crashed into the front ranks of the legions, the rear ranks, armed with bows, raised them to point almost directly upwards. Arrows flew high, slowed, and then gently curved in their flight to drop downwards, gathering murderous speed, onto the heads of the Franks. Behind the legions, the Plumbarii slowly reformed.

Glancing to her right, Aemilia could see that the front ranks of the archers, switching bow for shield and sword, had taken the full brunt of the Frankish charge whilst the rear ranks decimated the Franks, shooting high in the same manner as the legions.

The Auxilia in the meantime had charged out from the forest. The front ranks were locked in combat whilst the rear ranks lobbed javelins and arrows onto the Franks.

As the battle settled down into a grim and bloody melee, it looked as if the Roman line would break. The Franks in the center gradually pushed the archers back to the treeline, opening gaps between them and the Auxilia on one side, and the legions on the other. Above the murderous din of the fighting, Aemilia heard orders being called out again. With practiced speed, the rear ranks of the rightmost legion turned right and advanced into a new line at right angles to the front ranks, thus closing the gap between the legions and the archers. On the far side of the retreating archers, Aemilia saw the Auxilia perform a similar manoeuver to close up the opposite gap. The repositioned Auxilia and Comitatenses paused to regroup, then, with a rising yell, charged into the embattled warriors.

It was the turning point of the struggle. Already decimated and disorganized by the deadly missile fire, the Frankish center, confronted with a charge against its sides, broke almost immediately. From her vantage point, Aemilia could see the domino effect of the rout. The warriors in the center fell back, then, pressed by the Romans, turned and ran, creating a huge hole in the Frankish line. The Franks fighting the legions and the Auxilia, now exposed to outflanking themselves, fell back before facing about in full headlong flight.

But right ahead of them was the second line of warriors.

It had formed into a series of wedges, with gaps between one wedge and the next. The retreating Franks streamed into the gaps and rallied, connecting the wedges to form a solid, spiked wall soon to head straight for the exhausted Romans.

Overwhelmed as she was by the carnage around her, a part of Aemilia's mind was able to remain analytical, and she realized that Chlodovech had foreseen the course of the battle up to this point and had provided for it. A single line of Franks could not defeat the Roman infantry, but it could draw their fire, deplete their ammunition, wear them down. She also saw the purpose of the wedges: drive into the Roman lines and break their cohesion, exposing the rear rank shooters to close quarter fighting from the Frankish foot.

There was a lull in the combat as the two armies reformed. Before long, the Frankish line would charge. Roman arrow fire was now sporadic, and no more darts or javelins were being thrown. Archers hurried forward and feverishly pulled arrows from the ground or the bodies of dead Franks.

Everything now depended on the cavalry.

Looking to the left, beyond the infantry lines, she saw with amazement that the heavy cavalry had not yet moved. Further forward, the horse archers were galloping back from the Frankish cavalry who, even as she watched, stopped in their pursuit. She noticed Ennodius looking in the same direction. It was clear that the game of tag had been going on between the two bodies of horsemen for the duration of the infantry fight, whilst the rest of the Roman cavalry, and with them Syagrius's plan, had taken no step forward.

"Why won't the Franks charge?" she asked.

"They've seen the Illyricans—there," Ennodius pointed, indicating a line of horsemen that had half-emerged from the treeline on the hill that bordered the west side of the battlefield. "They won't come close."

"Why doesn't Syagrius charge them?"

"He's waiting for more cavalry to come up behind the Franks. They haven't appeared yet. I don't know why."

The horse archers veered off around the left of the heavy cavalry. At the same time the Illyricans emerged from the trees and wheeled to face the Frankish horse. The heavy cavalry began to trot forward.

"What's he doing?" asked Ennodius of no one in particular.

"I think he's going to charge, My Lord," a rider replied.

Ennodius worriedly scanned the approaching Frankish infantry. "He'll have to move fast."

There were about two hundred yards between the Roman and Frankish horse. As the Roman heavy cavalry covered the distance it picked up speed. The Franks waited, then, with less than a hundred yards between them and the Romans, they broke into a charge.

The two bodies of cavalry met and seemed to blend together. The Illyricans worked their way around the right flank of the Franks, and began targeting individual horsemen with their javelins. It appeared to be an even fight: the Illyricans could pepper the Franks with javelin fire and then gallop out of reach, but the Franks outnumbered the Roman heavy cavalry. The horse archers waited a distance away from the protagonists. Either they had run out of arrows or they were afraid to shoot and hit friend with foe.

The cavalry contest was still undecided when a vast shout arose from the Frankish infantry. The Romans had put a skirmish line forward to absorb the imminent volley of franciscas. Arrow fire was coming down more heavily on the warriors, though not nearly as thickly as it had against the first Frankish line.

Aemilia scanned the valley floor. The separate line of Franks that had formed the left of Chlodovech's army had not moved for the duration of the battle. That must be Chararic, she surmised. He won't fight for Chlodovech. There is still hope.

Metallic glints darted from the Franks to the Romans, who fell by the dozen. Then the Franks charged. The remains of the skirmish line tumbled back to the main line, which in its turn staggered back before the impact of the Frankish wedges. But for the moment it held.

Aemilia's eyes flicked back to the cavalry fight. The Frankish riders seemed to be nearly surrounded: Roman heavy cavalry to their front, Illyricans to their rear. She glanced at the distant line of Chararic's Franks. If he was to keep his word to Syagrius the time to do so was now. But the Franks did not move.

"My Lord! They're breaking through!"

Aemilia followed the rider's pointing finger. The archers, the weakest link in the Roman line, were buckling, Frankish wedges pushing through and fragmenting their line as they drove them back to the trees. This time there was no reserve to countercharge the Franks. Every man was committed to holding them where he stood.

Ennodius beat the saddle with his fist. "We need more time. We need more time!"

"Look!" The same rider pointed towards the distant cavalry fight. Frankish horsemen were beginning to flee, breaking through the Illyricans who turned to pursue them. "They're winning!"

Ennodius gazed at the cavalry, and then back at the crumbling infantry line, sparing a swift glance for the distant line of uncommitted Franks. He turned to Aemilia.

"You must get out of here," he said, pointing west. "That way. It's too late for the forest route now."

"What will you do?"

"I'm staying. I made a promise that I wouldn't run, remember?"

"But you could be killed!"

His face showed the hint of a grin. "That'll be your fault. You wrote the speech."

"No!" Aemilia cried out. "What can you do?"

"Plug a few holes until Syagrius arrives."

"But…"

"I've no time. Go!"

The fire in his eyes spoke as no words could. Yanking on her reins, she began to turn her horse around. Then she stopped.

"My message!"

Ennodius swore. "You!" he said to the nearest rider. "Go tell Syagrius that the garrison at Soissons have turned against him. Got that? The garrison have turned against him."

The rider nodded and reined his horse past Aemilia. "Come on!" he called back at her.

Aemilia looked one last time at Ennodius, a confusion within her, then dug her heels into her mount's flanks. The animal, already agitated by the bloody turmoil around it, needed no encouragement. The two horses flew past the ballistae, their crews now fighting the Franks hand-to-hand, until they were off the hill and clear of the battle.

"That way," the rider shouted, pointing south up the side valley, and then turned off north toward the embattled cavalry.

Aemilia did not stop. Away from Ennodius she was vulnerable again, a woman in a place of blood-maddened men. She found the Soissons road and galloped up the side valley until the palisaded camp came in view. Keeping a good distance away, she left the road and worked her way around the campsite, rejoining the road and resuming her gallop until she was out of the valley and had reached the treeline from which she had emerged earlier that day.

She brought her tired mount to a halt, turning it around so she could look back. There was the camp, motionless in the soft, overcast light. Besides the languid drift of smoke from a few campfires there was no other movement. All was quiet and still. The battle was as unreal as a nightmare after waking on a sunny morning. She dismounted, exhausted, and tethered her horse to a nearby branch. She needed to sit down. There. A dip in the ground that could serve as a grassy bench. She sat, her mind empty, frozen in its processes by a permeating numbness. She could not find any place in her for the human world. It was a foreign thing, not to be understood.

A small beetle crawled up a blade of grass beside her. She studied it, watching it use its feelers to find a path in the comic hit-and-miss way beetles had. It went about its business and it was good and necessary that it should do so. On the ground an ant crawled, carrying a tiny clump of earth. It threaded its way between grass stalks and finally disappeared down a hole from which other ants were emerging. She followed their movements as her numbness fractionally began to ease its grip. Little by little, she was able to bring herself to consider the human world again.

She looked over the valley. No sign of either Franks or Romans. Even the campsite was devoid of movement, save for the idle threads of smoke.

Should she stay? Her horse was weary and in any case she did not know if she could win a race against an experienced rider. Better to go now.

She had carried out her task to the best of her ability. She did not know if Syagrius had received the message, or even if he was alive, but now she simply did not care.

Ennodius, was he alive? Yes, that thought troubled her, breaking through the deadening wash that blanketed her mind. Lord God, look after him. He has the spark, more than I could ever have thought possible. Let him live.

Slowly, she raised herself to her feet. Making her way across to the horse, she untied the reins from the branch and then carefully mounted the saddle. Leaning forward, she stroked the beast's neck. "Come on then, one last journey," she said, and gently nudged it to a walk.

CHAPTER 22

She reached Soissons three hours later, glancing behind her all the way, but seeing no one. Entering the town gates, she left her horse with a soldier and mounted the stairway to the guard room where she found Tarunculus waiting for her. He took her outside on the battlement.

"Well?" he said, when they were out of earshot.

"I tried, father. When I got there the battle was about to begin. They took me to Ennodius—the Emperor. I told him. Later he sent a messenger to Syagrius." She did not want to talk, just lie down and close her eyes.

"You saw the battle then."

"Part of it."

"And? What happened? Did we win?"

"I don't know. I had to leave. Maybe. It was very bad."

Tarunculus looked at her intently, and his expression softened. "Aye, you've been through it, like a new recruit. You can't say for sure which way it went?"

"No."

"No matter. We'll know soon enough."

The two remained side by side on the battlement until the cold of their exposed position began to seep through Aemilia's garments, chilling her. She returned to the tower guardhouse and sat on a stool in the corner. Her eyes wandered around the room, examining its store of weaponry. Quivers of arrows leaned against the wall next to her. She tested the arrow points gingerly with her finger. They were honed to razor sharpness. The woodpile kept her puzzled until she saw a round cauldron in a corner. Of course. Boiling oil. There were the amphoras, full of it, not far away. She pictured the bubbling oil being tipped onto the Frankish warriors below. Her mind recoiled from the image. *You're getting morbid,* she thought. She ceased her examination and gazed through the battlement entrance at the gray skies beyond. Then, her back leaning against the wall, she let her eyes close and her thoughts drift. Time passed.

"There, sir! A rider."

Aemilia opened her eyes and glanced at the battlement entrance. Framed by the arched doorway, a soldier was pointing northwards. Tarunculus stood next to him, his hand shielding his eyes. She joined them and looked beyond the parapet. After a few moments she could make out a speck moving over the gray-green folds of the distant fields.

"There! Another! And a third!"

Aemilia glanced at her father. His mouth was a thin, grim line, his eyes narrowed to slits, fixed on the approaching specks that grew in numbers before his gaze. He did not speak.

The leading horseman finally reached the gates and paused, glancing up as if in response to a query, though no one said anything.

"It's lost! The battle's lost!"

Tarunculus called down. "The rest of the army?"

"Some of the cavalry got away. The infantry...." he shook his head and then urged his horse forward, not wanting to say any more.

Indeed there was nothing more to be said.

Tarunculus placed his hands on the battlement merlons, fingers gripping the stone like the claws of a captive falcon, eyes staring at the horsemen as they approached the walls, singly or in small groups. The afternoon wore on as the survivors trickled in: more horsemen, some archers, then later, scattered groups of militia with several wounded amongst them. There was no sign of Syagrius or Ennodius.

Aemilia, blue with cold, finally re-entered the guardhouse and sat on the corner stool, gathering her mantle around her. She observed her father through the entrance. He had not moved since the first sighting of the beaten army, the lines of his features deep and scored as if carved in stone. It cut her to the heart. His cause did not move her any longer. It had been blown out of her by a threat and a bag of money. But for a time it had been hers, and she could feel within herself the anguish behind his motionless face...*all for nothing, for nothing...take my heart and burn it...throw it away, away...*

One of the guards spoke something to Tarunculus that she could not catch, and pointed to the distance. He leaned forward, suddenly attentive. Aemilia rose up and rejoined him. Far away, a group of horsemen approached.

"Are you sure?" said Tarunculus to the guard.

"It's him, sir."

"Who?" Aemilia asked.

"Syagrius and his personal guard," replied Tarunculus, not averting his gaze from the knot of cavalry. Then he turned to one of the guards. "Sidonius. Anyone comes with an order to close the gates you get up here and tell me. Understand?"

"Yes sir."

"Now go wait at the bottom of the stairway."

The riders drew nearer, and Aemilia, after several moments examination, was able to recognize Syagrius in front, leading a troop of about a dozen horse. After looking through the faces, she spotted Ennodius at the back. They passed through the gateway without pausing or looking up, making, she guessed, straight for the barracks. As they passed into the town Tarunculus seemed to ease a fraction. "Good. He's through."

"What will he do?"

"With him here we can hold the town. The Franks won't spend the winter sitting outside the walls. We'll just have to tighten our belts in the meantime until they go."

"Will the Franks come here today?"

"Doubt it. They'll be spending their time divvying up the loot and celebrating. We won't see them before tomorrow."

For the next half hour Aemilia stood beside her father, watching the remnants of Syagrius's army stumble into the town. She was about to leave when the same keen-eyed guard who had first caught sight of Syagrius motioned to Tarunculus.

"Sir, look, over there."

Aemilia followed his pointing finger to a spot on the horizon, where, after a few moments scrutiny, she was able to discern some movement.

"More of ours?" Tarunculus queried.

"No sir...not ours."

"Damn! They're here already." Cupping both hands to his mouth, Tarunculus bellowed down at the approaching stragglers. "Get in now! They're right behind you!" Then turning to the guardroom he thundered, "Stations! Ready to close the gates!"

Some of the soldiers remained at the battlement, others ran to their various posts. Soldiers came up the stairs and began seizing bows and quivers. Several grabbed hold of logs of wood and took them out through the guardroom entrance, evidently intent on making a fire to heat up the oil. Aemilia tried to keep out of everyone's way. Better to wait, she thought, until the stairway was clear again before leaving. After a few minutes the to and fro bustle quietened down, each soldier now in readiness.

The last survivors of the army ran or limped through the gates as the Frankish host approached, a long column of horsemen and infantry that, once it came within a mile of the town, peeled off right and left to form a battle line, with cavalry in the center and infantry on the flanks. Aemilia saw that it was much a smaller force than the army she had seen in the valley floor earlier that day, and guessed that Chlodovech had come with only his picked men to seize the town, giving Syagrius no time to react. Slowly, in an ordered array, the Franks drew near to the town limits.

Tarunculus raised his arm in command. "Close the gates!"

There was a creaking and grinding below them, followed by a dull thump as the gate doors were closed and bolted. Tarunculus was giving orders rapidly now: "...I want the oil hot in half-an-hour...archers at the ready — first volley on my command only. No wasting arrows...make a fire in the guardroom in case of rain—we'll need fire arrows."

The Franks reached the outermost buildings and halted. There was silence for what seemed a long time. No one moved. Then suddenly, Aemilia heard footsteps running up the stairway. A centurion emerged from the guardhouse entrance.

Tarunculus turned to the sound. "Aulus? We're ready. They've stopped though. Seem to be waiting for something." He returned to his scrutiny of the Frankish host.

Aulus looked at him grimly. "Orders from Albinus. You're to open the gates."

Tarunculus turned back to him. "What?"

"Open the gates. The town's been given up."

There was a frozen silence. Then Tarunculus spoke, "Are you out of your mind?"

"Syagrius is deposed. Albinus is in command. Now open the damn gates!"

Tarunculus looked at him as if he had never seen a man before. Then the centurion turned to a nearby guard. "Are the gate crew at the winches?"

"Yes, sir."

The blow caught him completely by surprise. Tarunculus, breathing heavily, stood over the fallen centurion, who got unsteadily to his feet and took a step backwards, feeling his jaw. "Open the gates, you fool, if you don't want to get us all killed."

Tarunculus made no answer, but drew his sword. The centurion turned and re-entered the guardroom. He looked back a moment. "You're relieved of command. Albinus'll be back here with a guard." He descended the stairway and disappeared.

Tarunculus, the sword still in his hand, turned to the soldiers and said hoarsely, "Back to your posts." The men hesitated. "Damn you! Move!" he bellowed. They obeyed, slowly.

Aemilia spoke, uncertainly, "Father?"

"Yes?"

"Shall I go and find Syagrius?"

"Yes. Quickly. It could be a bluff." Tarunculus grabbed the sleeve of a guard. "Adeodatus, see she gets away."

She ran down the stairs, followed by the guard. On the street he unhitched the horse and helped her mount, passing her the reins.

"Can you manage?" he asked.

"Yes."

He shook his head. "Good luck, Miss, but I think the game's up."

She did not reply, but turned towards the street. Then the reins became still in her hands. Where was Syagrius? The barracks or the Residence? She glanced down at the soldier. "When Syagrius came through, did you see which way he went?"

"Aye Miss. That way." And he pointed south, past the forum to where the Residence lay.

She did not thank him but set off at once. She risked urging the horse to full speed as the streets were empty and her mission would be useless if it was not accomplished with the direst haste.

She reached the Residence in less than a minute. There was no guard at the front entrance and the door was open. Dismounting she looked through the doorway. No sign of anyone. She led the horse through the entrance and tethered it to one of the pillars in the entrance atrium, then turned to make for the main atrium and almost bumped into a slave carrying a heavy sack. She recognized him as one of the kitchen crew.

"Where's everybody?" she asked.

He looked at her with surprise. "Where'd you get the horse?"

"Loaned. Where are the guards?"

"At Syagrius's room. He's packing as fast as he can. They're giving him half-an-hour to get out."

"Where are you going?"

"Where do you think? Most've the slaves've grabbed what they can and made off already. You don't want to be here when the Franks come—it'll be a bloody massacre."

She shook her head. "I have to see Syagrius and get back to the gates as quick as I can. My father's there." She glanced at the horse.

The slave put his sack down. "You've done me a favor more'n once, Aemilia. Go find him. I'll keep an eye on the horse. But make it quick."

Thanking him, she hurried into the Residence and up the stairs that led to Syagrius's private quarters on the first floor. Half-a-dozen guards stood outside the door's ornate wooden panelling. She recognized Odo among them and approached him.

"I have to see Syagrius."

He shook his head. "No one's to see him."

"But I have to, Odo. I've come from my father on the north gate. The Franks have arrived and he needs to know what to do."

"Albinus's giving the orders now."

"He won't obey Albinus!"

The guards glanced at each other. Odo gave a nod. "All right." He gave a single rap on the door.

"What?" The voice was muffled by the door.

"Message from the north gate, sir."

The door opened. Syagrius stood, helmetless but still in uniform, with a thin film of sweat on his forehead, eyes wary and hostile. "What message?"

Odo indicated Aemilia. The eyes fixed on her.

Aemilia spoke, the words coming out in a rush: "My Lord, the Franks have reached the town. My father closed the gates but another centurion came and told him he must open them. He said the order came from Albinus. My father would not obey him and...sent him away. He must know from you what to do. He sent me to find out. I have a horse. I can go back to him with a message if you wish..." She stopped, not knowing what more to say.

"*You knew.*"

Aemilia was confused. "I don't..."

"She made a deal with Chlodovech. She must have, to get three months out of him. It was that meeting, wasn't it? You were there. *You knew all along.*"

Aemilia's eyes darted left, right, down, away from those burning eyes. Then she covered her face with her hands. "I didn't know what to do, My Lord. I didn't know why she wanted to meet him, only that I had to arrange it. I didn't know what to do afterwards. I was afraid she would be executed."

Syagrius shouldered past the guards and came close to her, almost touching her.

"It was *treason!*"

"I know! But I cannot be the cause of anyone's death!" She could speak no more, overcome by a fit of weeping. Then Syagrius straightened, moving a fraction back from her.

"Except mine, eh?"

Aemilia did not know what to say.

"Does your father still recognize me?"

"Yes, My Lord."

"Then my order to him is to keep the gates shut. That'll give me some time. He can fall on his sword afterwards if he chooses. Now go." And he returned into his room, slamming the door shut behind him.

Aemilia stood still, her mind in confusion, staring in front of her at nothing. Odo tapped her on the shoulder.

"It's true they're going to let them in now?

Aemilia nodded, hardly aware of the question. The guards shifted uneasily, glancing again at each other. "They'll make straight for here," one muttered. Then another dropped his spear with a clatter on the mosaic floor.

"What're you doing?" Odo demanded.

"I'm out," the guard said. "Stay here and get your throat cut if you like."

There was a fraction's hesitation as the other guards reached decision, then all likewise threw their spears down.

"You're under orders," Odo mumbled.

"Then you obey them," And with that they strode rapidly away toward the stairway.

"Bloody cowards," Odo spat.

"Are you the last guard here?" Aemilia asked.

"No. Galbus's keeping guard at the Lady's bedroom. They're staying."

"'They'? You mean Ennodius's with her?"

"Aye."

An idea came to her. Without another word to the taciturn guard she turned and hurried down the corridor, descending the stairway in leaps and continuing on until she found the other leading up to Lady Julia's bedroom. She mounted it three steps at a time. As she raced along the thought crept into her mind: *Are you doing this for your father or are you doing it for the Empire? For both,* she replied.

At the top of the stairs she paused to catch her breath and look down the passage. There, outside the Lady's door, stood Galbus. She waited until she had recovered her wind somewhat before approaching him.

"I must see Ennodius."

"Can't be done. They're not seeing anyone now. She's given strict orders."

"Galbus, listen. My father's holding the north gates. The Franks have come. He's been ordered to open them but he won't obey. Syagrius is leaving, but Ennodius is still Emperor. He must go to the gates and take charge. My father said we can hold the town against the Franks. It's our last chance, Galbus. Let me see him!"

The guard hesitated, looking away as if considering. A memory came to Aemilia.

"I was there when Chlodovech told her that if he found the gates shut he would cut her head off. They must be either shut properly or open properly, can't you see?"

That seemed to decide him. "All right, go in," he muttered, turning to open the door and neglecting to knock as he did so.

Aemilia strode past him into the room. Lady Julia sat in her ornate chair, dressed in her finest gown. Ennodius, in a plain tunic, stood by the arched window, his back to the room. Both turned to face her as she entered.

"What on earth?..." Lady Julia rose, her face a mix of astonishment and fury. "Who gave you permission..."

Aemilia cut her short, addressing Ennodius. "My Lord, there is trouble. You must come now." Ennodius said nothing, staring at her like a hunted rabbit. Lady Julia took a step forward. "What trouble, girl?"

Aemilia continued to speak to Ennodius. "The Franks have come. My father is keeping the main gates shut against them. He has been ordered to open them by Albinus, but he will not do it."

"Good God," Lady Julia uttered.

"My Lord Syagrius has said the gates must be kept shut, but he is leaving. You must come to the gates now, my Lord. Albinus is coming with a guard. But if you are there the soldiers will obey you and keep them shut. My father said we can hold the town against the Franks, but you must take command. I have a horse if you need it..."

"You insolent wretch!" Lady Julia's face was pasty white. "How...dare you!"

Aemilia turned to her. "Your Majesty, it is our last chance. The Franks will not stay outside during the winter, my father said so."

"You...upstart! Get out! Get out now!"

Aemilia did not move. "I will not leave until the Emperor comes with me." She turned to Ennodius. "My Lord, remember the coronation. They will obey you if you..."

With three swift steps Lady Julia approached Aemilia and struck her a blow across the face that sent her sprawling on the floor. "Out!" she ordered, her voice nearly a shriek.

Aemilia stood up and looked at Ennodius. He returned her gaze just for a moment, his eyes dull and heavy as she remembered them on their first meeting, and then, wavering, he turned away, resuming his post at the window. Aemilia backed towards the doorway. Lady Julia stepped forward, pushed her out and slammed the door in her face.

"Didn't go well," Galbus commented, whilst Aemilia rubbed her stinging cheek.

"No. I think you should go. The Franks will be here soon."

"I'll take my chances. Wouldn't want to be a coward on my last day as soldier. Seems that the Lady has an understanding with them in any case."

"Yes...she has. Good luck, Galbus."

"You too, lass. Where will you go?"

"I'll stay with my father." They shook hands, and Aemilia left him.

The horse was still where she had tied it. The slave was leaning against the wall, arms crossed. "Took you long enough," he grumbled, as she untethered the mount. "Get what you came for?"

"Not really," she said, leading it to the entrance.

She rode back at a trot until she was opposite the gate tower. There she stopped and dismounted, not willing to go any further. The great doors of the gate were still shut and there were no soldiers in sight. A few townsfolk were gathered in small groups, conversing, but most seemed to have decided to remain indoors. Time passed. Aemilia several times took a step toward the small doorway in the tower wall, but then stopped, returning to her place. Finally she heard the thud of hooves. Looking behind her she saw a knot of mounted troops approaching, the garrison commander at their head. They passed and halted at the tower, dismounting and entering under the narrow stone archway. Aemilia crossed the street swiftly and followed a few paces behind them.

She reached the top of the stairway and emerged into the guardroom. Albinus and his men were on the battlement with their backs to her. Before them stood Tarunculus, still gripping his sword. No one paid her any attention.

"Centurion Tarunculus, you are relieved of command. This gate is now under my personal orders. Men, do you acknowledge my authority?" There was silence for a moment, then several voices spoke: "...sir...yes sir..."

Aemilia moved up to just behind the commander. Tarunculus caught sight of her, and for a moment hope lit up in his face. Aemilia bowed her head and shook it slowly.

"You will now give up your sword."

Aemilia raised her eyes. The stark despair in Tarunculus's face smote her. He did not move.

"Drop it." It was a final warning. Tarunculus paused to look at the blade that had cut down a Hun from his horse in a battle now in so distant an age, then opened his fingers, letting it fall to the ground with a clatter.

"Open the gates."

Once the creaking and rumbling had ceased the commander spoke one last time. "You are all discharged from the army. Return immediately to the barracks. There you will be given civilian clothing and twenty siliquas each. You are commended for your loyalty. I wish the best of luck to you all. Dismissed." All moved off except Tarunculus, who remained stock still. Albinus, on the point of leaving, looked back to him, as if to say something, but then turned away and went on down the stairway.

In less than a minute the battlement was deserted. Tarunculus's eyes were fixed on his sword. Aemilia, watching him, suddenly remembered Syagrius's words. She stepped forward and, bending down, seized the sword and flung it over the edge. He stared at her. She moved next to him. "Come, father, we must go." He did not move. Taking him gently by the arm she led him down: a young girl and an old man with an uncertain step, the last defenders of an Empire that had been so long in the dying and was now, finally, dead.

PART IV:
PENURY

CHAPTER 23

Tarunculus was silent on the way back to the apartment, not seeming to care where he went, content to go wherever Aemilia led him. Once inside he sat down at the table and put his head in his hands. After a time he spoke. "Close the shutters."

She did so, and lit a lamp from a neighbor's fire to dispel the gloom of the darkened room. The flame flickered on the table, casting huge, dancing shadows on the walls. The two sat in silence for a while, then Aemilia spoke: "Father, I must get my things from the Residence." He did not reply. She rose quietly and slipped out, closing the door gently behind her.

The streets were deserted, as was the forum except for two figures who were breaking down the door of one of the plaza shops, evidently intent on doing some quick looting before the Franks arrived. She hurried past and went on to the Residence, finding it as empty as before. Having procured her small bundle of possessions and her precious books she quit the building and retraced her steps with speed. But she was too late. At the forum the looters were gone and the central space was gradually filling with groups of Franks, some standing, others sitting, talking among themselves and pointing to various objects, almost like holidaymakers. None of them, she noticed from her vantage point behind a pillar at the forum entrance, seemed to be emulating the vanished looters by breaking down shop doors themselves. They appeared to be content to wait. Aemilia guessed they were under orders not to touch anything in the town until their king had given the command.

They were dressed as colorfully and diversely as the Franks she had seen on the hillside three months earlier. Their weapons were also as diverse, if not more so. Some carried axes and the barbed harpoon-like javelins; others carried spears. A few had swords: some long, others short, almost like long knives. Most carried round shields, on their arms or slung over their backs. There was no sign of Chlodovech or his horsemen until, suddenly, she saw them coming through the opposite entrance at a trot, with Albinus at the Frankish king's side. Chlodovech put out a hand to stop the Roman, speaking a moment to him. Albinus dismounted, gave the reins to one of Chlodovech's men and remained standing at the edge of the crowd, whilst Chlodovech went forward with his guard onto the plaza in the direction of the basilica. Signing his guards to wait below he mounted up the steps and turned his horse side on. Pulling an axe from his belt he brandished it above his head. The men in the plaza gave a mighty shout: *Hoera Heer!* He replaced the axe and spoke to his men.

"My Franks, the town is ours, but remember these people are now our people. Take what you want but do not touch their homes or the churches. Bring it here and we will divide it up in four days' time according to the custom. Do not kill anyone unless he raises a weapon against you. *Franke verhef!*"

Hoera! the warriors cried.

Chlodovech guided his horse down onto the paving of the plaza. At the forum entrance Albinus fell behind him on foot. The troop of horsemen approached the archway where Aemilia stood. She moved well back behind the pillar and watched them pass. Chlodovech sat erect on his horse, his expression one of self-possessed satisfaction. He did not notice her and Aemilia felt no desire to make her presence known to him. The doings of the great were no longer her concern. She wished him well, however, as the horses disappeared down the street towards the Residence.

She felt no fear as she crossed the plaza, greeting the warriors as she passed. A few responded with rough politeness: "*dag, mejuffrou,*" but for the most part they did not pay her any attention. At the apartment she found Tarunculus exactly as she had left him. Stashing her bundle in a corner she sat across from him. "It's all right, father. They're not going to touch anyone's home." He did not reply.

There was still some wood and twigs in the kitchen. Using the lamp she made a fire and then prepared a soup from the few, sound vegetables she could find. Filling two bowls she took them to the table and placed one in front of Tarunculus. "Come father, eat." He made no response and she urged him again. "You need to keep your strength up."

He seemed to become aware of her. He looked at the bowl and waved it away, as a tired man would dispel a gnat. She did not insist further, but taking up her wooden spoon, ate her portion. When she was finished she took the two bowls back to the kitchen, pouring the contents of his bowl back into the pot on the brazier, in the hope that he might want it later. She tidied the kitchen and returned to the main room, unpacking her bundle and putting her things wherever seemed best. She was replacing the copy of

St. Augustine on its shelf when Tarunculus finally spoke.

"You should not have done it."

She glanced at him.

He looked at her sadly. "I couldn't kill myself now, but you should not have thrown my sword away." Rising up he walked to his bedroom, undoing the clasps of his chain mail corset and dropping it wearily on the floor. He lay on the bed, eyes on the ceiling. Aemilia resumed her task of putting the apartment in order, doing her best not to disturb him.

By the time she was finished, the evening shadows had lengthened into the gloom of night. She felt suddenly fatigued. Outside all was quiet, except for the occasional laughter and singing of a passing group of Franks. She looked in at her father. He was not moving and appeared to be asleep. The lamp in the kitchen shed a dim light on his face, casting in relief the deeply scored creases in his face that manifested age now rather than character. She hoped he was asleep, and able to put a few hours oblivion between himself and this most dreadful of days. She could not think ahead herself. Her senses were heightened to the details of existence around her: the silence of the town, underscored by the muted celebrating of its new masters; the dim and trembling light of the clay lamps in the kitchen and on the table of the main room; the coolness of the evening air and the modest glow of warmth from the brazier. Everything absorbed her, held her fast in the existing moment. There was no past, no future, there was just the present, and she found an unaccountable comfort in the thought.

The soft knock at the door came almost as a shock to her, pulling her back into the turbulence of human dealings. *Who on earth would want to see us now?* she thought, walking as quietly as she could to the doorway in order not to awaken her father. She crouched down to the keyhole. "Who's there?" she whispered through it.

"It's me. Ennodius," came the low-spoken reply.

"My father's sleeping now," she whispered again.

"Then come outside. I won't keep you long."

She unbolted the door and opened it slowly to soften its creaking. Ennodius stood before her in a plain tunic and cloak. She slipped through the door and left it open so that they remained in the light of the table lamp.

"How is he?" he asked.

"I'm hoping he'll be better in the morning."

Ennodius did not reply. He looked away from her for a few moments before speaking. "I'm sorry about that scene in the old girl's room."

"It doesn't matter."

"I wanted you to know that there wasn't anything I could do. Albinus planned the whole thing very carefully. If I hadn't played along I'd have been sent packing with Syagrius."

"Why didn't you go with him?"

"Was there any point in doing that?"

Aemilia glanced downwards. "No."

There was another awkward silence.

"What will happen to you?" Aemilia asked.

"We're leaving tomorrow. Chlodovech told the old girl he wants her out. He's given her some land near Paris for services rendered—part of Syagrius's estate. But you know about that."

"Partly, yes."

"I'll stay with her until I can get in touch with the family. They'll have me back. I'll take it from there. Who knows, I might even become a bishop. My grand-uncle was offered a bishopric after he was deposed. No reason why I shouldn't keep up the tradition."

"I don't think you'd make a good bishop."

"You said the same about my being emperor."

Aemilia said nothing, then looked at Ennodius. "What happened at the battle? Why did we lose?"

Ennodius's face twisted for an instant. "Does it matter?"

"It might."

"Well then, it seems the old girl's brand of diplomacy had caught on. Syagrius had a perfect trap waiting for the Frankish cavalry. They were supposed to charge our heavy cavalry from the front and then be caught from behind by some more heavy cavalry that were hiding further off. When the Franks didn't charge home Syagrius sent a signal for the other lot to come out, but they wouldn't move. Syagrius went off to find them but they'd disappeared. You saw what happened next. He came back, beat the Frankish cavalry anyway and then charged the Frankish infantry that were fighting the legions—they were the only part of the line that was still standing by then. It didn't work. Too many Franks. He was lucky to get out of it alive—we both were. The horse archers and Illyricans got away. The rest..." he shook his head. "It was a slaughter. The legions were wiped out. I don't want to talk about it any more."

"Thank you for telling me."

"Don't mention it. What are you going to do now?"

"I don't know yet."

"You've got nothing lined up?"

"Nothing for certain."

"Then why not come with me?"

Aemilia stared at him.

"I don't mean right away. Wait until I've fixed things up with the family and then come. I'll get you a position. Something easy. I can arrange a post for your father as well. It'll get you both out of a pickle."

It was like a sudden gift on a golden platter. Aemilia was drawn to it, powerfully. She looked at Ennodius steadily. The dull opacity she had seen in his eyes at the Residence was gone. They were more like she remembered them on the battlefield: a faint spark glimmered in their depths, almost impossible to discern, but nonetheless there.

"Come with me." His voice was soft. Something in her stirred in response, a warmth that was unlike the affection she had felt for him until then. No, that was not true: she remembered the moment during the battle when she had looked one last time on him and thought she would lose him. She had felt a fear that went beyond simple concern. *I am beginning to love him.* Love him, be with him, marry him....

Then she looked away.

"Do you still think you'll marry Symmachus's daughter?"

"No, but I imagine I'll be obliged to marry whoever the family line up for me. Does it have to matter?"

Not fear this time but pain clamped round her heart like a leaden weight. She forced herself to answer, not through any conscious desire to act morally, but simply because she could not do otherwise.

"It does matter. I can't come."

"Are you sure about that?"

"I'm sure."

He looked at her, as if waiting for something more, then he sighed.

"It wouldn't be any use," she said. "If I came I would be doing wrong and I would be unhappy and so would you, in the end."

The familiar grin appeared. "Don't count on my unhappiness—I'm not at your moral altitude just yet. I had an idea you wouldn't accept, though I can guarantee I wouldn't treat you like your old lecher of a master."

Aemilia felt herself coloring. "What do you mean?"

"He has something of a reputation, and you didn't run away from him for nothing."

"How do you know that?"

The grin broadened as Ennodius pulled out a folded parchment from within his cloak. "He says so, just here. He describes you as a runaway serf and insists on having you back. Accuses you of a number of other crimes in the bargain. It isn't too hard to read between the lines."

"How...did you get hold of that?"

"Now there's the question. It just so happens—I won't go into any unnecessary details—that the old girl was able to lay her hands on a replica of the senator's seal years ago, which makes it possible for me to read correspondence from him, make a duplicate with any necessary modifications, and keep the original. Obviously why she got hold of it herself. She was given a very innocuous letter three weeks after you arrived. I must add that it took a lot of persuasion"—he rubbed thumb and forefinger together—"to get the messenger to give the original to me. He was under strict orders to deliver it to her personally."

Aemilia was silent. Ennodius held out the parchment to her. "Here, a parting gift, if you like. I don't imagine anyone's going to bother about it now, but you never know."

She took it uncertainly, and then suddenly gave him a brief hug. "Thank you," she said.

"I'd like you to think there's some good in me." It was meant to sound flippant, but she noticed his smile was gone. His eyes strayed down the passage. "Time I was going. I took a bit of a chance coming here. We're supposed to stay in the Residence until tomorrow first light. It's off bounds to Chlodovis's lot, but they're probably tearing the rest of the town apart. Goodbye, Aemilia. Do you have any money?"

"Very little."

"Here." He pulled out a leather bag and put it in her hand. "That'll keep you going for a while. Good luck."

"God go with you," she said.

He hesitated, then turned and made off down the passageway. In a moment he had descended the stairs and was out of sight. Long after he was gone she was still standing outside. Might have been, might have been, if so much had been different, she thought. All a might have been. She looked at the letter in her hand. It would have to be burnt in the brazier before Tarunculus awoke. Glancing one last time down passageway she went back inside, closing the door gently behind her.

CHAPTER 24

The looting of Soissons went on methodically over the next few days. The Franks confined their attention largely to the more valuable items of the public buildings and the private dwellings of the wealthier citizens, also casually helping themselves to some of the wares of the forum shops. The apprehension of the town dwellers gradually abated as it became clear that they were not going to be massacred. They emerged and took up the threads of daily life once more, repairing and reopening their shopping booths once the Franks were finished with them. Within a very short time, Aemilia observed, the people took little notice of the passing warriors, who carried their booty to the forum with all the nonchalance of servants moving house.

The skies overhead had broken up into scattered light cloud, with little likelihood of rain, enabling the items of plunder to be piled up out in the open. Silver and bronze statues, ornate vases, chests filled with clothing, pieces of elaborately carved furniture, curtains, ornamental and real weapons and armor, and a kaleidoscopic variety of other bric-à-brac soon filled a large area on the central plaza, surrounded by Frankish guards, who spent more time poking curiously through the growing haul than keeping a lookout for possible thieves. Now and then they sauntered across to the booths for refreshment which, on Chlodovech's orders, they paid for.

"Aye, paid he did," said the fruiterer to Aemilia, whilst loading provisions into her basket. "Had enough Latin to understand money. I gave him half price, to be sure. If they're being polite, I reckon we keep 'em that way."

"Did they take anything from your shop when they came?"

"Not much. Some fruit—mostly they took a few bites and left it lying around. I call that a waste. But they left the scales and that's a mercy."

"I heard Chlodovis say they'll be sharing what they've taken among themselves tomorrow."

"That so? You can understand them I've heard tell. He say anything else?"

"Just that they must treat us as their people and not touch our homes or the churches."

"Well that's a blessing. Reckon he's one barbarian with sense. But I've always said that if I had to be under any barbarian, I'd choose the Franks. No damn tax-collectors among *them*."

"There's no news of Syagrius?"

"Not a word. He didn't stay around to face the music. Probably made for the coast and took a boat."

"Where would he go?"

The fruiterer made a wry face. "Anyone's guess. Britain perhaps. I hear Chlodovis sent some men after him. To Reims too. Reckon all the towns'll open their gates smartly now that the Great Lord's gone. Good riddance, I say."

Aemilia paid him from the money Ennodius had given her and returned to the apartment. She had not left it often since the arrival of the Franks. Tarunculus would not leave it at all. He rarely spoke, hardly seemed to acknowledge her presence and spent most of his time sitting in a wicker chair. She was finally able to coax him into eating a little broth. She kept the apartment clean and tidy, spending her spare time reading from his library after a request for permission elicited a nod. He manifested no gratitude or even awareness of her care, but it seemed that her company was something of a comfort to him. In any case she did not want to leave him alone for any lengthy period of time.

That evening she was sitting at the table perusing the *City of God* when Tarunculus suddenly spoke from his chair. "Get the *Reditu*."

It was Rutilius Namantianus's poem, extolling the greatness of Rome in her hour of darkness. Aemilia looked through the diamond-shaped pigeonholes. "Right hand side, top," Tarunculus indicated. She found the manuscript and returned to the table, opening and turning it until she found the passage. "Read it," he ordered. She did so.

Give ear to me, Queen of the world which you rule,
O Rome, whose place is among the stars!
Give ear to me, mother of men, and mother of gods!
Through your temples we draw near to the very heaven.
You do we sing, yea and while the Fates give us life,
You we will sing.

For who can live and forget you?
It were better for me to forget the sun,

For your beneficent influence shines
Even as his light
To the limit of the habitable world.

Yea the sun himself, in his vast course,
Seems only to turn in your behalf.
He rises upon your domains;
And on your domains, it is again that he sets.

As far as from one pole to the other spreads the vital power of nature,
So far your virtue has penetrated over the earth.
For all the scattered nations you created one common country.

Those that struggle against you are constrained to bend to your yoke;
For you proffer to the conquered the partnership in your just laws;
You have made one city what was aforetime the wide world!

O Queen, the remotest regions of the universe join in a hymn to your
glory!
For you to reign, is less than to have so deserved to reign;
The grandeur of your deeds surpasses even your mighty destinies.

She came to the end and fell silent. Tarunculus seemed unaware of her. His eyes were far away. His hand lay on the armrests of the chair, fingers moving restlessly. His lips moved, forming words, as if he was speaking to himself. And like flotsam rising from the sea of his own troubled thoughts, the odd word broke surface and became audible: "...place...among the stars...live and forget you...forget the sun...one pole to the other...one common country... "

Aemilia looked at him, then abruptly rolled the scroll up and returned it to its pigeonhole. She sat down again at her place, but read the book in front of her no longer.

The next morning Tarunculus ate breakfast with Aemilia and then took out writing materials once she had cleared the table. By the time she had finished the washing up he was busy with quill pen and parchment, showing no sign of his former lassitude. She judged it safe to leave him for a while.

"I'll be out for some time, father," she said, putting on her mantle, "I've a few things to do."

He glanced at her briefly. "You go on," he said, and resumed his writing.

The open space of the plaza was full of Franks. Aemilia guessed that most of Chlodovech's men were present for the dividing up of the booty. Round the edges a number of curious onlookers had gathered. Aemilia joined them.

Near her, under the shaded walkway running along the shopping booths, were two women with shawls, both middle-aged, one carrying a basket.

"How they be dividing it all up?" asked the one. "Reckon they'll start quarrelling?"

"Lord knows, Bertha," replied the other. "First sign of it and we're off."

"That's a fine piece of table right over there."

"I'm fancying that curtaining. See it?"

"No. Where?"

"By the chests. A big pile of it."

"Oh, aye. Lovely. Anyone can see why they didn't waste time rooting through *our* things. Truth to tell, it'd've been a mercy if they'd made off with the bed. I've told my man to fix the leg any number of times. You make hardly a move in it and over it goes. He's as lazy as sin, that's what he is."

"Well I always thank the good Lord for my Arbo. Bit of everything in him—carpenter, painter and whatnot. I can forgive him taking a jar more than he should on occasion. He don't get rough then, so it's no great trial."

"I'm only grateful mine doesn't touch the wine. *That* would be the final straw."

"He's in work?"

"Aye. He's got the sense not to loaf around *there*. I told him if he loses his job he's out the apartment. But when he gets home I can't do a thing with him. Reckons he's done his share at the potter's, he says. As if *I'd* spent the day sunning myself in the yard. It's a mercy the younger ones are still at home and can help with the chores. When they're gone what will I do then, I ask you, eh? What then?"

Her friend clucked in sympathy and then began a discussion on the merits of her own progeny. Aemilia's attention wandered back to the space in front of her. The booty was spread out in a long line down the middle of the plaza, around which the Franks were scattered singly or in groups. She could make out no sign of Chlodovech. The men were obviously waiting for him to arrive before beginning the proceedings.

Time passed. Aemilia went up to the nearest Frank.

"*Môre, meneer.*"

"Mejuffrou."

"Kan U vir my sê wanneer kom Chlodovech?"

"Hy sal nou kom."

"Dankie."

She returned to her place. The two women glanced at her and then significantly at each other. The one with the lazy husband made a sign with her head to the other and they moved off. Further down the walkway they stopped and glanced back at her, then resumed their discussion.

Aemilia waited another half hour or so, and was on the verge of making up her mind to leave when Chlodovech arrived. This time he came on foot and climbed up the basilica stairs a short way before turning to face his men. He was in military attire as before, with an axe hitched on one side of his belt and a sword on the other. His voice was powerful, and carried clearly through the still morning air.

"My Franks, the time has come for us to divide the spoils of victory equally among ourselves as is the custom. But before we draw lots I ask one thing." He signed to one of his men below, who brought up and placed on a step below him a large, beautifully painted vase.

"I ask you not to refuse me this vase in addition to my due part."

There was a murmur of surprise from the Franks. Then one warrior spoke up. "Why do you want it?"

"It was taken from the church in Reims. I wish to give it back to Remigius, whom I look on as a friend. Will you grant this?"

There was more murmuring, then the warrior who had asked the question spoke again. "My king, you have conquered your enemies. It is only right that you take whatever you want." A few Franks nodded and murmured in agreement. Suddenly another warrior strode forward and mounted the steps. Raising his axe he brought it down on the vase, shattering it.

"You are no Roman lord," he said. "Take only what is given to you by fate."

There was a frozen silence. Then Chlodovech spoke. "So be it. Divide the spoils." The warrior grunted in satisfaction and descended the stairs. Aemilia, looking at Chlodovech's face, remembered the words of the guard she had met on her first visit to the Franks: "He is good, until you make him your enemy..."

The distribution of the booty went on in an orderly fashion. It was divided up into roughly equal piles and then decided for by lot among the warriors at each pile. The system effectively prevented any bickering amongst the men, and in a short space of time every Frank was given his

217

portion. Soon the distribution turned to merrymaking as they gleefully examined and tried out their new acquisitions. One Frank put an ornate gladiatorial helmet on the wrong way round and began a game of blind man's bluff. Another draped curtaining around himself like a robe and commenced what was obviously an impersonation of a Roman senator. Wine was procured and soon many of the men were cheerfully drunk. The carnival atmosphere became a little rowdy and the townsfolk began discreetly slipping away, until Aemilia found herself alone among the Franks.

"Little Frank!"

Aemilia turned to the voice. It was the warrior, Merovec. "Good day, sir."

"What are you doing here?"

"I am just watching."

"But your mistress has left Soissons. Why are you not with her?"

"...I do not serve her any more."

"That is good. One should not serve a woman like that. You dance?"

"What?"

"You dance?"

"I know some dances, sir."

"Then come." He was slightly drunk and in high spirits. He turned, strode a few steps, and then looking back, signed her to follow. "Come."

She followed him through the warriors to the basilica steps. She glanced around but could see no one except Franks. Merovec found the group of warriors he sought and introduced her.

"This is the little Frank."

"*Ja?* The one who came out with the Roman lady?"

"Why you call her a Frank? Who ever heard of a Frank dressing up Roman?"

"Look at her eyes."

"What about her eyes?"

"They're gray. Look."

"Oh *ja.*"

"What is your name, little Frank?"

She was beginning to feel confused, as she always did when the center of attention in a group.

"...Aemilia."

"Amel-ja...that is a Roman name. Why did your mother give you such a name?"

"My father gave it to me, sir."

"Her father is a Roman from Rome," Merovec interjected.

"They were married," Aemilia added.

"There is no good in it," said the warrior who had questioned Aemilia. "Franks should marry Franks. It brings our blood down, marrying Romans!" And he spat on the ground.

"Radagad is right," agreed another warrior. "We should have the same law as the Visigoths. The Romans are a soft people. We should not mix with them."

"They can still fight, Lotar," said Merovec.

The other warrior pursed his lips and gave a nod in half-agreement. "They were not too bad," he admitted.

"The Alamans fight better," said the Frank called Radagad.

"They would have run sooner," interjected another warrior.

"No, they would stay longer."

"I say they're cowards. They would run sooner."

"It is no matter," Merovec interrupted, taking a goblet of wine and holding it up. "We fight the best."

The others took the cue and, refilled their cups from a flagon standing by, added its potency to the virile pride of their Frankish blood. Aemilia kept silent. Merovec had some sort of seniority in the group, but there was no telling how long before the wine dissolved that away. She was no longer at ease with them. Her mind was busy looking for a pretext to escape as soon as possible.

"Come dance for us, little Frank," said Merovec.

Aemilia colored up, eyes downwards. "Perhaps not, sir," she murmured.

"*Ja*, you must dance!" he insisted. "Wait." He turned away. "Chilperic! Come!"

A warrior, somewhere in middle age, approached the group.

"Get your flute. She is going to dance for us."

The warrior pulled a reed flute from a bag slung by his left side. "Here. What dance?"

"What dance can you dance?"

Aemilia glanced around her. Still only Franks in sight. "One dance, sir, then I must go." Merovec nodded, smiling. She turned to the older Frank. "Play any tune."

The warrior-minstrel placed the reed flute along his lips and began a lively melody, simple and with an obvious rhythm. After a few moments Aemilia was able to match it to a similar country tune she knew. Then she began to dance, a jig that she had done many times before around an evening campfire at the villa when the servants and slaves had gathered to celebrate one of the more major feast days. The warriors cleared a space for her and watched in silence. She was not an especially accomplished dancer, but the natural grace of her youth and the liveliness of her routine were quite enough to enthrall her audience, already disposed by the wine to being appreciative. She sensed it and gained in confidence, losing her feeling of unease. She was able to predict the end of the tune and conclude her dance accordingly, smiling as she did so.

"*Welgedaan mejuffrou!*"

"She is good."

"Do another!"

"One more, little Frank."

Aemilia acquiesced, and began a second jig. It was when she had become comfortable with what she was doing and could glance around her, that she became aware of a stocky figure in a tunic among the columns at the side of the forum. She had just a glance, before the intervening warriors blocked him from view, but it was enough to fill her with a sick apprehension. She finished the dance and made for a gap in the circle of warriors.

"No, you must stay," said Merovec.

"I have to go. I am late. Please."

He gave a shrug. "Go well then. Come back tonight. You shall dance for Chlodovech."

"I will see, sir."

The warriors stood back for her and she hurried through to the forum colonnade, but there was no sign of anyone other than a few Franks. She wondered if she had imagined it. It might just have been a Frank, she thought. I hardly had a glimpse. I'll know when I get back. She glanced around one more time at the festive army of Chlodovech and then made on reluctantly for Tarunculus's apartment.

CHAPTER 25

A human life is not a story, with a beginning, middle and end, but rather a constantly evolving progression of deeds and consequences, abruptly terminated by death. For Aemilia, the consequences of dancing for the Franks did not become immediately manifest. They waited, evil shadows in the wings, biding their time. What came home to her without delay, however, on the day Chlodovech's army divided up the spoils of their victory, was the reality of her predicament. She was cut loose, adrift in a world that was already poor and had just been struck by defeat in war. She could rely on no one for her sustenance.

Least of all her father.

He had not been in the apartment when she returned and she had passed an hour in fearful surmise until he finally came in. He gave no indication that he had seen her in the forum and she finally concluded that it was not him she had glimpsed. He did not ask where she had been; his mind was full of other matters. His slaves had disappeared, taking everything from his workshop, even the anvil.

"How do you know it was the slaves?" she asked.

"Nestor left this. *I* taught him to write, the bastard." Tarunculus shoved a scrap of parchment at Aemilia. On it was scrawled in crude letters: *Primus died quick. You die slow.*

He could not replace the stolen tools. His shop had made a great deal of equipment for the army on credit, with promises of payment after the battle. It was with those promises that he had procured the iron, wood and coal he needed. He was now heavily in debt, with no means of repayment.

After his fury had subsided Tarunculus sank back into the morose listlessness from which he had only just emerged. Aemilia tried talking to him but to little effect. Even if he could somehow lay his hands on the tools he needed he could never be an armorer again, and there were blacksmiths enough in Soissons. In any case he would be damned if he ever sank to shoeing horses. There was no other profession he could undertake.

"Won't you get anything for having been in the army?"

Tarunculus looked at her. "Don't be a fool, girl." And with a wave of his hand he ended the conversation.

The question, however, remained with Aemilia for the remainder of that day. It was whilst they were eating bread and fruit in silence during the evening meal that an idea occurred to her: go and see the Master of Scribes at the civil basilica and take up the job he had all but promised her, then give part of the money from it to her father as if it were a pension. The Master of Scribes, she was certain, would agree to play along. She turned it over in her mind that evening and resolved, in bed that night, to carry it out the next day.

The next morning she told her father she was visiting the church, though the excuse seemed hardly necessary since he showed no interest in where she went. When she left he had opened a scroll on the table, eyes gazing at it as if unable to see. She remembered the touch of sadness she had felt in the forum months ago, when the wind blew his words over the buildings to oblivion. It wrenched her heart now, watching him. I must help him, she thought. He can't carry on like this.

The main doors of the public basilica were wide open when she arrived, but the building itself was deserted. She walked down the central hall slowly, looking around her. There was no one in sight. Here and there an overturned stool interspersed with loose papers, seals, inkwells, lamps and other bric-à-brac attested to the thorough ransacking that the administrative center of Syagrius's realm had been subjected to. She passed through the side door and mounted the outside stairway up to the upper floor.

The higher level seemed as deserted as the ground floor until she perceived, in a corner of a booth, the Master of Scribes she had met a week earlier. He had chests opened and was rummaging through them, surrounded by heaps of scrolls and books and loose sheaves of paper.

"Sir?"

He spun around. "What? Don't startle me like that." He examined her cursorily. "What do you want?"

"You remember our last talk here, sir?"

There was a brief pause.

"Oh, yes. Back about the scribe's job?"

She nodded.

He raised himself from the floor and sat on a nearby stool, depositing a bundle of scrolls on the adjacent table.

"You've come at the wrong time. Nothing's settled yet. The Franks are moving off south today or tomorrow to make sure of the rest of the province."

"Isn't the war over?"

"No it's not. A fast horse came in yesterday. Paris won't open its gates. I'll wager a solidus it's that holy woman of theirs, Genevieva."

"Genevieva?"

"Yes. She must have persuaded them to hold out against the Franks— they would never have done it otherwise. And until Chlodovis takes the town he won't be making any decisions about the administration here."

"I remember her, sir. Wasn't she the one who did it before?"

"Yes, when Attila came. She told them to stay put. God would protect them. They got away with it then, thanks to Aetius, but they won't get away with it now. That woman is going to ruin us. It should have all been over after the battle: everyone ready to carry on with business as usual, the Franks happy to let things be—and now this comes along. Chlodovis won't like it, I'm telling you, he won't like it at all. Things could start getting very ugly."

"But why is she doing it?"

"How should I know? Probably because Chlodovis doesn't happen to be baptized. Puts him on the same level as the Huns, as far as *she's* concerned. God keep saints out of politics, that's all I have to say."

Aemilia was silent. Her knowledge of Genevieva was fragmentary and very much third hand, but she knew at least that saints of unimpeachable reputation like Germanus of Auxerre and Lupus of Troyes had been unstinting in their support of her. It was Germanus who had picked her out when he stopped at her home village, Nanterre, on his way to Britain to deal with the Pelagians and the Saxons. There were no convents in the area so he had encouraged her to live the life of a nun at home with her family. She had taken on the religious habit when she was sixteen with the blessing of the Bishop of Paris. After her parents had died she went to live with her godmother in that town, where her reputation grew steadily. Germanus had supported her against many who opposed her as a crank and a fraud until their opposition finally fell silent. And her prediction that Paris would survive Attila had been borne out. Paris was not the largest town in Gaul but it was large enough to constitute a prize worth taking: the Huns had been heading for it like an arrow to its target when Aetius, in the nick of time, deflected them from their goal.

"When I can see you again?" she asked.

The Master of Scribes threw his hands up. "Again, how should I know? It depends on how long Paris holds out and what kind of mood Chlodovis is in once he's taken it. All I can do is try to keep some sort of order until he comes back, in the hopes that he'll want to use my head and not cut it off." He paused, taking stock of her. "Nothing I can do for you until then."

She kept her face from expressing the leaden contraction in her stomach. "Thank you sir," she said, and left.

On the way from the basilica to the church she pondered what she had learned. If Genevieva was the saint that many held her to be, then she was right in getting Paris to resist Chlodovech. And if she was right then it would not fall to the Franks, just as it had not fallen to the Huns. She had passed through the town on her journey to Soissons. It was built on an island in the Seine, one of the major rivers of Gaul. It would be easy to defend, she thought, although she did not know how they would manage for food, unless they used boats to get it from somewhere. How long could Paris hold out? Months? Years? Certainly long, long after Ennodius's money had run out.

She realized that she had counted on employment at the basilica as a certainty, something she had taken for granted would follow if the battle was lost. She had made no plans in the eventuality of it falling through. She had no idea what to do now.

Wandering into the nave of the church she sat down on a bench along the back wall. For a long time she remained motionless, her gaze in front of her, until finally, making an effort, she wrenched her mind from the paralysis that had closed in on it. *Must start now,* she thought. Taking out the money pouch Ennodius had given her she emptied it on her lap and carefully counted the coins, replacing them in the pouch as she did so. Then she did some mental calculations. Used sparingly, the money would keep Tarunculus and her fed for three weeks, possibly a month—three weeks if she included other expenses, like oil for their lamps. By hook or by crook she would have to have employment by then.

Rising from the bench she made her way up the nave to the picture of the Madonna and Child. There were a few women there, lighting candles and making their orisons. After spending a few minutes in prayer herself she gently touched a woman on the shoulder. "Is the bishop here?"

"Not now. He's in Reims."

"Do you know when he gets back?"

"No idea, love. I heard tell that Bishop Remigius sent for him. He could be there a while."

She thanked the woman and arose, making her way slowly out the church. The sun shone down on the atrium, casting deep shadows under the architraves that rested on the tops of the pillars lining the central courtyard. Her eyes paused, taking in the contrast between the black shade and gleaming white of the sun-drenched capitals, and then settling on the movements of the pigeons that fluttered among them. Light and dark and movement and she could not linger here any longer but she did not know where to go: not to her sombre and bankrupted father; not to that harried Master of Scribes; not to Reims to ask the bishop for their livelihood, for she knew he could not provide that. She made her way through the entrance to the church atrium as if driven out by force, and stood in the great space of the forum, gazing around at the people who walked to and fro and took no notice of her at all.

She went across to the fruiterer she had visited many times before and, with great difficulty, asked if he had any work to give her. His former easy manner with her immediately became opaque and businesslike. No, he could not offer her anything. He had had an assistant once but could not afford one now. His sons helped but they were not paid for it. She understood the times they were living in. Yes, she understood.

She passed on to the next booth, one that sold pots and pans and other kitchen utensils. Its proprietor could not help her either, and told her not to waste his time. She went to the next booth, and the next, and the next. The manner of the replies from their proprietors to her request varied from cool and civil to short and impatient, but the content was always the same.

With less hope she tried the stalls in the central space of the forum and soon saw that hope extinguished. Leaving the forum she began working through the shops that lined the parallel streets. Their owners treated her query with a mixture of mistrust, irritation and surprise. She realized eventually that if they found themselves in need of an extra pair of hands they had their own means of getting it, and would not dream of taking on a stranger off the street, especially not a girl. One or two shop owners intimated that her services would come in handy, but not in the shop. She left their premises without another word.

It was well past midday when Aemilia stopped, exhausted, for a rest in a small square, taking a drink from a public fountain and then sitting on its edge. Her agitated mind danced amongst her options, settling on them and abandoning them one after the other. Could she approach any well-off family as a lady-in-waiting? She would have no chance without a reference. Even if Lady Julia's overbearing arrogance was known to the wealthy class of Soissons, they still would not take her without some recommendation, that she knew. And all they would have to do is write to Lady Julia or to Senator Avitus for her chances of employment, remote as they already were, to become non-existent. Working in a kitchen? That again, meant approaching a household of sizeable means without a reference. There might just be one in need of an assistant to the cook, but after a few moments' thought, she discarded the idea. Cooks trained their own assistants and never used girls. A stables somewhere? She would not know who to ask and in any case her post as stable hand at the Avitus villa had been a temporary and unusual one. She held out no hope of finding a similar position in Soissons. Become a copyist? Books were valuable and a good library was a prized possession, but the wealthy, who alone could afford books, would buy only those done in an immaculate calligraphy, and she knew her handwriting was not nearly good enough.

As her thoughts flitted through the possibilities, Aemilia became aware of a memory, a sense of déjà vu. She thought about it for a few moments, then it came to her: she and Lavilla examining and discarding one means of employment after another until eventually they had no ideas left. She smiled almost bitterly. Lavilla was better placed now than she.

The sun was still bright in the sky, beating on the courtyard with its hard, chiselled light. She knew none of the faces that passed her: they were expressionless, preoccupied with thoughts and affairs that had nothing to do with her. A sickening sense of being an alien crept into her chest, and with it a faint memory of her first day in this distracted and troubled town. The thought came unbidden: *Why am I here? What can I do for him now?* She waited, and mentally repeated the question, and waited again. In her mind there was only silence.

I must do something. But what? Go to Frankland? And what would she do when she got there? The few Franks she knew were going south to besiege Paris. Could she go north, amongst total strangers, with whom she shared only half their blood and none of their upbringing, and beg her bread? Her mind recoiled at the thought. Where else? Back to Avitus's villa?—no, impossible. Where to, then? She did not know.

The sun was low in the sky when, stiff from sitting on the hard stone of the fountain, she finally rose up wearily and made her way slowly back to her father's apartment.

CHAPTER 26

The news of Paris's resistance raised Tarunculus's spirits, as did the news that Syagrius had managed to escape to the Visigoths, who apparently were holding him in custody until they could decide what to do with him. Tarunculus was out frequently, sometimes for several hours at a time, though Aemilia had no idea what occupied him. It was nothing that brought in any money, at least, none she was aware of. She continued to purchase all the provisions they used.

The day after she saw the Master of Scribes, the Frankish army moved off south to Paris, leaving a detachment to garrison Soissons. Town life seemed to go on as usual, but as she walked down the streets in search of the cheapest groceries she could find, or followed up a recommendation to a shop "that might just need a pair of hands, lass, worth a try," Aemilia could sense tension in the glances thrown at any Franks who sauntered past. It was not something anyone spoke of directly, or even hinted at, but there it hung in the air: an uncertainty, a fear of the barbarians' unpredictability in time of war. The inhabitants of Soissons could trust the Franks only if the latter were absolute masters, faced with no real or potential opposition. Paris's resistance, just two days' march away, cast a shadow over Soissons' submission. The townsmen feared what the Franks might do if the war dragged on. Feared and resented.

It was this feeling of general unease, Aemilia conjectured, that had something to do with the sense of isolation she felt since Soissons had fallen. Largely though, she put it down to the fact that all the people she had had bonds of friendship with were gone. Vipsania and Sylvia had moved south with Lady Julia. Pollux according to rumor had left for Spain. No one knew where Galbus had gone. Most of the other slaves and servants of the Residence had scattered to the four winds, leaving the building itself virtually abandoned since the Frankish detachment guarding Soissons preferred the more spacious quarters of the barracks.

A few days later she had an idea. There was a small kitchen with a hearth in the insula, where food was prepared for the slaves who worked there. Aemilia approached the slave who did the cooking, the youngish woman she had seen hanging up washing on her first day in Soissons, who agreed to let her bake her own bread in it if she supplied the flour. She was about to leave for the bakery opposite the forum when Tarunculus stopped her.

"Where are you going, girl?"

"To buy some flour, father. I can bake our bread here and save us some money."

"How much money do you have?"

She opened her pouch, sifted through the coins, and told him.

"Well then, take what you need for the flour and give the rest to me. I've a debt to pay that won't wait."

She hesitated. "This is all we have for food, father. Couldn't you sell a book?"

Tarunculus's face was black. "It took me a lifetime to gather those books. Don't *ever* mention selling 'em again. Now give me the money and leave me to worry about food, d'you hear?"

Aemilia extracted several coins from her pouch and held it out to Tarunculus, who took it with a grunt. As she made for the door he said, his tone somewhat mollified, "Ease your mind, girl, I've got plans for the future. Everything will come right, you'll see."

She made her way down the street with her head lowered and her mantle pulled well forward so that none would see the wetness in her eyes.

She remembered the way to the bakery without difficulty and entered the courtyard. A grain cart, similar to the one she had travelled on, stood by the barn, but there was no sign of the driver nor of anyone else. She waited a few minutes under the arcade along the back wall of the mill room and then finally knocked on the battered door of the slaves' kitchen. A few moments passed. Finally the door opened. A sour, wrinkled face examined her suspiciously from behind it. Aemilia recognized the old slave cook.

"What d'you want?"

"Is the master here?"

"What d'you want him for?"

"I'm here on business."

The old woman looked her up and down. "Wait here." And the door closed with a thump.

Aemilia gazed over the deserted courtyard for several minutes until the door opened again. The old woman beckoned her in. "He'll spare you a minute."

She followed the cook into the kitchen and through another door down a passage until finally they came to an open door on the right. The old woman knocked.

"Enter."

Aemilia followed her into a small room with a table, covered with parchments, evidently the master's office. Rictiovarus (with an effort of memory she recalled his name) glanced at her. He was a balding man, stocky, with small eyes narrowed in a look of sharp cunning. She noticed a telltale slit in his left ear and realized, with a start, that he was an emancipated slave.

"What can I do for you, miss?"

"I've come to buy some flour."

"Stocks are a little low at present. How much are you wanting?"

"How much are you selling for?"

"Until I get some more flour in I've had to raise the prices. Three siliquas a bag."

She blanched. "I wasn't expecting that much."

"Nothing I can do, miss."

"Very well, then I'll buy a quarter of a bag."

"I don't sell less than a bag. It's not my policy to deal with private individuals, just breadsellers and establishments that bake their own bread." And he returned his attention to the parchment in front of him, the conversation for him at an end.

The old woman jerked her head toward the door. Aemilia glanced at her, and then set her feet more firmly on the ground. "Sir, I must buy flour. This is the last money I have. Please."

He looked up, and then leaned his elbow on the table and his chin on his hand, as if considering. "You're on your own?"

"I have a father, but he has no work."

"You neither?"

"No, sir. But I've worked in a stable and kitchen before." Some instinct prompted her not to mention lady-in-waiting.

He turned his attention to the old woman. "How is Olybrius?"

"He'll be dead in the morning, sure as I'm standing here, Master."

He raised a finger in Aemilia's direction. "How about her?"

"I'll have to try her out, Master."

"Do it, and let me know tomorrow." He returned to his papers, the dismissal now clearly final.

Back in the kitchen Aemilia turned to the old woman. "Was Olybrius the old man without any teeth?"

The old woman looked at her with a hint of surprise. "How d'you know that?"

"I was here before. I came on the grain cart from Reims."

The old woman shook her head. "People coming through here all the time. I can't be bothered remembering who they all are. Now here." She pointed at a large iron pot on the hearth. "Scour and wash that first. Afterwards you can prepare the vegetables. We'll see if you've worked in a kitchen or not, that we will."

Aemilia set to the task with a will, and after it was done, passed on to stripping and washing the vegetables. The old cook did not show any interest in her handiwork, but put her on to the next task, and the next, and the next. The sun was low in the sky when, stiff and weary, Aemilia spoke to her. "I must go. I didn't expect to be out so long."

"You can stay another hour and clean the floor, that is, if you want the job. Nobody picks and chooses their hours *here*."

It was nearly dark when Aemilia finally made her way back to the apartment. The door was locked and Tarunculus out when she reached it, and she had to wait nearly two hours before he finally returned.

"Where've you been?" he said, with a touch of irritation as he unlocked the door. She told him what had happened. "Aye, that's good," he said after she was done. "How much will you be earning?"

"I don't know yet, father."

"I don't expect it'll be much, but better than you being a dead weight round my neck."

There was a pile of parchments and writing materials on the table. Tarunculus sat at one of the wickerwork chairs and considered Aemilia. "You won't be staying there, will you?" he asked.

"They didn't mention me staying, father."

"Good. Then you can help me with this in the evenings."

Aemilia sat down wearily on the other wicker chair, and glanced at the one of the sheets on the table. She recognized the text on it immediately: it was one of Tarunculus's exhortations.

"We need to make as many copies of these as we can and pass them around to the right people." He leaned forward, voice lowered. "I've been seeing some army friends. Good men. They're not happy about the Franks. Syagrius will be getting help from the Visigoths, that's sure as sure. The last thing they want is Chlodovis becoming a big power in Gaul. They think they can have it all for themselves. It won't take much for them to step in. Paris is holding out. All it needs is an insurrection here so that the Franks have their hands full, and the Visigoths will be in like a bolt. They'll put Syagrius back in place to keep the Franks in line, and then..." he grinned, "...we can start all over again."

Aemilia felt a touch of fear. "Isn't that dangerous?"

He patted her hand. "Not if it's done right. We wait until an alliance between Syagrius and the Visigoths is public, *then* we rise. Meantime," he pointed at the parchments, "we've got to get the people ready. It'll mean work. A lot of work. We'll have to give it all we've got. Think you can manage, girl?"

Aemilia looked at her father. His eye was bright and in his face a vigor that was almost youthful. His mind, his resolution, the very heart of the man, had risen from the near death of defeat and resurrected its will to live. She could not find it in herself to refuse him. She nodded.

He clapped his hands on her shoulders and held her tight for a moment. "There's my girl! We'll have some supper first—no, sit yourself down. I'll be making it tonight. After that we'll start."

Supper was a brief affair. Afterwards lamps were placed on the table and the two got down to work. Tarunculus dictated a pamphlet to Aemilia after which they both made copies. They worked in silence with Tarunculus not stirring except to refill the lamps with oil. Time passed. There was no sound except the scratching of their quills. Aemilia found her eyes closing involuntarily. She stood up and paced around for a minute or two to wake herself up before returning to the table. She did not know how long Tarunculus intended to keep them at the task. Somehow she managed to keep awake and finish one parchment, and another, and another, as the hours dragged on and her hand grew stiff and sore from writing. It became a torment. She wanted to stop, to lay herself down, to sleep, forget. The words on the page leered at her, jostling about in a mind that no longer wanted anything to do with them—*Romans, countrymen hear me...our forefathers on the Capitol...that barbarian Hannibal...your duty...courage and guts...*

She turned her mind to the villa, the pine trees that lined the entrance avenue, but she could not remember them well. Her image of the villa itself was blurred: she could no longer picture it clearly. Nor could she recall the faces of its inhabitants. Senator Avitus was a vague malevolence, nothing more. Lady Avita, surely she could remember her? But the memory was indistinct, faint, eluding her attempts to fix and define it. Her own mother then? She tried to form a picture of her. It shifted out of focus, changing in detail as if it were a thing of the imagination. She could not remember her mother.

Eventually, after an age, Tarunculus grunted, placed his quill pen in the inkwell, and stretched his arms. "That's enough for one night. We'll carry on tomorrow."

Aemilia leaned back, her shoulders tense. She had done twelve copies, and calculated that they had been working for about four hours, possibly more. The old cook had told her to come at dawn the next day or lose her recommendation. In the few moments in bed before unconsciousness closed on her she murmured a prayer not to oversleep, briefly wondering if she had any desire to wake up at all.

CHAPTER 27

From that day on, Aemilia's mind was taken up with the struggle to keep up with the relentless demands made on her by the bakery, where she worked from before dawn to early afternoon, and by her father, who made her copy out pamphlets for the rest of the day until late into the night. She was young, with an optimistic temperament sustained by a bedrock of faith, and she did not fall prey to depression, though sucked into a poverty-driven cycle of exhausting labor that was doomed to be as endless as it was unremitting. The past receded from her memory and she did not allow herself to think of the future. Living only in the present moment allowed her to keep her equilibrium, and she did not indulge in any self-pity.

Fatigue, however, and the lack of empathy from those around her, gradually took its toll. The only interest the slave cook showed in Aemilia's work was when she made a mistake. Once, carrying a pot full of meal to the hearth, she stumbled, spilling a quantity of it on the floor. The old woman rounded on her at once. "Mind what you do! Think that meal's dirt?" On another occasion she picked up a wooden spoon that Aemilia had just washed. "Call that clean? Who ever taught you to wash, eh? Slatternly wench."

Aemilia was tired, her temper on edge. "I'm not a wench," she said.

"Not a wench! Listen to her talk. Just ready to dance for the first filthy barbarian that comes your way."

Aemilia looked at her. "What do you mean?"

"Just what I said. There's those who've got eyes and seen what they've seen. I call it shameful, doing a jig for those devils the moment they walk into the town. Didn't do you any good, eh, did it? No easy money from *them*, so now you come looking for it here. If I'd known at the time I'd never have recommended you. But now you'll earn your keep by hard work, that you will. Now wash this *properly*." And with that she threw the spoon at Aemilia, not turning to leave until it was thoroughly washed and

233

held out to her for inspection.

The realization that her time with the Franks in the forum was becoming common knowledge sat on Aemilia's heart like a cold stone. As she finished up the washing, she pondered over what she had learnt. She was sure her father did not know it yet, but how much time would pass before he did? What would he do then? A constricting uncertainty wrapped around her mind, imperceptibly adding to the deadening effect penury and labor were already having on her.

The master of the bakery agreed to Aemilia's request to be left free on Sunday. Possibly he found it more thrifty to pay her twenty-four stale loaves a week rather than twenty-eight. For Tarunculus it was incomprehensible that Aemilia should not spend all of that day copying out his pamphlets, and it was only with the greatest difficulty that she persuaded him to leave her free of the task until after midday. The whole bent of his mind was fixed on the insurrection he was planning. She sometimes thought he was obsessed by it. He spoke to her of little else and seemed, not unconcerned, but simply insensible to her predicament. He ate the bread or the frugal fare she was able to exchange it for without complaint or comment.

Several times a week the friends with whom he was making his great plans visited the apartment after sundown. One of them, a middle-aged portly ex-biarchus, seemed to be of the same stamp as Tarunculus, but the others struck her as being hangers on. They would nod in agreement when Tarunculus spoke, and ask him for a loan. To accommodate them, and pay off his creditors, he sold his shop. After that money was gone the number of his visitors declined. Aemilia wondered how many would side with Tarunculus when the time for the insurrection finally came.

When the visitors arrived Aemilia served them any available food and then sat quietly in a corner whilst they conversed. Much of their talk was anecdotal, each rivalling the others with his account of his military exploits in the good old days. Much of the talk was political: the use or uselessness of the various barbarian kings was analyzed. They spoke of the proclivities, friendships, mistrusts and inclinations of all the chief personages in Gaul with pontifical assurance, yet rarely, Aemilia noted, with agreement. Sometimes they discussed plans. Aemilia's presence did not inhibit them in the least, and they went over dates, places, those they could trust and those they could not, without reserve. No one paid the slightest attention to her except the fat biarchus who, on occasion, noticed her fatigue and urged her father to send her to bed. "The girl's falling off her stool, Tarunculus. Let her go lay her head down." She was grateful for those occasions, for Tarunculus usually made her do an hour or two's copying after his fellow conspirators had left.

When Sunday arrived she permitted herself to sleep in until an hour after dawn, then rose, dressed and went to the first of the two morning Masses celebrated in the church. She sat on one of the benches at the back of the nave, too weary to stand for long. The bishop had returned, but she felt disinclined to speak to him. There was nothing he could do for her, and she felt that telling him of her troubles would only uselessly importune him.

From the church she went over to the seedy insula outside the walls where Lavilla lived. Aemilia could no longer give her material help, but she felt she must at least not leave her on her own. In her former visits there had been friendliness without any real friendship between the two girls. Now, however, made equal by the same adversity, a comradeship of sorts grew up between them.

Lavilla's position had not changed since Aemilia had first met her, except that her Landlord, possibly motivated by the fact that the girl was honest and applied herself to her work, gave her two meals a day for her labor instead of one. She was genuinely happy to see Aemilia, and spent the latter half of the morning in talk that consisted chiefly of gossip. There was little depth to her personality and her character was somewhat colorless, but for Aemilia it was a relief to have the company of someone she could be at ease with, although she felt that living with the girl might prove something of a trial. As it was, she spoke to her far more unguardedly than she might have done had they dwelt under the same roof. But she kept the details of Tarunculus's plotting to herself.

Autumn gave way to winter and the year was near its end when the first snows fell. The winter was not a particularly hard one, but Aemilia felt the cold more than she had ever done in the past. She would wake up in the middle of the night, shivering, and gather her blanket around her, drawing her knees up to her chest in an attempt to create enough warmth to sleep again. Tarunculus did not have another covering to give her. They had no money and Aemilia could afford to exchange the bread she earned only for a little lamp oil to see by in the dark. Tarunculus never mentioned selling off any of his possessions and she did not dream of suggesting it again.

The nights of broken sleep left her mind in a wretched state by morning. It was almost more than she could do to force herself to get out of bed, wash herself, dress and eat a little bread before stumbling through the freezing snow to the bakery. She came to dread the bitter old cook, whose aversion for her seemed to grow as the weeks passed. Most of the other slaves shunned her. She did not blame them. The interminable siege of Paris, right in the middle of the province, combined with the uncertain attitude of the Visigoths, had sickened trade. Goods of every kind had become as dear as they were scarce, and the resultant hardship bred resentment like maggots. No one dared show a hint of it to the Franks who guarded the town, not with the main Frankish army two days' march away, but against it Aemilia herself had no defense.

"Frankish wench." She heard it often, from a passing slave shoving her aside in a passageway, from slaves shouting at her to get out the way as they loaded sacks in the barn, at the midday meal in the kitchen, when she tried vainly to sit quietly enough not to be noticed, and above all from the old embittered cook, often accompanied by a blow with a ladle. It took Aemilia a long time to discover her name—Cornelia—but she never used it when speaking to her. The cook being a slave and Aemilia a free woman, she could not use a title of respect when addressing her, and there was no other term available. It reinforced the barrier between them and the sense of alienation Aemilia felt between herself and the rest of the bakery staff, whose relations with the cook and each other were of rough and easy familiarity.

All of her efforts to bridge the gap of prejudice failed—there was too much ill-feeling. Rictiovarus had cut his slaves' rations. He was not a good master but in this instance they did not blame him: everyone knew his situation was precarious. It was the fault of the bloody barbarians, marching in like locusts, taking what they fancied, ruining the land. And here was one of them right among them. The Franks had had no time for her, and now she had come here with her tail between her legs. She would be kept in her place and taught a lesson, and go on being taught it, that she would.

Christmas day fell on a Thursday that year. The decree of Constantine forbidding work on that day was still respected, at least for non-slaves. The church was full and Aemilia could barely find a place to stand just inside the main entrance. The bishop celebrated the Mass and preached a sermon full of the joy of the coming of Christ into the world, the shepherds gathered in wonder around the crib in which the God-man lay, the triumphant singing of the angels at his Advent, the peace in the hearts of Mary and Joseph. As the sermon drew to its close Aemilia suddenly became aware of a tear trickling down her cheek. She dabbed it away with the corner of her mantle. It was followed by another, and another. Her throat constricted and became painfully tight. Her chest longed to heave the abrupt tide of anguish that rose within her. She turned, pushed her way through the people behind her and went out to the entrance to the deserted forum. There she stood, retched with sob after painful sob. A long time passed before she was able to compose herself, dry her eyes and face, and return through the atrium back to the arched doorway of the church.

After the Mass was over, she stood outside in the atrium and gazed around her. Its architecture was beautifully designed: gracefully fluted columns topped by finely-wrought Corinthian capitals bore up as lightly as a summer breeze the architrave that ran right round the central courtyard. She walked under one of the pillars and leaned against it. Here was a place between places, where no business was conducted, neither temporal nor spiritual—a sort of a limbo where, as long as she remained, nothing was expected of her, where no one stayed long enough to trouble her. She leaned against the pillar and gazed, her eyes above the heads of the departing churchgoers, at the sweep of ornate stone gathered around her, making of a moment an eternity in which her deepest desire was to be let alone and never to have to leave. She was unaware of time passing.

"Waiting for someone?"

It was the bishop. Besides one or two figures near the church doors, the atrium was deserted. A few moments passed before she was able to summon the effort to answer.

"No, My Lord. I'm just going."

He drew near to her and looked up at her face, his round, fat form shorter than hers.

"You're thinner than I last remember."

"Yes My Lord. It's been difficult—for everyone."

"Mm. Perhaps more for you than for some. Come. You need to sit down and get something solid under your ribs." He turned. She hesitated, then followed him.

The presbytery was situated behind the church. It was a large building, designed to accommodate all the priests, deacons and other clerics and servants that were needed for the various occupations of the diocese. He took her to the small refectory where the women of the establishment dined, and spent a few moments talking to a middle-aged nun, thin and with something of the bearing of a highborn. "Come and see me afterwards," he told her just before quitting the room.

The nun was kind to her, speaking to her with a mixture of charity and discretion, and leaving her be when she perceived that Aemilia did not want to talk. The food was simple but sufficient: wheaten porridge and greased apples. Aemilia ate her fill and listened shyly to the talk around her. The conversation revolved around their work, interspersed with some playful ribbing. Not all the women at table were veiled. One or two, it seemed, lived outside the presbytery and took their meals in it, helping the nuns with their daily chores. They knew each other well and their banter was good-humored. Little by little the shell of reserve that had grown over Aemilia during the past few months dissolved away and she smiled at the repartee around her.

"Have some more porridge, lass," said a fat, cheerful woman sitting across from Aemilia. "Do you good."

"No thank you. I've had enough."

"Go on," she said, encouragingly.

"Leave her be, Claudia," said an elderly nun sitting next to her. "You want to make her as fat as you?"

No one asked her any questions about who she was or why she was there. When the meal was done she asked the tall, thin nun if she could help clear and wash up.

"Not at all. You are a guest," she answered with a smile.

"Where can I find the bishop, Sister?"

"Go and wait in the church. I'll tell him you're there."

Once in the church Aemilia knelt by the Madonna and Child. The twenty second psalm came to her mind and she mouthed it wordlessly: *The Lord is my Shepherd; how can I lack anything? He gives me a resting-place where there is green pasture, leads me out to the cool water's brink, refreshed and content. As in honor pledged, by sure paths he leads me; though the valley*

*about my path be dark, I fear no hurt while he is with me; your rod, your crook
are my comfort...*

She felt a gentle touch on her shoulder. "Come, girl. We'll have a talk
outside."

She followed the bishop out to the cool shade of a portico. He asked
her about her health, clucking again over her thinness and paleness, and
then enquired in a general way about her father, and various trivia, leaving
her to open up in her own time.

She felt no reticence and without beating around the bush she told
him about their poverty and her failure to secure a position at the basilica,
about her father's plans, her work at the bakery, the hostility of the slaves,
her copying at night, her weariness, the bouts of black depression that
came upon her, her uncontrollable weeping that morning. She told him
simply, without embellishment. In ten minutes she was done. The bishop
said nothing for a while, but looked at her, and in his eyes there was a
deep, searching compassion. Then he gazed over the atrium's square, hands
clasped behind him, and made several grunts, as if deep in thought. "Mm.
Mm. Mm." Finally he turned back to her.

"I can't do anything practical for you right now. We already have more
working here than we can afford and in any case there's a rule about the age
of the women we take in. However, I can give you some news. I wouldn't
normally reveal it to anyone, but you can keep your counsel and I think you
need to know. What I say doesn't go beyond here, understood?"

She nodded.

"The good bishop Remigius interposed between Chlodovis and
Genevieva, whom as everyone knows is the driving force behind Paris's
opposition to the Franks. It would appear that Chlodovis has a tremendous
admiration for her. He counted on starving the Parisians out, but she
managed to slip a convoy of barges past him, get supplies downriver and
bring them back. Apparently he rather respected her feat and treated it as
something of a joke against him. He hasn't been pressing the siege too hard
and in any case it is quite a business for him just to keep his men in the field
through the winter. I think he was ready for any arrangement that would
end the affair quickly and cleanly.

"They've been talking for the last two months and they've nearly
finished hammering out a code of laws. The details have still to be worked
out of course, but the salient point is that the Franks and Romans will be
equal citizens, sharing the same privileges and rights. It will be drawn up in
a decree, duly signed by Chlodovis. Once that's done, Genevieva will open
the gates of Paris."

Aemilia's eyes were wide. "This is—wonderful."

"Isn't it just? Expect it all to happen in the next few weeks. Once Paris has surrendered to the Franks, Chlodovis will return here. Which brings me to your situation. He is going to make Soissons his capital, which means that that Master of Scribes will need someone fluent in Frankish pretty soon. You should see him again."

"Yes...I will."

He grinned at her. "Think you can last until then?"

"Yes, I can, My Lord."

"Good girl. Come and have breakfast on Sunday."

She was about to take her leave when a thought occurred to her. "My father will take it very badly."

A strange, hard glint came into the bishop's eye. "He'd better take it well. He won't have any other choice. That reminds me—this is also confidential, mind—the Visigoths are handing Syagrius over."

"Handing him over?"

"Yes, as a prisoner to the Franks. It seems Chlodovis wanted him and wasn't taking no for an answer."

"What will he do to him?"

The bishop looked her with surprise. "What do you think he'll do? Syagrius will be executed."

CHAPTER 28

hen Aemilia returned to the apartment just after midday she found her father busy at the table with parchment and quill pen.

"Have you had lunch, father?" she asked.

"Aye, girl, I made some soup—it's in the pot. Help yourself."

She took a clay bowl, ladled in a portion from the pot on the brazier, and sat at the table opposite Tarunculus. She said a short grace to herself and began to eat in silence whilst he wrote on steadily. She was nearly finished when he put his quill pen back in the inkwell and leaned his chin on his hand, considering her. "All well at the church?" he asked.

The question surprised her. He had never asked her anything about her religion before. "Very well, father. The church was full."

"Aye." He relapsed into silence, eyes wandering over the parchment in front of him. After some moments he returned his attention to her. "You've been looking under the weather lately. Not ill, are you?"

"No."

"That's good, then." Another silence. "I don't want you to think I've been driving you too hard. All this"—he indicated the papers in front of him with a sweep of his hand—"is having its effect. People are listening, girl. They're listening. Even Aulus is coming round. It won't be long before we're ready. We just need the Visigoths to make their move and we'll have the Franks out of here quicker than you can blink. And when that's done I'll make up to you for all the work you've done for me."

Aemilia looked down at the table. Tarunculus stretched out his hand and put it lightly on hers. "You've been a good daughter, don't think I can't see that. I'll be a good father to you, you can be sure of it."

She said nothing. Tarunculus removed his hand and glanced away, as if not quite at his ease.

"Father," Aemilia asked after another pause, "what if...what if the Visigoths don't come. What will you do then?"

He did not answer her. She hesitated, and went on. "Is it that bad that we can't just carry on? Nothing's really changed. People can still work, and live as they did before. We can do the same."

"And what do you see me doing?"

"The highborns have guards."

"Spend the rest of my days chasing poachers and runaway slaves? Not bloody likely. I'm a soldier, not a gatekeeper."

"There's still the Eastern Empire. If we can find the money to get there..."

He pointed a finger at her. "Don't think I haven't thought of it. Twenty years ago, I'd've done it too, but I'm not fool enough to think they'll glance at an ex my age now. Not a chance in Hades, girl. Besides, I don't hold with the East—a bunch of soft Greeks playing at Roman, that's what they are. My loyalty's to Rome, not to a port on the Black Sea. I've spent my whole life fighting for Rome and I'm not about to change. This old dog isn't learning any new tricks." He leaned back in the chair with a smile. "In any case I won't be needing to go anywhere just yet. We'll get the Franks out of Soissons, you'll see, sure as I'm sitting here."

"Father," she leaned forward, a new kind of urgency in her voice, "the Visigoths may not come."

His eyes held hers a moment, then dropped. He moved a finger over the scored wooden surface of the table. "Then we'll just have to do without them."

"But..."

He held up a hand, silencing her.

She realized that any further talk on the subject would anger him. She picked up her spoon and bowl and took them to the kitchen to wash, and then returned to the table to help with the copying. She was about to commence with the first manuscript when Tarunculus interrupted her. "Not today."

She glanced at him in surprise.

"I'll tell you when I need you. You can be off for now."

He wanted to be alone. She put on her mantle and made for the door. "Shall I make supper later?" she asked.

"Aye."

Once outside Aemilia stopped under the archway of the insula entrance and wondered what to do with herself. She would have to be gone until the tenth hour, in about three hours' time. The ground was covered with a foot of snow, which made walking anywhere except on the cleared streets an unappealing prospect. She had already visited Lavilla that morning. The

church, without the press of people to give some warmth, would be as
cold as ice. With nothing else to do she decided to go and see the deserted
Residence. She had not been back to it since her last hurried entry to secure
her possessions before the arrival of the Franks, and the walk at least would
keep her warm.

The streets were quiet from the Forum to the Residence and Aemilia's
mind was tranquil, thinking on nothing in particular. On reaching the
Residence entrance she found the door shut. She tried it. It was bolted from
the inside. Somewhat nonplussed she debated for a few moments what
to do, finally deciding to try knocking, not able to imagine who would
answer. In the center of the thick wooden door, a bronze lion held an iron
ring in its mouth. She grasped the ring and brought it down hard, several
times. There was silence for a minute or two, then a muffled voice spoke
from the other side. "Who's there?"

"It's me, Aemilia."

The door opened slightly, the face of a young boy appearing in the gap.
Aemilia recognized him as one of Syagrius's stable hands. She racked her
memory for a few moments before the name came to her, Germanus...no,
Gerontius.

"What you doing here?" the boy asked.

"Just come to visit," she replied. "Are you the only one here?"

He shook his head, opening the door wide. "No. There's Pertinax and
Staterius. We have to look after the Residence until Chlodovis comes back.
That's what Chlodovis told Staterius."

"Is Staterius here?"

"Aye. In his office. You want to see him?"

"Yes. Are you managing all right?"

"Suppose so. But it's more work'n before. Lucky we haven't got horses
any more."

She followed him into the central atrium. They stopped at the door of
Staterius's office. It was closed. The slave boy knocked.

"Come in."

He pushed the door open. Inside, the old chamberlain sat at his desk, a
glowing brazier next to him. "Close that door," he said to the boy. "Aemilia.
This is a pleasant surprise."

"Good day, sir," Aemilia said.

"Gerontius, go and bring some wine. Aemilia, be seated." He indicated
a stool near the desk. She complied, feeling a trifle uncomfortable. "Now,
then," he said, once the boy had gone, "how are you?"

"Well, thank you," she said. "I really only came to see the Residence, sir. I didn't expect to find anyone still in it."

"No matter. A visitor makes a pleasant change. The two boys are competent enough at their chores, but they're not much company for an old man. You're still with your father, I take it?"

"Yes, sir. We stay in his apartment. I work at a bakery now."

"Not as lady-in-waiting I imagine."

"No. In the kitchens."

The chamberlain gave a sad shake of the head. "We must take whatever we can in these times."

"Are you still chamberlain here, sir?" Aemilia asked.

"It would seem so, in a manner of speaking, though everything has yet to be finally decided when Chlodovech returns." Aemilia noticed that he used the Frankish pronunciation of the name. "From what I can gather he intends to take up Residence here, at least for a time. He intimated that my abilities in organizing an establishment like this would come in useful. I may add," he said with a hint of a smile, "that it was a relief to hear it. It is difficult for someone my age to attempt any new profession."

"How did you find him?" Aemilia asked. She knew, like everyone else, that Chlodovech had stayed at the Residence during his few days in Soissons.

"Oh, quite agreeable," the old chamberlain answered. "Certainly he was in high spirits and drank more than perhaps was good for him, but that was to be expected. Broke a few items of crockery, but nothing worse than what I had seen before during a few more boisterous evenings here—and elsewhere. In any case, I was well treated."

"Are any of the others staying on?"

"That remains to be seen. There were only three of us here when Chlodovech instructed me to keep the Residence in order until his return. For the moment, you understand, I cannot take back any more without his approval. There have been a few who have returned to make enquiries. I have told them to wait until Chlodovech's return, when I shall be in a position to recommend them." Aemilia realized that he had implicitly included her in the group of those who had 'returned to make enquiries.' She smiled.

"I don't think, sir, that there is any post vacant for a lady-in-waiting."

Staterius raised his eyebrows in a wry expression. "It would seem not." He seemed to hesitate a moment. "Perhaps though, if all turns out as we hope it shall, I could put in a word for you as employable in some other capacity?"

"Thank you sir, but I don't think it will be necessary. I hope to get a position at the basilica once Par..." She stopped, flushing. The chamberlain looked at her curiously. "I mean," she said, "once everything has been settled."

"Indeed. We get very little news here. It would be a relief to know with certitude that...everything has been settled." She looked down, feeling her cheeks redden. The old chamberlain smiled. "If I may say it, you always struck me as a girl capable of discretion. That is something to be respected." He stood up. "Come, let us find that laggard and have a cup of wine before you go."

He opened the door for her. She passed through and then paused, looking back. "Sir, everything *is* settled, but I can't..."

"I quite understand," he said, holding up a hand. "We shall speak no more of it."

In the kitchen the chamberlain, the two slave boys and Aemilia gathered round the warm glow of the hearth, each holding a cupful of wine. At the boys' request Aemilia described her chores in the bakery kitchen, leaving out any mention of the bakery slaves' treatment of her.

"Sounds hard," said the one called Pertinax.

"No harder 'n what we're doing," countered Gerontius.

"Reckon it'll be easier, sir, when Chlodovis gets back?"

"I would imagine so," the chamberlain replied.

"Don't know what it'll be like having a Frank as a master," Gerontius went on. "Reckon he'll whip us each day?"

"I doubt it. I haven't heard that Franks treat their slaves any worse than Romans do."

"You mean," Aemilia interjected, "you're still slaves?"

Staterius looked at her. "Of course. Transfer of ownership took place the day the Franks arrived." Aemilia was silent. "Does that surprise you?"

"I don't know, sir...I didn't think that Franks had slaves."

"Oh yes. Not many, but some of their notables have a few in their households. They are no different in that respect from Romans, just a little less extensive in their practice of it."

Aemilia looked away. "I just thought that slavery would stop when they came." She glanced at Staterius. "Do they have serfs too?"

The chamberlain's look, again, was curious. "Not that I know of. That pertains to senatorial families who possess very large tracts of land. The Franks, I believe, have other arrangements."

Aemilia gazed at the glowing embers in the hearth. "Do you think they will become like Romans?"

There was a pause before the chamberlain replied. "Who can say? I rather feel that the truth of the matter lies in mutual admiration. Many who would call the Franks barbarians envy, even admire them. The Franks and other barbarians"—he paused—"for want of a better word, in their own way admire Romans. I see no evidence that they intend to do away with Roman institutions. Perhaps they will eventually imitate the Roman way of life, more or less. I cannot say I would regret it. A very preferable alternative to anarchy."

Aemilia looked again at Staterius. "Sir, are you happy to be a slave?"

The chamberlain drained his cup and examined it a moment. "Is a goat happy to be a goat, or a horse to be a horse? One accepts what one is born into. It is foolish to wish for anything better if nothing better is to be had. I have seen that kind of discontentment in free men as well as in slaves. It is to be avoided. A discontent succeeds only in making a tolerable, even agreeable, occupation, onerous to himself, and himself onerous to others. For myself, I have led a life that, if I may say, has not been without interest—one, I think, that many free men would be happy to exchange for theirs. I am content."

There was a silence. Staterius turned to Aemilia. "Before you go I would like to show you something. You two, about your chores. I will be along shortly to check on your progress."

He led her from the kitchen back to his office. Along its walls bookcases held piles of manuscripts, scrolls and rows of books. Staterius lifted aside a pile of papers and picked up several sheets from beneath them, placing the sheets on the table.

"Do you recognize this?"

She started involuntarily. It was the second, polished text of the speech she had written for Ennodius, with here and there a line crossed out and several words written above or on the side.

"I find it curious," the chamberlain continued. "I am well acquainted with the writing of Master Ennodius, and this script differs from his on several points, although the additions are in his hand. It is also unlike that of my Lord Syagrius." Aemilia said nothing. "I found it in a sealed chest in my Lord's bedroom. The chest had been broken open by the Franks. Any items of value had, of course, been removed."

"It is the coronation speech," Aemilia said, not knowing what other comment to make.

"Yes, and a fine piece of oratory, if I may say so. Here," he picked up the parchments and held them out to Aemilia. "A memento of your...very beneficial sojourn here."

Aemilia did not want the speech but neither did she wish to offend the old chamberlain. She took the parchments. "Thank you, sir."

Staterius took her to the entrance and opened the door for her. She went through it and turned to wish him goodbye.

"One last thing," he said. "I would not like you to take my words in the kitchen in the wrong spirit. I maintain that a man must be content with the lot that fate has ordained for him. However do not think that you are fated to be a kitchen maid to the end of your days, or, for that matter, a lady-in-waiting. I think you are capable of a good deal more, and in the times we live in, anything is possible. Do bear that in mind."

"I will, sir. Goodbye."

"Goodbye, or rather,"—his eye lightened with humor—"*totsiens*."

PART V:
SUNDERED

CHAPTER 29

The New Year came and went. One day, in the latter half of January, Aemilia was returning home from the bakery towards dusk, having been kept in by Rictiovarus to help the bakers with an extra order for bread. Though the sun had already set, there was enough light in the clear evening sky for her to see her way without difficulty. Her feet crunched on the coarse, crystalline snow as she walked along, her mantle wrapped tightly around her. It was very cold. Near the arched entrance to the Aurelian Flats she noticed the portly figure of the ex-biarchus, a regular visitor at Tarunculus's evening meetings, standing outside and slapping his arms against his body to keep warm. He caught sight of her and came over.

"When's he get back, d'you know?"

"No, I don't, but he shouldn't be too long."

The old man's eyes darted around, showing his agitation.

"Is something the matter?" Aemilia asked.

"You haven't heard the news?"

"What news?"

"They're bringing Syagrius back," he leaned forward conspiratorially, "as a prisoner."

Aemilia was silent a moment, and then involuntarily glanced around for a sign of Tarunculus. "When?"

"Don't know. He's already on the road they say, with a Frankish guard. He'll be here in a few days."

"But that means..."

"Aye. The Visigoths are out of it."

"What will you do?"

He did not answer, except to look more uneasy. He looked around one more time. "I've been waiting here for an hour. I must be off before I freeze. You'll tell him?" Aemilia nodded. He turned to go and then paused.

"Tell him too I had a tip-off from Aulus. Word of the meetings here's getting around. He'll have to go to the cemetery for the next one."

251

"To the cemetery. I'll tell him."

The old man made off down the street without turning back. Aemilia entered the insula and climbed the stairs to the passage outside their door, walking up and down it to keep warm. She wondered how she would break the news to him. It would be the extinction of any real hope he might have had. Perhaps he already knew, which was why he was late. She paced back and forth, hugging herself, her body tense with cold. Finally he arrived, his frosted breath hanging in the air as he panted after his climb up the stairs.

"Waited long?"

"Not too long, father."

"Aye then, we'll stoke up the fire and warm ourselves, eh?"

She waited until they were seated with bowls of soup at the table before nerving herself to speak.

"Polybius came by earlier."

"He did? The meeting's only in two days. He get the day wrong?"

"No, he had something to tell you." She stopped. "The next meeting must be in the cemetery."

Tarunculus paused in the action of lifting his spoon to his mouth.

"Why?"

"Syagrius is being brought back."

"Brought back?"

"...as a prisoner. The Visigoths have handed him over."

There was a long silence after that. Tarunculus put his spoon back in the bowl and placed both his hands on the table, as if steadying it. Looking at him, Aemilia was reminded of that afternoon on the walls, when they watched the tattered remnants of Syagrius's army stumble through the gates. He did not move, or say anything. She felt something within her give way with pity for him. A giant beaten to its knees by sledgehammer blows, resisting with all the might of its ironcast will as it is crushed inch by inch, baffled like a child in seeing its resistance overcome, and mute in the bewilderment of its suffering. She could not remain silent. She touched his hand.

"Father, it's over. There's nothing anyone can do any more. You've done your very best, no one's done more than you, but you must leave it now. You must leave it."

He looked at her, silent.

"We can carry on. I've heard that the Franks will treat the Romans well—Chlodovech said they must look on the Romans as their own people. We can keep up all that's good and fine and noble that we got from Rome. They don't mind. Staterius said that they admire Romans. He said they may

even one day live like Romans. He said..."

Tarunculus's fists crashed like mallets on the table. "NO. NO, NO, NO." His voice rang in her ears, shocking her to silence. "*Never*, d'you hear me, *never* will I accept it. *Never*. Bloody, brute barbarians...in *our* town, *our* Empire, that *we* built, *we* made great, *we* spilt our blood for. *I will never accept it*." His eyes on her bulged with fury.

"How can you understand it? You're half a bloody barbarian yourself. You'll serve the first ape in a wolfskin that comes in and calls himself king. It's all the same to you. But me, I am Roman," he raised his fist and crashed it down again on the table, "and I will *never* accept that those goatherds rule me. *Never*, d'you understand?"

Aemilia said nothing, trembling.

"And do not ever try to get me to lick their boots again. You are of *my* family and you will honor everything *they* stood and worked and died for. *Is that clear?*"

She nodded, eyes wide with fear.

"Now finish supper and get the writing things out. We have a lot of work to do. I told you we'll manage without the Visigoths if we have to, and by all the gods that's what we're going to do. We'll need to make more pamphlets and pass them around to as many good people as we can, people with some backbone in them. Once there's enough support we'll jump the garrison and take the town. Chlodovis is getting nowhere with Paris and he'll do no better here. We'll have him out by the spring."

After supper they worked in silence. Aemilia wrote, line after line, page after page, whilst the tightness across her chest gradually eased and the pounding in her head slowly faded. Her father did not speak or look at her. Her fingers and wrist became cramped, and she paused from time to time to stretch her hand in an attempt to loosen its stiffness. The hours passed and still neither of them said a word. The letters on the manuscript she was copying became a dance of black lines, living bars of a cage that agitated and slid and pressed on her mind, confining her ever closer in an airless space with no room to breathe, no room to move or turn or see beyond its suffocating limits. Her eyes became red as she struggled to focus on what she was doing, fearful of making an error. The parchment they used was expensive, and Aemilia was certain that Tarunculus had sold off more than one book in order to procure it. She could not afford to spoil a single sheet.

She became lightheaded. The tightness in her chest returned, as did the throbbing in her head. The movements of her arm became slow and heavy. Tarunculus gave no sign to indicate when they would stop. To start a new page, a new line, even a new letter, became an effort of will, a will deadened by not knowing when it would be freed from its toil, like a horse pulling a cart full of rocks along a road that has no end, with no respite except to collapse and breathe its dying gasps whilst its back was cut by a whip. Finally, she put the quill pen back into the inkwell.

"Father," she said, too tired to need to summon her courage. "May I go to bed now?"

He raised his eyes to her from the sheet in front of him. "Aye, girl. You've been at it long enough. Go rest."

As she stumbled to the kitchen Tarunculus put out his hand and stopped her. "Don't take too hard what I said earlier, eh? You're a good girl."

She murmured something and made for her bed, falling asleep almost as soon as her head touched the pillow.

Two days later Chlodovech arrived at Soissons with his prisoner, having left his army at Paris. A large crowd lined the street from the south gate to the forum. Aemilia stood by Tarunculus and watched the procession go by: Chlodovech on horseback, erect in the saddle, his face impassive; behind him, strung out in pairs rode his guard, and between two of them, occasionally stumbling in the effort to keep up, came Syagrius.

His hands were tied by a rope which was fastened to a saddle, pulling him along. He wore a poor man's tunic and was barefoot. As he passed close Aemilia had a few moments to study his face. He was pale and his features seemed shrunken, as if life had already left his body. His eyes gazed on the ground ahead of him, seeing nothing. His jaw sagged open and he breathed heavily. Aemilia wondered how long he had been obliged to walk. She looked at his feet. They were dark red, probably frostbitten. She glanced around at the bystanders. They were utterly silent. No one wept or cheered. No one moved. She guessed what was in the stillness: the shock of finally comprehending that the world that had been theirs for half a millennium was irrevocably gone, as if it had never been, a corpse limping obscenely by, to be buried with horror and quickly forgotten. Let the dead bury the dead. For the living there is but life. Syagrius was already a ghost.

She started, feeling a touch on her shoulder.

"Follow them and see where they take him, girl. You're quicker than I."

She nodded and pushed her way back through the press of bodies until she found a side alley. Continuing along it, she turned into a street that ran parallel to the one used by the column of Frankish horsemen, and walked along quickly in the same direction. She guessed that Chlodovech

255

was making for the barracks, the only building in Soissons with prison cells. If Syagrius was to be executed that would be the place to do it, in the courtyard before the assembled garrison and guard.

Or possibly he meant to make an example of his fallen enemy in the forum. Aemilia quickened her pace to a run. When she felt she had gone far enough, she turned back down another side alley and rejoined the street. Yes, the Franks were well behind her. She continued down the street toward the forum, her lungs cut by the sharp winter air, and reached it with several minutes to spare, leaning against an entrance pillar and painfully catching her breath.

After a time the Franks arrived, dragging along their stumbling captive. The gathering crowd left a passage for them and a large space in the center of the forum, but Chlodovech did not stop. Over the flagstones the horses stepped, a steady staccato of hoof-falls, accompanied by the labored breathing of the bound prisoner, eyes glazed with despair from clinging to a life that would soon, soon be ripped from him.

I have caused his death. She could not help it. The thought took hold of her mind, repeating itself with increasing force, filling her with a wave of nausea. *I have caused his death.* It had been with her from the moment Syagrius had divined her part in Lady Julia's betrayal, but she had refused to give it a moment's reflection. The bishop had counseled her to let the Lady's treason be, but he had not known that treason, unrevealed, would breed treason, that the knowledge that Chlodovech was prepared to bargain with traitors in Syagrius's camp would leap, like sparks from a brush fire, among Syagrius's commanders, and lead in the end to his ruin.

"*My Lord!*" The shout was hers. Syagrius turned his head in the direction it had come from. His eyes fell on her, recognizing her, and the corner of his mouth twisted slightly, showing, through the pain and despair, the trace of a sardonic grin. Then he was past, followed by the Frankish guard. The crowd closed behind the last of the horses and followed them to the barracks. Aemilia waited until they were far ahead before following after. She could not bear to let Syagrius see her again.

Outside the entrance to the barracks the crowd was thick. The iron-grill gates were closed. Aemilia stood some distance away under an arcade and waited. Time passed. Eventually the crowd began to disperse. Aemilia asked a passerby, a tall, powerfully built man with the look of a blacksmith, what had happened.

"Looked inside, lass, but didn't see anything."

"They haven't executed him?"

"Not in the parade ground at any rate."

Aemilia remained where she was until there were only a few bystanders outside the gates, before approaching the thick, iron bars of the grill. On the other side two warriors stood, keeping guard. She spoke to one of them in a low voice: "*Verskoon my.*"

He glanced at her in surprise. "*Ja, mejuffrou?*"

"*Wat doen hulle met Syagrius?*"

"*Niks vir nou nie.*"

"*Is hy nie dood nie?*"

"*Nee, maar hy het nie meer lank om te lewe nie,*" and he grinned.

Not dead yet. She felt a tiny rush of relief. She thanked the guard and turned, walking quickly at first to put distance between herself and the curious stares of the remaining loiterers. Then she slowed down, and made her way back to the apartment, her eyes on the patches of dirty snow, over which she stepped gingerly as if picking her way through a quagmire. She had nearly reached the forum when the idea came to her, at first dismissed as lunacy and then gradually growing into a conviction: she would have to do her utmost to save Syagrius's life, no matter how hopeless such a task might be. She would have to see Chlodovech.

CHAPTER 30

The old cemetery of Soissons was at least three hundred years old. It had been law throughout the Empire that the dead be buried outside municipal limits. As imperial authority weakened, the burial law and with it the old cemeteries gradually fell into desuetude, and newer burial plots sprang up in the spreading vacant areas of ground within the depopulated municipal limits. The traditional graveyards, more distant and inconvenient, crumbled into decay.

At Soissons the old cemetery was rarely used for burials, but was still tended by the burial guild, who assigned a caretaker from the more frequented cemetery nearer the town to go every now and again to clear away excess growth and raise up fallen tombstones. The office of caretaker had been held for the last thirty-five years by a certain Publilus Aptatus, an ex-*Limitaneus* who lost his post in the army when the segment of imperial frontier he guarded ceased to exist. Publilus was among the group of disgruntled ex-soldiers who met at Tarunculus's apartment, and he was the only man in Soissons who was familiar with the layout of the Christian catacombs that ran labyrinth-like beneath the tombstones, monuments and mausoleums of the cemetery grounds.

Aemilia, during one of the evening meetings at the apartment, had asked him about them.

"Aye, they're big enough," he had told her. "Story is they made 'em so that their graves wouldn't be dug up and desecrated. Also they'd meet there in times of trouble and have their Eucharist and all that, in secret. No good for hiding but easy to get away from if there was a raid."

"How's that?" Aemilia had asked

"Lot of ways out, some of 'em hard to find from the top. I reckon they made 'em that way."

"Are they full of tombs?"

"Oh, aye. They're in the walls, dug out like."

"Are there martyrs there?"

259

"A few. You can tell 'em from the palm branch they carved on the stones."

Tarunculus had overheard the exchange. "Damn good place to meet if we have to. Christians are good for something after all."

The idea had stuck, and now, with the warning from Polybius and the arrival of Chlodovech, Tarunculus sent word around that his quarters were no longer to be considered a safe meeting place. The next meeting, on the same day as Chlodovech's return, was to take place at the cemetery.

It was in the dead of night when Aemilia woke from a deep sleep, feeling a gentle shake of her shoulder. Tarunculus stood over her, holding a lamp. "Come, girl, rouse yourself. We must be going."

"Where to?" she murmured, half-asleep.

"The old cemetery."

Aemilia slowly tied on her sandals, her mind dull from the fog of sleep. Wrapping her mantle round her, she followed Tarunculus out the apartment along the passage and descended the stairway, stumbling once about halfway down. Tarunculus turned quickly.

"Step quietly now."

The bitter winter air cleared her mind. Publilus was waiting for them under the archway. Together they made their way to the west gate which they found open and unguarded: the Franks did not man the town walls and the gates were no longer closed at night. Passing quickly through it they made their way down the thick darkness of the deserted streets until they were beyond the last buildings and found themselves in open country, whose barely visible features were varying depths of blackness under the faint light of the cloud-obscured stars.

"This way," said Publilus.

"You're sure?"

"I'm sure."

Guided mainly by the sound of his footsteps crunching on the thin covering of snow, they followed him off the main western road down a narrower cart track, and then from there onto a footpath. As Aemilia's eyes gradually adjusted to the dark she was able to make out the shapes of the trees around her. They came to a mass of regularly shaped blackness. Aemilia raised her hand to it. It was a stone wall. Beside her near the ground there was a scraping of flint and then a tiny flicker of flame.

"We can risk a light here," said Publilus, raising a lamp up to the archway before him. In its glow Aemilia discerned a rectangular doorway, with an inscription carved in a stone plaque above it. In the poor light the writing was not clear, but she could make out a name: CVRATIA

CLODANILLA and a number: XX.

"Died young, she did," said Publilus, noticing her scrutiny. "Only twenty. Probably in childbirth. Husband spent a tidy pile making this mausoleum for her."

He took a large ring of keys from his belt and inserted one into the heavy iron-framed wooden door. Turning the key he pushed the door, which gave way with a drawn-out creak.

"Come."

They entered the mausoleum. Within its confined space Aemilia had a flickering view of a sarcophagus against the opposite wall, figures carved in relief on its marble sides. The roof and walls were covered with a pattern of reddish painted lines, breaking up the surface into geometric shapes within which were loose brushwork scenes. She had not the time to examine anything for Publilus gestured them towards another sarcophagus to the right. Whilst Aemilia held the lamp he and Tarunculus carefully lifted off the lid, placing it on the ground. They looked inside. At one end of the sarcophagus bottom a vertical stone shaft led to a floor of what looked like a tunnel perhaps six yards below. Iron rungs, evidently meant as a ladder, projected down one side of the shaft.

"Down there."

"Are the rungs firm?" asked Tarunculus.

"Aye."

Stepping in, Tarunculus sat down next to the aperture and dropped his legs into the opening, getting a purchase with his feet on the rungs before easing himself into the shaft. Slowly he descended to the bottom and then stood, looking up. "Right, I'm down."

The old ex-soldier turned to Aemilia. "You next, lass."

She climbed down as Tarunculus had done and then waited until Publilus joined them. "Not the easiest way in," he said with a grin, "but it's the one way out only I know about. The Christians must've built the shaft to get away from a raid in a hurry. This part of the tunnels was blocked off till I guessed it was here and opened it up. If we need to run we come back here."

Holding the lamp high, he went down the tunnel, followed by Tarunculus and Aemilia. The space between the tunnel sides was narrow, just wide enough to let through one man at a time. Two would have had to turn sideways to pass each other. Openings were carved into the gray stone of the walls, two feet in height and about the length of a body. They were all empty. Further on the openings were sealed shut with stone or marble slabs, covered with crudely scratched or more elaborately carved inscriptions.

Their guide reached a junction of four tunnels and took the rightmost one, and then a left tunnel after that. They reached a fork—the openings in the walls were empty once again—and took the left branch. A few moments further on Publilus motioned them to stop. In the silence they heard voices up ahead. He turned to them.

"No worry. It's the others."

The tunnel opened into a chamber about the size of a room. The walls, more finely shaped than the crude and irregular passages they had passed through, were filled with slab-covered niches, the same shape and size as the openings she had seen in the tunnels. At one end of the chamber stood a small, squat altar on which several lamps had been placed. Aemilia glanced upwards. The stone roof sloped up to a square aperture covered with a metal grate. Above it a shaft rather like the one she had climbed down led to the surface, a fact she deduced from the faint twinkle of a star.

There were about a dozen men in the chamber. Some she recognized from the group who had met at Tarunculus's apartment, but others were strangers to her except—she noted with surprise—the centurion who had ordered Tarunculus to open the gates to the Franks. Aulus. That was his name.

"Welcome friends," said Tarunculus.

Some murmured greetings back, but not, Aemilia noticed, with any great heartiness.

"All here?"

"There's a few missing," said a young, heavily-built man Aemilia did not recognize. "Polybius told me he's not having anything more to do with us. I don't know about the others."

"Damn cowards," said Tarunculus. "We'll do better without 'em."

"What's the news on Syagrius?" asked a lanky man, with slightly protuberant eyes.

"Alive still," said Tarunculus. "He's locked up in the last cell, lower level."

There was a murmur amongst the group.

"How do we get him out of there?"

"I've got a plan," said Tarunculus.

"How much longer before he's executed?"

"Stycoricus tells me one, maybe two days."

"How long has *he* been prison guard for?" This came from Aulus.

Tarunculus glanced at him in surprise. "Two months. Why?"

The centurion crossed his arms and regarded Tarunculus with a sceptical tilt of the head. "How did he get the job?"

"I told you. He can speak their lingo. He's an ex, by Hades. One of us."

"Sure of that?"

"Aye, I'm sure." Tarunculus's fists were clenched, his head jutted forward. "A damn sight more than *you* were when the Franks arrived. You couldn't wait to let 'em in."

"I didn't have a choice."

"Aye, you did. You could've told that traitor Albinus to go hang himself and helped hold the town against the Franks until they froze in the snow. They wouldn't've stayed for a siege and you know it."

"They've stayed outside Paris."

"That's because they think they've nearly won. If we'd all stood by Syagrius Chlodovis's men would've told him to call it a day and go home, sure as I'm standing here. You don't lose a war because of one battle. D'you think Scipio gave up because Hannibal beat Rome three times and his own father'd been killed? *He* didn't. He knocked the stuffing out of 'em in Spain and then we know what he did next. He went over..."

Aulus interrupted him. "What's your plan, anyhow?"

Tarunculus seemed to come to himself. "Aye, listen. Stycoricus's ready to help us out. He wants us to make a diversion at the barracks. Somewhere by the gates. While that's going on he'll let Syagrius out his cell and take him up onto the main walls. They'll both climb down with a rope ladder— he says he's already made one. We'll have two horses ready to get 'em off to Paris. He told me the Franks aren't keeping a close siege on the town. They'll get through easily. Once Syagrius's in Paris we can start organizing an insurrection here."

"Here?" said the lanky man. "With what?"

Tarunculus looked at him. "With men who've got backbones and who see that their Lord is back in command. Chlodovis'll be off to Paris the moment he hears Syagrius is in the town. How many men d'you think he'll leave here, eh? If we made up our minds, we could jump them, easily. D'you know how many ex-soldiers are still in town? Nearly a thousand! If he leaves a garrison of two, three hundred men, what's stopping us, eh? What's stopping us?"

A few of the men had their eyes and attention on Tarunculus, but most looked away, arms crossed or clasping their sides.

Aulus looked hard at him. "What kind of a diversion are you talking about?"

"We'll set fire to the barracks stables."

Several breaths were drawn sharply.

"What?"

"They'll kill us!"

"They'll burn the town down!"

"We can do it," said Tarunculus. "Torches soaked in oil and thrown at the stable roofs. They're straw-covered. We'll throw them from ladders against the barrack walls. The Franks'll come out smartly to save their horses. We can easily get away while they're busy with that."

Aulus shook his head. "It's insane."

"There's no other way," Tarunculus replied. "Stycoricus told me there's too many Franks hanging around upstairs. He's got to have 'em out the main building before he makes his move."

"Even if we do pull it off, what's to stop them massacring the town as a reprisal?" That came from a young man Aemilia did not recognize.

"They won't. Aemilia, tell 'em what you told me."

Aemilia was confused. "What?"

Tarunculus glanced at her. "You know. What Chlodovis said about treating the people here."

She gathered her wits. "He said...he said that these people are their people...and not to touch their homes."

"How'd you know that?" said another man she did not recognize.

"Lass speaks their lingo," interjected Publilus.

Several of the group looked at her curiously. "Well, what about it, then?" said Tarunculus. "I'm off to the barracks tomorrow night. Who's with me?"

Aulus stepped forward. "Now listen to me. I didn't come here to join any mad, half-baked scheme of yours. The game is up. Syagrius is a dead man, no matter what you do. And you'll be too if you go any further. I came to warn you. The word's getting to the Franks that there's a group. You start anything and we could all be in a lot of trouble. Give it up, you hear me?"

Tarunculus turned on him. "I should've cut your head off on the wall," he said through clenched teeth. "I should do it now, you bloody spy."

"If I was a spy you'd be dead already. I came to tell you, give it up before they get any more suspicious. I'm going now. Who's coming with me?"

Tarunculus looked Aulus in the eye. "Off to squeal to the Franks?"

Aulus looked back at him. "I don't rat on my men."

Tarunculus stepped up close to him, looking him up and down as if measuring him for a fight. "You're a coward and a traitor. Anyone who joins you is a coward and a traitor too. Whoever's a real Roman can show it now. The rest crawl back into your beds, or under 'em if you prefer."

There was a few moments' silence. "I'm in," said the lanky man with the protuberant eyes. Two or three other voices spoke up. "Me too...count me in." But most of the group kept quiet.

Tarunculus turned to the group. "Those coming with me, stay. We've got details to plan. Rest of you be on your way."

"I'd come along," said Publilus, "but I'm too old for those kind of games. Come to think of it," he continued, looking Tarunculus over, "so are you."

"Damn you, I'll manage," Tarunculus growled.

Slowly, in ones or twos, the men left through the chamber entrance through which Aemilia had entered. Ignoring them, Tarunculus gathered his volunteers around the lamplit altar and drew a parchment out from inside his tunic, on which Aemilia could make out some sort of a street plan. Aulus, about to exit, turned a moment to Tarunculus.

"If you're mad enough to do it, then watch your back. It's getting known at the barracks that you're a troublemaker." With that he left.

Aemilia stood by one of the vault-lined walls. Tarunculus, busy with his confabulation, paid her no attention. Publilus, after glancing at the parchment for a minute or two, took his lamp and sauntered over to where she stood.

"Come, lass. They'll be at it for a while."

"Where are we going?"

"To see some martyrs."

She followed him through the entrance she had entered the chamber by. The two went down the network of tunnels, turning right and left until Aemilia lost all sense of direction. Finally they reached a low entrance in the side of a tunnel wall.

"In you go."

Aemilia entered a chamber, smaller than the one she had come from, and looked around. They were in a tiny cube of a room, with a concave vaulted ceiling covered with the same geometric pattern of red lines interspersed with loosely-painted scenes she had seen in the mausoleum. The brushstrokes were large, as if applied in haste. She studied them. One depicted a youngish man carrying a sheep on his shoulders. Of course. The Good Shepherd. Another showed a bearded man standing before wavy bluish lines—a river or watercourse—with a dense crowd behind him. Moses crossing the Red Sea. And another, drawn with more care, showed a woman, shawl over head, arms outstretched in front of her. That puzzled her. The head was done with great skill. She was sure she was seeing the likeness of someone real, who had died long since and was buried here.

There were niches, one above the other, in the walls, all covered with pale gray marble slabs. She studied one. On it was carved the outline of a boy standing under a dove, with the superscription PANCRATIVS IN DOMINO. Pancratius in the Lord. And a little below it: VIXIT ANNOS XIIII. He lived to his fourteenth year.

"Here." Publilus beckoned her over. He was bending down beside a nich whose slab had a crack running almost across its length. "Someone gave this a good, hard knock. During a raid, I reckon."

Aemilia drew in a quick, deep breath. On the milky surface of the marble a palm branch was carved, and below it was scratched the outline of a woman, and the legend: FAVILLA IN DOMINO, followed by VIXIT ANNOS XXIII. She lived to be twenty-three.

"She was a martyr?"

"To be sure."

Below the inscription was carved in crude letters PETI PRO ME. Pray for me, misspelt. Someone who had come, decades, maybe centuries, before to ask the martyr for a favorable word with her Master in heaven.

"It's loose." Publilus pushed against the bottom half of the slab. It gave slightly. He shoved the piece of slab further in and then gripped the top half from underneath.

"No, don't."

He glanced at her. "If we don't someone else will."

With a heave he lifted the marble out and dropped it on the stone floor. He held the lamp up inside the cavity. A skeleton lay, covered with crumbling remnants of cloth, its former color corroded into a dark gray. Publilus searched the length of the space. There was nothing else.

"No jewellery, coins, nothing," he muttered. "Wait..."

On the bones of the left hand there was a ring. He gripped it with finger and thumb and was about to slide it off when Aemilia took hold of his arm.

"We can't take it. We must respect her."

The old man held his lamp close to the ring. "Look, girl, it's bronze. Not worth more than six folli, but one fine day a grave robber's going to find it and he won't be minding a pin about respect."

"Then let me have it."

He looked at her, and at the ring, hesitating. Then easing the ring off the finger he passed it to her. She took it and examined it. On top of the ring was engraved the labarum: the two letters X and P superimposed, the Christian symbol for the name of Christ. Fine, barely discernible letters ran round the ring band. She scrutinized them closely. CONIVGI CARISSIMI. To a most beloved wife. A gift from her husband. She held the ring, gazing at the faint inscription, for several moments, and then closed her fingers round it, hiding it from view. She turned to the old ex-soldier.

"Shouldn't we be getting back?"

"Sure, lass. They'll be done soon."

They returned to the main chamber to find Tarunculus and his knot of volunteers still gathered round the map on the altar. Aemilia waited to one side. A quarter of an hour passed, then the group broke up. Tarunculus beckoned Aemilia over.

"I want you to do something for me."

"Yes father?"

"I need you to get a message to Stycoricus at the barracks."

"A message?"

"Aye. He won't be off duty before tomorrow night and it's too risky for me to go there. He wants a letter from us for Syagrius to convince him our plan is genuine and not a Frankish trick to get rid of him."

Aemilia said nothing, feeling a tightening of fear in her throat.

"Don't worry, girl. You'll have no trouble. Just tell 'em you have a basket of cakes for him from his family. You can pass yourself off as his sister if need be. Now listen carefully. When you find him tell him we'll be setting fire to the stables at the third watch of tomorrow night. Got that? The third watch of tomorrow night. He must be ready to get Syagrius out then. Now repeat what I said."

Aemilia did as bid.

"Good. You can make the cakes tomorrow morning and take 'em to the barracks in the afternoon. You never told any of 'em I was your father, did you?"

"No. I just said my father was a Roman."

"No harm in that."

"What shall I tell them at the bakery, father? I'm supposed to be there tomorrow."

"Leave it to me. I'll fix it. Time we were going."

Aemilia wanted violently to speak to him, to convince him that his plans were ashes, that Paris would soon fall, and that no one, from the highest to the lowest, save the handful of impressionable stragglers he had managed to sway, cared a jot for his cause. She followed him in silence back to the shaft they had descended by. Beneath it he paused a moment to turn to her. She opened her mouth, desperately, then closed it again. She had not the words nor the courage.

"Aye, my girl?"

"Nothing."

It was whilst they were walking home in the motionless quiet of the dark that the idea came to her: see this Stycoricus and get him to abandon his plan to free Syagrius, and then see Chlodovech and plead on behalf of the fallen governor. Would she have any chance with Chlodovech? She did not know, but she had no other choice. She would have to make the attempt.

CHAPTER 31

Making cakes posed a problem as Aemilia did not have the ingredients nor any means of buying them. She eventually decided to bake a simple loaf of bread instead. It would look incongruous taking plain bread to a jailer, but no more so than taking cakes to one. She would just have to hope the Franks were unsuspicious.

Baking the loaf was a straightforward matter and it was midmorning when she carefully levered it out of the hearth with a wooden pallet before wrapping it in a cloth to keep it warm. She decided not to wait until the afternoon before visiting the barracks, thinking that the excuse of taking hot bread to her dear relative would better justify her going there in the first place.

Tarunculus was in the apartment when she re-entered with the wrapped loaf.

"I'll go now, father," she said, showing it to him.

"Good. I've written the letter. Here, hide it in your dress."

She took the small piece of parchment from Tarunculus and rolled it into a narrow tube. Then taking hold of a twine cord round her neck she drew it up, revealing the bronze ring from the catacombs.

"What's that?" Tarunculus asked.

"Something I found last night at the cemetery."

She pushed the rolled up parchment into the ring and dropped it back inside her dress, concealing it. She then put the wrapped loaf in a small wicker basket, placed her mantle over her head and faced her father. He looked at her approvingly.

"Perfect, lass. They'll never suspect a thing. Now, repeat one more time what you must say."

She did so. Tarunculus gave a nod.

"Good. Off you go now. Come straight back as soon as you're done."

She looked at him, eyes wide. "Yes, father."

Seeing her fear his expression softened, and he placed his hands on her

269

shoulders. "Don't be frightened, lass. They're a simple lot, the Franks. If they weren't I'd never have asked you to go. You'll be fine."

She hesitated a moment, then, still holding her basket, she suddenly hugged him.

"There, my girl. This'll soon be over, you'll see. Don't be worrying about anything. Off you go. Be back soon."

"Goodbye, father."

As she turned to leave she did not see him sit down heavily at the table, looking after her with troubled eyes. Nor was she to know that he remained unmoving for many minutes after she had gone, finally giving a shake of his head as if dispelling an unwanted thought.

Walking down the snow-cleared streets, Aemilia turned over in her mind what she could tell the Frankish guards at the gate without actually lying. Only once in her life—when she first met Tarunculus—had she been driven to tell a serious lie, concealing the fact that she had run away from Avitus, and she did not want to have to do it again. She reached the barracks gates and found the same guard she had spoken to the day before.

"Good morning, sir," she said in Frankish.

"*Mejuffrou.*"

"I have come to see Stycoricus. He is a guard in the cells. He and my father were comrades. I've brought him some hot bread." She raised up the basket and opened the cloth, revealing the loaf that steamed faintly in the sharp winter air.

"Oh, *ja*. I know him. He speaks Frankish like you." The guard opened the gate and let Aemilia in, closing it behind her. "You go through the archway over there, then you find the steps that take you below the ground. He is there."

"Thank you."

The main barracks edifice was built around an atrium. There were few warriors outside, the cold air, she guessed, having kept most of them indoors. A few individuals moved about on some errand or other. One large Frank, with a spear and shield, leaned against the wall next to a gray, stone doorway. She approached him and asked if this was the entrance to the underground cells.

"Why do you want to go down there?"

"I have something for the guard, Stycoricus," she said, and showed him the bread.

"*Ja*, go," he said, giving a jerk with his head, "but not too long. Nobody is supposed to be down there."

The stone steps led downwards to a narrow passage, dimly lit by a single, large oil lamp hung from the low, arched ceiling. At the end of the passage was a heavy wooden door pierced by a small square aperture covered with a grill. Below it an iron clapper was fastened to the worn and irregular surface of the wood. She took hold of the clapper and brought it down several times, producing a sharp, metallic knocking. She waited.

"*Ja, ek kom,*" came a voice from within, followed a moment later by a face at the grill.

The shock was almost a physical blow. The light was poor but nonetheless she recognized him instantly: the cavalry officer she had first met on her arrival at Soissons and later encountered in the basilica. The same opaque eyes and discolored teeth. What was he doing here?

He examined her curiously for a moment or two. "Who are you?"

It occurred to her that her back was to the light, casting her face into shadow. "I've come from Tarunculus. I have a message."

His eyes immediately flicked behind her, confirming that she was alone. Then a key grated in the lock of the door and it swung open with a creak. He stood before her, dressed in a discolored tunic and sandals. He held a ring full of keys attached by a small chain to his leather belt, from which was slung a sheathed knife.

"Did you bring the letter?"

"Yes."

"Give it to me."

"Wait...I must talk to you."

There was a pause, as he examined her more intently. "You're his daughter. Lady Julia's girl. Did Syagrius know you?"

"...yes."

"Then come in. Talk to him and tell him the plan's for real."

"No. It must not happen."

"Eh?"

"You must call the plan off. I will speak to Chlodovech for Syagrius."

He looked at her curiously. "Did you father tell you that?"

She dropped her gaze. "No."

His voice became hard. "Listen. Chlodovech hates Syagrius's guts. He'll kill him tomorrow, and nothing you can do will change that. Nothing. You hear me?" Aemilia remained silent.

"Syagrius's only chance is to do whatever I say. If you don't convince him of that he's *dead.*" He underscored the word by drawing a finger across his throat. There was a pause as he waited for a reply before resuming: "Come on. There's no time. Anybody could come down."

She followed him into the passageway beyond the door, as narrow as the one before it but with cells on either side closed off by hinged gratings. She could see no prisoners in them until they reached the last cell on the right. In the dirty, yellow glow of an oil lamp she made out a figure sitting on the floor against the wall, indistinct in the gloom.

"Someone to see you," said the guard.

There was movement as the head raised itself towards the grated entrance. Then the figure heaved itself to its feet and slowly approached the light.

"My Lord," Aemilia murmured.

His face was haggard and pasty, but his eyes, lit with the strength of hope, fixed on her. "Is it true, then?"

"Yes, my Lord." She glanced at the guard. "There'll be a diversion tonight at the third watch. They'll set fire to the stables. You are to go over the town walls where horses will be waiting, and go on to Paris from there."

"How am I supposed to get past the siege?"

"My father says it's not very close. It will be easy to get through. Here," she continued, remembering, "I have a letter for you."

She drew out the ring with its rolled up parchment and gave the parchment to Syagrius. He opened it and tilted it towards the weak lamplight. After a few moments he nodded, and gave it back to her. "Keep it. Better that there be no risk of it being found here." Suddenly he winced. "My feet. I can't stand for long."

"Do I take a message back, my Lord?"

"Just to say I've understood and I'll be ready. Have some bandages packed with the horses, and salve too."

"Yes, my Lord."

He was turning to resume his place by the wall when he paused, and glanced back at her again. "I was hard on you over Ennodius. His mother told me you intended to marry him and that he could not resist your charms."

Aemilia's eyes widened. "That's not true! I made him agree to meet me only in Her Majesty's apartment! I never had any intention of...you must believe me, My Lord!"

"Don't worry," Syagrius replied. "I know how much I can trust that woman." For a moment he showed the ghost of a smile. "He can marry you with my blessing if he chooses. Also more than he appears to be. Go now."

At the wooden door she stopped to bid the guard goodbye.

"It's brave of you to do this for him," she said.

"Least I can do."

"Were you with him in the battle?"

"All the way through, and coming back too. Didn't leave him for an instant. Reckon it was my job to keep an eye on him."

"You came back with him?"

"That I did, all the way to the barracks. That's where Albinus jumped us. Nothing I could do."

She hesitated, something nagging her. Oh, the loaf, she thought. "I must give this to you," she said, holding it out to him, "I told the Franks that's why I came here."

"Obliged. I'll give it to the governor. Reckon he can do with it more'n me, eh?"

He shut the door and she heard the key turn in the lock. The sound of footfalls signalled that he had gone back down the passageway. She remounted the worn, stone steps and bade the Frank at the cells entrance goodbye.

"Thank you for letting me see him," she added.

"You bring me hot bread next time," he said, grinning.

The Frank at the barracks gate let her out without comment and she walked back slowly to the apartment, a preoccupied expression on her face. There was something wrong, something that the cavalryman-turned-jailor had said. She had reached the street by the Aurelian Flats when it came to her: *All the way through, and coming back too. Didn't leave him for an instant.* She made an effort to recall the day of the battle: her standing next to Tarunculus in the cold autumn breeze on the battlement above the gate, watching the beaten remnants of the army trickle into the town...a small group of horsemen approaching, Syagrius with what was left of his guard, no more than a dozen men...she examining their faces, not seeing Ennodius immediately, finally recognizing him at the back of the group. Had she looked at them all? She was sure she had, and she was equally sure she had not seen the jailor among them.

Why had he lied? She did not know, but now the unease she had felt on encountering him at the cells coalesced into fear, a certainty that he was not to be trusted. She picked up her pace and covered the remaining distance to the flats almost at a run.

Tarunculus was waiting in the apartment for her.

"All go well?" he said, letting her in.

"Father, something's wrong."

"What happened? Did you see Stycoricus?"

"I did. No one stopped me, but I don't trust him, father." She told him of the jailor's lie. Tarunculus frowned, considering for a moment, then he clapped a hand on her back.

"Don't be bothering about it, girl. Just a soldier's yarn. Everybody in the army wants to be the one who saves the general's life. I've heard tales taller than that. Don't lay anything by it."

"Father, it's not just a soldier's story. He's not right. He'll betray you, I'm sure of it."

Tarunculus's expression began to blacken. "Then why aren't I sitting in a cell right now? Stycoricus's known long enough what we're about. He's had any amount of time to sing to the Franks. Why hasn't he, eh?" Suddenly he hesitated. "Has he got the letter?"

"No. Syagrius read it and gave it back to me."

"Stycoricus didn't take it from you?"

"No."

"There you are then. That was his chance to get proof, if he needed any. Enough of this nonsense now."

"But Father..."

"I said enough."

Aemilia bowed her head, her eyes wet with tears. Tarunculus regarded her and then went on, voice grim, "Stop this old maid's terrors and show some backbone, girl. You're a Cornelian, by the gods. Act like one. Now pull yourself together and tell me exactly what happened. You said you saw Syagrius. What did he say?"

Aemilia recounted the details of her visit, answering Tarunculus's queries until he was satisfied.

"Good," he finally said. "Tonight we get him out."

For the rest of the day neither of them left the apartment. Aemilia busied herself with diverse chores: preparing the midday meal, washing up, cleaning the table and furniture, sweeping the floor, finally, with nothing else to do, listlessly reading a scroll of Virgil's *Georgics* in one of the wicker chairs. The agitation in her mind rose and subsided, like slow-moving waves breaking on rocks, growing in size and force as the hours passed. Images flashed through her mind, faint memories that gradually became clear with the effort of recall: Tarunculus in the catacombs: *He's an ex, by Hades. One of us...*the road outside Soissons: *Ten miles further away from town and I'd have cut your throat for what you just said...*a face, inscrutable in the gloom of the prison: *Didn't leave him for an instant. Reckon it was my job to keep an eye on him...*Tarunculus, smiling: *Don't be bothering about it, girl. Just a soldier's yarn...*in the basilica: *we don't know anything. But a little bird told me that Her Mightiness isn't the only one who can make a deal with the Franks...an ex. One of us...*the scorn of a slave: *Half of 'em are bandits too. Picked up by patrols and recruited, just like that...One of us, by Hades, one of* *us*....waves rising and falling, and rising higher and higher, until nothing could calm them; fear mounting and mounting until she wondered how she could sit in the chair and hold the scroll open before her and not scream with terror at her father.

She looked across at him. He seemed not to notice her, absorbed in preparing the torches to be thrown on the straw roofs of the barracks stables. Using the table as a work surface, he wrapped a linen strip tightly around one end of a short wooden baton. Once that was done he dipped the clothbound end of the baton into a small amphora of oil, until the linen was thoroughly soaked, before stashing it into a canvas bag on the floor next to the table. When a score of batons had been done he closed up the top of the bag and tied it with twine. His preparations completed, he passed the rest of the time alternating between gazing out the window and pacing back and forth in the apartment. He did not speak. The afternoon shadows were lengthening when there was a soft knock at the door.

Taking a knife from the kitchen Tarunculus went over to the door. "Who's there?"

"It's me," came a low voice.

"Who are you?"

"Amniatus."

Tarunculus opened the door, revealing the lanky youth Aemilia had seen in the catacombs. "Curse you," he said with irritation, "can't you give your name right away?"

"Sorry. I've got the horses. It took all the money you gave me. I'll take 'em out with a cart at sundown and have 'em by the walls tonight." Aemilia glanced at the bookshelves. Three or four scrolls gone. That would have been enough to purchase horses.

"Good. Third watch, don't forget. Don't come too early but be on time. Take a water clock if you have to."

"I will. Reckon he'll make me a centurion for this?"

"Sure to, lad. But be off now. Remember, third watch."

Tarunculus closed the door and turned to find Aemilia directly behind him.

"Father, listen to me. This is a trap of some kind. I'm certain of it. You mustn't go."

"I told you not to discuss it any further."

"Father, listen. Ennodius told me that the battle was lost because some special cavalry didn't attack when they were supposed to. I'm sure that man was part of it. That's why he lied about being with Syagrius. He never came back with the army. There's something else I haven't told you.

When Soissons was given to the Franks—that was done by Lady Julia. She arranged it with Chlodovech. That man—he knew it. He told me she wasn't the only one who made a deal with Franks. He knew but he didn't tell Syagrius. You can't trust him, don't you see? Father, you mustn't go."

Tarunculus stood motionless, eyes fixed on her. "How did you know about Lady Julia?"

Her gaze fell to the floor. "I was with her when she...when she arranged it with Chlodovech."

There was silence for a moment. Then she reeled back, the force of the blow knocking her against the wall. For a few seconds she lay on the floor, dizzy and confused, before looking up at her father.

"My own family. My own flesh *and blood*."

He gripped the kitchen knife with his hand. She stared at him, not speaking, for several moments. Then, with a thud, he drove the knife into the table.

"Aulus has water for guts, but he won't betray us. Neither will Stycoricus. He's a soldier, by the gods, and a man. You, raised a serf by a Frankish slut...I'll settle with you when I get back."

He seized the bag with the torches and strode over to the door. Drawing the key from the lock he left, slamming the door behind him. Aemilia heard the key turn in the lock and then the sound of fading footfalls as Tarunculus made off down the passage.

She did not move for several minutes until the growing pain in her jaw and at the back of her head dispelled her lightheadedness, then, getting slowly and unsteadily to her feet, she made her way across to the door. She tested it. It was locked. She moved over to the table and slumped into a wicker chair. She sat for a long time, making no movement, until finally she bent forward and bowed her head onto the table, wetting its surface with tears as her sobs racked in her throat.

CHAPTER 32

The daylight was fading when Aemilia finally stirred herself. She went over to a window and looked out. It was early evening. The streets were quiet, their sides piled with the dirty slush of melting snow. The winter air, still carrying some of the warmth of the afternoon sun, was fresh. She leaned out and looked down. Below the ledge of the windowsill the wall went straight downwards to the pavement stones twenty feet below. Without a rope there was no way of getting to the ground. The blankets would not be long enough. She turned her gaze to the right. The sun had sunk below the lines and angles of the apartments, filling the western sky with an orange glow that fused into pink, then mauve, then deep blue as the eye travelled overhead from west to east.

Should she call for help? It would mean getting a stranger to break the door down and let her escape, never to return. She could go to Chlodovech or Merovec and be done with her father. The more she considered it the more it became clear that it was the only sensible thing to do. Why stay? And was there not danger in staying? She must go. There was nothing more she could do here.

A woman, middle-aged and poorly-dressed, passed by below. She should call her, ask her to find a slave to break the door down and set her free. She took a breath and opened her mouth to speak. The woman went by and continued down the street, disappearing beyond sight round a corner.

Aemilia turned from the window and sat at the table, holding her fists to her temples, her mind an agony of indecision. *I'm insane. If he comes back he will kill me.* But he had not killed her when he had had the chance to, when he had held the knife in his hand as if he would drive it through her chest. *He will whip me with his cane like the slave at the villa.* But he had not done that either. One blow and he had left. He needn't have gone: it wasn't yet time for the diversion at the barracks. *He will never forgive me. He will despise me as a traitor.* To that she had no answer, but was she justified leaving him because of it? *Yes. What good can I do him now? Why stay here and be a kindling for his hatred, day after day?*

She moved back to the window. It was nearly dark and the street, cold in the night air, was deserted. She would have to scream now to get the attention of the nearby flat dwellers if she wanted to escape. She gripped the wooden frame of the windowsill. She could not do it. She gave a sigh, almost a sob, and drew back. Going through to the kitchen she put more wood on the glowing embers of the brazier and blew gently until a small fire flickered. Then, lighting the oil lamps from the fire, she closed the shutters of the windows and put her mantle around her.

She knelt on the floor and, crossing herself, spent a long time in prayer. *Show me what I must do. Help me to do it. Do not abandon me. Protect him. Keep him safe.* Finally, when it had become quite dark, she rose up wearily and moved a chair over to the brazier, then sat to keep warm and await the return of her father.

The scratching of a key in the lock awoke her. She felt cold. The fire in the brazier was dead, but the lamps were still alight. She listened. The scratching resumed, as if the holder of the key had difficulty in making it turn in the lock. She stood up and went into the main room, standing by the table. Why was he so long in opening the door? The scratching continued and then there was a click as the levers turned. She put her hands on the table to steady herself, her heart thumping as if it would burst in her chest. The door opened slowly, creaking faintly on its hinges.

Fear surged up within her. He stood before her, features clearly lit by the lamp on the table.

"Hello, love."

It was *him*. The hard, opaque eyes took her in, gloating, the brown and yellow teeth showing through his grin. The same knife at his side, the same discolored tunic. Even the same bunch of keys. *God help me.*

"Why are you here?"

"Well, now, that's a story," he said, turning to close the door behind him. "Seems your dad's in a spot of trouble."

"Where is he?"

"Taken the place of me noble lord Syagrius. Caught red-handed trying to bust him out. He's not dead yet," he went on, seeing her shock. "Reckon the Franks'll get him to squeal on his mates a bit before they cut his throat. A sad business."

He stepped up to the table. She shifted sideways to keep it between them. "You betrayed him."

"Not me, love. The fool pulled off his diversion. Got a lovely blaze going in the stables. Didn't help Syagrius though." He edged around the table.

She moved in the opposite direction. "Why didn't you give him away earlier?" Anything to keep him talking.

He stopped. "Now that's a good question. Don't mind if I tell you. Before the battle me and the lads, we see which way the wind's blowing. They send me to go and talk to Chlodovech. I say, 'We'll come over to your side if you make it worth our while.' He likes the idea and promises us five solidi each. After the battle we go to him for the money. The bastard gives us solidi made of brass. He laughs and tells us one trick's worth another.

"So I look around and all I come up with is this stinking jailor's job. Only thing the Franks'll give me seeing they don't fancy sitting underground all day. Prisoner in, prisoner out. Nothing on 'em. Nothing to squeeze out of 'em. I'm nearly for going back to the bandit trade when they bring in Syagrius."

He tapped his head. "So I use my noggin. I know the highborns've all got a pile stashed away somewhere where only they can find it. They want something handy and portable in case the barbarians come. I tell Syagrius, 'Tell me where the loot is and I'll spring you.' He doesn't believe me so I come out and find your dad and play old soldiers with 'im. He takes it like a fish on a hook. He gets you to come and give Syagrius the letter and Syagrius tells me where the money is. A smart bastard he was, letting the fishes look after it. Then I wait for the third watch and when the fuss starts upstairs I go to his cell and tell 'im let's get going, and he comes out and I give it to 'im, in the belly. *He* won't be squealing on me. They come and I tell 'em he grabbed my keys. Meantime the Franks catch your dad—they tell me he tripped up running away. He can squeal all he likes. I've got a dead man to prove who's side *I'm* on. All a smart bit of work, don't you think?"

Aemilia could say nothing, her gaze fixed on the malignant satisfaction of the face across the table.

"One question you haven't asked, girlie," the jailor said, edging around the table again.

"What?"

"You haven't asked why I'm here."

Aemilia did not answer, glancing around in mounting panic for anything that might serve as a weapon. There was the knife in the kitchen, but he stood near the kitchen door now, putting it beyond reach.

"I've come for my reward. Your dad's dead tomorrow and you won't have a friend in the world except me. I could kill you now in the line of duty. Don't worry. I'll look after you, lovie, good and proper. But I'll be wanting that note, the one you brought."

It was still in the ring around her neck. Aemilia did not want to give him any excuse to come nearer. "It's gone. I burnt it."

The grin turned into a leer. "I think I'll be checking that."

He lunged round the table. She dashed round the opposite side, making for the kitchen. He caught her and spun her around, grabbing the cord around her neck and pulling it up to reveal the ring with the rolled-up parchment. With a jerk he broke the twine and dropped the ring and parchment onto the floor.

"That's business taken care of. Now for pleasure."

There was the sound of a dull thud. The jailor's eye's widened and his mouth opened as if to cry out, but no sound came. A moment passed and then a noise like a gurgle or hiccup forced its way up from the depths of his throat, accompanied by a trickle of blood that ran from the corner of his mouth. He collapsed heavily onto the floor, revealing an axe sunk deep into his back.

Aemilia stared at him, frozen, and then looked up. By the front door, his arm still extended from the axe-throw, stood Merovec.

Aemilia's body began to shake. She stared at the Frank, saying nothing. He strode forward. "You are not well," he said, "go, lie down. I will take this pig-breed out."

She did as she was told and went to the bed in the room adjoining the kitchen, sitting on it and watching through the doorway as Merovec wrenched his axe from the back of the dead jailor, wiped it on the body's tunic, and then dragged the corpse out of the apartment. When he came back in again she was still shaking.

"It is all right. He is gone now."

"Sorry...hard to speak..."

Taking the blanket from her straw mattress in the kitchen Merovec draped it around her shoulders. "You stay warm. Wait a while. Then you will be well."

"...thank you..."

After a time the shaking subsided. Merovec stood by her, waiting. Finally, she looked up at him. "Why did you come?"

"Chlodovech did not trust that pig-breed. He told me to follow him after he killed Syagrius. He comes here. I wait outside the door and listen to him talk until he goes for you. Then I come in and kill him. Putting his hands on a woman, and a Frank! Such a one does not deserve to live." He turned and spat on the pool of blood.

There was another silence, then Aemilia spoke again. "What will happen now?"

"I must tell Chlodovech everything. You must come with me. Do not be afraid. I will speak for you."

"...my father?"

Merovec shook his head. "I cannot say what Chlodovech will do with him, but I do not think he will spare him."

"Will Chlodovech listen to me?"

"He will give you an ear, but will that help your father?" He shook his head again. "He did a very stupid thing. We must go to the barracks now. Chlodovech is there. Are you well?"

"I am well."

She stood up. Stepping carefully around the congealing blood, she made for the front door.

"You forget this."

She turned. Merovec had picked up the ring, still threaded through the twine. The parchment was gone. He held the ring out to her. She took it from him and, tying a knot in the twine, placed it back around her neck. Holding the ring a moment she read the inscription: CONIVGI CARISSIMI, and glanced curiously at the Frankish warrior. Searching the floor with her eyes, she spotted the parchment against the wall and picked it up. Merovec glanced at it with a momentary curiosity, not understanding its import, and went on to the door. For a moment she debated what to do with it and then closed her fist around it. Chlodovech would have to be told everything. It was known she had been at the barracks in any case. She paused to close the door behind her, taking from the keyhole an oddly shaped key, and then followed Merovec down the passage, skirting the body that lay on the floor outside.

CHAPTER 33

By the time they reached the barracks Chlodovech had already returned to the Residence. Tarunculus was in an underground cell and could not be seen by anyone. He was the only one of his group to have been caught. Aemilia followed Merovec from the barracks over the frozen ground, the night air sharp in her lungs as she panted in the effort to keep up with the warrior's stride. At one point he stopped and glanced back at her.

"I go too fast?"

"You are big. I am small."

He smiled and went on, slowing his pace.

Arriving at the Residence they found the main door shut. Merovec rapped several times with the knocker. They waited, then a voice came through the wood, "*Ja?*"

"It is Merovec."

The door opened. A Frank, holding a pitch torch, glanced out and then opened the door wide. "He is waiting for you."

He led them through the darkened Residence to the *triclinium*, the large banquet-room where Syagrius had entertained his guests. Two guards stood outside the entrance which was lit by torches in holders fixed to the wall. Merovec opened the door and went in, followed by Aemilia, whilst their guide remained outside. Aemilia took her place a little behind Merovec, and looked around. The couches on which the guests had reclined were gone, replaced by a long wooden table on which goblets and a pitcher of wine had been placed. At one end of the table Chlodovech sat in a high-backed chair whilst a dozen or so warriors occupied the benches on either side. To the wall behind the chair a bronze head of a wolf had been affixed, its jaws open. From its neck a pennant hung which, Aemilia realized, would fill with the wind blowing through the wolf's mouth when the head was carried in battle. Above the table, oil lamps hung from the ceiling, giving the room a weak but adequate illumination.

283

Aemilia felt a touch of the same surprise she had experienced on first meeting Chlodovech. His youth was almost incongruous as he sat in discussion with the older Franks around him. He glanced up at the arrivals.

"*Ja* Merovec. What news?"

"He is dead. I kill him."

Chlodovech shrugged. "What did he do?"

Merovec indicated Aemilia. "He put his hands on her. She is the daughter of the one we catch."

Chlodovech looked at her, his face showing immediate recognition, and signed her with his hand to approach. "Come."

She came up to the end of the table opposite Chlodovech and stopped. He examined her keenly, eyes narrowed. "What do you have to do with this?"

Her mouth was dry. "I knew...what my father was doing, my Lord."

"She plotted with him," said one Frank.

"She can go to him," said another. "Tomorrow we cut both their heads off."

"She was at the prison in the afternoon," said a third.

"Yes." Aemilia interjected. "I came to give a message to the jailor. It was this." She opened her fist, showing the note.

"Give it to me," said Chlodovech.

The Frank nearest Aemilia took the crumpled parchment and passed it up to his neighbor, and so on until it reached Chlodovech. He perused it for a few moments, then dropped it on the floor. His gaze returned to her. "Why did you do this?"

"I could not do otherwise, my Lord. My father would not listen to me."

"Why did you not tell me, or one of my Franks?"

She held his gaze. "I cannot be the cause of my father's death."

The Franks murmured amongst themselves. Some looked at her curiously, others with hostility. Did one or two expressions show comprehension? She was not sure.

Chlodovech glanced away, as if considering her reply. Then he regarded her again. "You say your father would not listen to you."

"Yes, my Lord."

"What did you tell him?"

She paused with the effort to remember her exact words. "I told him what you said in the forum, that these people were now your people. I told him that the Franks would treat the Romans well, that life could go on as before. I said he must leave it, that there was nothing anyone could do any more. That we could keep all that is good and fine and noble that we got from Rome. He became angry with me. I could not say any more."

There was a moment's silence, then Chlodovech's features relaxed. "*Ja*, you tell the truth."

Several Franks glanced at him in surprise. "How do you know?" said one. "Her tongue is smooth."

"She is telling the truth," Chlodovech repeated. "I know when a man is lying to me. Have I ever been wrong in that?"

No one contradicted him. Aemilia, taking advantage of the momentary silence, spoke up: "What will happen to my father?"

The face became hard again. "I must know everything of his plotting. I can allow no threat against me in my kingdom."

"My Lord, I will tell you." Beginning with the meetings at the apartment, she described all she knew about the group of Tarunculus's fellow conspirators, their characters, their varying motives, their rambling talk, omitting only their names. She described the scene in the catacombs, the warning of Aulus, the defection of most of the conspirators, the impressionability and naïvety of the two or three who stayed with Tarunculus. When she related the lanky youth's hopes of becoming a centurion, one or two of the Franks chuckled. Omitting the blow Tarunculus had given her on leaving, she finished by describing the jailor's arrival at the apartment.

"I hear that dog when he talks to her," Merovec interjected. "It is as she says."

There was a silence. Chlodovech toyed with his goblet. He glanced up at her again. "What do the people think of me?"

The question surprised her. She hesitated before replying. "My Lord, when Syagrius was here I think most wanted to see you as lord in his place. Syagrius put heavy burdens on them and had no care for their good. He was...too high above them. They believed their life would be easier if you were here."

"And now?"

"I think...they are afraid. They want an end to the war. Until you are a master without enemies they fear what you may do to them."

Chlodovech grunted. "*Ja*. It is as I thought. These people wish for a lord who does not doubt them." He put the goblet down and placed his hands firmly on the table, as if reaching a decision. "Your father's plot is nothing. It is the folly of an old man. He shall not die." Some of the Franks started in astonishment. "I shall show these people that I fear nothing from them. But he shall stay in his cell until I see fit to let him go. Let him think on what it means to oppose me."

Chlodovech rose up. "Tomorrow we go back to Paris. When the town is mine we return to Tournai. My cousins Chararic and Ragnacar send me a message that I must give them a portion of the land I took from Syagrius, though they did nothing to help me win it."

"What will you do?" asked Merovec, with the hint of a grin.

"I will go to them and give them the land they ask for," said Chlodovech, slapping the knife strapped to his belt, "two yards of it!"

The warriors guffawed with laughter and the meeting broke up. As the Franks made their way out Chlodovech called Merovec over to him.

"I leave you in charge of Soissons. Do not seek out the men she spoke of, but if you hear of any more plots, you know what to do."

Merovec grunted, and gave a nod. Aemilia, gathering her courage again, spoke up, "My Lord, may I visit my father?"

"*Ja*," he said, then grinned, "but do not bring messages."

Merovec accompanied Aemilia back to the apartment.

"What do you do now?" he asked. "You have other family?"

"No," she replied, "but I have work. I will stay here and look after my father until Chlodovech frees him."

"That may be a long time," he said. "I take him now," he went on, seizing the body lying in the passage and shouldering it as if it were a sack of flour. "Go well."

"Go well."

He turned and left. Aemilia spent the next hour scrubbing the floor by lamplight until she had removed every trace of blood she could see, after which she cleaned the area of passage outside the door. She then sat in a chair and waited for dawn. When the blackness of the night sky began to lighten in the east she ate the remains of a loaf in the kitchen and made her way across to the bakery. The old cook answered her knock at the kitchen door.

"Where were you yesterday?"

"My father kept me in."

"Think that's an excuse? You'll work today for nothing. Next time don't come back. Now start with the floor."

Several hours later Aemilia was kneeling on the ground cleaning out the ashes from the hearth when Rictiovarus strode in. "You."

She turned to face him. "Yes, sir?"

"Your father's the centurion?"

"Yes, sir. He is."

"The Franks have locked him up. You know that? For setting fire to the barracks."

"...yes, sir."

"And you've got the nerve to come back here. Get out. Get out now."

She rose hesitantly to her feet. Rictiovarus stepped forward and seized her arm, propelling her to the door and shoving her outside with such force that she nearly lost her balance.

"Get going. Off my premises."

She turned and made her way out the entrance. *That's that,* she thought, feeling a little bemused, but otherwise tranquil. She did not worry about how she would earn a living. So much had happened in the last day that her mind had become as it was on the day the Franks occupied Soissons: content to live in the present, instant by instant, not giving a thought to the past or future.

She returned to the apartment. There was a little flour left. She mixed it with water and leaven to make dough and took it down to the small insula kitchen to bake. The slave girl who had allowed her to use the hearth was there.

"Heard the news? There's been a big to-do at the barracks. Somebody setting fire to it, they say."

"Yes."

"The Franks'll be angry now. They'll kill us all."

"They won't. I spoke to them. They don't think anything of it."

"That so? They say you can speak Frankish and all. What else did the Franks say?"

"Chlodovech said he doesn't want us to be afraid of him."

"He did?"

"Yes."

Aemilia was disinclined to talk. The slave girl in any case had other chores and left the kitchen a few minutes later. As the loaf baked in the hearth Aemilia sat on a stool and waited, gazing pensively at the floor. The placidity of her mind gradually gave way to unease as she thought of her father. Should she visit him at all? Would he not resent her, curse her for a traitor, throw the loaf she brought him back in her face? She could leave it with the guard, to give to him. Wouldn't he prefer that? But he was alone now, his friends scattered, his lord dead, just her to care whether he lived or died. She couldn't abandon him, not now. She would have to see him, just once. If he did not want to see her she would not come again.

The smell of baked bread brought her out of her preoccupation. She sighed and, taking a wooden spatula, eased the loaf out of the hearth into a cloth, putting it into the basket she had taken the previous day. She returned to the apartment, put on her mantle and with difficulty locked the door with the strange key the jailor had used to open it. Then she set out for the barracks.

When she explained her errand to the guard at the barracks gate he was implacable. "You can leave bread for him, but you do not see him. Nobody sees him."

"But Chlodovech said I can."

"He says nothing to me."

She wondered what to do next. She did not think Chlodovech had changed his mind about her; clearly his permission had not yet filtered down to the rank and file. There was nothing for it but to wait. Then she remembered something.

"Is Chlodovech still at the Residence?" she asked.

"No. He is gone," the guard replied.

"Does Merovec rule in Soissons now?"

The guard looked at her curiously. "*Ja.*"

"Where can I find him?"

"He is here."

"He knows me. Can I see him?"

The guard opened the gate and pointed at the main barracks building. "Over there."

"*Dankie.*"

Her knock at the main doors was answered by a Frankish warrior, who bade her wait whilst he conveyed her request. After five minutes the door opened and Merovec stood before her.

He wore a white tunic fastened with a belt from which a sheathed knife hung on the left side. His trousers were bound with leggings below the knee, in the Frankish fashion, and he wore leather shoes. A dark green cape was fastened by a brass clasp at his right shoulder. His head was uncovered. His plaited blond hair hung down behind his shoulders. Aemilia realized that he was not much older than Chlodovech. The fact of his being a warrior had made him seem a maturer man.

"*Ja,* little Frank."

"I came to see my father. I brought him some bread." She lifted her basket and opened it, showing the small loaf she had baked.

He looked at it. "That is not much."

"It is all the flour I have left."

"You cannot buy some more?"

"I have no more money."

"But you said you have work."

"Not any more." She dropped her gaze. "They told me to go away."

Merovec put his hands on his hips. "*Ja?* Why?"

"They know my father is in the cells for setting fire to the barracks. They think...they will be in trouble."

The hands on the hips closed into fists. "I give them trouble. They must respect a Frank."

She looked up. "No, leave them. I did not like working there. I am glad I left."

"What do you do now?"

She glanced at the paving stones again. "I do not know."

"You have no other work?"

"No. I hoped to get work at the basilica. The..."—she groped for the right term—"...man who does writing there wanted me to work as an interpreter between Franks and Romans. But that can happen only when the war is ended."

"There is no war here." There was a silence as the Frank put fist to chin, considering. Finally he continued: "Chlodovech told me to watch Soissons for more plots. He did not tell me to make anyone interpreter. Still, there is a need for one. I can speak Latin but there are many words I do not know. There are things the people must be told. I must have them made in writing and put up where the people can see them. There will be other things too..." He turned his head and called within the building. "Chilperic! I am going out for a short time."

"*Ja,* good," came the faint reply.

Merovec strode out the door. "Come. We will go to the basilica."

"Can I see my father afterwards?"

"*Ja, seker.*" He paused a moment then continued: "He is well. We did not hurt him."

The two made their way out through the gates, Merovec giving a wave to the guard who nodded back.

"When did you learn Latin?" Aemilia asked.

"After Chlodovech became king. He tells me that Franks are no longer servants of the Romans but that one day Franks and Romans will be one people, and must understand each other. So I find a Roman—a dark Roman, not like your father—and tell him if he will stay at my hall and teach me Latin I will give him what he needs. He has been with me for five years."

"You have a hall?"

"*Ja.* A small one. I have a village beyond Tournai. Our family is respected since my grandfather became a man of the king's household. Childeric gave him the village. Chlodovech promises me another after I marry and have a son."

"Are the villagers your slaves?"

Merovec glanced at her. "Franks are not slaves. I am their eorl. I must settle their disputes and protect them in war. For this they give me ten votes in the village council and a tithe of their wheat. But they are free men."

"So they own their land?"

"I do not understand why Romans speak so much of 'owning'. The land was not made by men. It is there to be worked. The men who can work it do so. If they cannot, they give their place to those who can. What a man grows he keeps, save the tithe he gives to his eorl, but the land is not his, just as the sky and the sea are not his. "

"I understand. It is very different from what Romans do."

"You are from a village?"

"...no. A villa. Everything belonged to a Roman lord. I did not like him." She went on to describe the villa and her life under Avitus. Soon they were passing under the great, ornate lintel of the basilica's main doors. There were several people within, Aemilia noticed, though far fewer than she had seen on her first visit.

"Where is this man who does the writing?" Merovec asked.

"He should be over there and up the stairs."

Ignoring the curious glances, Aemilia led Merovec over to the side door then up the steps to the ambulatory above the basilica's great central space. Once inside at the top, Merovec paused to lean on the railing and look over the edge.

"*Ja*, it is big. Will I break my legs if I jump?

She joined him. "I would not try it."

He looked at her. "You think I am a coward?" He heaved a leg over the railing.

"No!"

Merovec laughed and brought his leg back down. Realizing her own leg had been pulled Aemilia pursed her lips in a frown, but Merovec grinned, seeing the hint of mirth in her expression.

"I scare you. Do not worry, little Frank. I am brave but not a fool."

"The man who writes is over there," said Aemilia.

The Master of Scribes was at the same table as when Aemilia had first met him. He was reading a scroll, head bent. He looked up at their approach and gave a start, clumsily rising to his feet. "Excuse me. Morning. What can I do for you?"

"You choose the people who do the writing?" said Merovec.

The Master of Scribes glanced at Aemilia and then back at the Frank. "Yes, My Lord, I do."

"Take her. I rule in Soissons while Chlodovech is at Paris. There are some things the people need to be told, but I do not know all the Latin for it. She will be my interpreter. It will be her work."

"Certainly, My Lord."

"One thing," said Merovec, his eyes narrowing. "Where she worked before she was not treated well. She will be treated well here. Understand?"

"I understand, My Lord."

"Good," said Merovec, turning to Aemilia and lapsing into Frankish. "We start now. The people must be told that they need not fear Chlodovech's anger for the burning of the stables, but that from this day on any man who plots against Chlodovech will die."

"The Romans would say it differently," said Aemilia.

"Then write how they would say it."

Borrowing a pen, parchment and a stool, Aemilia sat and wrote a draft of the decree, conferring with the Master of Scribes on the exact wording. His strained deference gradually relaxed as he became involved in the composition and in the end he was animated, even dogmatic, over the correct terminology of the enactment. Finally, with his approval, Aemilia rewrote and read the final draft to Merovec, translating the words he did not understand.

"Many words to say a simple thing," he remarked, but nodded his approbation. "Good. Now it must be put where the people can see it."

"I'll do that right away, my Lord, and have criers announce it." The Master of Scribes held out a quill pen to Merovec. "If you could just make your mark here. To show it is from yourself."

"What mark do I make?"

"A letter will do."

Aemilia drew an 'M' at the bottom of the first draft. Merovec clumsily imitated it on the second, adding an ink blot. He grinned at Aemilia. "Some day you teach me to write, *hein?*" He turned back to the Master of Scribes. "She comes with me now. Later she will come back here. Give her what money she needs."

"Only too happy to, My Lord. I'm pleased to have her."

On the way back to the barracks Aemilia was silent. As they approached the main gates Merovec turned to look at her.

"You do not speak. You are not happy?"

"No," she replied. "I am quiet because I am happy."

"Oh, *ja*."

He accompanied her as far as the doorway leading to the cells. "Let her see him whenever she wants, Alberic," he told the guard.

The warrior nodded and turned to open the door.

"I leave you now," said Merovec to Aemilia. "You will come tomorrow?"

"I shall. You will be here?"

"*Ja*. Ask for me at the big doors. Go well, little Frank."

"Go well."

He turned and strode away. Her eyes strayed after him for a moment or two before she turned to follow the guard down the dim passage to the cells. She noted that she was tranquil at the thought of seeing her father, whatever his reaction to her might be. The ship was coming home to its port and nothing could prevent it now. The rock and storm of human turbulence were behind it, vanished into the mists. She had a father to care for but he would eventually be released, and would be supported. She could carry out her original plan and get the Master of Scribes to make over part of her pay to him as a pension. Merovec would agree to it, she was sure, and if it was entered into the records as such it would not be a lie. After that, her future rolled open before her like a gently undulating field. As she waited for the guard to open the passage door leading to the cells, she did not realize in the inexperience of her youth how rarely life is simple and how calm waters and sunny skies are all too often the eye of the storm.

CHAPTER 34

Tarunculus was locked in the same cell Syagrius had occupied. The fact did not surprise Aemilia: it was the darkest cell in the malodorous, dimly-lit corridor, the furthest from the thick wooden door that led to air, light, the free world above. It was the natural hole in which to throw those who had fallen foulest of authority. The Frankish guard stayed only long enough to point out the cell to Aemilia before returning to the surface, leaving her alone.

"I'm here, father."

He did not reply. It took a few moments for her to make out his shape, sitting against the wall in the shadow. She waited. He did not move or speak.

"I've brought some bread."

Silence, then the ragged intake of a breath drawn in pain or despair, she could not tell which. There was a slight movement as his head turned to look at her and then turned away again. She put her basket down by the iron bars of the cell and hesitated, wondering whether she should push the loaf through onto the filthy floor beyond or wait until her father came to take it, if he would come at all. The silence began to weigh heavily on her.

"I've...I've spoken to Chlodovech..." Another movement as the head turned towards her again. "He says you will not die...but you must stay in the cells for a time."

"He said that?" The voice was low, gravelled with weakness.

"Yes. You'll be free again."

There was another silence.

"What does it matter? He is dead."

Aemilia could think of nothing to say.

"You were right. Why did you come? What am I to you now?"

"You are my father."

"What kind of a father have I been to you, eh? What kind? What have I ever done for you? As much as I did for your mother. You should leave me, as she did. She was right to leave. You could do no worse."

Aemilia took hold of the bars, bringing her head close. "I will not leave you. I'm your daughter. I love you."

The intake of breath was almost a sob. Aemilia waited, but he did not speak. She went on, gently: "I'll come tomorrow, with some more bread, maybe some soup. If you want me to bring anything, just say." He did not reply. She left the basket with the loaf next to the bars of his cell and made her way back up the passage, holding open the wooden door for a few minutes to let a little fresh air down into the darkness, before continuing up to the sunlit entrance.

"I left him some bread," she told the guard, "I will bring him some more food tomorrow."

"*Ja, goed.*"

She returned to the civil basilica and found Vegetius, Master of Scribes, upstairs at his desk. He was genuinely pleased to see her and immediately proposed a salary that was the equivalent of ten times what she had earned at the bakery, and which he reduced only slightly at her insistence. He then drew up a long list of administrative needs for Aemilia to take to Merovec. Everything that had concerned the former civil service and governmental structure of Roman Gaul was to be confirmed, rebuilt, or scrapped, as soon as possible. It was early afternoon before he was finally done. Aemilia leaned back in her chair and gave a sigh.

"I don't know how much of this he can do, or even how much he'll understand. I'll do my best."

"You've done very well, so far, Miss. Just get done what you can. A cup of wine before you go, and something to eat?"

"Yes, please."

Over her meal Aemilia told Vegetius of her plan to support Tarunculus. He was sceptical.

"I could do it, presuming the Franks agree, but I don't know if it'll work. Only in exceptional cases were ex-officers ever given a pension and that's all been stopped now. You don't think your father will suspect something?"

"He might, but...I still think he would prefer it this way, even if he knew."

Vegetius's appraising glance had a touch of respect in it.

"Very well, Miss. With the Franks' approval I'll see it's done in the official manner. Anything else?"

"No. Just that."

"Then it's time we settled your wages." Opening a bag tied to his belt, he counted out fifteen siliquas.

"But that's a week's pay," said Aemilia, "I've worked here only one day."

He took her hand and placed the coins into it. "Don't argue with the administration. I pay by the week. Buy yourself a new dress. I expect my staff to be well-attired."

Aemilia smiled and put the money in her own pouch. Vegetius saw her to the main doors of the basilica.

"I'll be back as soon as I have replies to this," she said, indicating the parchment he had given her.

"As soon as you can, Miss, but no sooner," he said, holding up a hand in farewell before re-entering the basilica.

Aemilia stood in the center of the plaza and let the faint warmth of the low afternoon sun sink into her face. For the first time in many months she had time on her hands, and she had no inclination to do anything except breathe in the cool winter air and gaze at the cloudless sky above and thank a Providence that had finally smiled upon her. Later she would buy flour and vegetables and bake a loaf of fresh bread and make a hot soup for her father. She would take a lamp and a book and read to him. Then she would see Merovec and learn more about life in his village beyond Tournai, where there were no slaves, and where he was lord without being master. But now...now, she was content just to let the light cool breeze and the warm afternoon sun wash over her, whilst her eyes followed a few pigeons that fluttered to and fro about the great open space of the plaza. When the spring came and the snow melted she would walk under the trees again and hear the soft rush of the wind in their branches high above her and be at peace. *I wasn't made for life in a town*, she thought. *A village will do for me.* Then she caught herself and had a momentary flush of embarrassment. *Not so quick. Maybe he already intends to marry someone else.*

But for a long time afterwards her thoughts lingered on the village beyond Tournai.

Over the next few days her life settled into a new routine. In the morning she visited Tarunculus, bringing him food—usually soup with bread, on occasion some honey cakes. He spoke little and showed no gratitude for her visits, but she sensed he took comfort in her presence. Once she brought a book from his library, one of Seneca's histories, and began to read with the aid of an oil lamp she had brought for the purpose. He interrupted her after a few lines.

"No. Take it away. I'll hear no more of it."

She did not bring a book again, but left the oil lamp behind in his cell.

Once she had seen her father, Aemilia would call on Merovec. They discussed business at a rough wooden table in the main dining hall of the barracks, interrupted now and then by a slave or a Frank with a request. Merovec deferred as much as possible until the return of Chlodovech, but settled pressing issues with decision and, Aemilia noted, with a good deal of natural insight.

"Why does he want guards for the basilica?"

"He keeps the pay for the basilica staff there and he is afraid thieves will break in and steal it."

Merovec pondered for a moment.

"I cannot give Franks for this. While Chlodovech is at Paris there are many things the staff cannot do, *ne?*"

Aemilia agreed.

"Then tell him to choose the strongest of them to be his guards. I will give them the weapons they need. But they must not carry them outside the basilica."

Once his decisions were made, Aemilia wrote them out and had Merovec mark the documents with his letter. One day he asked her: "How do you write my name?"

She showed him on a blank sheet of parchment.

"Do it again."

She complied.

"Now I try."

She showed him how to hold the quill pen and dip it into the inkwell. His first effort was a blotchy mess, his second not much better.

"Ach, I do not have the fingers for this."

"You are holding the pen wrong. Here, like this. Always make the lines down and to the side—so. See?"

After a dozen attempts he was able to make a creditable signature.

"Here," she said, replacing the parchment with a document, "write your name just there." He did so.

"That is good! Not a single blot." He glanced up at her with a smile. She smiled back at him.

"I learn quick?"

"Very quick. I was slower."

"Who taught you?"

"My mother. She taught me how to read first, then I began learning to make letters when I was five. The first word I wrote was my name. Then I learned to write my mother's name. I was so proud when I could do that. My mother was proud too. She gave me a honey cake as a reward."

The conversation continued as they left the barracks and strolled towards the basilica. "...I say one day I will learn to read. Chlodovech learned to read after he became king. He said it was one good thing we could learn from Romans. With words on paper we could remember all the deeds of our great warriors. The bards pass many things on, but there is much more that would be remembered if it was written. I looked but I could not find a Roman who could write and teach me to write too."

"I can teach you, if you wish."

"*Ja.* I will make it part of your work."

"...the hall is smaller than the basilica, *seker,* but it is bigger than a cottage. It is thirty paces by ten. My mother and my two sisters live there, as do our servants.."

"Are your servants paid?"

"We do not use money there. We give them food, lodging and all else they need. They work the land, keep the hall in order, weave the cloth, and do all such things. They are always free to go if they wish, but they are happy to stay. On midsummer's eve we kill a pig and have a feast. They may drink as much mead then as they want. We dance until dawn. It is a good time."

"...there is a lot of forest there, and the land is flat, but there are some hills. I sometimes climb the hill near our hall early in the morning and watch the sunrise. It is a beautiful thing to see. I cannot tell it to you. The sky is all colors and the light from the sun is like a mist. The trees are like green mist coming from the ground. Truly there is no better a land. I shall be happy to return to it."

"I should love to see it."

"*Ja,* little Frank, but the Romans also have beautiful things in their towns, *ne?*" They stood in front of the basilica's façade: great, fluted pillars crowned with delicate Corinthian capitals that supported an ornate architrave. "We have nothing like this in Frankland."

"I would prefer the sky and the sun and the trees."

"Oh *ja?*" He glanced at her. She returned his glance and looked away, feeling her cheeks redden. A few moments passed, then she looked back at him, at his eyes that rested gently on her. "Yes, I would."

On Candlemas Day Paris surrendered. The occupation of the last independent town of the defunct Western Empire was tranquil. Chlodovech, as Aemilia learned a few days later from Vegetius, entered through the gates to meet a crowd that welcomed him with goodwill. On the day of the capitulation, a proclamation was put up declaring Romans and Franks to be equal citizens before the law, under the same obligations and possessing the same privileges. The proclamation, brought by the messenger who carried the news of Paris's capitulation, was to be made public in Soissons without delay. Aemilia read it to Merovec, translating where necessary.

"Good," he said. "It is finished."

On her next visit to the cells, Aemilia broke the news to Tarunculus.

"'Equal citizens'? Don't you believe a word of it. That was a trick to get 'em to open the gates. The only thing that'll be equal is how they carve up the booty between 'em. You'll see." But he spoke listlessly, and lapsed again into his morose taciturnity.

"I brought some honey cakes this time father," she said, opening the basket to show him. Tarunculus sat next to the bars on a small stool that Aemilia had persuaded Merovec to give him. The lamp in the corridor had been moved to just outside the cell, and she could now see him clearly in its yellow light. He had visibly lost weight and the skin on his face seemed to have undergone a decade's aging and begun collapsing into a mass of wrinkles. The lines of his features no longer showed the strength that had so cowed her on their first meeting. It was an old face, weary of life, its spirit nearly extinguished.

Tarunculus took the cake Aemilia proffered him and began to eat. It was a small relief to her that he still had an appetite. Then he paused, and looked at the half-eaten cake in his hand.

"As good as your mother's." There was a silence. "I did not do well by her. I could have had your grandfather's case thrown out, you know that?"

Aemilia kept still, but felt her heart constrict within her.

"It's been on my mind to tell you. Lepidius's case...it depended on a witness he bribed to say he saw your grandfather making a deal with the Visigoths. He thought it would stick because your grandfather was hunting in the countryside that day. Lepidius knew he liked to get away from the town from time to time. What he didn't know was that I was with him. I went to him and asked what in Hades was he playing at. He told me to shut my mouth or I'd lose my commission and never get it back. I told your grandfather. He said he would take me into his business, treat me as a son. But I couldn't do it. I could not give up the army. So I left Tours and let him get convicted. Your mother never forgave me for that."

Her mind was a writhing mass of thoughts, and nothing to say. Then something came to the surface. "She forgave you, father, I'm certain of it. She never spoke ill of you. If she hadn't forgiven you I would have known."

"That so?"

"I don't know why she didn't come back to you, but it wasn't for that reason."

Tarunculus was silent.

"Father, it's past. Think no more of it."

"*You* say that? Think of the life you've had, girl."

She extended a hand through the bars. "It doesn't matter, father." He looked at it and then moved his own a fraction toward hers. She took hold of it.

"You're a good girl."

She gave his hand a gentle squeeze. "Everything will be well, father."

"Aye. Be off now. A young thing like you shouldn't be down here so long. Go get some fresh air."

"I will. I'll come by this evening."

"You do that." Just three words, but as Aemilia left the barracks and made her way home, and for a long time after that, they lingered with her. She had reached him at last.

CHAPTER 35

Chlodovech's return to Soissons was delayed by an outbreak of Saxon raiding in the west of his newly-extended realm. The snow was thin on the ground, allowing the Saxons to move freely over the countryside, pillaging country villas and farms and threatening Soissons itself. Taking his veteran warriors, Chlodovech hunted their warbands down one after the other, as February gave way to March and an early thaw melted the meager layer of snow, encouraging the first buds of spring to push above the earth.

By Soissons, a small river—the Aisne—meandered past the town and on through the wide valley for about sixty miles before finally joining the Seine just below Paris. The thaw had melted its covering of ice and the water sparkled: cold, clear and brilliant beneath the young spring sun. Late one morning in the second week of March, Aemilia was sitting on a warm rock on the riverbank, a short distance from a track that dropped down to a pebbly ford. It was her first sortie outside the town since winter. The Saxon menace had faded and she judged it safe to venture out beyond the walls.

The water reflected the copse of trees on the other side of the river, the perfection of its image disturbed now and then by a circle of ripples as a trout rose to the surface, looking for the breadcrumbs she threw from the half-loaf she had brought with her. The shapes of the fish gleamed in the water, their sheen like silver in the refracted light.

She threw the breadcrumbs distractedly. Her mind, as it had done habitually over the past few weeks, dwelt on Merovec.

She loved him. It was a love like and unlike the love she had felt for Ennodius. Ennodius, for all his sophistication, had been—how to put it? —only half-grown within himself, needing to be drawn out of his childish self-absorption. It had been accomplished, and for a moment on the battlefield when with burning eyes he told her to go, he had become a man. But it had been only a moment, and in the collapse of defeat he had fallen back to his former atrophy—fallen back but not quite fallen back. He had come to her and given her money, and he had resolved to leave his mother. The spark had not gone out, she was sure, but it was still only a spark. How long before it finally became a steady flame? *If I had married him I would have been trying to bring him up, almost like a mother, and I do not want that.* Providence had been wise after all, separating them. Ennodius would stand on his own feet and become master of his own house. The thought gave her a feeling of contentment and she wished him well.

Her mind passed to Merovec. Merovec was like an oak, with wood as hard as iron solidly planted in the ground, and fresh leaves above bending gently in the breeze. Her love for him was as settled as the sky was blue and the fields were green and the sun shone with white light. It was natural, inevitable, and in its solidity needed no great displays of affection. A look, a word, a gesture, were enough to convey the depth, not only of her love, but also of his, for she knew that he loved her in the same way.

They had not yet spoken of marriage. Aemilia, raised a Roman, did not fully understand Merovec's mind, and could only guess he was waiting until the time was right. In the meantime he treated her with an affection mixed with respect. It was uncharted territory for her but a territory she very much liked. He would propose marriage eventually, probably when Clodovech returned to Soissons. She wondered if there was there any practical difficulty holding him back. Money perhaps? A dowry? Was she supposed to give him one or was he supposed to give one to her? *I hope it's not money. Why would we need money to marry?*

Another fish momentarily disturbed the water's surface. Something nagged in her memory, a fragment of conversation. She made an effort to remember. Something about fishes, but what? He gave it to the fishes? No, not that. He let the fishes look after it...

Then it came to her. The dead of night, in the apartment. The jailor, gloating, telling her of his cunning in getting Syagrius to reveal where his money was hidden: "...a smart bastard he was, letting the fishes look after it..." That was it. He had hidden his treasure where the fishes were. What could that mean? Had he hidden it in the river? In that case she would never find it. She mused on the subject for a few more minutes before deciding to broach it with Merovec.

Later that day in the barracks mess room she told him about it. "Maybe he hid it under a bridge," he suggested. "There are not too many bridges close by. We go and look?"

"Alone?"

Merovec grinned. "You are afraid of me?"

"No, but it would not be right."

"I know this. In Frankland a man must walk with a young woman in front of his neighbors' eyes until they are married. I bring a slave. He will carry the gold."

That afternoon Aemilia returned to the barracks with a basket containing provisions for the afternoon sortie: bread, cheese and a few greased apples. She found Merovec with a young boy standing by. She recognized him: it was Pertinax, one of two stablehands who had been helping Staterius at the Residence.

"Are you working at the barracks now?"

"Yes I am...Ma'am," the boy replied, unsure of Aemilia's status and deciding to take no chances.

"Never mind 'ma'am'. How is Staterius?"

"He's doing all right. More slaves came back and he's got all the help he needs. He reckoned the barracks needed a groom for their horses so here I am." Aemilia ceased her questioning, sensing his unease in the presence of Merovec.

"Go bring three horses," Merovec told him, "the brown with the white feet, the black and the gray."

"Is he happy here?" Aemilia asked, once the boy had gone.

Merovec pulled a wry face. "He works well, but he fears me like a Roman lord. It is the same with all the slaves. I do not like it much."

"Maybe he will change."

"It will be better if he does. You bring food in the basket?"

"We will be gone for the rest of the day."

"*Ja, dis reg.*"

The three of them rode through the east gate on the road toward Reims. Like all grooms Pertinax could ride, albeit badly. Taking the mule track Aemilia had originally used to find the Frankish encampment, they rode north for two miles until they found the first bridge—a ramshackle wooden affair that was evidently no longer fit to bear the wheeled traffic it had been designed to carry.

They dismounted. Avoiding the rotting planking, Merovec stepped gingerly along the main timbers, crouching down now and then to look underneath them, passing over the bridge on one side and then returning on the other. "Nothing," he said, when he had reached the bank. He removed his axe and knife, stripped off everything except his trousers and then dived into the water, swimming beneath the wooden supports and disappearing underwater from time to time to examine the riverbed below. Finally he emerged, dripping.

"There is no gold here," he said, drying himself with his cloak.

Remounting they decided to follow the river across country to the next bridge. Aemilia and Merovec rode side by side, Pertinax behind them. The sky was cloudless, the warm sun offsetting the freshness of the cold spring air.

"...my grandfather became a kingsman after he saved Childeric's life. They were hunting a boar near our village. My grandfather was their guide. Suddenly the boar breaks cover and catches Childeric's horse with his tusks. The horse rears and throws the king. The boar is charging him when my grandfather spears it, right through the heart, from twenty yards. 'You throw a spear well,' he tells my grandfather. 'It is how I hunt boars,' my grandfather says. 'An arrow does not always stop them.' He became Childeric's kingsman there, in the forest, and Childeric made him eorl of his village. My grandmother said it was foretold. Thor thundered when he was born, to show he was marked for great things."

"...we do not have temples, like the Romans. There is the sacred tree in Eben forest, but I have not been there. That is where the shamans go. We gather the harvest firstfruits for Frea, to thank her for blessing the land, and burn some of them at midsummer. That is when we have the feast I told you of. Some consult the shamans to know what will pass and some go to them for medicines. I do not need to know the future and I have not had a day's sickness. But if a shaman comes, I give him welcome. They have strange powers and it does not do to anger them."

"...there are several priests in Soissons. They are not like shamans: one does not need to fear them. I know the chief priest. He was kind to me. He said he would protect me if I was in danger."

"You were in danger?"

"...Yes. At one time Syagrius threatened to put me in prison. I knew too much about something he was doing. He did not want me to speak about it to anyone else."

"He deserved to die."

"He was sorry in the end. He said so to me in the cells."

"...when the day is over the fighting ends. The warriors who died come to life again, then all have a feast in the great hall of Valhalla. The next day they go out and fight again."

"Why do they do that?"

"It is what warriors do. What other life can a warrior have after death?"

"What happens to women after death?"

"They do not say."

"...when the world ends the Christians will all be given their bodies back. But there will be no more pain, no more sickness, no more death. They will live with God forever..."

"...they say a great sea will rise up and cover Valhalla, ending all things. I asked a shaman if the gods could prevent it. He told me no..."

The second bridge was made of stone: a flat walkway running over thick stone supports connected by arches made of precisely shaped stone blocks. It did not take long for Merovec to ascertain that there was no treasure hoard under or anywhere near it.

"I think this is a story," he said rubbing himself dry.

"Maybe," Aemilia replied. "Perhaps we should eat now."

They sat on the edge of the bridge and shared the basket's contents. Pertinax sat a short distance away, eating the share of food Aemilia had given him. The sun was lowering toward the west and it was cooler, with a hint of the coming evening in the late afternoon air.

"There is no more?" Merovec asked, when they were done. "If I had flint and a hook I could catch a fish and cook it over a fire."

"If we were at the Residence we'd have no problem with fish, My Lord," said Pertinax. "You could just take one from the pool in the entrance atrium."

Aemilia and Merovec looked at each other.

"We are fools," he said.

"Yes," she replied.

They remounted their horses. The mule track from the bridge led to the northern gate of the walls. Merovec glanced at Aemilia.

"The first to the gates gets the gold, *hein?*"

She looked at him a moment, then dug her heels into her horse's sides. The remainder of the journey was completed at full gallop, Pertinax prudently keeping to a walk far behind. Merovec reached the gates well ahead of Aemilia. She reined in next to him.

"Not fair. You have a bigger horse. Next time give me the black."

"Come, I am the better rider. But you are not too bad, little Frank."

"I teach you to write. You teach me to ride. Fair?"

He grinned. "Fair. One day you will be nearly as good as me."

She glanced back down the road. Pertinax was still out of sight. "We wait for him?"

"He can go to the barracks himself. Let us find the gold, *né?*"

They completed the final leg to the Residence at a more sober pace. Merovec's knock at the door was answered by Gerontius. He glanced at them in surprise. "My Lord...do you want to see Staterius?"

"No," said Aemilia. "We want a spade, now."

The pool in the atrium held only about a foot of water. Jabbing through the pebbles with the spade, it did not take Merovec long to hit something hard. He cleared away the pebbles to reveal the dull gray of a lead chest three feet long by a foot in width and a foot and a half deep. With the help of two slaves from the knot of curious onlookers, Merovec heaved it up onto a space at the edge of the pool. The chest was not locked, but kept shut with leaden bolts. He knocked them back with the edge of the spade and lifted the lid. The waterlogged interior was filled to the brim with gold solidi that gleamed as if new despite having spent months, perhaps years, underwater. There were gasps from the slaves. It was an enormous fortune.

"Why did he not take it with him?" Merovec asked.

"He did not have the time," Aemilia replied.

Under Merovec's orders a cart was commandeered to move the chest under Frankish guard to the barracks. There it was emptied and the money counted—nearly 10,000 solidi, the fruit of twenty years' hoarding of an entire province's surplus revenue.

"We keep it until Chlodovech returns," said Merovec. "He shall decide what to do with it."

Three days later a messenger arrived at the Aurelian flats from Tours, with a letter for Aemilia. She gave him a few folles, asking him to wait in the courtyard for the reply, and then broke the seal and sat down to read. It was from Ennodius, and was dated early December.

My dear Aemilia,

Something, a whim perhaps, prompts me to write to you. I am now with the august senator in your old villa. He had some unflattering things to say about mother which I heartily agreed with, so we are on the best of terms. He did not ask after you.

The old girl was careful to choose a villa on prime land at a convenient proximity to Paris and civilization, making it the perfect place for Chlodovis to bivouac his men for as long as this siege lasts. The efforts of the old girl to maintain her temper whilst a lot of less than immaculate Franks wandered around the place breaking things was priceless to see. It was something of a struggle for me to decide whether I should stay and watch the fun or finally break with mater and try out a new arena. In the end the new arena won. Her villa building is not large and the thought of sitting confined there indefinitely with the old girl was simply not to be entertained. Sylvia and Vispania are to be pitied.

I do not think I will become a bishop after all. Besides the fact that there seems to be no episcopal see available at present, I have concluded that the vocation would not suit me. I have decided that I must marry into money and settle down. The excellent senator might just be induced to adopt me and make me his heir—it flatters him to have another ex-emperor in the family—or failing that, I should be able to raise enough money from him and any future in-laws to buy a small villa of my own. I do not think I am ambitious, but one must live in the manner one was born to.

I would have sent you some money with this letter but I do not trust the messenger. I cannot do more than wish you well. You were good for me. Perhaps one day I shall be able to repay the favor.

By my hand,
Ennodius Avitus

Aemilia thought for a few minutes then, taking a quill pen and parchment, wrote her reply.

My Lord,
Your letter arrived just before the Ides of March. I send this letter hoping it will reach you more quickly than yours reached me.

You asked if you could repay me. You owe me no debt, but there is one favor I ask of you. Could you send this messenger to Her Ladyship's villa and tell Vipsania and Sylvia that I think I may be able to help them before too long, and then send him to tell me they have received the message? It is perhaps foolish for me to ask this, but I do not want them to go where I could not find them again. Nothing is clear yet, so I can say no more.

With all my heart I wish you happiness. I pray you will find the right person to marry, not just for money but also someone you are able to love. I do not think a marriage made purely for money would be good for you. You are capable of more than that.

By the time your messenger returns to Soissons, my situation will be clearer.

Farewell.
Aemilia

She rolled up the parchment and then melted a piece of red wax in a spoon held over one of the lamps, pouring it over the edge of the paper. She hesitated a moment. What would she use for a seal? Then she remembered the ring around her neck. Lifting it out she pressed the head of the ring into the soft wax, leaving a reversed impression of the Chi-Rho monogram. She blew on the wax to cool it then took the letter down the stairs to the Insula courtyard, in search of the messenger.

Giving him a siliqua she promised him five more if he returned speedily with a reply.

"Very kind of you ma'am," he said. "Lost my horse and then got held up by the Saxons raiding and all. Won't be so long next time, I'm sure."

"Do your best," she replied.

Later that day she asked Merovec, "Can Chlodovech take slaves away from a Roman Lord?"

"If he wants to, who will stop him?" said Merovec. "Why do you ask this?"

"Just a thought," Aemilia replied.

CHAPTER 36

In mid-Lent Chlodovech returned with his army to Soissons. The discovery of Syagrius's hoard filled him with immense satisfaction. He stood by the atrium pool as Merovec described the search and discovery of the treasure.

"I give most of it to my Franks as spoils, even though it is not war booty," Chlodovech said, when Merovec was done. "They stayed with me all through the winter. They have earned it. To you I give four hundred solidi." Turning to Aemilia he added, "From the day I met you you have brought me good fortune. May the gods always smile on you." He glanced briefly at Merovec and then left for the barracks.

Merovec waited until they were alone. "The money that Chlodovech has given me: I give you half."

Aemilia looked at him in surprise. "No. I already have plenty of money."

"I know Chlodovech. It is what he would wish. Come." They walked through the peristyle to the main garden. Merovec stopped and turned to Aemilia. "When your father comes out of his cell, what will he do to live?"

"I will look after him. If Chlodovech agrees, he will have part of my wages as"—she hesitated, searching for the Frankish equivalent of 'pension'—"money for being in the army. Vegetius is willing to do it."

"*Ja,* but if you leave your work, what will he do then?"

Aemilia looked at him. "What do you mean?"

"In Frankland it is the custom for a man to give a dowry to his wife's family. I give this money to you for your father, as your dowry."

She gazed at him. He took a step forward, taking her gently by the shoulders. "You will be my wife?"

A heart as full as an apple tree in bloom. "Yes. Yes," She came to him and embraced him, leaning her head on his chest. He held her to him, then placed his palm against her cheek, raising her face to his. "I have wished this since I first saw you, coming out the trees, alone. A little thing, but full of courage. You took my heart then, little Frank."

All that I could ever have wished for, and more, and so much more. How I am blessed. "I have loved you for a long time," she murmured. "A long time."

For many minutes after that there was no need to speak. Finally they left the garden, her hand in his. Returning through the peristyle they met Staterius, who took in the situation at a glance. "Good day, My Lord...Aemilia."

"Soon you will have to call her 'My Lady,'" said Merovec.

"Nothing would give me greater pleasure," Staterius answered, smiling. "I would be honored to attend the wedding."

That gave Aemilia pause. She turned to Merovec. "Will you marry me in the church?"

"It is better to wait until we return to Frankland and marry at the village."

"But there is no church in your village."

"Why do you want a church?"

"Christians always marry in a church. The priest brings the blessing of God on their marriage."

"This is important for you?"

"Yes."

Merovec pondered a few moments. "It is no matter to me. We will marry in the church here, but we must have the marriage feast at the village. The shaman will not like it, but in this I am not the shaman's servant."

Aemilia hugged him. "Thank you."

"We must marry soon. There is trouble in Frankland. We leave Soissons with Chlodovech in two days' time."

She seized him by the hand. "Come. We will speak to the priest now. He will marry us today."

On the way to the church Merovec spoke to her: "You cannot wait to marry. Why did you not tell me sooner?"

"I did not speak of it because you did not. I did not know what to think—perhaps you were to marry someone else."

He nodded. "*Ja.* Irmingard will be very unhappy. But I get my goats back, so it is not so bad."

She stared. He held her look for a moment, then grinned.

"Why, you..." With her finger she poked him under the ribs.

"Ai!"

The two entered the church. There were a few worshippers within.

Leaving Merovec in the nave Aemilia questioned an old woman who was refilling the oil lamps above the picture of the Madonna. "He's in the presbytery," came the reply. "Go through the vestry door."

The door was shut. Aemilia knocked, and waited. After a minute it was opened by one of the nuns. Aemilia recognized her.

"Hello, sister. May I see the bishop?"

"You certainly may," said a voice behind the nun. The familiar tubby form came into view. "Aemilia! We haven't seen you for some time. Is the nuns' cooking that bad?"

"There's nothing wrong with the cooking, My Lord. I've come to ask you something. I'm to be married. Today, if you can."

"To the Frank who has been in charge of Soissons whilst Chlodovech was away?"

For a moment Aemilia was at a loss for words. "...yes, My Lord. But how..."

"...did I know? It's hardly a secret that you and he have been courting. I know, I know, you're his interpreter and you've been very correct about it, but it isn't difficult to read between the lines. I've been expecting this visit for some time. I must admit I've been rather impressed by your man's handling of affairs in Soissons. A combination of decision and good judgement. Important for a man in authority. But to get to the point. He has a good nature and he will make a good husband for you—not that you've come for my opinion, of course."

Aemilia flushed.

"He isn't baptized, I take it?"

"No, My Lord."

"Did he create any difficulties over marrying in church?"

"No. He just said that the marriage feast must take place at his village."

"That's sensible. It would be hard on his family not to have anything to do with the wedding. Mind you don't let any of their shamans start their pagan incantations over you. You don't want to get mixed up in that devilry."

"I won't. I don't think he likes shamans very much."

"Good, good. We might make a Christian of him yet. A word of warning: don't try too hard. No man likes being nagged by his wife into doing what's good for him, and I don't imagine the Franks are any exception. Just make sure he agrees to have the children baptized, and let prayer, example and time do its work. If he's interested he'll ask questions when he's ready."

"Yes, My Lord."

"Right. That completes the marriage instruction. Where is the fellow?"

"He is in the church. You want to marry us here? Now?"

"Not as fast as that. I want to talk to him and let him know exactly what he's in for."

The bishop took Merovec into the presbytery, telling Aemilia to wait in the vestry. About half-an-hour later they returned.

"Agreed then," the little man said. "Tomorrow afternoon at the ninth hour. I'll have everything ready. It will not take long."

Aemilia waited until they were outside. "How did it go?"

"I like your priest," said Merovec. "He talks straight. He does not play Roman games. But he is very ugly. Now I understand why he cannot marry. He asked me about your father. Shall I speak to Chlodovech for him?"

"Do you think he will free him?"

"I think he will."

The two of them went on to the barracks. It was midday when they arrived. Chlodovech was dining with his closest men in the same room Merovec had used to conduct business with Aemilia.

"*Ja*, Merovec," he said, and leaned back to sign to a waiting slave. "Bring him a knife and a plate."

"I have something to tell you," Merovec said. "I am getting married tomorrow."

Chlodovech slapped the table and turned to the Frank sitting near him on his right. "What did I say? Come, pay up."

The Frank, an older man with more than a touch of gray in his moustaches, pulled out a purse. Opening it, he extracted half-a-dozen siliquas and passed them to Chlodovech. Aemilia looked on uncomprehendingly, then glanced at Merovec, and caught the hint of a smile. "He likes to make bets," he murmured to her.

"Did I not say you bring me good fortune?" the king said with a grin to Aemilia. "I wagered a month."

"How was I to know he is off his head?" the older Frank muttered.

"You are not marrying in your village?" Chlodovech asked Merovec.

"No. We marry in the church here. But we will have the wedding feast in the village."

Chlodovech gave a shrug. It clearly was of no concern to him. "Make a place for her too. She will be our guest for this meal."

A short while later—after the group had reduced a large pheasant and half-a-dozen chickens to insignificant remnants—Chlodovech raised his goblet. "To Merovec. May his sons be as their father." The Franks raised their goblets to him and then drained them. Chlodovech refilled his from a pitcher. "I come to your wedding tomorrow, *ja?*"

"That is an honor for me."

"And she? Her family will come?"

"She has only her father—he can give her away?"

Chlodovech paused, considering, then drained his goblet. "There has been no trouble in Soissons?"

"No. Nothing."

He looked into the goblet for a moment. "I will think on it."

At the end of the meal Aemilia took Merovec aside, "Do you remember that loaf Chlodovech gave me the day I first came?"

"*Ja,* I remember."

"I gave it to a girl who had no work. Will you let her come with us to Frankland? I wish to see her now if you agree."

"*Ja, seker.* We will make room for her. She will be a help to you."

Aemilia looked at him, then suddenly kissed him. "You are good."

He smiled, and put his hand to her cheek. "You have many things to bring?"

"No. Nor she."

"Still, it is a long way. We will need a cart. I will find one. You come later?"

"*Ja.* Before sunset."

"Go well, little Frank."

"Go well."

It was all Aemilia could do not to run all the way to the miserable insula where Lavilla dwelt. It took her some time before she finally found her on her knees, scrubbing the floor of the fetid lavatory room with a rag and a wooden basin of dirty water.

"Aemilia!" the girl said. "I can't stop. The landlord could come in any moment. I'll talk to you later."

Aemilia picked up the chipped basin and threw its contents with a splash over the floor. "He can do it then."

Lavilla stared at her, open-mouthed. "Are you out of your mind?"

"No. But you are out of here. No more of this work. I'll pay off your landlord for the next two days, then you're coming with me."

"Where to?"

"Frankland," Aemilia said, pulling her up off the floor, "to find you a husband."

CHAPTER 37

The next morning Tarunculus was released from the cells. The weeks of inactivity had stiffened his joints and as he walked from the barracks back to the insula, his limp was pronounced. He refused Aemilia's offer of help and her suggestion that she find him a stick.

"I'm not done yet," he said.

They entered the apartment and Tarunculus sank into one of the wickerwork chairs with a sigh. "By the gods it's good to be back in my own home. You've kept it tidy. Good girl. Any of the books missing?"

"No, father. I always locked the door when I went out. There's some bread and fish ready. You must build your strength up."

The early morning light was soft in the room and a sense of domestic peace hung in the air. Tarunculus stretched out his stiffened knees and glanced up at her, all the former uneasiness gone from his eyes, now full of the bond between them. Father and daughter, at long last reconciled over the past, behind them and gone.

Suddenly she realized what the news of her marriage would do to him. The joy that had filled her mind when Merovec declared his love for her had swept every other consideration into oblivion. She had assumed that her happiness would justify itself to everyone, even to her father. As she looked at Tarunculus across the table the folly of her thinking finally dawned on her. Marry a barbarian: marry a man high in the favor of the barbarian king who had conquered his world and killed his lord. Go and live in a village of barbarians: dress, eat, live as a barbarian. No, he would never accept that. She could not tell him, but she could not delay telling him, not even for a day.

"Something wrong, my girl?"

"I..."

He leaned forward, extending his hand. She hesitated, and stretched hers towards him. He placed his hand gently on it. "Don't you be worrying about anything girl. I've had my time to think things over. We won't be

315

setting fire to any stables again, eh?" He gave the hint of a grin.

"What will you do, father?"

"I've been passing ideas through my head. Maybe that notion you once had of doing guard work in a villa isn't so bad after all. Think you could write to the senator and see if there's a post going?"

"It won't be necessary. You'll be getting a pension. From the basilica."

"A pension?"

"The Master of Scribes told me. I work there now as a translator. They're to make a special case of you."

Behind the wonderment in Tarunculus's face Aemilia could detect no suspicion.

"You're not pulling my leg, now?"

"No father, it's the truth."

He leaned back in his chair, and began to laugh.

"By all the shades in Hades. Who'd've thought it? I sit in a dungeon and when they let me out I get a pension. A pension! No man can read the Fates. Someone wrote that. By the gods it's true!" He was silent for some moments, his mind full of the news. "D'you know how much?"

"Five solidi a year."

"That's more than a soldier's full pay." He glanced at her. "You had something to do with this?"

Aemilia did not want to lie. "Being his translator helped."

"Oh, aye." He fell silent again, then laid his hand on hers. "I'll not begrudge you working for them, girl."

"It was the only work I could find, father. They threw me out the bakery after you were arrested."

"Did they? Afraid of their necks, the damned cowards. You've seen none of the group since I was put inside?"

"No one."

"Cowards too. Wanted to keep their heads on their shoulders." He glanced at her again. "I think you also had a hand in me keeping mine, eh?"

She looked downwards, saying nothing.

"Well, that's the second time you've kept me out of the underworld. There won't be a third. Syagrius is dead. Paris is taken. There's nothing left to fight for." She noticed the heaviness in his voice and the gloom in his eyes. "No news?" he went on.

She thought of her imminent departure, and how to tell him of it. "Nothing, except that Chlodovech is going back to Frankland. There's trouble there."

"Oh? What kind of trouble?"

"I don't know," she said, her unhappiness at having to break the news of her marriage making her deaf to the tiny dart of unease within her. "I think it's his cousins."

"The ones that didn't support him?"

"I think so."

"Is he taking his army back with him?"

"Yes." She thought of Merovec and a marriage that could not be delayed.

The sudden slap of the hand on the table jolted her out of her preoccupation.

"*That's it then,*" said Tarunculus. "They've started fighting each other. I knew they would." He saw her surprise. "Don't you see? We still have a chance. But this time we'll be careful about it. No trusting anybody we don't know. No sudden moves. Let 'em tear each other apart until it's unliveable for the people here, *then* we organize a rising. We'll tell 'em: stand up for Rome or let the Franks pluck you like a hen. That's how I'll say it: pluck you like a hen. If they're cutting each other's throats what d'you think they'll do to you, eh? *That'll* wake 'em up. We'll start making pamphlets today, and be damned careful who we give 'em to. Nobody we don't know. It'll take time but we've got time, all the time in the world. We'll start now. By the gods, that changes everything. It's good news, damned..."

"*Father!*"

There was silence, as father and daughter stared at each other.

"I can't help you any more." She spoke haltingly, as if the words were difficult to enunciate.

"Why not?"

"I'm...getting married."

His eyes were fixed on her, with all the naïve bewilderment of a child. "What?"

"I'm getting married—today—to one of Chlodovech's men... Merovec."

She could not continue. His eyes remained on her. He did not speak for what seemed an age.

"You are marrying a Frank?"

"Yes."

He looked at her a moment longer, then dropped his gaze. There was nothing she could say, no word of justification or explanation that would be of any use, this she knew. But she could not say nothing. She had to try.

"He is a good man, father. He spoke for you, when you were arrested, and yesterday, to have you released. He owns a village. He has a hall." She remembered the money Chlodovech had given him from Syagrius's hoard. "He's rich."

Still he did not look at her. "You're marrying him for his money." It was not a question.

"No, father...I love him. It's the truth. I wouldn't marry for any other reason."

He raised a palm for silence, but did not speak. She waited a few moments and then turned away miserably. She stood in the kitchen, wondering what to do, finally nerving herself to lay out the meal she had prepared for him. He did not move, nor seem to notice her as she laid the plates, knives and bowls with fish, bread and strawberries on the table. Finally she brought a dish of honey cakes she had baked the previous afternoon, and placed it with the rest. He glanced at it, then took one, examining it. "As good as your mother's." She was wrung by the sadness in his eyes and in his voice. There was nothing she could say. The moments passed.

"You are leaving with him?"

"Yes, father. Tomorrow."

He fell silent again. She sat in the wicker chair opposite him and waited, hands clasped together in her lap.

"You tell me only now."

"It was decided only yesterday, father, we..."

"Do not call me your father. A father—a *Roman* father—is the one who decides whom his daughter will marry. Or he gives his permission. You call me your father? Then you don't have my permission, you hear?"

She hung her head.

"Marry a bloody, stinking, ignorant barbarian? Have you lost your wits? You'll not see this savage again, *ever.*" The table shook under the weight of his fist. His anger was rising. She could not prevent it, and she could not hide her mind. She looked up at him.

"I'm marrying him today."

The two hard, burning orbs glared at her a moment longer, then, with one swift movement, he rose, overturning the table with a flick of his hand. She sprang up in fright.

"I *forbid* it."

She turned for the door, but he lurched over the upturned table and grabbed her, shoving her violently away from the doorway. Throwing open the chest nearest the door he pulled out a Centurion's cane, the one she remembered seeing at his shop.

"D'you know what happens to an upstart daughter?" he said. "Exactly what happens to a wife."

Her eyes were fixed on the cane. "You beat her."

"Aye, I bloody well beat her. What I did was *my* decision to make and *hers* to follow. I told her to come, bring her mother if she wanted to. She told me to get out. By the gods, I beat her! It was her duty to obey her husband, and it's yours to obey your father. Now—I want you to vow you will never have anything to do with the brute and his money again. Make a vow, by your Christian God, *now.*"

Aemilia looked at him in frozen horror. An image flickered briefly in her consciousness, of a bloodstained body hanging from a tree.

"*Vow, damn you.*"

"No."

The first blow sliced into her cheek, making her stagger back. As she raised her arms the second blow caught her on the elbow. She retreated into a corner and turned away from him, hands over her head. Tarunculus followed, thrashing her with the cane, the odd words forcing their way through his grunting rage, "You...bloody well...will...obey...bloody well... obey..."

Finally he stopped, fatigue momentarily overcoming his fury.

"Will you vow?"

"No."

"Get out. *Get out.*"

She struggled to her feet and stumbled for the door, nearly falling as he wrenched it open and shoved her outside, slamming it behind her. She made her way unsteadily down the passage, weeping. At the stairs she paused a moment to compose herself. Then, fearful that he would come looking for her, she descended the stairway as quickly as she could and hurried on to the barracks, oblivious to the curious glances of passers by.

The Frankish guard at the barracks gate recognized her. "*Wat het U oorgekom, juffrou?*"

"*Niks. Merovec is hier?*"

"*Ja. Daarin,*" he said, pointing at the main entrance.

Aemilia did not knock at the door, but pushed it open. She caught sight of a slave. "Where is Merovec?"

The man glanced at her, startled. "In his bedroom. I'll take you there, ma'am."

The bedroom was the former private chamber of the garrison commander with a heavy wooden door. The slave knocked softly on it.

"*Ja, kom.*"

Aemilia pushed the door open. Merovec had his back to her. As he

319

turned she flung herself against him, weeping uncontrollably.

"Aemilja, what..." He stopped speaking, seeing a dark purplish weal on her face. Gently, he held her back from him and examined her. Seeing the marks on her hands he pushed back the sleeves of her dress and saw the weals on her arms. His face became expressionless.

"Who has done this to you?"

Aemilia, her throat racked by sobs, could not speak.

"Has your father done this to you?"

"...yes..."

Carefully, he made her sit on his bed. Against the wall a massive, two-handed war axe was leaning. Once before, he had dared Aemilia in fun to lift it. She had barely been able to, using both her arms. Merovec went over to the wall and picked it up with one hand as if it were a twig. He turned to face the terrified slave.

"Find a physician to treat her. I will be back soon."

He made for the door, the slave jumping aside to let him pass. As he passed through the doorway he felt two hands grasp his arm.

"*Do not hurt him.*"

He did not turn to face her. "I will not hurt him. I will cut him in half."

Aemilia moved around in front of him. "No, *no*. Leave him. If you love me leave him!"

He looked at her, and saw the desperation in her eyes. The resolve of his hard, cold rage wavered a moment.

"Only death can wipe out such a deed. Let me go."

"No. I beg you. I could not bear it."

The tension between them was like the silence of a storm about to break. Then, with infinitesimal slowness, Merovec lowered the huge axe.

"Very well," he said at last, "but hear me, little Frank. You will never see him again. Do you swear this?"

She looked at his eyes and knew she could not hesitate. She nodded. "I swear."

"If I see him but once, either near or at a distance, I will kill him. You," he faced the slave again, "will tell him this."

"Yes, my Lord." He glanced in query at Aemilia.

"Aurelian Flats," she said. "Go." He turned and ran.

Neither of them spoke for a full minute. Suddenly Merovec twisted around and swung the axe against the doorframe. The blade cut right through the wood, burying itself deep in the adjacent stone. Then he strode off.

The wedding was a simple affair. Staterius and Vegetius acted as witnesses. The two slave boys, Gerontius and Pertinax were present, as was Lavilla. Chlodovech came with half-a-dozen of his warriors. He glanced at Aemilia and then at Merovec, but did not question her condition. There was no one else in the Church.

After the brief ceremony Aemilia took the bishop aside.

"Your father?" he asked. She nodded. He said nothing, but shook his head.

"My Lord, I want you to do something for me."

"Anything you wish."

"Keep an eye on him. Let me know how he is. I can no longer see him, otherwise..." she gave a slight tilt of her head towards Merovec. "I never will, in any case. What happened was too....too...."

"I understand. I'll do it. You'll be in my prayers, Aemilia. May your new life be a happy one."

She smiled. "It will be. I have no doubts about that."

"Go well," he said, and gave her his blessing.

The slave had delivered his message and gone. He was alone again. He turned back from the door and glanced round the apartment. The table lay where he had overturned it, the plates, cutlery and food scattered over the floor among the fallen chairs. A slave could clean it all up later. She should do it. Damned if *he* would.

His eye wandered over his library, his treasure: the riches and memories of the world he had spent his life in arms for, like his father, and his father before, and his father before him. He had no son and she was gone to live in a filthy village like a pig in a sty. She was no longer his daughter.

He noticed, on one of the top shelves used for books, a book with a strange cover. He went over and pulled it out. It had a cross engraved on the front. He opened it, and after perusing through several pages, finally recognized it as a Bible. Her own book. He threw it on the floor in contempt. As it fell the pages splashed open and several sheets of folded parchment fell out. He hesitated, with half a mind to ignore them, then bent down and picked up a sheet. He recognized her handwriting. He read several lines and realized with a start that it was the coronation speech. He picked up the other sheets and read them through. The corrections were not in her hand. They reminded him of something. He jogged his memory, then after a closer look at the cross bar of the T's, he went over to a pigeonhole and pulled out a manuscript. It was a letter, written to him by Ennodius, requesting the loan of several of his books. He compared the calligraphy of the letter to the amendments in the speech. There was no doubt. They had been done by Ennodius.

Slowly, Tarunculus stepped over to a fallen chair, righted it and sat down. The anger in his eyes faded, to be replaced by a look of disbelief.

"...she wrote it..." The words were a barely audible murmur.

Memories began to surface: her care of him after the battle was lost; her hours of copying pamphlets at night, never once complaining; her fearful but resolute face when on the point of taking that dangerous message past the Franks to Syagrius. The memories rose up, gradually shifting their focus to his own response: never reciprocating, never showing real gratitude, merely reiterating a promise that one day he would be a true father to her.

He had a peculiar sensation of standing outside his own body, examining himself as if he were a stranger. He gave a sudden jolt, as though he had been struck, and dropped the sheets he had been holding. He raised his hands to his temples. "You fool. You bloody, bloody fool. You bloody, bloody fool."

It was as near as he ever came to admitting what he truly was.

The cart was nearly packed. The early morning light hung in the air like a sense of expectation as the army made its final preparations for departure. The huge convoy was gathered in the great space of the plaza. Wagons piled high with booty were interspersed among several thousand Frankish warriors. Aemilia's own vehicle was to travel just behind the king's guard, as befitted her new status as kingsman's wife. Lavilla stood beside her as slaves loaded the last few items of Merovec's spoils. She was as excited as a kitten with a ball of wool.

"I can't wait to go. Look at him. Over there. *He's* handsome. Do you think he's married? When are we going? I can't wait."

Aemilia smiled at her but did not reply. Her eyes ran over a group of horsemen, standing by their mounts. She spotted Merovec, in conversation with a fellow rider. As if aware of her scrutiny, he glanced at her, and smiled. After a few moments he walked over.

"All ready to go?"

"*Ja.*"

"Where is Pertinax?"

"I do not know."

"I told him to be here early. I do not have the time to find another driver now."

At that moment the young slave boy came up, holding a bandaged wrist. "Sorry I'm late, my Lord. Fell on my arm and had the physician look at it."

"It is broken?" Merovec asked.

"No my Lord, but it's sore. I can't use it much right now."

"Can you drive the cart?"

"I'll try, my Lord."

Merovec took the slave boy's arm and squeezed the wrist gently. The boy winced in pain.

"No good. You cannot use it for several days. I will not let you drive one-handed."

"Want me to find someone else, my Lord?"

"There is no time." Merovec considered a moment. "I will hitch my horse to the cart and drive it myself. You stay here. Tell Chilperic I say you must not work for a week."

"Sorry, my Lord," said Pertinax, with all the misery of a child on the first day of holidays.

"I am sorry too. Go." The slave boy scampered off with alacrity.

Aemilia looked up at Merovec. "So we have to be together for the whole journey."

"*Ja*. Maybe the gods, or your God, wished it so?"

"Maybe."

A short time later Chlodovech mounted his horse, his guard following suit. He took a hunting horn from his belt and blew a loud, clear note, then, raising his arm and extending it in front of him, he set off at a walk, followed by his horsemen.

The column slowly made its way to the northern gate. Chlodovech's horse passed under the stone archway first, followed by his guard. Behind them came Aemilia, sitting on Merovec's left with Lavilla on his right. Aemilia glanced up at the great stone frame before her, then down at the small doorway below that led up to the battlement. Something stirred in its shadows: an indistinct figure, half-concealed.

The cart was nearly at the gateway. The figure emerged from the doorway and for a moment the eyes of father and daughter met. A moment full of anguish at the comprehension of a precious bond that had been formed and abused and lost forever. As the cart passed under the shadow of the stone arch, Aemilia's glance left him. With Merovec at her side she dared not turn her head to look back, but she knew her father's eyes were on her as the cart creaked slowly away from Soissons down the road to Frankland and gradually disappeared from view. She never saw him again.

Finale

AD 496

The winter air was cold and clear. The ground was frozen but free of snow. There was no wind.

The horses came down the road at full gallop, their nostrils steaming. There were a dozen of them, heavy warhorses carrying armed riders, one of them holding the bronze wolf-standard, the sign of Chlodovech's kingsmen, its pennant lashing like a tail in the breeze.

Between them rode a woman, her fine blue cloak and dress showing her to be of Frankish gentry. She rode as well as the men around her, who were evidently her guards. As the troop crested a low rise she raised her hand to halt them.

"There it is," she said. In the distance, just below the line where the land met the sky, lay the outlines of a town. It was not large, and the walls were short, enclosing only its inner core.

"Two miles, maybe three," said one of the escort.

"We can wind the horses when we get there," she replied.

They started off again, urging their mounts to the limit as they made their way down the last approach to the town. Soon they reached the outermost buildings, one of the men blowing a horn to clear the way.

The few townsmen on the streets stood back as the troop of horsemen thundered past. In less than a minute they reached the forum and galloped on directly towards the presbytery of the church. At the entrance they halted and dismounted. Leaving her escort, the woman stepped quickly to the door. She raised the iron knocker and brought it down firmly, three times. After a moment the door was opened by an elderly nun.

"Yes?"

"Is the bishop in?"

The nun hesitated a moment, then her eyes suddenly widened in recognition. "Aemilia!"

"How are you, sister?"

"Very well, very well. My, what a surprise to see you. After all these years! You're looking in the pink." Her eyes strayed beyond to the knot of riders standing beside their tired horses.

"My escort," said Aemilia. "My husband didn't want me to travel alone."

"Well, well. Quite a Lady you've become. Come in. Bring them in too. They'll need a cup of wine after their journey. You've travelled far?"

"From Reims."

"Ah. You were at the baptism?"

"Yes. Chlodovech is a Christian at last. So are his men—including my husband."

The old nun gripped her hand. "That is a great blessing for us. Heaven knows how long we've prayed for it."

"It is, sister. I'll tell you all about it, but I need to see the bishop now, if I may."

"Of course. Sister Claudia will show you where he is. Sister, there you are. I think the bishop is in the church. Take the Lady to him. I'll look after your men." She ushered her through the door and then turned back to the Franks. "Come in and have some wine and something to eat."

The thin light from the overcast winter sky fell lightly from the high nave windows onto the marble floor. The bishop was kneeling in prayer before the Madonna. The nun pointed him out to Aemilia then left. She knelt a little behind him and said a few prayers herself. Finally he rose from his knees. His wad of hair was graying and lines of maturity were etched around his eyes. Otherwise he was as she remembered him.

"My Lord?"

"Aemilia. You've come."

"As quickly as I could. Am I in time?"

He looked at her with compassion. "No. He died a week ago. I'm sorry."

She dropped her gaze to the floor. "I could not come earlier. The messenger reached my village after we had left for Reims."

"It was Providence. No fault of yours."

She studied the flooring a moment longer then looked up. "Were you with him when he died?"

"We brought him here. The sisters nursed him. I was with him at the end."

"Did he...say anything?"

"He did. He bequeathed his library to you a fortnight before his death.

He was lucid only for moments by that time, but he got me to draw up a will. He had just enough strength to sign it."

"He didn't say anything else?"

"If you're asking me whether he converted, or formally showed repentance, then the answer is no. But it's impossible for me to say what was going on inside his head. He'd become...odd."

"Odd?"

"Yes. I judged it better not to mention anything to you in my letters. His pension was paid to him regularly, he was never in any real trouble and until two or three months before he died his health was good. There was no sense in having you worry uselessly over him."

"Can you tell me now?"

"I was counting on doing just that. You've just arrived? Then, come, have a little refreshment first."

There was a good fire in the hearth situated in the center of the refectory hall. The Franks were gathered at one of the tables, their conversation jovial from the warmth and the pitcher of wine between them, whilst the bishop and Aemilia sat in two wickerwork chairs drawn up near the blaze. He asked her about the great baptism that had taken place that Christmas Eve at Reims, three days previously. "Remigius must have foreseen it, all those years ago. *I* certainly never thought it would happen. Difference between a saint and a fool. How many of his men were baptized with him?"

"Three thousand."

"Good Lord." He inclined his head towards the Franks. "And them...?"

"Them too. Not just full of the joy of wine, My Lord."

The little fat man chuckled. "I hope they all know what it means."

"Some do. Merovec does. We spent a long time talking about it. I think he would have been baptized even if it wasn't for the battle at Tolbiac, but that really convinced him. He told me he was with Chlodovech when the Alamans broke Chlodovech's army. Everything was lost, then Chlodovech prayed to God and suddenly the Franks rallied. Merovec said he'd never seen anything like it."

"It's a rare miracle. If Chlodovech hadn't been blessed with a saintly wife like Clotilda, I wonder if it would have been granted him..."

"He's not a bad man, My Lord. He let her baptize their children."

"True, but it was Clotilda's God he prayed to, which shows how much he thought of Clotilda."

She smiled. "He's very fond of her, My Lord. Like Merovec is of me."

"Merovec isn't here, I take it?"

Aemilia's face clouded. "No. I told him not to come. It was enough for him to let me see my father. He is a good man, but he has never forgotten what...happened."

There was a moment's silence between them. Then Aemilia looked up. "Tell me about him, My Lord."

The bishop paused a moment before speaking, as if casting his memory back.

"Nothing visibly changed with him after you left. He kept on producing those pamphlets of his and trying to give them to whoever he could find to take them. I think he may have been reported to the Franks once or twice but they didn't do anything and no one bothered after that. Eventually the locals had enough of him and tore up the sheets of parchment he tried to give to them. Several times he was given rougher treatment—we had to tend his cuts and bruises on one occasion. He didn't thank me for it, but railed against me for being a Roman that had sold himself to the filthy barbarians. I didn't lay much by it. I think kindness affected him in a way he didn't want to reveal.

"He left the townsfolk alone after that and took to accosting strangers—travellers, visiting merchants and the like—telling them that they had the sacred duty to save Rome from the barbarians and if they were men with backbone they were sure to triumph as their forefathers had done against the Gauls. Since the strangers he spoke to were usually Gauls themselves it took them quite a while to work out what he was talking about. He would ramble, and quote disjointed bits from Livy or Horace or whoever. Not coherent in the way he used to be.

"He was no longer the town eccentric—he was more like the town idiot. He dressed very shabbily and let his beard grow. You might have mistaken him for a beggar. He was an old, tired wreck of a man when he finally fell ill. If he hadn't had an iron constitution to begin with I think he would have died long before now.

"Someone from the Aurelian Flats told me he was ill. I had him carried here. We spoke together a number of times. He was very troubled. I did all I could for him, and I could see it touched him. I have a feeling that in the end he was softened enough for God's grace to work in him, but that's his and God's secret, Aemilia. I'm sorry I can't tell you more."

"Thank you. I needed to know the truth."

"His books. They were brought here for safekeeping. What would you like me to do with them?"

"I've thought about it. I'll send a cart and have them brought to our hall in Frankland. I'll have a room built specially for them. I'll use them to educate my children. The eldest two can already read and write."

"Very good. In fact, excellent."

"Once my children are grown up," she continued, "I would like to bequeath the books to the church in Soissons. In gratitude for all you've done for me."

"We'll take good care of them."

Later, as she mounted her horse, a thought came to her. She turned to the bishop. "I may have many children. It could be a long time before they are all grown up. Do you want the books now?"

His face broke into a smile that made him seem suddenly years younger. "No rush. No rush at all," he said, giving her a final wave. "The Church won't go away."

Of the barbarian kingdoms built on the ruins of the Western Roman Empire none would survive except that of Chlodovech. During his reign and after his death, the Frankish kingdom grew in size and power, eventually becoming a great empire. After the death of Charlemagne, the empire crumbled, its fragments coalescing into blocks that later became France, Germany, Italy, Belgium, Holland, Luxembourg, Switzerland, Denmark, Austria and Czechoslovakia. Its civilization, a fusion by the Church of Roman and Frankish culture, has endured to the present day.

Roman Britain was conquered by the Saxons, who in their turn were conquered by the Normans, a fief of the Frankish crown.

Visigothic Spain was overrun by the Arabs. Karl the Hammer, grandfather of Charlemagne, shattered the Arab army at Poitiers, enabling the Spanish to begin a 700-year war of reconquest.

The Eastern Roman Empire would last another 1,000 years. In AD 1453, its capital city, Constantinople, was stormed by the Turks and it disappeared from history.

GLOSSARY

Aetius – 396-454. In his youth, he was kept as hostage by the Visigoths and later, the Huns, with whose king, Rugila, he became friends. After the death of the Western emperor Honorius in 423, he used the Huns to contest the succession of Valentinian III to the throne, eventually accepting the young emperor. Made commander-in-chief in Gaul, he successfully limited barbarian expansion in the area. After the death of his rival, Count Boniface in 432, he became the effective ruler in the West. With the help of the Visigoths, he defeated Attila at the Battle of the Catalaunian Fields in 451. Fearful of his power, Valentinian III stabbed and killed him in his court at Ravenna in 454.

Alamans – An alliance of German tribes that occupied Roman lands west of the upper Rhine. In 496 they were defeated by the Franks in the Battle of Tolbiac, during which Chlodovech converted to Christianity.

Alaric II – King of the Visigoths from 485-507. He was defeated and killed by Chlodovech in the Battle of Vouille.

Ambrosius – Ruler of southern Britain. It is probable his father, Aurelius Ambrosius, was the last Roman governor of the province of Maxima Caesariensis, in southeast Britain, around 417-420.

Augustiekins – Romulus Augustulus, last Roman emperor. Installed as emperor by his father, Orestes, in 475, he was deposed ten months later by Odoacer, dying some time before 488.

Auroch – An extinct type of wild cattle, with a shoulder height of 6 feet and a mass of nearly a ton.

Avitus – 385-456. Of a Gallo-Roman senatorial family, he studied law before serving under Aetius, becoming Praetorian Prefect of Gaul in 439. He persuaded Theodoric II, king of the Visigoths, to join Aetius against Attila in 451. Created Supreme Commander of the Gallic field army by the Emperor Petronius Maximus, he became emperor with Theodoric's support in 455 after Petronius's death. He could not gain the support of Ricimer, the Italian Supreme Commander. After disbanding his own troops to alleviate famine in Rome, he was deposed by Ricimer, dying shortly afterwards.

Biarchus – Junior officer below a centurion in rank

Burgundians – After occupying Roman territory on the left bank of the

Rhine, the Burgundian tribe was defeated by Aetius in 436. Enlisted by Aetius as federates, they were settled around Vienne, later aiding Aetius against the Huns. Gundobad became their sole king after murdering his brother Chilperic, father of Chlodovech's wife Clotilda. Chlodovech defeated him in 500, after which time the Burgundians were vassals or allies of the Franks.

Candidatus Guards – The emperor's personal bodyguards, named after their white uniforms.

Catalaunian Fields – Site of the battle between Aetius and Attila in 451, ending in the defeat of the Huns and their withdrawal from Gaul.

Chararic – Cousin of Chlodovech, he joined him at the Battle of Soissons but took no part in the battle. Chlodovech later captured him and his son, forcing him to be ordained a priest and his son a deacon, and ordering both to be tonsured. When the son persuaded his father to grow their hair long again Chlodovech had them killed.

Childeric – 440-481. He succeeded his father Merovech as king of the Salian Franks around 457. As federate, or ally, of Aegidius he defeated the Visigoths in 463 and later helped Count Paulus against the Visigoths and the Saxons. According to Gregory of Tours, he was exiled for eight years by the Franks for taking their women, eventually regaining his throne before his death.

Circitor – Lowest non-commissioned officer rank in the late Roman army.

St. Clotilda – 475-545. Wife of Chlodovech. In 493 her father and mother were murdered by her uncle, Gundobad, who became king of the Burgundians, sending her into exile. Received by the Franks, she married Chlodovech in the same year. Her efforts to persuade him to accept the Catholic Faith finally bore fruit in 496, when he converted during the Battle of Tolbiac and was baptized on Christmas Eve that year. She bore him five sons, one who died in infancy, and a daughter. After Chlodovech's death in 511 St. Clotilda retired to the Abbey of St. Martin at Tours. Her later life was troubled by the discord between her sons, culminating in the murder of two of her grandchildren by her third son, Chlothar. After her death at Tours she was buried alongside Chlodovech in the Abbey of St. Genevieve at Paris.

Comitatenses – Roman troops forming part of the mobile field army.

Count – Latin *Comes*. An official, military or civil, directly appointed by the emperor.

Euric – 415-484. King of the Visigoths after the death of his older brother Theodoric II in 466. He extended Visigothic power into Spain, and by 476 controlled nearly the entire peninsula. He declared his complete independence from Rome in 475.

Fabrica – Imperial factory for the manufacture of military equipment. Each fabrica specialized in a particular item.

Follis – Unit of Roman currency equal to 1/180 of a solidus.

Francisca – Curved throwing axe, used rather like a tomahawk.

St. Genevieve – 422-512. Born of a Frankish father and Gallo-Roman mother, St. Genevieve lived the life of a nun from the age of 15 after the encouragement of St. Germanus. She moved to Paris and was made responsible for the consecrated virgins there by the bishop. When the Huns invaded Gaul, she persuaded the populace not to flee the city, and by her prayers Attila was diverted to Orleans, after which he was defeated by Aetius. Under her influence Paris resisted a siege by Childeric and later by Chlodovech. The latter founded an abbey for her in which she was later buried.

St. Germanus of Auxerre – 378-448. Ordained bishop of Auxerre after holding a post as provincial governor, he visited Britain around 429 with St. Lupus of Troyes to combat the Pelagian heresy which was rife amongst the British clergy. He defeated the Pelagian bishops in a public debate and later led the Britons to victory against a Pictish and Saxon army. He returned to Gaul and may have visited Britain again in the 440's. He met and encouraged St. Genevieve in her desire to live a religious life. He died in Ravenna while petitioning the emperor for leniency towards Armorica in Gaul, against which Aetius had sent the Alans on a punitive expedition.

Honey cake – A popular Greek and Roman delicacy. Here is a recipe:

Ingredients: 3 large eggs, 7 ounces runny honey, 2 ounces Spelt flour/ordinary flour.

Method: Heat oven to 170º C or 330º F. Whisk eggs until stiff. Add the honey gradually. Gently fold in the sifted flour. Pour the mixture into a greased cake tin. Place in the preheated oven. Cooking time 45–55 minutes. Check after 40 minutes. When done, the cake is a rich golden brown color.

Illyricans – Javelin-armed light cavalry.

Legion – The late Roman legion numbered approximately 1,000 men and came in two kinds: the *limitaneus* legion, assigned to guard the frontier, and the mobile *comitatensis* legion, used to counter a barbarian incursion by pitched battle.

Limitanei – Roman frontier units, generally assumed to be of inferior equipment and quality. However several Limitanei legions were transferred to the elite *Comitatenses* mobile armies, and were known as the *Pseudocomitatenses*, implying that their fighting ability was not as inferior as is often supposed.

St. Lupus of Troyes – 383-478. Initially a lawyer, he renounced his possessions and entered Lerins Abbey before being elected bishop of Troyes in 426. He accompanied St. Germanus of Auxerre on his first visit to Britain in 429. He is credited with saving Troyes from destruction by Attila in 451.

Magistrate – an elected official that could hold a civil or military post.

Majorian – 420-461. Western Roman Emperor from 457 until his death. He made efforts to reconquer Gaul, Spain and North Africa, but after the fleet he created was betrayed to the Vandals, his popularity declined, and he was deposed and killed by his commander-in-chief, Ricimer.

Nummus – Smallest unit of Roman currency, theoretically equal to 1/7200 of a solidus. It was effectively worthless and out of circulation by 486.

Odoacer – 433-493. Commander of the barbarian foederati, or allies of Rome, in Italy. In 476 he deposed the last Roman emperor and became effective king of Italy, though nominally under the authority of the Eastern Roman Empire. In 488 the Ostrogoths under Theodoric invaded Italy. After years of inconclusive warfare Odoacer agreed to share Italy with Theodoric. At the banquet held to celebrate the alliance, Theodoric killed Odoacer with his bare hands.

Plumbarii – Roman skirmisher troops who threw large, lead-weighted darts that had a greater range than javelins.

Ragnacar – King of Cambrai, a man of loose morals as was his favorite, Farron. He was defeated by Chlodovech in battle, captured and executed.

St. Remigius – 437-533. Born into the highest levels of Gallo-Roman society, he was elected bishop of Reims when 22 years old. After his

victory over the Alamans at the Battle of Tolbiac, Chlodovech asked
Remigius to baptize him at Reims, which took place on Christmas Eve
in 496. Chlodovech gave him grants of land in which he established
many churches. His brother St. Principius was bishop of Soissons until
505.

Ricimer – 405-472. Of noble Suevic and Visigothic origin, he spent
his youth at the court of Emperor Valentinian III and fought under
Aetius. In 456 Emperor Avitus made Ricimer supreme commander of
the Western empire, by then reduced to Italy and a portion of southern
Gaul. After defeating the Vandals, he deposed Avitus and became the
de facto ruler of the Western empire. From 456 until his death he made
and deposed a succession of Western emperors.

Rutilius Namantianus – Of a distinguished Gallic family, he held the posts
of Secretary of State and Prefect of Rome. He wrote his famous poem,
De Reditu Suo, during a voyage from Rome to Gaul in 416.

Seker – Frankish word for "certainly," "sure."

Serf – Latin *colonus*. Tenant farmers who worked the large country estates,
or villas. Technically free, they could not leave their estates and could
be flogged. They paid rent in the form of a portion of their labor or
produce. Many of the poorer class became serfs to escape the crushing
burden of late Roman taxation.

Shaman – pagan priest/witchdoctor with some resemblance to the Celtic
druids, though little is known of their cult.

Siliqua – Unit of Roman currency equal to 1/24 of a solidus.

Solidus – Roman gold coin.

Spangenhelm – barbarian helmet whose distinctive feature was four metal
strips that joined at the top to form a pointed crown.

Stilicho – 359-408. Born of a Vandal father and Roman mother, he rose in
the ranks of the army under the Emperor Theodosius, who appointed
him commander-in-chief. Under Theodosius's son, Honorius, he
defended Italy from barbarian incursions for ten years. After the
barbarian invasion of Gaul and Spain and the military revolt of Britain,
he was arrested and executed.

Tolbiac – Site of a battle between Franks and Alamans in 496. The battle
initially went against the Franks, who were on the brink of defeat until
Clodovech invoked the Christian God of his wife, Clotilda, vowing to

be baptized if he gained the victory. At that point the Franks rallied and went on to rout the Alamans. Chlodovech kept his vow and was baptized on Christmas Eve, 496.

Tournai – Originally Roman Tornacum. A stopping place on the Roman road from Cologne to Boulogne. In 432 it came under Frankish control. King Childeric I was buried there. It remained the Frankish capital until 486.

Valens – 328-378. Eastern Roman emperor, killed by the Visigoths at the Battle of Adrianople.

Villa – large, self-sufficient country estate owned by a wealthy family, often of senatorial rank.

Visigoths – A barbarian tribe that was settled in the Balkans by Eastern Emperor Valens before defeating and killing him in 378 at the Battle of Adrianople. They moved into Italy, sacking Rome in 410, before finally settling in southern Gaul, where they created an independent kingdom around Toulouse.

Wolf standard – Commonly known as the draco, it consisted of a cast-metal dragon, wolf, dog or even fish's head with an open mouth through which the wind filled an attached windsock pennant. Originating from Dacia, it became widespread amongst Rome and her adversaries.

If you enjoyed this book, you might also be interested in these other high-quality works from Arx Publishing...

Belisarius: The First Shall Be Last by Paolo A. Belzoni
"The book strikes one as a conservative rallying cry to the 'Christian West' today....Not that the book deliberately carries a political message. On its own terms, it is an ambitious tale, filled with action, spectacle, and intrigues of all kinds....Painstakingly authentic in its historical, military, and religious detail, assiduously researched and replete with facts."
—*John J. Desjarlais, CatholicFiction.net*

Leave If You Can by Luise Rinser
"Speaking of treasures, I loved *Leave If You Can*. It is a very good book to form people in an understanding of a vocation. And there are some powerful lines in it in that regard. People may think that one always is holy and attracted to religion, but that is often enough not the case. One can be called and have an aversion. That's why I think the book has a lot to teach. In that respect, it is a true story."
—*Sister Magdalene of the Hearts of Jesus and Mary, OCD*

Angels in Iron by Nicholas C. Prata
"The novel's principal strength is its attention to historical detail and the unrelenting realism with which the battle scenes—and there are many—are described....In addition to being an exciting action/adventure yarn and quite a page-turner, *Angels in Iron* is valuable as a miniature history lesson....This is a book that belongs on the bookshelf of every Catholic man, should be read by every Catholic boy (11 or older, I would say), and stocked by every Catholic school library."
—*Latin Mass Magazine*

Crown of the World: Knight of the Temple by Nathan Sadasivan
"*Knight of the Temple* is written in a style of historical fiction that was prevalent in American Catholic literature several decades ago and follows in the footsteps of such Catholic classics as *The Outlaws of Ravenhurst* and the novels of Louis de Wohl, but with greater intensity. *Knight of the Temple* is a really excellent work, fraught with tension, that hooks us for part two."
—*Phillip D. Campbell III, Saint Austin Review*

The Laviniad: An Epic Poem by Claudio R. Salvucci
"The author successfully writes in the style of the ancient epic in modern English. Lovers of classic tales will really appreciate the poetry and the plot. The poem reads easily and naturally with the flow and flavor of the ancient epics."
—*Favorite Resources for Catholic Homeschoolers*

For further information on these titles, or to order, visit:
www.arxpub.com

CPSIA information can be obtained at www.ICGtesting.com
Printed in the USA
BVOW020617130112

280403BV00001B/12/P